D0069569

Praise for the novels of Jamie Freveletti

"Just terrific—full of thrills and tradecraft,
pace and peril….Outstanding."
—Lee Child, *New York Times* bestselling author
of *Worth Dying For*

"[Her] crisp writing, clever plotting, and memorable
characters…will satisfy even the most finicky of readers.
On every page you'll find just the right blend of menace
and normality—all of it written by a master."
—Steve Berry, *New York Times* bestselling author
of *The Jefferson Key*

"Exciting….Caldridge's grit, ingenuity, and courage
should win her new fans."
—*Publishers Weekly*

"A breathless, hair-raising read, one of the most gripping
thrillers I've read in a long, long time."
—Tess Gerritsen, *New York Times* bestselling author
of *Ice Cold*

Also by Jamie Freveletti

THE EMMA CALDRIDGE SERIES
(in publication order)

Novels

Running from the Devil
Running Dark
The Ninth Day
Dead Asleep

Ebook Short Stories

Risk
Gone
Run

✦

THE COVERT ONE SERIES

Robert Ludlum's The Janus Reprisal
Robert Ludlum's The Geneva Strategy

✦

NON FICTION

Anatomy of Innocence:
Testimonies of the Wrongfully Convicted
(contributor)

Calexia Press LLC
525 W. Monroe St., Suite 2360
Chicago, IL 60661
www.calexiapress.com

ISBN: 978-0-9835067-1-3

Library of Congress Control Number: 2017949564

Book design by Prideaux Press
Cover design by Bookfly Design

Publisher's Cataloging-In-Publication Data
(Prepared by The Donohue Group, Inc.)

Names: Freveletti, Jamie.
Title: Blood run / Jamie Freveletti.
Description: Chicago, IL : Calexia Press, [2017] | Series: The Emma Caldridge series
Identifiers: ISBN 978-0-9835067-1-3 | ISBN 978-0-9835067-2-0 (ebook)
Subjects: LCSH: Women biochemists--Africa--Fiction. | Chemical weapons--Africa--Fiction. | Revolutionaries--Africa--Fiction. | World politics--Fiction. | LCGFT: Thrillers (Fiction)
Classification: LCC PS3606.R486 B56 2017 (print) | LCC PS3606. R486 (ebook) | DDC 813/.6--dc23

BLOOD RUN

Jamie Freveletti

CALEXIA PRESS

For the readers
Thank you

1

Three Hundred Miles East of Dakar, Senegal

Emma Caldridge gazed out the open SUV window at the beauty of the savannah, unaware that in the tall grasses a man lurked. She rested her folded arms on the door's edge while she watched the baobab trees fly by. The dry wind, filled with the smell of pounded dirt and grass and sun, whipped her hair around her face.

For his part, the man in the field smelled only the dirty oil and grease of the rocket-propelled grenade launcher on his shoulder. The wooden heat shield, smooth from years of use in the wars of Africa, nestled against his neck. He watched the black Escalade approach, its wheels kicking up a dust cloud, and noted the woman leaning out of the rear passenger-side window. Her light brown hair flicked and spun in the wind. For a brief second, he regretted having to kill her, because his primary source of income came from kidnapping and a Westerner paid well. But the Arab had commissioned this job, and no one crossed the Arab.

The Escalade rocketed past and he rose up, his sudden movement startling a couple of grasshoppers into fleeing.

He ignored them as he stood among the swaying grass to aim. Right before he pulled the trigger, he glanced behind him, a reflex from years of experience, because he knew the weapon would shoot hot gas and smoke from the back as the grenade launched.

Emma glanced in the rearview mirror in time to see the man rise into view, the long weapon pointed at her. She jerked back inside and hit the button to close the window. The bulletproof window began its electrical slide up just as the man fired. She saw the backblast explode out from the weapon and heard the whistling of the rocket.

The armored car took the first hit on its hatch door. A Kevlar net spread across the back deflected the grenade, and the heavily plated vehicle absorbed the impact with a creaking, shrieking, metallic sound. She pounded on the glass divider between her and the driver.

"Go, go, go," she yelled at him.

The top-heavy vehicle lurched forward and careened around a tight corner and Emma tumbled across the back seat and slammed into the opposite door. Her arm hit the row of rocks glasses set in holders and the top half of the nearest one sheared off. The broken section flicked into the air. She glanced back and saw more attackers on various vehicles emerge from the high grasses on the side of the road.

The now closed window thudded near her head as a bullet hammered into it. Emma jerked back, afraid that the bulletproof glass would shatter. It dented with the force but held. She was relieved to see the lack of spalling, because it meant the glass was resistant to a higher level than the guns being fired, at least for the moment. Multi-hits in a twelve-centimeter triangle would cause it to fail. It was the driver's ability to keep the car moving that would spread the hits across the vehicle, giving them a chance for survival. But he was also the one they would try to kill first.

The woman in the plush bench seat in the row behind Emma started screaming. The third occupant in the car was Jackson Rand, the billionaire owner of Rand Laboratories.

"Climb in the back," he said. "The walls and windows are bulletproof."

The woman scrambled over the seat and into the cargo portion of the extended car. Rand joined her and they pushed the luggage aside to make room for them both. He collected the screaming woman into his arms and shielded her with his body. She was his secretary of ten years, as she'd proudly told Emma by the light of a campfire.

The heavy car shuddered when a second grenade exploded near the roof, and another rain of bullets hit the driver's side window. It failed in a shower of tiny glass slivers and shrapnel. Emma watched in horror as a splash of red washed over the clear divider between the driver and the passenger area.

"The driver's been hit," Emma said to the two others.

She pressed the button to lower the glass divider, like those found in limousines, to access the front seat. She was glad that it still moved. That meant that the car hadn't yet lost power. She knew that a car taking fire, even an armored car, had seconds to escape the first hit. A vehicle that didn't move while under attack would eventually be breached, no matter how extensive the armoring.

The lowered partition revealed the driver slumped over the wheel. Blood poured from his left ear and the glass next to his head was shattered by multiple rounds in a tight firing pattern. The man remained still and the SUV was slowing. Emma slid through the narrow opening, scraping her ankle across the metal lip, and leaving a skid mark of broken skin.

She shoved the chauffeur back to an upright position and as far as she could against the door, then squeezed herself into the seat with him. She hammered her left foot on top of his, which was still on the gas pedal. As she did, she leaned against his body to gain better access to the steering wheel. To her profound relief, the heavy vehicle picked up speed.

They were on the RN1 between Kayes in Mali and Tambacounda in Senegal, which was the only passable road for miles and a route notorious for its potholes. The SUV's run-flat tires would have fifty miles left in them after being hit by a bullet or flattened by a puncture, but not at the speeds that they were traveling. The vehicle hammered into a pothole and it jerked, throwing Emma against the driver's body. She tamped down the revulsion she felt being pressed so close to a corpse and concentrated on driving. The man's position in front of the steering wheel forced her into an awkward angle, and she prayed that the road stayed straight because, if it didn't, she would need a longer reach to maneuver it. The driver had a gun in his right hand, and Emma kept her left hand on the steering wheel while she used her right to pry it from his fingers.

"Can you shoot?" she yelled back to Rand.

Rand's head appeared in the partition's opening. He reached a hand through and placed it on the driver's shoulder, jerking it back when he touched blood. He stared at his hand in horror.

"I said. Can. You. Shoot?" Emma ground out the words. Rand tore his eyes from his bloody hand and shook his head.

"Not that well. But I can drive."

That's an understatement, Emma thought. Rand owned a racing team and rumor was that he occasionally raced his own Indy car in lesser venues.

"Then you drive and I'll shoot," Emma said. She wanted more than anything to keep the car moving and kept her attention on the road.

A quick glance in the side mirrors revealed four attackers—two on motorcycles and two in a battered convertible of undetermined make. The SUV's faster pace had increased their distance from the convertible, but that was a mixed blessing because the trees lining the road left little room to maneuver and even less to escape. The faster they went, the more Emma needed to concentrate on driving. A herd of goats rambled across the road far ahead and she laid on the horn to make them move. A skinny goatherd plodding behind them looked up at the noise and started waving a long stick to hustle them across.

Rand pulled off his jacket and squeezed through the opening. He was slender, about six feet tall, with wavy, precisely cut, dark hair that reached the top of his collar. He landed in the passenger seat and fell against the door as Emma turned a tight right corner. More bullets hit the back window, and Emma swerved to keep them from attaining that multi-hit jackpot that would shatter the glass completely. The motorcyclist on her left edged forward and she swerved that way to force him off balance. He braked, choosing to fall back rather than be pushed off the road. The second motorcyclist appeared in the right-hand mirror and aimed a weapon at them. He began firing. The gun kicked up with each round, ejecting silvery cartridges into the air. Emma heard the thuds as the bullets hit, but couldn't tell if they were concentrated in one area. The attack reached the seven-minute mark.

"Get close. I'll rise up, you maneuver under, and put your foot on the gas as soon as you can," Emma said to Rand. He slid next to her, and she moved over him and onto the passenger seat. She was forced to lift her foot off the pedal, and the SUV began to slow. The driver's body stayed slumped against the door. Rand put his foot on the gas, and they accelerated again as he settled into position. His longer reach gave him a better angle on the steering wheel, but his face revealed his distaste at being flush up against the dead driver. Emma turned to watch behind them.

"New car just entered the road ahead," Rand said.

Emma glanced up and saw a heavy sedan bounce up onto the road in front of them from the dirt shoulder, raising a cloud of dust. The red brake lights glowed. She had little doubt that it was a blocking vehicle.

"Ram it."

Rand nodded, never taking his eyes from the action. "Hold onto the gearshift. I'm going to accelerate into the right rear tire well to spin it."

Emma snapped on her seatbelt, grabbed at the shift to hold it in place, and placed a hand on the dash to brace against the impact.

Rand corrected, lifted his thumbs off the steering wheel, and aimed at the vehicle. They surged forward and hammered into the smaller sedan. Rand's aim was true, and the reinforced radiator cover and bumper acted as a battering ram. Emma's teeth cracked together with the force of the whiplash as her body moved forward, was caught by the belt, and then reversed backward. She heard Rand's secretary scream. The car in front of them spun off the road and slammed into a baobab tree, but the SUV took the hit with a minimum of damage and surged forward. The remaining shards of the driver's side window shattered and fell onto the dead man in a shower of glass. Wind streamed into the car and Emma's hair whipped with the force, covering her face, and blocking her vision. She scraped it back and twisted it to keep it in place.

The road curved around some trees. Rand took the bend well, despite the heavy vehicle's lack of agility. When they were once again on the straightaway, Emma saw a disabled bush taxi sitting dead center on the road ahead of them. Two men crouched at the wheel well changing a tire, and a large group of passengers milled around or lounged on the grassy shoulder. Rand leaned on the horn as they barreled forward. The people scattered. The man holding the tire upright let it go, and it wobbled into their path. Rand shot through a narrow channel created by the bus and the tire on one side, and a still running group of passengers on the other. The SUV's right tires fell off the road onto the shoulder, and the vehicle vibrated and shuddered as it did. Rand muscled it back, nearly clipping an ancient red pickup truck that carried a jumbled cargo of old metal. The pickup's driver laid on the horn in an extended blast.

The attacker's convertible cleared the pickup but pulled onto the shoulder with a lurching, uneven motion that indicated a blown tire. After a quick glance behind them, both motorcycle drivers slowed to a stop, abandoning the chase. One turned back to assist the convertible. Emma kept her eyes on the side-view mirror until the attackers appeared as dots in the distance. After another minute more, they disappeared from view.

"They're not following. Blown tire on the convertible," Emma said.

Rand nodded, keeping his eyes on the road. Emma inhaled a deep breath in an attempt to stop her body from shaking, slow her breathing, and calm down. The whistling wind and the roaring engine were the only sounds. Emma glanced at the body of the driver, still slumped against the door.

"Is it just me or is the engine louder than it should be?" Emma asked.

"I think the muffler kicked loose on one of the potholes," Rand said.

"You okay?" she asked.

"I'm not hit. But I'd really like to stop and move the driver."

Emma didn't blame him. "Perhaps in a few minutes. Let's try to get some distance between us first. Is a tire blown?"

Rand nodded. "Dash indicates left rear."

"They're run-flats?"

"Yes. At least fifty miles."

"That Kevlar net on the back saved us. Otherwise, I'm pretty sure the grenade would have pierced it."

Rand shook his head. "It's not Kevlar. It's a new fabric that we're developing to compete. Not as heavy as plating, and when it 'catches' an RPG it acts as a buffer."

"Someone in your R&D department deserves a bonus for saving the boss," Emma said.

Rand took a deep breath and nodded. Emma turned to talk to the woman behind them.

"Are you all right?" The woman was still on the floor with her back pressed against the far seat. She swallowed and nodded. "Do you have a cell phone that will get a signal?" Emma asked her. "Mine hasn't since I landed here."

"I think it will," the woman said. "But I don't know who to call. We're nowhere near Tambacounda and Dakar's even farther. I don't know the emergency number in Dakar, if there even is one."

"Dial this." Emma recited the digits. "The man's name is Edward Banner. He's the owner of a contract security company that works with the Department of Defense. Tell him where we are and that we were just ambushed."

Rand glanced at her. "Where to? And let me know when you think it'll be safe enough to pull over and move the driver's body to the back of the car." Rand sounded calm but a muscle bunched in his jaw, revealing his stress. Emma did her best not to look at the corpse.

"Let's hear what Banner has to say first." She kept her eyes on the side-view mirror and the gun in her hand. "For now, you can just keep driving. And, while you do, you can explain to me what just happened. That was a professional crew and this is your car, so they weren't after me."

"They're after me." Rand's quick answer surprised Emma. She had expected him to be puzzled, or at least outraged, by the attack. He was neither. She frowned.

"Why?"

"I know too much."

"About what?"

"Everything."

The cryptic answers made her want to shake him. "Please be specific."

Rand shook his head. "I can't."

"I thought this was a humanitarian mission. Registered and approved. No one should be shooting at us."

They were only miles from the border with Mali, and Rand Pharmaceuticals was to provide the vaccines that would inoculate the country's children against polio. She hadn't expected an attack when she'd agreed to be part of this mission.

"It's more than that," Rand said.

"How much more?" Emma asked.

"Enough to keep those attackers on the hunt. They won't quit. And, if they do, others will take their place. They won't stop until we're dead. And once we're dead, they're going to destroy everyone else."

2

Emma struggled to keep her anger at bay. She hated the thought that she'd been duped into the charitable mission, but until she knew the facts she needed to keep a cool head. Rand's secretary put her hand through the partition.

"It's Mr. Banner," she said.

"Thank you, Ms...." Emma let her voice trail off. In the panic, she'd forgotten the woman's name.

"Sinclair...Rhonda Sinclair."

"Thank you," Emma said again as she took the phone.

"What are you doing in Senegal?" Banner asked.

Just hearing his calm, steady voice emanating from a quiet office somewhere in the United States gave Emma a bit more hope than she'd had in the past half hour. She wanted to yell, "Get me the hell out of here!" into the phone but reined in her first impulse. As a former military officer and current head of Darkview, Banner managed crews in hot areas around the world and did it without breaking a sweat. Emma sometimes took assignments from him, and neither of them acted in panic. This attack had been so sudden and unexpected that she was having a hard time wrestling her emotions to the ground.

"You've traced the phone," she said, modulating her voice to match his even tones.

"I'm at the DOD's offices. Routine procedure. Calls are recorded, as well. Why are you there?"

Rand waved a hand to get her attention and pointed to the gas gauge on the SUV's control panel. Emma leaned over to get a closer look. They had less than a quarter of a tank. Emma nodded her understanding and sat back.

"I'm on a humanitarian mission with a group that's sponsored by Rand Laboratories. We were just leaving a nearby village, after a presentation on vaccines, when we were followed and attacked."

"Who's we?"

"Jackson Rand and his secretary, Rhonda Sinclair. The driver is dead. Mr. Rand has informed me that they may be attacking him for reasons that he can't—" She looked over at Rand. "—or won't reveal."

"All right. That's interesting. How can I help?"

"I need backup and bodyguards. Do you have any available?"

Banner also maintained a network of paid contract security personnel spread across the globe. They were the best in the business.

"I don't have anyone in Senegal. They're all to the east, in Mali, since the last insurrection broke out."

Emma's initial relief fled with this response. "I'm on the RN1 headed to Dakar through Tambacounda."

"I can see that from the transmission, but I have bad news for you. The insurgents have blocked every road out in a five-mile radius around Dakar, with repeated blocks on major incoming arteries starting at Thiès. The first outer rim is roughly an hour and a half from Dakar."

"Which insurgents? From Mali or the MFDC in Casamance?" Emma watched Rand's head jerk toward her at the word "insurgents." He shot her an alarmed glance. Emma switched the cell on speaker so that he could follow the conversation.

"Both, actually. A second arm of the same group that's operating in Mali ringed Dakar, and the MFDC is pissed at the intrusion. They're on the march to intercept, along with the Senegalese forces. We expect shelling to begin soon. The whole thing has formed up very quickly, though there's been chatter about it for months."

The driver's corpse twitched, and Rand yelled an incoherent oath and jerked away. The SUV swerved.

"I heard something," Banner said.

"That was Mr. Rand. The driver's corpse moved," Emma said.

"Is he alive after all?" Rand asked.

Emma shook her head. "It's a motor system response, nothing more. He's dead."

"Are you talking about the driver?" Banner said.

"Yes," Emma said. "They targeted him first."

"Pros, then," Banner said. "Not just a bunch of locals firing away at random, hoping to score a hit."

"Absolutely," Emma replied.

"Can you get back to the N2 at the Mali border? Don't go over the border, because that's where my guys are and the situation there is full-on war, but you can take the N2 north to Mauritania."

"Isn't that a death sentence as well? Mauritania's a mess."

"I agree it isn't great but the Al Siva in the Islamic Sahel forces there are scattered, with more distance between them. You just might be able to thread your way through. But be careful, ASIS makes its money off kidnapping and targets Westerners."

"We're not going to thread anywhere unless we can get some more gas," Rand said.

Which wasn't a surprise given the vehicle. Emma had questioned the use of the massive, modified SUV. West Africa's roads were marginal at best, and assistance between villages was nonexistent. Most of the humanitarian missions used old Land Rovers or Mitsubishis, but those weren't generally armored. Now Emma understood why Rand had insisted on that particular car. He must have been worried about just such an attack. She would demand some answers from him later but, first, they needed to focus on getting out of the danger zone.

"What about the train to Bamako?" Emma asked. "Didn't some company buy the rail line and vow to restore it?"

"Yes, but they went bankrupt years ago. Your only other option is bush taxi."

Which might not be a bad option, Emma thought. Bush taxis usually jammed thirty people into a minibus licensed for sixteen and, if the three of them worked their way into the middle of the vehicle, they could be well hidden from anyone on the road.

"We'll probably run out of gas soon. There was a bush taxi with a blown tire behind us and pointed toward Dakar. Maybe we'll flag them down when they show up and try to talk them into turning around."

"Warn them that if the insurgents take Dakar, they're expected to push outward. If you can get through Mauritania and north to Marrakesh, you're home free."

"That's twelve hundred miles from here."

"I know. Sorry for that," Banner said.

Rand shot her a serious look. The car's dashboard made a dinging sound, and a gas pump icon appeared on the display.

"Ten miles left," Rand said.

"Shall I call you on this number or your cell?" Banner asked.

"It's Ms. Sinclair's. Mine's been spotty. I'll have her text you Rand's, as well."

"Good enough. I'll try to get someone to meet you in Nouakchott, Mauritania."

About five hundred miles away, Emma thought. Better, but still a long way through dangerous territory.

"That's almost a ten-hour drive. Easily three times that if we're stuck using bush taxis," Emma said. "But I'll take whatever help I can get."

"Are you armed?"

Emma nodded, then caught herself when she realized that Banner couldn't see her. "The driver had a pistol." She looked at Rand. "I noticed that trunk in the back. Any weapons in there?" Rand shook his head. "And that appears to be it," she said.

"Well, at least it's something. I'll keep you posted by text and let me know when you've crossed into Mauritania."

"Will do," Emma said. She ended the call and handed the phone back to Sinclair, who leaned through the partition to accept it.

"What about the heli service? Should I call them?" the secretary asked.

Rand nodded. "Worth a shot."

Sinclair disappeared into the back of the car to make the call.

"You have a helicopter nearby?" Emma asked. Rand had flown into two different villages by helicopter several days before.

Rand shook his head. "It's a service I've chartered on prior trips. We didn't use it this time because it flies out of Dakar and we're out of range now. The bus and limo seemed a better way to go." The entire mission consisted of twenty-five aid personnel from various countries. Most had left in a bus three hours before Rand's ride. Sinclair appeared once again in the window.

"They said they're sorry, but they're in Dakar and swarmed with people begging to be flown out of the war zone. He said people will pay anything. They're offering outrageous sums."

"You tell them I'll top their highest offer and throw in a new helicopter as well," Rand said.

Emma raised an eyebrow. Being a billionaire had some clear advantages. She heard Sinclair relaying the offer to the charter company.

"They said that they would love to accept but they would have to fly over the insurgents' perimeter to get to us, refuel, and then fly back over the perimeter out of the danger zone. They're not willing to risk it. From Dakar, they're going to head out over the ocean, south to Banjul and then out over the water again, landing to take on fuel as needed. It's the safest evacuation route."

"Ask them if there's anyone they know who'd be willing to take the risk. Planes, helicopter, anything," Rand said.

Sinclair relayed the question. "They said most have already left and the rest are in the process of leaving. They don't know anyone crazy enough to try it."

"I do," Emma said. Both Rand and Sinclair looked at her in surprise. "Ask them if they know Wilson Vanderlock and whether he's in Africa right now."

Sinclair asked the question. "They said they do know him and Vanderlock's crazy enough to try anything, but they think he's in South Africa, not West Africa. They'll leave a message for him. What do you want them to say?"

"Give him my name and both our phone numbers, and have him contact us the minute he can," Emma said.

Sinclair relayed the message and hung up. Emma sat back and mulled over their options. Rand glanced at her.

"Who's Vanderlock? A member of Banner's security group?" he asked.

Emma shook her head. "Freelance. He's South African. Used to fly the khat drug route from Kenya to Somalia."

"Drugs?"

"Legal drugs. At least here in Africa."

"The charter company thought he was crazy. Is he?"

"Not insane crazy. More like a risk-taker crazy."

"Would he be willing to help, despite the risk?"

"Yes," Emma said.

Rand gave her a focused look. "For money, or for you?"

Emma again checked the rearview mirror before answering. "Both, I guess."

"And if we had no money?" Rand seemed keenly interested in the answer. Emma looked him in the eye.

"Then he might do it for me. But money doesn't sound like it's a problem, judging from your offer to the charter company."

"There are some things money can't buy." Rand raised his hand off the steering wheel. "Not many things, but definitely some. And we're going to learn that lesson right now because money can't buy us a refill." The warning lights on the car dash started beeping repeatedly.

Emma leaned over to look at the display. They were on empty. Rand pulled the car off the road and over to a stand of trees. He maneuvered into the shade and killed the engine.

They sat in the sudden silence and Emma took stock. They were in a war zone with no gas, no food, and no assistance in sight. They did have a band of professional assassins chasing them, insurgents massing from every direction, a corpse, a gun, a phone…and access to more money than the gross domestic product of Senegal for the year.

Which could buy them absolutely nothing.

3

Emma threw open the door and got out. Now that the immediate danger had passed, she once again wanted to throttle Rand. He emerged from the passenger side and held open the back door for Sinclair.

"What the hell is going on?" Emma said. She ground out the words. Rand put his hands on his hips, and his expression turned stony.

"You're not involved. It's my matter to handle." He looked every bit the arrogant billionaire CEO in his creased navy twill pants, gray polo shirt open at the throat, and rubber-soled boat shoes. His tanned, angular face; expensive haircut; and straight, white teeth contributed to the overall polished look. Emma stepped nearer, getting close until he was forced to take a step back.

"Tell me how you think you handled it. I'd really like to know because, when someone shoots rocket-propelled grenades at the car that I happen to be riding in, it escapes me how you can claim that I'm not involved. Are you insane?"

He paced back and forth. "They're after me. You leave now and they won't follow you. I've got this under control. Why do you think I used the armored car?"

"Whatever you think you've got under control, it's not apparent to me." She pointed to the car. "No car, no matter how well armored, will survive a sustained RPG attack. We were just lucky that the netting on the back deflected it enough to soften the damage."

"I told you, that netting was added by me in order to defend against just such an occurrence."

"That netting was a lucky break, nothing more. If they'd had a few additional grenades, the next one, or the one after that, would have breached it, and we all would have gone up in smoke. Incinerated. If I'm going to be shot at, I'd at least like to be shown the common courtesy of being told why."

"It's not something I can reveal." He set his jaw and stared at her in defiance.

Emma stepped even closer until she was within inches of his chest. At that distance, she could smell the mixture of cologne, sweat, and a vague hint of spice around him. This time, rather than step back, he stood his ground.

"Listen, you son of a bitch, you're in Africa, not on Wall Street. While I'm sure you're hell on wheels in a boardroom, you're so far out of your element here as to be laughable. If you knew assassins were after you, then you had no business letting either me or Ms. Sinclair ride with you. It's that simple. But now that you've embroiled us in your mess you'd better start telling me what's going down or I *will* leave you here to rot, be eaten by animals, or have your head blown off."

Emma watched a mixture of emotions race across his face as he thought about what to say. From the corner of her eye, she saw Sinclair standing ten feet away with an expression of horror on her features.

"What makes you so competent here? You're the head of a chemistry lab, not a soldier. Seems to me that you're not so much different from me." Rand's breathing was rapid as he challenged her. Something in his delivery, though, was unconvincing. As if he knew what she was, and was aware of her background and reputation. Or at least enough to know that she'd been in many tight situations and had fought, fired, or blasted her way out of them. And then it occurred to her in a burst of clarity why she'd been asked to join the mission.

"You deliberately recruited me for this trip, because you decided that you needed someone with my unique skill set, didn't you? I always wondered why Rand Pharmaceuticals, a company a thousand times the size of Pure Chemistry, would go out of its way to invite me on this mission. It was you, wasn't it? You knew that I sometimes take work for Darkview and that I'd be a useful asset to have around if your hit men came sniffing at your heels."

Rand inhaled and let his breath out slowly. "I asked you to join because your reputation as a chemist with knowledge of plants, both healing and poisonous, as well as chemical reactions, is becoming well known in the community. Your background in weapons and quick thinking in tight spots is also becoming legend."

"So, you thought you'd offer for me to come along, never tell me of the risks, and hope I'd handle it when the worst happened."

He narrowed his eyes. "I've paid you very well for this trip. More than a chemist at your company can make in a year."

"You have no idea what I pay my chemists."

"I know exactly what you pay your chemists."

Emma sucked in her breath. Her employees routinely signed nondisclosure agreements, and no one should have known what they worked on and what they were paid. Pure Chemistry had lost three bids in the past year and, in all three cases, she had the distinct impression that a competitor had hacked the company computers. She'd wiped them clean and installed better firewalls, and yet the hacks kept coming. She'd had some sleepless nights this past year over the situation so, when the company was tapped to assist in this federally funded program, she leapt at the chance. Now she wondered how much Rand knew about her company and the hacks.

Emma hewed to a strong moral code but now knew better than to expect the same from Rand. He'd used her. She wanted to pummel him into the dirt but, once again, she took hold of her emotions. She'd drill down on the specifics of the situation once they were out of danger. For now, they needed to keep moving before their attackers reappeared.

"Are either of you runners?" she asked.

Sinclair nodded. "I do, but slowly. Three miles every other day."

Rand shook his head. "Not at all. Spinning and swimming."

Both answers suggested some level of fitness for the march ahead, but what was still an unknown was their ability to sleep rough. While Rand and Sinclair had hopped in and out of villages by helicopter and chauffeured car—followed by a safari outfitter, who brought tents, cots, and provisions for their trek across Senegal—many times Emma had opted to accept the hospitality of the various villagers. For her, the incongruity of traveling in a cushy SUV and then sleeping in a spacious tent, when the villagers themselves were sleeping in mud huts, detracted from the core mission, which was to convince the population to vaccinate their children, sleep under mosquito netting, and use insect repellent to avoid malaria.

But, while Rand lacked a sense for the average African's— or any average person's—experience of the world, he had a clear view of the value of his company's vaccine. He spoke bluntly to the parents. "Either vaccinate them or watch them die. It's not a question, and I can't imagine how you can stand there and say no," was his steadfast response to naysayers.

He'd watched her closely at times during the two-week trip. Sometimes too closely, and Emma found herself staring back at him in an open challenge. Only then would he glance away without revealing his true thoughts. Women gathered around him in admiration, both for his looks, but also for the air of power and wealth that he carried with him. The wealth, in particular, acted as a potent lure. He'd arrive in a vast dust cloud, with the rhythmic chopping and roaring of the copter's blades, jump out of the door and stride toward the gathered villagers. Even wizened old women would preen when he turned his attention on them to discuss vaccinating their grandchildren and great-grandchildren. To Emma, he reeked of someone who'd never known hardship. He moved through the world in a bubble of power purchased by several generations of great wealth built upon the backs of workers, busted union efforts, and railroad ties laid across America over a hundred years ago.

Now he rubbed his face, and Emma noticed that his nails were buffed to a manicured shine. Oddly enough, on him, it wasn't effeminate but was just another incongruent piece of the man's entire presentation. Incongruent because he exuded the impression that to mess with him meant taking a beating. Probably financially, but possibly physically, manicured nails or not.

"Two months ago, I was preparing to ship the vaccines for this trip. Our quality control personnel usually pick lots at random to test. They tested fine and were shipped. When we got here, there was some sort of foul-up at the border and customs claimed that they were going to have to open the container before allowing us to take delivery. I went down personally to address the matter since I didn't have any shipping personnel in Senegal. The containers had been opened and the boxes removed and they were stacked on the dock. I managed to get the product released, but I noticed, as we were loading them on the truck, that two lots had been placed to the side by one of the customs guards. Almost as though he was hoarding them. I didn't like it and, when he wasn't looking, I grabbed them and mixed them in with the others. Later, I retrieved them and saw that the boxes had been opened and resealed poorly with clear packing tape."

"And?"

"And then I took out a single vial and sent it to our facility in Dubai to be tested. I got the results a week after we'd begun our mission. It tested positive for smallpox."

Emma frowned. "It was actually the smallpox vaccine?"

Rand shook his head. "Not the vaccine. Smallpox, the disease. The vial was filled with live smallpox. Had we used it, we would have revived one of the greatest scourges this world has ever seen."

4

I don't believe it," Emma said. "The last existing stores of smallpox are secured at the Centers for Disease Control in Atlanta and a lab in Russia. They're heavily guarded. If they *had* been stolen, two of the largest nations in the world would have been in an uproar, and we would have heard about it."

"Believe it," Rand said. He got a cynical look on his face. "You don't think that those vials of smallpox that were found in a closet in the old National Institutes of Health building were the only misplaced vials, did you?"

"What's he talking about?" Sinclair asked. Emma knew of the incident.

"Just a couple of years ago the NIH discovered over three hundred vials of various deadly agents in one of their old buildings. Several were over sixty years old and had been overlooked in a storage closet for years."

"The NIH hired Rand Pharmaceuticals to properly store and dispose of those vials," Rand said. "It was supposed to be top secret. Select Rand employees handled the transfer to a secure facility."

"So, are you implying that you kept them instead? Why?"

Rand put his hands out.

"Within days of the discovery, which hit the news if you recall, I began getting threats on my life and blackmailed to hand the vials over. It was as if someone had breached the CDC firewalls and learned that it was Rand Pharmaceuticals assigned to secure them."

Emma began to pace. "Smallpox dies in heat—and within twenty-four hours, when exposed to the air."

"Those vials dated from the 1950s and they were still live after being kept in a closet for over thirty years. A fact that was also dutifully reported worldwide." Rand sounded bitter. "Those reports probably sealed my fate. That the virus survived should have been a secret."

Sinclair's eyes widened in horror. "Please tell me that's not true. How could they have survived all those years? Vaccines are supposed to be stored in cool containers and never, ever exposed to heat. If they're so unstable—and most contain viruses, in order to work—how can a virus itself remain viable?"

"What were these closets like? Were the vials kept in cold storage all those years?" Emma asked.

"Not at all. It was exactly what the newspapers reported—a *closet*. Locked, yes, but not temperature controlled. And, even though the building itself had air conditioning, there had to be times during those past thirty years that the electricity went down, or the system was shut off for servicing...something. Yet, the virus remained alive."

"Did your scientists protect themselves when handling it? Have you notified the authorities?"

"Yes, and of course we notified the authorities. They directed us to retain the sample so that they could analyze it and determine which lab was breached. We were also told to cease the mission immediately."

"That's why you ended it so abruptly." A devastating thought came to her. "Oh God, do you think any of the vaccines that we administered in those villages contained smallpox?"

Rand swallowed. "I don't think so. I personally checked each of the remaining boxes, and none appeared to have been altered. Even so, I pulled several more random lots from boxes that retained an intact tamper seal and sent them along with the tampered group. Those were clean. All the other boxes were present and accounted for and remained sealed with our tamper seal. I think they were clean as well. I just wish we had learned of this earlier because I wouldn't have used any of it."

Emma nodded. "Okay, give me an idea of who you think would do this, starting with your competitors. Who would want you or Rand Pharmaceuticals to fail?"

Rand snorted. "This has nothing to do with competition. It's bioterrorism. Someone learned of our mission and decided to piggyback on it. What better way to hide a biological agent then to intersperse it with other similar agents?"

"I'm not arguing that the plan was ingenious, just that I don't think Rand was singled out at random. There are any number of vaccination missions being conducted throughout Africa at any time. Yours was the one that had the potential to move large quantities of vaccines over an expansive area. Somebody had to infiltrate Rand, learn which vaccines were targeted to be shipped to Senegal, identify just that shipment, open the crate, find the vaccine stores, and tamper with two."

Rand said nothing but he didn't need to. Emma could read in his eyes that she'd analyzed the situation correctly. She stalked to the SUV and yanked open the door. The driver's body fell sideways and his torso curved toward the ground. Blood dripped from his head wound into the dry earth.

"Help me get your first victim into the back."

Rand set his jaw and walked over to the car, while Sinclair covered her face with her hands and started to cry.

Emma grabbed the corpse's shirt at his back and curled a hand around his armpit, while Rand did the same on the other side. They slid the body out and lowered it to the ground. As they did, a small, disc-shaped device dropped onto the ground. Rand bent down, picked it up, and turned it over before he held it out to her. Made of hard plastic, it was black, the diameter of a hockey puck but not as thick.

"What's this?"

Emma turned the disc over and held it up to study it more closely. The black plastic became slightly more transparent in the sun's rays, and she could see the circuits inside it.

"It's a GPS locator. It sends out a signal that can be tracked. Like those services that locate and recover your car when it gets stolen. Generally, it's stuck to the bottom of a car in an inconspicuous place."

Emma reached down and searched the driver's pockets, taking care not to look at his ruined face. She found a frayed wallet with nothing in it except a chauffeur service business card and a wad of hundred dollar bills. She showed them to Rand.

"Did you pay him in American dollars?"

Rand shook his head and crouched next to her. "I did not."

"How did you come to employ him? Did *you* hire him?"

Again, Rand shook his head. "I did not. The SUV was ordered from a facility in Johannesburg and shipped to Senegal. We received it the night before last, and two of my employees took it to the chauffeur service's garage, where they arranged to add the netting. The service called the next day and said that their regular driver had come down with dengue fever and they were sending us a freelance operator." Rand jutted his chin towards the body. "This guy showed up."

"Did this guy bring the gun?"

"I brought the gun," Rand said.

"And he brought the hit men," Emma said.

She put the disc on the ground, stood, and stomped on it with the heel of her combat-style boots. After several raps, it lay in pieces in the dirt.

Rand straightened and waved away a fly hovering near his ear. The creature made several large looping curves downward and landed on the driver's face, near the blood.

"So someone got to the limousine service," Rand said.

Emma rocked her hand back and forth. "I don't think so. At least, it doesn't appear as though the service was in on it. If they had the car in their garage, it would have been a simple matter to attach the disc to the undercarriage. The fact that he was carrying it in his pocket makes me think that whoever is after you compromised the driver, not the service."

Emma watched him absorb the information. He seemed shaken but even more determined than he had been earlier.

"Can I guess what you're thinking?" Emma asked.

Rand sent a wary look in her direction. "Give it a shot."

"You're thinking that you're going to get revenge on whoever is after you. Make them pay."

A glint of satisfaction came into his eyes. He nodded but said nothing.

Emma checked to make sure Sinclair was far enough away so she wouldn't be able to overhear what she was going to say next. No sense in further upsetting the already distraught woman.

"Forget it. Hitting back means you're standing in the kill zone, which is stupid. Right now, you need to run. You can regroup and fight back later. With a plan."

He snorted. "I'm no coward. They're going to pay for this."

Emma felt her frustration mounting. "Listen, I'm all for making people feel the consequences of their actions, but few people have dealt with violence at this level. I have, and I'm here to tell you that people who'll do this don't think the way we do. They have no conscience. Nothing bothers them. You kill their partners in crime, guys they've known for ten years and who you'd think they care about, right? They'll put on a show of grief but, in reality, if someone else had offered them money to rat out, or even kill, their partner they'd have done it in a heartbeat. You'll never get the satisfaction that you're looking for that way."

"Sounds like capitalism at its finest," Rand said. "If you knew what goes on in the boardrooms of America, China, and any other world power, you'd be appalled. I'm used to betrayal, treason, theft, embezzlement, and now," he pointed to the driver, "attempted assassination. I'm not going to just roll over for them. Would you?"

"I'm not suggesting you roll over, just that you acknowledge what you're dealing with," Emma said.

He gave her a curt nod. "Point taken."

Emma took a deep breath to maintain her calm. His quick, almost flippant response made it clear that the point wasn't taken, at least not in any meaningful way. He was still acting as though he was the master of all he surveyed. Even if what he surveyed was a flat savannah dotted with trees.

"Help me get him into the back. Can you open it?" Emma said.

Rand took the key fob from his pocket, pressed a button, and the car's back door clicked.

"We'll have to make room," Rand said. He went to the rear of the car and started removing the luggage. Sinclair wiped her eyes and joined him. They stashed the bags in the shade of a nearby tree, where Sinclair stayed with them, while Emma and Rand returned to the body. Emma grabbed the man's legs and waited for Rand to lift the torso. The body sagged, and Emma staggered with the weight, even though the man was slender. Together they moved him to the car and fitted him into the back behind the second row of seats.

They closed the door, and Rand stood a moment, staring at it, his face grim.

"Tell me why these men are after you," Emma said.

Rand glanced up.

"I have a theory, not hard facts," he said.

"I'm listening," Emma said, "but we don't have the time for long stories. Those assassins will be back. Give me the Cliff Notes version."

Rand nodded. "Okay. Rand Labs has been developing that netting for three years. We're making it in various formats—netting, tarpaulin, and mesh screening. Once our final testing is complete, we'll begin selling it. We already have interest from the military establishment of several countries. The fiber content is patent protected, and the process to create the material is a trade secret. We're fighting on all fronts to stop unauthorized use but, several months ago, Chang Pao Zian, the head of one of China's largest manufacturing companies, stole the details of the manufacturing process. I've sued him in federal court, and he vowed to beat me there and to, as he put it, 'Crush you under my heel boot into the hard earth below.'" Rand swung his arm to indicate the SUV. "This is the result."

5

So, tell me who, besides this Chinese competitor, wants you dead."

Rand rubbed his forehead. "The list is too long to be of any use. Every major player in the pharma industry, every medical device player, two newspaper moguls, and an ex-girlfriend who married the head of an international bank. When she discovered he was playing around, she claimed that she was too...with me. He's vowed to destroy me."

"I didn't ask who wants to crush your business, I asked you who wants you dead. There's a difference," Emma said. As a scientist, she dealt with logic and disliked drama. Rand struck her as the type of man who dramatized everything in order to feel important. "What guy is fool enough to try to kill someone over a woman that he was already betraying anyway? Why would the guy care?"

Rand gave her a wry look. "I know you'll think I'm arrogant, but the billionaire set is the nastiest, filthiest, most corrupt group of people you'll ever meet. Many sold their souls to get on the Forbes list, and most will do anything to stay there. They take nothing lying down and just because they cast something off doesn't mean anyone else can have it."

"So says the man who threw two women to the dogs," Emma pointed out.

He nodded. "Touché. I'm not lily white, either, but I'd like to think I limit my competitive streak to mostly legitimate competition. I undercut sales margins, and I fund research for new and improved products. We invest billions in a few drugs, in the hopes that one will earn out."

"Just a benign worker bee who just happens to have two assassins on his tail," Emma said. Rand opened his mouth to respond, and she waved him off. "Let's discuss this more later. Right now, we have to get out of here. The problem is, how and which way?"

Emma started pacing as she thought and Rand moved to stand under the shade of the baobab tree, where Sinclair stood and fanned her face with a sheaf of papers that looked like a company memorandum. The car took the full heat of the sun and Emma couldn't help but think about the driver's body baking in the back.

"Get Nassar on the phone," Rand said to Sinclair, who started punching buttons on her cell. While she did, Rand turned to Emma.

"Nassar is a Saudi prince and business colleague. He has a fleet of planes at his disposal and can amass a troop of bodyguards in a heartbeat."

Sinclair handed Rand the phone, and he paced away as he spoke into it in low tones. After a moment, he waved Emma over.

"He says that he's sending a group from Pakistan. The Maraad. Do you know them?"

Emma nodded. "They're ruthless and efficient, and I don't trust them for a moment."

"I don't see that we have any choice," Rand said. "Nassar says that they're loyal to him and willing to risk it."

Then Nassar is a snake, Emma thought. "What's his plan?" she asked.

"If we can get to the Mali border they'll meet us there."

Emma shook her head. "Don't trust them."

Rand frowned, annoyance clear on his face. "I've known Nassar for years. He's been solid and dependable. He's a Saudi prince, for God's sake, so he can't afford to mess with me because he knows that I'll scream bloody murder to my friends in Washington."

"I'm not talking about him, I'm talking about the Maraad."

"I'm going to take him up on his offer," Rand said. "It's all we've got."

Emma had no intention of being anywhere near Rand when Nassar's crew came calling, but she had no control over Rand.

"You're free to do as you wish."

Sinclair gave her a piercing look and, when Rand turned his back and walked away, still cradling the phone in his hand, she came to stand next to Emma.

"What do you know about them?"

Emma batted at a fly that was swooping around her face. "They marched into a town at the India-Pakistan border, near Kashmir, in search of a wealthy Pakistani businessman that they thought was being held there. They shelled the town, killed most of the men, and then raped the women."

Sinclair swallowed, her eyes wide. "Did they get the man? Was he there?"

Emma nodded. "He was there all right but, when they found him, they called back to the family members that bankrolled their sack of the town and demanded more money. They got the money but never delivered the man. They killed him instead."

"So they cheated everyone."

Emma nodded. "Yes."

"Will you go to the border with us?"

Emma sighed. "I will, but only because it gets me nearer the route that I need to get through Mauritania. I'll disappear before the Maraad shows up."

"Do you think there's a chance that Mr. Rand is right… that they'll stay loyal to Nassar?"

"I suppose anything is possible, especially when dealing with a Saudi prince who has vast resources at his disposal, but I won't stay to test the theory."

Rand finished his call and returned, handing the phone back to Sinclair.

"We need to get out of here. They're going to fix that tire and come looking for us," Emma said.

Rand nodded. "I know. I've been trying to decide the best path to take."

"We leave the road and any chance of a bush taxi is gone. Still, I think we need to get away from the truck. When they come, they'll check it," Emma said.

Sinclair began fanning herself again. "There's not much around here to hide behind." She scanned the horizon.

Emma had to agree. Sun-bleached scrub grass lined the road, giving way to a brown dirt field dotted with trees. The expanse of browns and yellow made for a stunning contrast against the blue sky. The air smelled of hay and baked dirt.

"I wonder how long it will take for someone to pass us," Rand said. He looked at his watch, which appeared expensive enough that, if pawned, would feed an African family for several years. Emma's own watch was a sturdy running model with a lap counter, chronograph, and a glow switch for nighttime viewing. Not fashionable, but practical. She'd left her fashionable watches at home in Miami Beach.

She marched back and forth, debating what their next move would be. An ultramarathon runner and sometime trail endurance competitor, her first desire was to run as far and fast as she could before the assassins could regroup, fix their vehicle, and follow. But the reality of Africa weighed on her. She could run, but not into the emerging crisis at the capital, and not into the scrub all around her, without supplies of water and food. Also, racing across the country would work for her, but Rand and Sinclair might not be able to keep up.

The sputtering of an engine in the distance made her pause. Rand heard it as well.

"Salvation?" he asked.

Emma didn't answer. Instead, she checked the pistol.

"Maybe you get into the vehicle. Lay on the floor. It's dead but still armored," she said to the two. She crouched next to the car's wheel.

The bush taxi they'd seen earlier came into view. Painted turquoise blue—with bright yellow trim and complete with haphazard rust holes, dents, and a roaring engine—the minibus bulged with people, luggage, and three goats tied to the roof area and cordoned off with makeshift wooden slats. Even from a distance, Emma could see that it was packed full. She stepped out from behind the wheel and waved the taxi down. It came to a halt next to her in a flurry of dust. The driver, a skinny man with a missing canine tooth and wearing a polo shirt faded from red to pink, leaned out. Next to him sat a large woman in a colorful dress with a head wrap equally as colorful.

"*Salaam alaikum.*" Hello. Emma greeted him in Arabic, as she waved away the bits of grit thrown up by the truck wheels.

"*Wa'alaikum salaam,*" the man said, as a delighted smile spread across his face.

Emma itched to get straight to the point, but such direct conversation was considered rude in West Africa. So, she reined in her impatience and began the elaborate required greeting process. While the driver's words didn't reveal his ethnicity, the majority of Senegalese spoke Wolof, and so she switched to the few words of greeting that she knew in that language.

"*Na'nga def?*" How are you?

"*Jaam rek. Yow nag?*" I'm in peace, and you? "You speak our language! You need a ride, lady?" he added in English. "If so, I must tell you the same that I told the men down the road. We are full."

"Were the men driving a car with a flat tire?"

He nodded. "These men did not look friendly to me, and so I just waved them off and kept moving. Like you, they were not African."

"Were they fixing the tire?" Emma fervently hoped that they were not.

He nodded. "They had the car up on a jack and a spare ready. I would not wait here for them to appear."

"I understand, but our car is also not working, as you see."

"Do you wish to go to Dakar?"

His gaze took in her clothes—a dark blue linen shirt with the sleeves rolled up, khaki shorts in a technical fabric, and black combat-style lace-up boots that were made by a running company. He also flicked a glance at her watch, which she'd expected. The serviceable running watch wouldn't scream money as Rand's did, but just being a Westerner in Senegal meant that she'd be charged ten times more than the Senegalese passengers, if she was lucky, that is.

She shook her head. "Not to Dakar. The fighting has started."

The woman smacked the driver on the shoulder and directed a stream of Wolof his way. The man winced and responded in rapid fire. When he was done, he exhaled in irritation.

"She says she didn't want to leave her village and the danger is my fault. She acts as though I should know when the world tilts," he said to Emma. "I will continue through Tambacounda to Koumpentoum. And then we will see."

Emma heard the sound of a baby crying from somewhere in the bowels of the bus. No other sounds came from the packed passengers, and none seemed impatient at the delay. Emma had always admired the Africans' tolerance for delay. The rhythm of the day in Africa matched no other rhythm she'd encountered. Time was flexible and plentiful.

"I would like to return to the N2. I'll head to Marrakesh through Mauritania," Emma said.

"That's very dangerous. You might be safer waiting in Tambacounda for the fighting to stop."

"And if it doesn't?" Emma asked.

The man frowned. "Then nowhere is safe."

"Still, I need a bush taxi. Are there any coming?"

The man nodded. "Usually. But full, of course."

"Yes." Emma sighed.

Bush taxis between destinations were always full because they wouldn't leave until every seat, and then some, were taken. They had no schedule and, if you paid your fare in the morning, you would have to wait until the remaining seats were purchased. Emma heard the SUV door creak open and close and Rand walked up to stand next to her. The woman in the headscarf leaned across the driver to get a better look at the new arrival.

The driver locked onto Rand's watch. Rand gave the usual greeting in Arabic, and both the man and woman responded.

"How far to the nearest village?" Emma asked. The man and woman conferred.

"Only seven kilometers that way." He waved to the west. "Follow that thin trail there. When it disappears, you will have three kilometers left. Look to the dead tree for direction. There is sometimes a bush taxi at the village."

"Then that is where I'll go. I thank you for your help. Peace," Emma said.

"And to you," the man said. He put the taxi into gear and started to move away. Two of the goats bleated in distress as the truck picked up speed.

"You told them about the fighting?" Rand asked.

Emma nodded. "I did."

"And they don't care?"

"He'll stop before Dakar."

"I was hoping they'd turn around and take us with them."

"Me, too," Emma said. "We'd better head to the village. He said the attackers were busy fixing their tire. I don't want to wait for them, or nightfall."

Rand turned and headed to Sinclair, who stood again under the tree with the luggage.

"The SUV is stifling hot...and with the driver," she said, swallowing hard, "I couldn't stay in there.

Emma glanced at Rand, who flicked a look at her but said nothing.

"There's the trail," he said.

A beaten path was visible through the grass. Emma looked at what they'd carry.

The luggage carried by Rand, Sinclair, and Emma was a study in contrasts. Both Rand and Sinclair had hopped in and out of capital cities throughout the trip and so carried regular suitcases. Rand's consisted of a metal roller bag made of what appeared to be titanium. It was a lot like the man—sleek, expensive, and giving the appearance of indestructibility. Sinclair's conservative black roller bag looked solid, dependable, and well used. Emma's clothes were packed in a large technical backpack, which was equipped with a ventilated bottom for carrying wet shoes and several outside pockets for easy access to tools, maps, and her compass. A rolled sleeping mat and a lightweight sleeping bag were attached to the bottom. Inside, the clothes were sealed in compressed plastic travel bags. She'd traveled and camped around the world, and was well versed in the various insects that could nest in one's shoes and clothes. Pulling on a pair of socks with a scorpion nestled inside was not her idea of a good morning.

"Do you intend to drag the luggage?"

Both Rand and Sinclair nodded.

"I don't have anything smaller or more lightweight to use," Rand said. "The path looks well worn, so they should roll easily enough, at least while the trail holds out."

Emma wasn't interested in arguing. She shrugged into her backpack and slapped a safari hat on her head. Sinclair did the same with a straw number and prepared to pull her bag. Rand reached down, telescoped the handle on his luggage, and straightened. Emma checked her compass just for good measure.

"I'm ready," she said.

They started out. The hot sun beamed down, and a few young locust jumpers leapt out of their way. Emma fought the urge to run but increased her pace to a brisk walk. Both Sinclair and Rand kept up. The only sounds were the rolling luggage wheels as they bumped along the path and the breeze as it rattled the shrubs and tree branches. The Harmattan trade winds blew across Africa from the Sahara Desert during the dry season, creating clouds of dust and violent sandstorms. While they were not as strong as they'd been in previous days, Emma knew that they would only increase when they reached the border.

If they reached the border.

6

Baston Tobenga's cell phone rang just as he was completing his morning prayers. While not a devout Muslim by any means, he'd long ago learned that the appearance of caring went a long way to ensuring his acceptance among the men in his camp. The telephone screen indicated that the Arab was calling. Tobenga nodded to the others and pulled out his phone as he moved away to a quiet corner.

"What is it?" he asked.

"He escaped." The voice on the other phone was soft, which belied the actual menace of the caller. The Arab was as vicious as any African strongman that Tobenga knew.

"Hard to believe," Tobenga said. He kept his voice neutral, but inside he felt the adrenaline beginning to surge. It would not do to cross the Arab.

"Believe it. Send a second crew."

"Why? The first are closest. Are they all dead?" Tobenga doubted such a thing would befall them all. They were four of his best, and every one of them had completed successful assassinations the world over, against some of the toughest targets. A soft CEO of an American company could not match them in ferocity.

"No, but they will be when I reach them. Send a second crew."

Tobenga set his jaw. "To kill them before they complete their task is foolish. It will take me several hours to assemble another crew and then I have the logistics of getting them to Senegal to deal with. No, let the first crew finish the job. It's not like he can fight. He's a weak American bureaucrat."

"So you haven't heard," the Arab said.

Tobenga felt his body tense even further. "Heard what?"

"He travels with Emma Caldridge."

The name meant nothing to Tobenga. "A woman? Even less to worry about."

The Arab swore. "Fool. She sometimes works for Darkview and Edward Banner. Does that jog your memory?"

Tobenga swallowed. That Rand would have employed a Darkview security officer was something he hadn't counted on in preparing for the hit. Darkview personnel were known for their skills and, more importantly, their intelligence. The latter attribute was one that few hired mercenaries possessed. Darkview's competitors had many ex-soldiers in their employ, but most were used to following orders, not giving them. Banner hired personnel with various skill sets, which created a wealth of experience and knowledge across many fields, and all were leaders.

"Is she former American military?"

"No. A chemist. And ultra runner. She was competing in the Comrades Marathon that was bombed a few years ago." Normally a chemist would strike no terror in Tobenga, but any Darkview operative was to be respected.

"So, Rand hired a Darkview chemist as a bodyguard?"

"It's doubtful that Rand knew she worked for Darkview. He asked her to join in his charity mission. Her company did work for Rand's pharmaceutical holdings. Either way, she's armed. Your crew reported that they were fired upon."

Not to Tobenga. They'd told him everything was fine, but taking just a bit longer than usual. He wondered how the Arab got his information.

"I'll cover this, you needn't worry. He will be killed," Tobenga said.

"And her?"

"And her, too. Or sold. Either way."

The Arab hung up. Tobenga punched some numbers on the phone. It was answered in seconds.

"Kortya?" he said.

The man on the other end grunted.

"What's going on? The Arab said you failed."

"The Arab is an ass. Someone tipped Rand. He travels in an armored SUV."

Tobenga's eyebrows flew up. An armored vehicle was one of the last vehicles he'd expected Rand to use.

"And the helicopters? Couldn't you shoot them down?"

"He only used two. We expected him to fly into the village today from Tambacounda, but the distance was too far for the helicopter and he drove."

Tobenga had to agree. Someone had tipped Rand off.

"The Arab wants you and the crew dead. Kill Rand and the woman with him and get out of Senegal for a while. Where is he?" Tobenga asked.

"We don't know. We found the driver dead in the car, but Rand is gone. Either he grabbed a bush taxi or took off. But don't worry, we'll get him."

"Is he coming my way?" Tobenga was stationed in the second ring from Dakar. Not close enough to draw fire from the Senegalese forces, but still giving the appearance that he wanted to fight for freedom. He'd let the others die and—when they'd taken their casualties—he'd move in, finish the job, and loot the city.

"Maybe. Are you afraid of him?"

Tobenga snorted. "Never, but I have my hands full watching the front lines. I don't need to watch my back, as well. I expect you to get him."

"Relax. He's a dead man. But first I'll need some supplies. I'm coming in."

"Fine. Come here and stock up, but then get back on Rand's trail and kill them all. And, after you're done, don't forget to drop out of sight for a while."

"The Arab doesn't scare me. Besides, the days are long, and the fighting begins. Soon we'll see who survives."

Tobenga nodded to himself. Accidents happened all the time in war.

7

Two hours into the walk they came upon the village. A village in havoc, that is. Several women carried luggage to a waiting bush taxi, this one a vintage Peugeot 504 sedan, where the men were busy roping baggage to the roof. One—a rangy man in his thirties with thin, short dreadlocks to his ears and wearing a faded blue t-shirt—was holding a towering stack of luggage in place while discussing the logistics of strapping over twenty pieces onto the car's sloped roof. He spoke French with an English accent that declared him to be a foreigner. He glanced up as Emma walked toward him. She watched him take in Rand, Sinclair, and the bags they dragged before returning his attention to her.

"Did the Ritz Carlton's shuttle break down?" he asked in British-accented English. Emma bit back a smile.

"Our car blew a tire, and we were told that there might be a bush taxi available here."

He shook his head. "Not likely. We've got nine people slated for this one, and the other has twelve."

Emma glanced behind him, where thirty others were haggling around the driver of what might have been another Peugeot 504. She couldn't see beyond the throng but—if it was a cinq-cent-quatre, as the locals called the car—it would carry ten at the most. Twelve sounded unlikely, unless two were infants.

"He have a lot of money?" One of the men helping the dreadlocked Englishman pointed to Rand. Dreadlocks flicked a look at Emma, and it was clear that he was trying to gauge if she understood French. Emma kept her face impassive. She spoke French fairly fluently but wanted to take Dreadlock's measure.

"Probably, but who would you boot? Your mother? Auntie? Grandmother?"

The man shrugged. "My mother-in-law, for sure." Two men nearby laughed, and another spoke in rapid Wolof.

"I'm Emma Caldridge," she said to Dreadlocks. "And they," she waved in Rand's direction, "are Jackson Rand and Rhonda Sinclair."

"Carnegie Wendel. People call me Carn," he said. "I'm sorry you had to walk all the way here for nothing but, as you can see, we don't have enough transport for the village, much less strangers." Several women balancing luggage on their heads walked by, followed by a stream of children and two goats being led by twine leashes. A helper on the far side of the car tossed a rope over the towering stack, and Carn caught it and pulled it tight.

"Why are they leaving?" Emma asked, though she suspected that she knew what the answer would be.

"There's fighting in Dakar, and the rumor is that it will soon spread outward. They fear the villages will be sacked."

"By the ASIS?" Emma asked.

Carn looped the rope through the handles of several pieces of luggage and held it in place while he waited for another man to thread the other end through the car windows.

"Not the ASIS so much. You and I are more likely to be

targeted by them than any Africans," he looked her over, "though, since I'm black, I might be left alone. But you—and those two—are definite ASIS targets." He grasped the second end of the rope and began tying off the stack. "They're mostly afraid of the insurgents from Casamance, who are known to burn entire villages just for fun."

"I'm going to ask the Toubab what he will pay," the other man assisting Carn said, this time in French. "If it is much, then I'll tell my mother-in-law it's better for my future that she should walk." He strolled away and toward Rand, who was drinking water from a woman's earthenware pitcher. Emma wondered how much Rand had paid for the water. She shrugged out of her backpack and laid it on the ground.

"I'd better go over there. He doesn't speak French," Emma said.

Carn nodded. "They'll take him for a lot if you don't."

Emma had seen Rand in action, while he negotiated with villagers to convince them to allow vaccination, so she knew that Carn was wrong. No one took Rand for a ride. She followed the taxi driver and caught up with him as he began his pitch.

"Good afternoon to you and your friends. I hope all is well with you and your family," the driver said in French.

Rand handed the woman the pitcher. "Do you speak English?"

The driver shook his head. "No Anglaise," he said.

"Can you translate?" Rand asked Emma. She'd been translating periodically for Rand during the trip, so he was well aware of her ability.

"He wants to know how much you'll pay for a space in the taxi."

"In CFA?"

Emma shrugged. "He might take euros as well." The West African franc was the usual currency, but euros were often accepted.

"I have both on me, as well as dollars, but not enough to buy the entire car, which would be my first choice. Do you think he'll take a note for the rest and then give me the car?"

"I doubt it. That car is his only way to survive."

Rand rubbed the back of his neck. "Start at five thousand, then."

It was the equivalent of ten dollars and about triple the usual three-dollar fare. Emma turned to the driver.

"He says he and his family are well, thank you, and wishes you peace."

"Peace upon him."

"He wishes you peace," Emma said to Rand, who gave a quick nod in response.

"I see that your friend is on foot. Does he wish to purchase a seat on the taxi?"

"He does," Emma said. "He's offered five thousand."

"CFA?" The driver pronounced it *say fah*.

"*Oui*, CFA," Emma said.

"I am so sorry. It must be at least twenty-six thousand CFA."

"Twenty-six thousand, or about fifty dollars," Emma told Rand, who frowned.

"That's absurd. Tell him eight thousand and I need three seats."

Emma translated and the driver shook his head. He didn't have three seats, he explained. Only one and, because it was already taken, he would have to split the fare with the one who had the prior claim.

The haggling continued, with Rand raising each bid in small increments and insisting on seats for all of them. When they reached twenty dollars per rider, the driver agreed to ask for more volunteers to give up their places.

Rand sighed. "What are my odds?"

"Depends. He definitely has at least one. It's his mother-in-law's seat. Will the others give up their safety to get more money than they've seen in months? Hard to say. I'm surprised that you're bargaining. Quite different from the helicopter conversation."

"Once it was clear they wouldn't sell me the car, it's best to bargain. Otherwise, I'll look like a fool. Is it the ASIS that they're afraid of?" Rand asked.

"No. Apparently, while we Westerners fear the ASIS, the Africans fear the insurgents more."

The driver returned with an older woman in a bright dress and traditional head wrap. She walked with an upright posture and seemed more than capable of walking.

"This is my wife's mother. She will not give up her seat but urges you to allow one of your female companions to ride along and share her seat," Emma translated.

"How much?" Rand asked.

"The same," the driver said.

Rand snorted. "That was for a full seat, not a half. I'll pay you half."

Surprisingly, the driver relented.

"Which one of you two will ride?" he asked Emma and Sinclair. Sinclair shot a look at the taxi.

"It doesn't look as if it'll make it out of the village, much less all the way to the border."

Emma had to agree but—while the taxi would be extremely uncomfortable—running in the hot sun, while being sandblasted by the trade winds, would be much worse. Of the two of them, though, Emma suspected that she was the only one truly qualified to attempt the run.

"Not me. I'll run it. Given the roads and the state of his transportation, I'm likely to make it there before the taxi does anyway," Emma said.

"Are you sure?" Sinclair asked.

Emma nodded. "I'm sure."

"Then I'll see you both at the border. In Kidira."

8

Rand and Emma helped Sinclair squeeze into the packed Peugeot. The car creaked with a groaning sound as the weight of eight other adults was added in addition to Sinclair. Both cars were overburdened, and only one of the passengers in each car was an infant. Sinclair was the last to be jammed into the front passenger seat, where three others already sat. Carn tried to close the door, but he only succeeded in pushing against Sinclair's side.

"Hold on, we're going to press you inside," he said, as he waved to Rand. "Give me a hand, will you?" Rand stepped up and put both palms flat on the Peugeot's door. "Now push slowly," Carn said and he added his strength to the endeavor. The passengers shifted and somehow the door closed. Rand stepped back with an astonished look on his face.

"I would never have believed it possible," he said to Emma.

Sinclair winced. "The chicken in the car's footwell is pecking at me," she said, as she craned her neck to see downward through the many legs.

"Shove it a bit with your foot," Carn said. Sinclair shifted and the chicken squawked.

Carn slapped his hands together. "You're off, then. Safe travels."

The Peugeot sputtered to life and, when the driver put it in gear, it lurched a bit before the gears engaged and it finally moved out.

"Sounds like the transmission's slipping," Rand said. Carn nodded.

"Been that way for as long as I can remember."

Rand gave him a quizzical look. "How long has that been?"

"Two years," Carn said. "I came as an aid worker and stayed on."

"Your contract was renewed?" Emma asked.

Carn shook his head. "No. It was a woman."

Emma was just about to tease him about falling prey to a female, but the look on his face stilled her tongue. It was a mixture of sadness and despair. He spun around and went back toward three houses that lined the village's main pathway.

Rand watched him go. "Not a happy ending."

"So it would seem," Emma said.

"Think it was malaria?"

"Or HIV…or childbirth. Hard to say."

"I hope not childbirth," Rand said.

"I agree. That would be awful."

He sighed. "So much sorrow here."

"Africa is the world of many sorrows, isn't it?"

Rand stood with his arms akimbo. "It doesn't have to be that way," he said in a harsh tone.

Emma reached down to retrieve her backpack. While she agreed with Rand, the troubles in Africa sometimes felt overwhelming. "We should move on. I'd like to find a safe place to stop before night falls. The last thing I need is to be out on an open plain with no shelter."

"I don't have a tent, and my bag certainly isn't right for walking," Rand said.

"I'm going to ask Carn if anyone would be willing to sell you a backpack."

Rand nodded. "Meanwhile, I'm going to change into some technical gear and running shoes."

Emma nodded and headed toward the house that Carn had dodged into. It was a simple structure, with one large room on entry and a doorway on the left that Emma assumed led to a bedroom. Carn stood next to a wooden kitchen table with three mismatched spindle chairs. The wall behind him contained cabinets, a sink, and an ancient white refrigerator in one long line. Two women dressed in head wraps were talking to him in rapid French, and he was listening with a serious look on his face. He glanced up when she stepped inside.

"Trouble?" Emma asked.

"Big trouble. The insurgents are attacking Red Cross stations. Burning everything in sight and killing the aid workers."

"He must leave. Now," the closest woman said to Emma. She had dark eyes and what Emma could see of her hair, under the head wrap, was white. Yet her skin was smooth and unlined. "Go with her," the woman said to Carn.

"And the rest? What happens to you?" Carn asked.

The second woman waved a hand in the air in dismissal. "We'll head into the bush. They'll not find us. We have this." The second woman when to the sink and opened the cabinet below. She angled out a short gun. Emma did her best not to gape at it. It was an AK-47 with a retractable butt. The woman extended the end and held the gun crosswise before her.

Carn, too, looked astonished. "Where in the world did you get that?"

"My grandson. He stole it from some insurgents while they slept. That was some years ago." She cocked her head to the side as she thought. "In the Congo. He was lucky to get out alive." She handed the gun to the first woman before bending over and reaching again into the cabinet. When she straightened, Emma saw that she held a Beretta. She extended it, grip out, to Carn. "This one you take. I'd give you the other, but we have more bullets for this one, and you'll need bullets. We know how to be economical. We'll only shoot when required."

Emma wanted the AK, but she had no bullets for it, either.

"I don't believe in weapons. This war isn't mine and I'm not allied with either side. They'll have to fight without me," Carn said. A look of frustration passed over the first woman's face.

"When elephants fight, the grass gets trampled."

Carn pressed his lips together and shook his head. The woman sighed and held the pistol out to Emma.

"And you?"

Emma took the gun from her. The metal was cold against her palm. "Thank you."

The woman gave her a curt nod. "As a Westerner, you're worth a lot to them. They will sell you if they catch you... after they rape you."

Emma held the gun up. "With this, I have a chance."

The second woman lowered a sling around her neck that ended in a bulging woven sack. She settled the strap crosswise across her body. Carn picked up another bag and waved the women out the door. Once outside, the hot wind dried Emma's lips, and she squinted against the glaring afternoon sun. Rand stood a few feet away, now clothed in lightweight cargo shorts and a long-sleeved shirt made of a technical fabric in a dark color. His expensive loafers were gone and, instead, he wore bright green and yellow neon running shoes. The watch remained. He glanced at the gun in Emma's hand.

"Excellent. We need all we can get. The villagers told me that the forces that are headed this way are moving fast."

An ancient Mitsubishi drove up, stacked with mismatched luggage roped onto the roof, which tottered in a curving tower and looked like a sagging question mark. The passenger door opened and a man waved the two old women inside. After much pushing from outside the car, and maneuvering from within, the women were settled in the back seat and the door pressed closed. They drove away in a cloud of dirt and muffler noise. An arm appeared out of the window, and the small, delicate hand of a child waved goodbye.

The village was empty. Only Emma, Rand, and Carn remained.

9

W hy didn't you go with them?" Emma asked Carn.

He inhaled deeply and exhaled just as slowly. "When the insurgents discover aid workers in the villages they're becoming even more brutal. One of the men said it's to set an example and to send the message to the villages ahead that they must offer up any Westerners in their midst. I'd just put everyone at risk."

"With your looks, they may assume you're Senegalese," Rand said. "Or at the very least African."

Carn shook his head. "My Wolof is terrible. One word out of my mouth and the accent would give me away."

"Would you like to join us?" Emma asked.

Carn nodded. "Where are you going?"

Emma waved down the road. "Back to the border. From there through Mauritania to Marrakesh."

Carn grimaced. "Can I change my mind? Mauritania's not a whole lot better than here."

"I know, but I don't have any other ideas," Emma said.

Rand stepped closer. "I do. How about if I put out a request for a mercenary force to act as our bodyguards? Offer to pay double? Would your friend Banner be able to get the message out?"

Carn brightened. "You know Edward Banner?" he said to Emma.

"I do. How do you know him?"

"About two months ago, he sent a group of his security personnel to a nearby town to act as an escort for some supplies. The insurgents were attacking the convoys at night and taking all the provisions. Banner loaned the guards and never charged our organization. I rode with him in the lead truck."

"We've already been in contact with him, and he said that he can't spare any personnel for us, but promised to get someone to meet me in Nouakchott."

Carn's hopeful look fled. "That's a long, dangerous way from here."

Emma nodded. "I know. I'm sorry. I won't be offended if you decide to strike out on your own."

"No, I'll join you. Wandering in the bush alone is for fools."

"And my idea? The mercenaries?" Rand asked.

Emma pulled out her phone and powered it on. After a moment, she was relieved to see a signal load. She dialed Banner and he picked up on the first ring. She assumed he was aware she was the one who was calling and launched right into her request.

"Mr. Rand would like to get the word out that he's willing to pay exorbitant amounts to any mercenary guards willing to provide security for our trip to Mauritania. Do you know any who'd be willing to take the job?"

"Only the Dysann Group, but their reputation isn't the best," Banner replied. She had the phone on speaker and she watched Carn scowl at the name.

The Dysann Group was known for employing men that were rejected by Darkview and the other, more reputable, contract security companies. While Dysann paid very well, working for them heightened the risk of bodily injury or death. Their employees would make a lot of money, but were expected to go to any area that Dysann chose to send them, no questions asked. Their loss rate was triple that of other contract groups, and rumor was that they could be easily swayed to switch sides mid-mission, if the right amount of money was offered.

"I guess we're stuck."

"Okay, then. I'll put the word out. Has your situation changed?"

"Not really, but I do have a second weapon."

"Well, that's something. Keep moving. All night if you have to. The insurgents are laying waste to every village they encounter. It's a rampage."

"Where are they now?" Rand asked.

"One hundred miles away."

"Which direction?" Emma asked.

"Every direction, but the group marching from the Mali border are south of the N2 so, if you head that way, you might miss them in the dark. Can you keep your phone on? Do you have enough juice for it to last through the night?"

"I do. And I have a solar charger, so I'll recharge it when the sun rises."

"Good. I'll use it to track you. If one of my men gets free, I'll let them know your coordinates. Believe me when I say that, if there's even a slight chance to get help to you through the enemy lines, I'll do it."

Tears sprang to Emma's eyes at his words, and she swallowed to control the sudden surge of emotion.

"Any other tips?" she asked, her voice rough.

"You'll hear the insurgents before you see them. They're led by drummers. They think it chases off evil spirits."

"Who are they kidding? *They* are evil spirits," Emma said.

Carn waved Rand toward him. "Come with me. I have a spare backpack." The two men walked away. Emma switched the phone off speaker.

"Are they moving through the night as well?"

"They are."

"Then they're beating the drums to drive the animals before them."

"That's a good point. No sense getting attacked."

Emma walked over to her own backpack and shifted the phone to her other hand while she rummaged through a pocket for her compass.

"Tell it to me straight. How many fighters are there?"

Nothing from the other end of the line.

"Banner, you there?"

"Twenty thousand, all told."

Emma sucked in a breath. No guerrilla force in Africa anywhere could amass that many fighters. She'd expected Banner to say two, maybe three, thousand, and that they were spread between the various groups in different locations, so that she wouldn't have to face them all at once.

"How the hell did they get that many? They must be from several tribes, and they typically don't work together. Tribal animosities run deep."

"We think there must be some government…some foreign government…working in the background, funding them. No African strongman that we know of has the kind of resources that can amass such a force, much less pay for the logistics of arming and moving them."

Emma finally found the compass. It had a dial rimmed with glow-in-the-dark dots, and a large needle pointer, and was encased in a leather holder with an attached carabiner.

"Not to mention feeding them. How are they arranging to do that?" She took off the safari hat, stuffed it into the pack, and grabbed a vented baseball-style running cap.

"They're stealing it from the aid shipments sent from the West. They've taken over the supply lines and are halting the cargo at key points along the route, killing the aid workers and looting the food."

"And the civilians?"

"They were starving before, now they're dying."

Rand and Carn appeared from around the back of a house with a thatched roof. Rand's suitcase was not in sight and he now wore a backpack.

"Listen, Rand's headed this way, so I don't have a lot of time, but can you ask Stromeyer to check into him? Get me some information?"

Carol Stromeyer was the vice president of Darkview, and former military, as well. She'd spent most of her career in acquisitions, procurement, and logistics for various US military installations around the world. As a result, she was unparalleled in her ability to find, procure, and requisition anything, despite immense bureaucratic entanglements. Her research capabilities were legendary, and she was responsible for managing Darkview's DOD contracts.

"Will do."

"In the meantime, I'll shake the truth out of Rand."

Banner rang off, just as Rand and Carn stepped up.

"I heard my name. What's up?" Rand said.

Emma bent down and put the phone in a side pocket of her own backpack. She stood and fixed him with a look.

"Tell me why you have assassins on your tail."

Carn looked stunned. Rand shot him a glance before turning back to address Emma.

"I told you, it's most likely a competitor."

"Did you say assassins?" Carn asked. Emma waved him to silence.

Rand's face took on the set expression that Emma already recognized meant that he wouldn't tell her. She turned and walked away. After a moment, Rand and Carn caught up.

"He wants to bury me, I told you that," Rand said.

"Liar," Emma replied. She picked up the pace and began plotting how to survive.

10

Tobenga's day turned bright when he saw the embassy caravan driving toward him. He'd been encamped in the second ring outside Thiès and following by radio the shelling from the first ring into Dakar. His men had finally breached the Senegalese army's forces, taken Dakar, and hacked down the doors to the United States embassy, only to find shredded paperwork blanketing the floor and the offices empty.

Now, Tobenga watched from a high ridge as the caravan of SUVs wound its way down the single best road out of Dakar and wondered how they'd managed to dodge his perimeter. Someone had been bribed, that much was certain. He made a mental note to find the traitor. The three white Suburbans were pocked with gunshots, and the first car's passenger window had a jagged hole in it.

They'd taken some fire at least, Tobenga thought. Still, he wanted to throttle whoever had allowed them to escape. It was his job as a lieutenant with the ASIS to secure enough hostages to keep the coffers full, and a load of US embassy personnel was sure to bring bags of cash and worldwide notoriety. The Arab would be thrilled at the capture.

Tobenga tallied up the soldiers who surrounded him. Three seasoned warriors with AK-47s, and RPG-7s capable of firing over a distance of close to five hundred meters; ten fighters at ground level with various semiautomatic weapons, mostly AK-47s, but some with pistols only; and six teenage boys with no training and little ability to follow commands. The last he'd taken from villages near the border of the Republic of Congo, and they'd proven to be more hassle than they were worth. Tobenga was planning to set them free to wander home because he hated having to feed such useless idiots. Kortya walked up to stand by his side.

"Have a look," Tobenga said and handed over his binoculars. Kortya gave a grunt of satisfaction.

"Consulate plates."

"*United States* consulate plates," Tobenga said. "The passengers in those cars are worth a fortune in ransoms."

Kortya looked dubious. "I thought the Americans refuse to negotiate."

Tobenga nodded. "They lie and say that, it's true, but they also carry kidnap insurance for just this situation, and they let the hostages' relatives access it. That way a ransom is paid, but the government can claim deniability."

Kortya went back to watching the convoy. "Think they have any arms?"

Tobenga stroked his beard. This was, of course, the question. "I would think at least a couple of guns. Probably handguns. No AKs and no one who can shoot with any accuracy."

Kortya threw him a surprised look. "Most embassy personnel are undercover CIA. What makes you think that they can't shoot?"

"I'm not saying that they can't shoot, I'm just saying that we shouldn't expect anyone who can hit a target. They've been sitting at desks too long, and most don't practice after they land in Senegal. Would look strange for embassy personnel to be caught training for a gun battle. I suspect whatever skills they had have grown rusty."

"I still think we should hit the lead with an RPG and see what happens," Kortya said.

Tobenga shook his head. "I need some kept alive."

"Those cars are armored. We hit the trunk and the car will stop, but the people likely won't die. Besides, how are we going to stop them otherwise? The AKs won't do it, and our forces are too scattered to overwhelm them in numbers."

"Ah, you're right, but hit only the lead car."

Kortya nodded and barked an order at the nearest soldier. "Put a rocket in that first car. We want to see what form of insect comes out."

The man nodded, shouldered his weapon, aimed, and fired. The warhead shot out of the weapon, and the resulting backblast exploded from the breech and flared ten feet behind. The grenade hit the first SUV on the hood, and the car exploded into flames. The back doors flew open, and three men tumbled out of one side, two women out of the other. All held guns. The second car swerved around the first and accelerated, shooting down the road and away from Tobenga's view.

"See? Armored," Kortya said.

"Tell him to do it again with the second car. When they emerge, kill a few from the first to get our point across."

Kortya relayed the order and the soldier fired again. The rocket hit a precise spot on the hood and, with the resulting explosion, the second car bounced once on its suspension. A second group of people, also armed, spilled out and began running back to the first car. The ground level soldiers stepped closer and began firing shooting three in the back and two more in the shoulders and head. The bodies jerked as each bullet entered and two fell straight down. A third, wounded but not dead, rolled to his back and raised his gun to fire, but died in a hail of semiautomatic fire. The soldiers ringed the remaining five survivors. Tobenga watched as they threw down their guns and raised their arms. The entire attack was over in a few seconds.

"Nice and quick," Tobenga said.

"Why'd you kill the ones in the front car, but not the ones in the second car?" Kortya asked.

Tobenga looked up from dialing his cell phone. "Because the lead car is the advance scout used to flush out danger and most likely held low-level personnel. With any luck, there are a few high-ranking officials in the back car." He heard the Arab answer and he put the phone to his ear. "We have some US officials from the embassy. They were fleeing in consulate vehicles."

"Excellent," the Arab said. "In SUVs?"

"Yes."

"There are cameras on the front and back of those cars. Secure any footage of the attack."

"How do you know that?' Tobenga asked.

"I was a guest of the embassy just a few days ago. They picked me up. Let me know when you have the footage. We'll release it to the media in the West. You did well. Now get Rand."

The Arab hung up.

11

Edward Banner sat on the sofa in the living room of his home on the outskirts of Washington, DC and watched as Carol Stromeyer paced the room's length. In her forties—with dirty blond hair, blue eyes, and clear skin devoid of makeup—Stromeyer's straight posture and trim figure gave evidence of her military training.

On the cocktail table in front of him were two folders, both open to reveal a 4 x 6 photo on one side and a dossier on the other. The man in the first folder Banner knew well—Cameron Sumner, a sharpshooter and contract employee of the DOD's Southern Hemisphere Drug Defense Department. Thirty years old, slender, with dark hair and an even darker personality, Sumner was an intense man who could fly a plane and shoot with a sniper's accuracy, although he'd never been in the military. He worked at the tip of Key West in the Air Tunnel Denial program, a joint effort between the United States and Colombia that was charged with the task of identifying and intercepting planes attempting to enter US airspace under radar. When not working there, he took the odd assignment from Darkview. Lately, he'd been refusing all additional work, opting to remain in the Keys and go about his business, but Banner knew that he would respond if approached in the proper manner.

The second dossier contained a photo of Jackson Rand. Rand's dossier ran to three pages, single spaced. The photo of an unsmiling Rand, who was ten years older than Sumner, showed a man—sharply dressed in a bespoke suit and tie striding down a city street—two other dark-suited and somber-looking people flanking him.

"Who are the wingmen?" Banner asked. To his relief, Stromeyer stopped her pacing and looked at him.

"Rhonda Sinclair, his assistant, and Brenda Rion, his attorney." She tilted her head to the side as she gazed at him. "Why do you look so relieved?"

"Because you've stopped pacing. You were beginning to remind me of a caged lion."

She inhaled deeply and lowered herself into a nearby leather club chair. As she did so, Banner rose to a side bar and reached for a decanter of what he knew was her favorite drink. He poured a shot into a rocks glass and walked over to hand it to her. She took it with a wry expression.

"It's just that I can't stand the fact that we're sitting here fiddling while the world burns. We need to intervene in Senegal, and you need to get the secretary of state to agree to it."

"She won't because she can't. The president won't let her."

Stromeyer took a sip of her drink and closed her eyes as she swallowed. She opened them and smiled at him. Her smile warmed him the way it always did.

"Use your considerable charm," she said.

He snorted. "Like that's going to help." He returned to the sofa and tapped on the photo of Rand.

"Tell me about him."

"Well, that's one fascinating individual. Raised in a small town in Iowa, undergrad at Harvard, and then again at Harvard for a business degree…which he didn't complete.

Took a job as an investment banker on Wall Street, moved to manage a hedge fund, and fifteen years ago left to accept a position at a mid-level pharmaceutical company. His Wall Street buddies were scratching their heads until he arranged to buy the company. Within ten years, it rose to become one of the fastest growing pharma labs in the world, and he took it public in a spectacular fashion. He's been married twice, claims to have learned his lesson, and swears he'll never marry again. As you can see, he's nice looking, and the ladies flock to him."

Banner shrugged. "To him or his money?"

"Both, I assume, but his latest companion is the heir to the Corlean cosmetic company, so I don't think she needs his checkbook."

Banner raised an eyebrow and took a sip of his own drink. "A match made in billionaire heaven."

Stromeyer nodded. "The rich are like royalty in that they tend to marry among themselves."

"But he claims to be done with marriage, so what does she get out of the deal?"

"Rumor is that she wants to buy a small cosmetics ingredient company that he controls."

Banner shook his head. "Wonder what that pillow talk sounds like at night."

Stromeyer smiled again. "They say shared interests keep a relationship alive. Wouldn't you want to discuss your day with your girlfriend?"

Banner pinned her with a direct look over the rim of his glass. "I can think of better ways to spend my time in bed."

She held his gaze for a moment, and it seemed like the air in the room shifted and warmed. She sipped again and broke contact.

"He's managed to amass quite a few enemies along the way," she said. Banner felt a stab of disappointment that she'd moved the conversation back to the mundane, but he shook it off and focused again on Rand.

"Does he deserve his enemies?"

Stromeyer shrugged. "Hard to say, but there's no denying he's ruthless in business. When his first wife's father added him to the family company, he took the job and, within two years, had his father-in-law ousted by the board. When the wife protested, he filed for divorce. When she refused his first offer, he arranged to freeze every account of hers on the pretext that she'd been moving money into offshore accounts. She retaliated by calling the IRS on him, but that ploy failed because they filed jointly and the IRS hit them both with penalties. He paid his end of the deal, but continued to insist that he was unaware of the accounts."

"Did they take the divorce all the way to trial?"

"No. His lawyer said that no jury would believe that a man of his education and experience wouldn't be able to keep track of his own personal funds. They settled out of court, on the eve of the trial, and there's a confidentiality agreement, so we'll never know the actual terms."

"Any other trouble?"

Stromeyer nodded. "The latest involves another wealthy woman. He was dating Hermine Sahna, the heir to a portion of an Arab sheik's fortune. She's twenty-eight, beautiful, and well educated. When he refused to marry, she cut bait and headed to George Tribault, the banking king. He left her when she claimed to still be seeing Rand for the occasional hookup. Two months ago, the men ended up in the same club and an argument ensued. They say that the club's doormen had to be called to break up the two."

"Isn't he a bit old to be getting into bar fights?"

"My take on it is that his competitive streak is so strong that he needs constant challenges. Like a shark that must continue moving forward or die. The women and fighting feed that urge."

"So why does this wealthy CEO playboy brawler engage in an expensive vaccination program in Africa? The whole humanitarian thing seems out of character."

Stromeyer shook her head and took another sip before answering. "Since Bill Gates started his charitable foundation, the new prestige activity among the billionaire set is to expend massive sums in charitable giving, leaving the impression that you're so wealthy you can afford to give it away and still maintain your private jet, boat, helicopter, and enormous homes."

"Kind of like the old adage among the railroad barons, 'If you have to ask you can't afford it'?"

"Exactly like that. But what I can't figure out is why attack him there? It isn't as though he hides from the light. Far from it. If someone wanted to assassinate him, they would have ample opportunities while he's walking down the street in New York."

"But, in West Africa, there would be far fewer chances to get caught. Those countries are known for having fragmented, underfunded governmental infrastructures that would be happy to label him as just another tragic victim of the insurgency and move on."

Stromeyer looked dubious. "Maybe, but I can't help thinking that he's being attacked there because his killer is based there. Anyway, it doesn't solve our immediate problem, which is to get Caldridge out safely."

The phone on a side table rang, and both Banner and Stromeyer jumped at the noise. The display read *Private Caller* and he picked it up immediately.

"Mr. Banner? This is Secretary of State Plower's personal assistant. The secretary would like to speak with you. May I put her on?"

Banner sat up a bit straighter. "Of course."

"Hold, please." Stromeyer threw him a puzzled glance, and he put his hand over the mouthpiece.

"It's Secretary Plower."

"It's ten in the evening, so something's not right," Stromeyer said. Banner just nodded.

"Banner?" Susan Plower's voice came through the earpiece.

"Yes," Banner replied.

"I'm sorry to call you at home, but it's an emergency. Is this line secure? Or do I need to wait until you can get to one?"

"This line is solid. And Carol Stromeyer is here, so I'll put you on speaker." He flipped on the speaker and Stromeyer leaned forward to listen.

"I need you to help me get some embassy personnel out of Senegal and to locate several stolen vials of smallpox virus."

Stromeyer gasped and Banner swallowed.

"Did you say smallpox?"

"I did."

"Wait a minute. Backtrack. Are they both in the same place?"

"No. The embassy personnel are in the hands of the ASIS, and the smallpox is in the possession of Jackson Rand, the CEO of Rand Pharmaceuticals."

12

Tell me about smallpox. I admit, I know little. I thought it had been eradicated," Banner said.

"I emailed you a dossier that lays out the scenario," Plower replied.

"OK. We'll read it carefully," Stromeyer said. Banner nodded.

"Good. Let me know if you have any questions. In the meantime, you have my approval to requisition one helicopter and at least four or five personnel," Plower said.

"I assume you're hiring us because the US can't openly dispatch the military."

"That's correct. And the governments of Senegal, Mali, or Mauritania have not agreed to let us intervene. We're suggesting that they allow our military in on a consulting basis to the local forces, but they aren't exactly thrilled with that idea either. I'm working on it. In the meantime, read that dossier and let's talk again soon."

Plower rang off. Stromeyer printed out the dossier and handed it to Banner.

"Let's start with some facts about smallpox. It's an ancient scourge, like leprosy, and it's transmitted by coughing and expelling it into the air. One-third of people who got it died.

The reason that you think it's been gone forever is because the last known case in the US was in 1947, in New York, and it was declared eradicated in 1979."

"And we no longer vaccinate for it."

Stromeyer nodded. "Correct."

Banner flipped through the dossier and paused at a chart. He held the page up for her to see.

"This looks ominous. Explain it."

"That's a possible scenario whereby smallpox is used for bioterror. You can see here," she pointed to a place on the chart, "that the US has stockpiled a lot of smallpox vaccine. Smart, right?"

Banner nodded. "Very smart. Was this done in case of a potential terrorist threat?"

"Yes. We have enough vaccine to quickly ramp up and vaccinate over two million people. We'd target the children first and those adults who never received the vaccine. We don't know if the vaccine's protection continues for those adults who were previously vaccinated, but the response scenario assumes that they would still have a better chance of avoiding infection so they would be last in line for vaccination."

"Sounds like it would work to stop a widespread outbreak."

Stromeyer looked uncertain. "A person can be infected for a few days and not know it, and it's during that time that they're still mobile. In the past, the way to contain an outbreak was to 'ring' it by vaccinating the fifty or so people around the infected person. But, these days, given the wide-ranging ways of many people, including air travel, this method may not be nearly as effective as it once was."

Banner held up another chart. "What's this?"

Stromeyer went to the wet bar and refilled her glass. She held it up for him to see. "Would you like some more?"

He still had a third left, but if she needed a bracing shot to describe the next graph, then he might need one to hear it. "Sure." He held up his glass. "Top me off before you give me the bad news."

She filled his glass halfway and replaced the decanter. She returned to her chair and settled in.

"So, that chart projects a possible scenario involving not just a terrorist use of smallpox, but one in which the existing real virus is bioengineered using synthetic materials to become hundreds of times more lethal."

He raised an eyebrow. "It already kills a third. How much more lethal?"

"Somewhere in the range of Ebola."

He inhaled. "That almost always ends in death."

"Yes, and so would the synthetic."

"Paint the picture of what that would look like."

"I don't have to. The dossier does it on page twenty-six."

Banner flipped to the page, which showed a young child from Bangladesh in the 1970s covered with sores so prevalent that her skin was no longer smooth but instead a bumpy mass. Only her eyes remained untouched and, in those eyes, was a look of despair that no child her age should have experienced. Banner felt his throat tighten with tears and he blinked them away. The dossier suggested that millions of preschool children would be infected first, because of their immature immune systems.

"Can this synthetic feat be accomplished?" he asked.

She rocked her hand back and forth. "We're not entirely sure. By a premier facility in the US, Europe, China, or Russia? Perhaps. By someone like an insurgency operating out of a third world country? Not likely. At least not without the help of a premier facility."

Banner stared at the chart, which listed the various countries in the world that might be swayed to assist in an insurgency's use of a synthetic pathogen. Then he noted the dollar figure next to the conclusion of what it would cost to bioengineer a synthetic, highly virulent equivalent. The cost was in the hundreds of millions. He pointed to the figure.

"None of the insurgencies that are currently surrounding Rand and Caldridge have this kind of money to throw around."

"They get more every day from ransoms. That CEO from Mexico just paid thirty-six million to get his wife back."

"I'll grant you that. But most will go to an offshore account or to stockpile arms, not to bioengineer a virus that may or may not work in the end. Plus, if it costs so much, why not use Ebola? They're much closer to the area of transmission for that particular virus."

"Ebola is tougher to spread through the air. We're pretty sure it's possible, but more research is needed. Whereas smallpox is highly communicable and the incubation period is long, which provides time to expose the most to it. And, as for the money," Stromeyer said, as she pointed to North Korea on the chart, "that one will pay."

Banner took a sip of his brandy and relished the burn all the way down. The eyes of the child haunted him. He would do anything to stop such misery again, and he knew that if the virus fell into the wrong hands the countries listed in the dossier, including North Korea, would pay for it, and eagerly.

"But do they have the knowledge to create the synthetic? North Korea isn't known for its microbiology labs."

"The dossier concludes that the country would kidnap a specialist and threaten them or their loved ones, or both, with death, in order to get them to cooperate. Not only one specialist could do it. It would have to be a team. And, on that team, there would have to be a chemist."

Banner locked eyes with Stromeyer.

"Caldridge."

13

Cameron Sumner stood in the Air Tunnel Denial's control tower and watched as the Gulfstream private jet lined up with the airstrip for landing. He sipped his coffee and mulled what his response would be to the request that he knew was coming.

"Who's on the jet?" Sumner's colleague, Jorge Sabatin, asked.

"Edward Banner, CEO of Darkview."

"The contract security company? Then he's probably going to throw some freelance work your way. You know this, right?"

Sumner nodded. "That would be my guess."

"Money's good?"

"Very good. But the risks are generally quite high."

Sabatin nodded. "That's why the money's good."

The jet hovered a second off the ground before lightly touching down and beginning a smooth deceleration.

"Nice work. Who's the pilot?" Sabatin asked.

"Probably Banner," Sumner said.

Sabatin rose and stretched. "Well, I'd like to stay and meet this guy, but I've got a conference half an hour away and twenty minutes to be there. Adios. Watch your back."

Sumner nodded and watched as Sabatin disappeared down the stairs. Banner emerged from the plane and spoke to a member of the ATD's ground crew, who waved in the control tower's direction. Sumner put his coffee cup on a nearby counter and headed down the stairs. At the bottom, he opened the door just as Banner reached it.

As always, Sumner was struck by Banner's manner, bearing, and demeanor. Forty-five years old, with dark hair just beginning to show slivers of gray, ramrod-straight posture and perfect features, Banner was the darling of photographers in the Beltway and beyond. When he'd been required to testify in a televised congressional hearing, ten of them followed him daily, despite the fact that his testimony was only tangential to the issue at hand. Afterward, he received fan mail from gushing women who declared their love. Sumner knew that Banner found this fascination with his looks to be superficial and silly and, more often than not, he refused interviews or assignments that would require him to give a press conference. On the odd occasion when he did address the media, he took pains to keep conferences short and informative. Usually, he asked Stromeyer to handle them.

Banner broke into a smile and stuck his hand out. "Good to see you."

"You, too. Come on up." Sumner leapt up the stairs and led Banner into the control tower.

"Catch any drug planes lately?" Banner asked.

Sumner pointed to a white board attached to a far wall. Written on it were the months of the year and next to each month was a tally. For the current month, it read "24" and it was only the first week.

"I hope that doesn't mean that you shot down twenty-four."

Sumner shook his head. "No, that's twenty-four intercepts.

After we hail and warn, most scramble to turn around and then the guys on the Colombian side take over. This year we only had to engage four that refused to respond but instead kept flying."

"Result?" Banner asked.

"I shot them down and fished the pilots out of the ocean later. The one that died pulled a gun in the transport van on his way to jail."

"Stupid man," Banner said.

Sumner shrugged. "He knew that he'd likely be killed in prison. The cartel doesn't let them survive long. They're afraid that they'll turn state's evidence."

Banner scanned the room and pointed to a shelf that held a series of what looked like model helicopters. "Are those radio controlled?"

Sumner smiled. "Those are drones." He walked over and handed one to Banner.

"I've seen the actual drone fighter jets, of course, but only heard about these. Looks like a toy," Banner said.

"A very expensive toy. Each one carries a small camera that can see a six-inch object from fourteen thousand feet. We use them to find the downed pilots, and to watch for incoming boats and the makeshift submarines that the cartel sometimes uses for transport."

Banner handed it back. "Are we winning the war on drugs?"

"No. But I like to think we're putting a dent in it." Sumner placed the drone back on its holder. "So how bad is it?"

Banner sighed. "Bad. Did you see the evening news last night?"

Sumner shook his head. "I don't watch television news, but I did read the paper online and saw the headlines. Is this about the embassy officials?"

"It is, and Caldridge is involved. So, naturally, I thought of you."

Sumner shook his head. "Caldridge is on a humanitarian mission in Senegal. Vaccination program. We just Skyped two days ago and she was getting ready to return here."

"She was attacked on her way back to Dakar while riding with Jackson Rand and his assistant. They escaped, but now they're ringed in by insurgents."

Sumner's pulse kicked up. He turned away and pretended to fiddle with a drone in order to regain his composure. While he did, Banner walked over to a nearby chair and lowered himself into it.

"I'm sorry to drop that on you so quickly, but I need your help."

Sumner listened while Banner laid out the problem, which sounded like the usual desire for power and money, wrapped in a package of poverty and guns. He leaned against the counter, crossed one leg over the other, and waited until Banner was finished.

"Getting past the insurgents is going to take some fancy flying, which I know you do on a daily basis here. I'd like to fly you to Mauritania first. She's headed there, as well. With any luck, you can meet up in Senegal, and she can help with Rand and the hostages the rest of the way back," Banner said.

"And in the meantime? What if she's taken or the embassy personnel's situation gets worse? Do you have anyone on the ground?" Sumner asked. "What about Vanderlock? He can fly as well as I can. Isn't he South African?"

"Last I heard, he's somewhere nearby. But he'd have to fly over the perimeter to get to her, too. I don't have clearance for Locke with regard to the embassy personnel. Rand's offered anyone who attempts the trip a new helicopter and, if he's learned of it, I can't imagine Locke passing up that offer. But, the reality is that there are no helicopters to be had. The rest of my available personnel are in Mali, and the military is of little assistance because, technically, the president hasn't agreed to enter the fray. The official stance is—"

"America does not negotiate with terrorists."

Banner nodded. "You got it."

"But he's sending a Seal team covertly, right?"

Banner inhaled. "I don't know. All I do know is that Darkview's been asked to run a small crew in, to attempt a rescue of the embassy officials, and Stromeyer's been able to requisition a military helicopter."

"Are you going to send it to Locke?"

Banner shook his head. "You'll get first crack at it. We'll bring it into Nouadhibou from Marrakesh in the next three days."

"Why so long?"

"Right now, they're busy painting over the US insignias and removing all traces of its origins and then we bring it down along the coast over water." Banner rose. "Will you do it? If so, we'll take the Gulfstream to Frankfurt, refuel and fly on from there."

Sumner nodded. "Let's go."

14

Of all the hellholes Sumner had the bad luck and misfortune to visit in the world, Nouadhibou, Mauritania was one of the worst. Djibouti was better and that, in Sumner's opinion, was about as low a standard as one could use. He'd flown in from Germany via Casablanca, landing at the airport in the morning. Banner had stayed on in Casablanca to finalize plans for the helicopter delivery. Before Sumner left, Banner informed him that Mauritania had little industry and what industry it did have was controlled by a few. Slavery had been banned in 1981, but the practice still occurred. While technically illegal, nearly twenty percent of the population remained in slavery. Banner warned Sumner to stick to the main cities, if at all possible, because the rest of the country was nothing but sand.

As Sumner stepped off the small cargo plane, the heated desert air hit him like a blast from a blowtorch. He looked around for a sign of his contact person but saw no likely candidates. Two checkpoint guards lounged under a lean-to at the end of the airstrip. His phone started buzzing the moment he turned it on.

Not a good sign, he thought.

"We've got a problem." Banner's voice was surprisingly clear, despite Sumner's obscure location. "Two problems, actually."

"Okay, give me the worst of the two."

"Your cover's been blown. We've intercepted some texts between suspected ASIS members ordering a small force to intercept you in Nouadhibou. They've identified you as a high-value hostage. We think they're currently on the N2 from Senegal and headed to Nouakchott. That road runs along the coastline, so avoid the area. You need to get out of there and to a safe location for a bit. Just long enough for them to decide they were wrong."

"*Donnez moi un cadeau!*" a small boy of seven or eight yelled as he ran next to Sumner, who reached into his pocket and pulled out a piece of gum, handing it to the boy before waving him off. Out of the corner of his eye, he saw one of the two checkpoint guards push off the wall and start toward him. Sumner pretended not to notice, putting his head down and continuing toward the terminal.

"And the second problem?"

"The helicopter can't be flown from Djibouti to Nouadhibou. The military is concerned that the route will be watched and the chopper's true provenance discovered. We're going to try and fly it around the trouble and bring it in from the south."

"In that case, Locke will be closer. Give it to him. I don't see how you'll get it to me without taking fire, anyway."

"We could bring it in over water, along the coastline."

"That'll take too long. Besides, there's no guarantee I'll be able to fly it through the perimeter and, with my identity blown, there's no telling where I'll be. I'm going to find another way in."

"Don't do that. The whole plan here is to use the helicopter to get them out safely and, if you go in, you'll just add to the list of people I have to rescue. Get a little bit out of town, go to ground, and wait until you hear from me. I'll think of something."

The guard began waving Sumner toward him.

"I'll do my best," Sumner said. "A guard is coming toward me, so I'm out."

Sumner clicked off the phone as the guard came within ten feet of him.

"Passport," the guard said in broken, but passable, English which surprised Sumner. He fished his passport and visa out of the side of his backpack and handed them over.

"You speak English?"

The man shrugged. "*Un peu,*" he replied in French. A little. "You need an additional visa. Come with me to the office." The guard delivered this sentence in French and handed Sumner's papers back to him with a frown.

Sumner glanced around. The few other passengers on the cargo plane had shuffled off and away, and only Sumner and the guard remained on the tarmac. He wasn't sure if the guard's demand was a trap designed to get him alone, so that the ASIS could stroll in and kidnap him, or just a common ploy to obtain a bribe from a Western tourist.

Sumner reached into his pack and removed a money clip. He carried four—each was a slim case, and each held different amounts of cash. Sumner had used the tactic before—carry a small wallet as a decoy. If a mugger appears, and demands it, he thinks he's been successful and takes off. Sumner opened the wallet in such a way as to allow the guard to see all of the bills inside. They amounted to only five dollars American, but that was a large sum in this poor country. As he suspected, the guard locked onto the sight of the cash.

"I'll pay for any extra visas here. Okay?" Sumner held out the cash with an innocent look. He knew that no additional visa was necessary but was willing to play along, if it meant mollifying the guard and avoiding a prolonged stint in the office. It worked. The guard took the money and jerked his head to the side, dismissing Sumner.

Sumner veered to the right, heading toward a small place between the building and the tarmac. He doubted that the guard would stop him and, if all went well, he would wait a bit in town and then buy another flight out of Mauritania and have no one notice his lack of an entrance stamp. He walked along the wall and emerged in the front of the airport and was confronted with his first dilemma.

The airport was about a mile from the city center and, between the two, was a flat expanse of sand, dust, and piles of garbage. The sand and dust he'd expected; the garbage, not at that level. It was a large pile, five feet high and twenty feet wide, as if several garbage trucks had upended their payload and driven away. The stench was vile but, despite that, or perhaps due to it, he saw three thin donkeys foraging. One used its front hoof to pound at a nearby bag, opening a large hole and spreading the contents of the half-emptied sack around. A second donkey raised its head to watch Sumner, a pink plastic bag hanging from its lips as it gummed whatever detritus was left on it. The third ignored Sumner completely.

He skirted the pile and headed toward the town center, keeping a steady pace. As he did, he rooted around in his pack for the navy head scarf and *boubou*, a robe that West African men wore over their pants. He put the pack down while he pulled the boubou on. He was almost finished wrapping the scarf around his head when the small boy from the airplane tarmac reappeared.

"*Donnez moi un cadeau!*" the boy said again but this time with a smile.

"No presents this time unless you take me to the market." The boy seemed to understand, because he nodded, took Sumner's hand, and started toward town. The boy's palm felt warm and surprisingly fragile in Sumner's, but the boy himself appeared to be well fed. Sumner assumed that he was not dealing with a street urchin.

They walked toward the town and onto a narrow dirt street lined with two- and three-story houses, most made of earthen materials with flat roofs but interspersed with solid structures made of rock. Electrical wires crisscrossed overhead and a transformer hummed ominously. Sand piled up against the walls, along with more garbage bits and pieces. A plastic bag carried by the wind blew past them both, coming to rest on a pile of sand near a closed door. Sumner felt rivulets of sweat running down his sides and soaking into his waistband. They were at the walls of the second block when the boy froze. He stared with large, frightened eyes. Sumner looked, as well, but saw nothing that would cause such alarm.

"What is it?" he asked in French.

"Azhan," the boy whispered.

Sumner froze in turn. Azhan was the name of one of the bloodiest and deadliest ASIS leaders. A jihadist, he routinely cut off limbs, stoned, or tortured—to gain control of the villages that he sacked. Sumner crouched down and pulled the boy lower next to him.

"Where?" he asked.

The boy pointed to a window about ten feet from them. There was no glass in the frame, just a piece of burlap on a rod, which had been pushed aside to let the breeze circulate.

At first, Sumner saw nothing but, after a moment, a man in a red and white headscarf passed by, before disappearing from view.

A woman screamed in a long, drawn-out wail.

"*Maman!*" the boy cried and, before Sumner could stop him, he took off running toward the house.

15

Sumner dumped his backpack on the ground and quickly removed the gun he'd stored in a front pocket. He pulled off the large plastic zip bag that he'd placed it in before takeoff and checked the weapon. The plastic bag, a suggestion from Banner who'd fought in the Sahara before, had kept it free of sand and dirt.

He rose, grabbed the pack by one of the straps and ran to the window's side, pressing his back against the cinderblock wall. The heavy pounding of fists on flesh made it clear what was happening.

The woman screamed again and Sumner grabbed the sill and hauled himself through the opening, falling into the house head first. He landed on a countertop and slid the rest of the way to the floor, taking a set of glasses and a wire dish rack with him. Two of the glasses shattered, and a shard of glass cut deep into one of his fingers.

He was in a short, exceedingly narrow galley kitchen that opened into a small living area that measured only about twelve square feet. His feet and legs were splayed across the face of the cabinets, and his shoulders were pushed against the wall on the other side. He twisted his head to look into the living room.

In the far corner, a woman was curled into a ball with her arms wrapped over her head. Azhan stood over her, his legs wide set and his arms swinging, as he delivered punches with both fists. The woman's dress was stained with blood, and she didn't move as he continued to pummel her. The boy crouched against a far wall. Azhan only stopped long enough to watch Sumner slide in from the window.

Sumner had landed on his right side, pinning his gun hand. As he rolled to free his arm, Azhan took one long leap toward him, leading with his booted foot. Sumner dodged the heel by jerking to the side but hit his skull against the wall. The kick glanced off Sumner's ear and scraped the skin on his cheek. The man reached for Sumner's throat, slipped, lost his balance, and landed on Sumner, pinning him to the floor. Sumner needed to get free of the man's weight and the enclosed area, if he was going to have a chance to fight. He heaved upward, leading with his elbow, which he shoved into the soft part of Azhan's stomach. The man grunted and rolled off. Sumner scrambled to his feet but Azhan did, too. He kicked Sumner's gun from his hand. It hit a cabinet in the narrow space and ricocheted off, flying into the living area, and clattering against the legs of a small chair.

Now their positions were reversed, and Sumner's back was to the living room and Azhan was trapped in the narrow kitchen. Sumner reached down, snatched a piece of broken glass off the floor, and slashed it upward. Azhan jumped back, and Sumner kept the pressure on, swinging and forcing the man backward until he was pressed against the kitchen's far wall. Azhan's eyes had a slightly deranged look and he was breathing heavily. A bead of sweat rolled down his face into his beard. Sumner stood at the opening to the main room, using his body to block the exit. Keeping his eyes locked with

Sumner's, Azhan reached down and slid a wicked-looking knife from his waistband.

Sumner knew that there were few things deadlier than a knife fight in a restricted area. His jagged piece of glass was far inferior to the well-balanced weapon in Azhan's hand.

"Give me the gun, now!" Sumner hissed to the boy behind him.

Azhan lunged forward, pushing off his back heel and stabbing at Sumner's midsection. Sumner jumped back, curving his spine to keep his stomach from the blade, and causing his robe to billow with each leap. He parried with a swing of his own makeshift weapon. He kept up the pace, holding the jihadist in the narrow space in order to contain him long enough for the boy to retrieve the gun. Sumner could hear the man's harsh breathing, and smell the pungent scent of spice and smoke on his breath. Several times the knife came perilously close to slicing open Sumner's stomach, and each slash opened long tears in his robe.

The man was slender and sinewy, and could fight and fight well, as the well-placed kick had proven. Sumner felt a bead of his own sweat roll down the center of his back and soak into the band at his waist. His fingers ached from the strain of holding the slender piece of glass tight enough to avoid losing it and his throat was dry from his own gasps.

Azhan increased the pace of his slashes. He nicked Sumner twice, once on the forearm and again higher up, where he opened a jagged cut. Sumner hissed at the pain and retaliated with a stab into the other man's bicep. Sumner twisted the piece of glass as he yanked it back and was rewarded with the sight of blood flowing down the other man's arm. Azhan acted as though he hadn't noticed and slashed even faster, gaining another two feet closer to the end of the galley. It was obvious to Sumner that, if the man were able to clear the narrow area, he would have a far greater advantage, mostly due to his superior weapon.

From the corner of his eye, Sumner saw the swirl of a colorful robe and felt the cold metal of his gun thrust into his palm. Azhan screamed in rage and leapt at Sumner. Sumner shot the man in midair, but not before he felt the knife on his shoulder, and once again Sumner flew backward under the weight of his attacker.

Sumner lay on the dirt floor under the jerking body of the dying jihadist. Blood flowed everywhere, soaking into his robe and Sumner couldn't tell if it was his or Azhan's. He heaved the body off, and it rolled onto the floor next to him. He stayed flat on his back while he tried to catch his breath.

The woman stepped closer and stood over him. Her nose bled, and the skin around her dark eyes was already beginning to swell from the beating she'd taken. Her long hair hung down on one side of her face where it had fallen out of a clip. The boy was glued to her, his face buried in her robes. She stared at Sumner with a mixture of concern and wariness.

Sumner rose to a sitting position and immediately regretted the quick motion because the room began to spin. His head settled, and he pushed up and stood, swaying slightly while he took stock. He had several superficial slashes on his arms, one deeper, more painful cut on his stomach, and a puncture wound at the top of his shoulder where the knife tip had entered. This last cut was a near miss. The man had been aiming for the area where Sumner's neck met his shoulder, a vulnerable location. If one was stabbed there, instant death would ensue. Sumner limped back to the kitchen and leaned across the counter to look out the window. His pack was still on the ground.

"Ask the boy to get my pack. It's outside against the kitchen wall," Sumner said in halting French. He couldn't remember the word for "outside" and had used "exterior" instead. The woman must have understood because she spoke in low tones to the boy and pushed him in the direction of the small house's front door.

The boy was back in a flash, clutching the pack. Sumner found his cell phone, limped over to the body, and snapped a photo that he added to a text to Banner that read, IS THIS AZHAN? Banner called seconds later.

"I'm sorry to have to tell you this—because there's a $2 million reward for the person who captures or kills Azhan— but that's not him. That's his lieutenant."

Sumner exhaled a long breath and leaned against the wall. "If that's only his lieutenant then I hate to think of what Azhan can do. This one was a very, very tough fighter."

"Azhan's better than any of his men, so bear that in mind, if you do encounter him. He's bright, resourceful, and completely dedicated. Are you injured?"

"Yes, but I'll live. I'm going to get out of here. I'll reconnect later."

Sumner clicked off the phone and turned to the woman. "Do you have a car I can borrow? I'll pay you well." His French was appalling, and he knew that he'd mangled the sentence.

"No car. Only the train. But please take us with you. Azhan will come and kill us both."

She spoke in English and held the boy by the shoulders in front of her. He watched Sumner with large, sad eyes.

"Azhan will come here? How do you know?"

"Because I am his wife."

Well, that's just great, Sumner thought. He'd managed to tumble into a viper's nest. But the fact that this nest was Azhan's told Sumner more about Azhan's influence in the region than any dry statistics from the DOD could have. Traveling through the area safely would require far more convoluted measures than he'd thought. He immediately discarded any idea of openly boarding a plane at the airport. Likely it would be monitored and Sumner's presence telegraphed back to Azhan.

"Is that his son?" Sumner asked, indicating the boy.

The woman shook her head. "Azhan wished to marry me, so he killed my husband...who was this boy's father. I refused and ran away. That was eight months ago."

The last thing Sumner needed was two civilians trailing behind him while Azhan chased them down, but leaving them meant certain death for both. Sumner's head pounded and he felt a bit dizzy.

"Do you have any bandages? Fresh water? Aspirin?" he asked.

The woman shook her head. "Water only."

"Then please get me some."

She gave an order to the boy in French, and he went to a small box and removed a pitcher. He turned to head to the kitchen, probably to retrieve a glass, but looked at the dead man and stopped.

"I don't need a glass," Sumner said in French.

The boy nodded in obvious relief and brought the water over. It wasn't cold, but it appeared to be clean. Sumner gulped more than he should have, used even more to rinse down the wounds on his arms, then splashed some on the stomach cut. He left the shoulder wound alone.

The woman went into a hallway and returned with a handful of white rags. "The cloths are clean and can be used for bandages."

Sumner wrapped the cloths around his arms and then rewrapped his head scarf around his head, leaving his face free. His light eyes and skin would give him away. He removed a pair of sunglasses from his backpack.

"I'll pull the scarf higher and put on the glasses when we get outside. I need to head inland for a couple of days, and we need some form of transportation out of here. Do you know anybody who has access to a car?"

She shook her head. "It's not safe to drive a car through the desert. The towns are far apart and no one else is on the roads. If the car breaks down, you could wait for days before someone passes by to help. Many have died that way."

"Does the train travel along the coast? Near the N2 from Nouakchott? If so, I can't risk it."

She shook her head. "No, it heads inland through Choum. If you want to get to Nouakchott, you'll have to take a truck from Atar. It travels on the N1."

Sumner liked the sound of a train, except for the fact that Azhan or the ASIS might have spies in the ticket office that would tip them off.

"Where can we catch this train?"

"It's an iron ore train. It leaves from the station, which is north of the city. I'm told it is the longest freight train in the world. There are two passenger cars, but they're often full. If you travel in the ore cars, there is no ticket. They are empty and free."

"Perfect. When does it leave?"

"It's due at fourteen thirty this afternoon."

"We need to hide until then."

The woman nodded. "There's an abandoned shack near the edge of town. Risan," she said, indicating the boy, "and I have used it before."

Sumner rose and picked up the backpack. Even that weight made his injured shoulder ache.

"I need gauze and alcohol. If I give him the money, is it safe for Risan to go to the store and buy it?"

The woman nodded. "I think so."

"What's your name?" Sumner asked.

"Aaliyah." Sumner introduced himself, and Aaliyah looked at him with a quizzical expression.

"You are American. Are you a soldier? Why do you come here?"

"I'm not a soldier. I came to help a friend in trouble."

"I hope that he's not at the border with Mali. There is great trouble there, most of Azhan's making."

Sumner didn't correct her assumption that his friend was male. The less known about his mission, the better.

"There's trouble everywhere, it seems." Sumner looked pointedly at the dead man on the floor before waving Risan to the front door.

Aaliyah wrung her hands. "I hope Azhan doesn't hurt your friend. He believes that he can do anything."

Sumner waved her to the door. "My friend will show him differently. Let's go."

16

The iron ore train to Choum appeared at five in the evening. It seemed that only Sumner noticed that it was over two hours late. He had used the time to patch his shoulder wound as best he could and prepare for what Aaliyah said would be a fourteen-hour trip. She packed a small bag with food, some of Risan's things, burlaps sacks to cover their backpacks against the sand, and utensils for making tea. Sumner questioned the need for tea-making equipment, but Aaliyah just shook her head.

"No one travels without tea," she said with a ghost of a smile.

Sumner would have liked to have some whiskey to dull the pain, but he knew better than to carry any open liquor in a Muslim country, and so popped some aspirin and hoped for the best.

When they reached the area where they would climb on board, Sumner was astonished to see over ninety people gathered along the rail line. Some milled about, while others waited patiently at intervals along the track with their goods stacked next to them, including crates with live animals. One man led a string of goats on a rope. Children ran around their parents playing tag, goats bleated, a stray dog barked excitedly at a crate of chickens, and the people laughed and talked as they waited.

"I didn't expect to see this many," Sumner said.

"It's the only safe and free way to travel in this direction. I must warn you, though, it's not comfortable."

Sumner didn't care about comfort, he cared about safety, and the myriad of people made blending in easier.

"How do we board?"

"You must climb into the cars. It's easiest if you have family members here to see you off because they can lift you up while those in the car pull you in."

Before Aaliyah could finish, a cry went up through the throng. The train pulled into view, chugging slowly in their direction. Sumner shouldered his pack and helped Risan into his. What he wasn't prepared for was the mad dash that ensued as the train pulled alongside. Men and women, along with all their relatives, began pushing and struggling to get into the empty hopper cars. People yelled at each other, the dog's barks gained in speed and pitch, and the children howled in excitement. Bags and rolled rugs were tossed in, and goats followed, bleating in distress as they were lifted off their feet and pulled by their horns into the hoppers. Sumner lifted Aaliyah up, and she grabbed the edge and swung into the car with little trouble. Risan was next, and Sumner thought the boy weighed next to nothing, even with his pack attached. Sumner removed his own pack and tossed it in before him. When he reached up to the car's edge, a large woman grabbed at his arm.

"*Aidez-moi, s'il vous plait,*" she said.

A man, presumably her husband, reached down for her hand. He grunted and groaned as the large woman scrambled to rise high enough to get a grip on the car's edge. Sumner laced his hands together, and she stepped into them, putting her whole weight on him. He nearly staggered with the load, as the woman was far north of two hundred pounds. Her husband was leaning halfway out of the car and trying to pull her upward by the arm, while Sumner was below and trying to raise her higher, when the train began to move. The woman shrieked, and Sumner gritted his teeth and threw the woman upward. Aaliyah and the woman's husband clawed at her, hauling her bodily over the edge.

Sumner started jogging alongside. He found a foothold at the base of the car and reached for the lip at the top of the U-shaped metal ore hauler. The husband wrapped his hand around Sumner's wrist, pulling him upward. Sumner swung a leg over the edge, sat a moment, and dropped into the metal car.

Four more passengers clambered into the haulers. The high sides of the car kept the worst of the windblown sand from hitting them directly, but it still sifted down upon them as the train traveled. The car's metal walls were cool to the touch, and iron ore dust was everywhere, but Aaliyah said that it was still far preferable to riding in the hauler when it returned loaded. In that case, they would be compelled to sit on a shifting bed of rock and gravel.

The four new passengers were men—one young shepherd heading to Atar, who jumped to do the bidding of an older man with him; and three other men who greeted them but otherwise remained silent. Sumner noted that all but one carried equipment for making tea. He studied the last man. The lack of tea materials wasn't the only anomaly about him. He also wore pants in a dull army green, and his boots were standard army issue. He kept his face covered and, like Sumner, he wore sunglasses against the sun and the iron ore dust whipped up by the moving train.

Aaliyah's bruises had swollen and turned an angry purple, but she kept her face covered, and none of the men spent any time looking at her. Sumner didn't like the idea that a stranger would see them together and assume he'd inflicted the blows, and, for one of the first times, he appreciated being able to hide one's face without raising curiosity. Aaliyah gladly accepted some of the aspirin he'd purchased. He put his pack back on his back and wore his gun nestled in a holster at his armpit. He unbuttoned his shirt underneath the trailing edges of the scarf so that he would have easy access to it.

The husband and wife rolled out a small carpet and began to prepare tea. Two of the men claimed their own space with a carpet and assembled a hookah with three attached pipes. They placed their tobacco on the small pan and lit it, before settling in to smoke. They offered the remaining pipe first to Sumner, who shook his head, and then to the husband, who accepted.

The train rolled on through a stark landscape that Sumner found to be beautiful and haunting. That man could eke out a living in such a barren desert area seemed to be a triumph of endurance. The dry air sucked moisture from him and his various wounds ached, but he still stood occasionally to watch the landscape sweep by. They passed several houses—wooden shacks, some with straw roofs, and others with flattened boards warped with heat, and dried and cracked from the constant blasting of grit. One of the other passengers described a trip where he had ridden the train during a sandstorm.

"I pissed sand for weeks," he said. His lips twisted in a wry, gap-toothed smile.

While the car bed made for a hard and unforgiving surface, Sumner found the ride to be less uncomfortable than he'd expected. There was the occasional lurch when the hopper would give a violent jerk, accompanied by a horrendous, shrieking sound. When it first happened, Sumner could have sworn that the train had derailed, but the car rumbled forward again as usual. He was grateful for both the head scarf and his sunglasses, but it still seemed as though iron ore dust permeated everything.

Night fell, and Sumner removed his sunglasses but kept his scarf wrapped around his mouth. He noticed that the man wearing military gear also removed his glasses, before he settled alone against the far wall of the car and watched the rest of them in silence.

As night fell, the desert air turned cold. Sumner, Aaliyah, and Risan huddled together under a threadbare shawl and did their best to capture their own body heat. Risan fell asleep against Aaliyah's side. Halfway through the night, Sumner asked Aaliyah to teach him how to make tea, and she did. They sipped the warm liquid under a blanket of stars.

Through it all, the man without the tea utensils watched them through lidded eyes.

17

Three hours into their hike, Emma came to the conclusion that of all the unpleasant conditions nature could throw at you, being blasted by a hot, dry wind filled with gritty dust had to rank up there with the worst of them. They trudged ahead on a trail that Carn claimed would cut nearly three miles from their trek to the N2. The rocky, beaten earth puffed brown dust around their shoes and, every half an hour or so, one of them would halt to shake out tiny bits of gravel that had worked their way inside. Rand stopped for the tenth time and bent to untie his laces.

"I keep telling myself to ignore it, but it's amazing how the smallest thing can be infinitely annoying," he said.

"It's not good to ignore it. We have a long walk ahead of us and should do everything we can to preserve our feet," Carn said.

"Spoken like a true runner. Are you one?" Emma asked.

Carn shook his head. "Just a man who's lived in Africa long enough to know that you're not going to be driven most of the time and so your feet are needed to walk long distances."

Rand retied his shoes, stood up, and stretched. "Okay, ready."

They resumed their pace, a brisk march that had Emma sweating and wet despite the dry air. Rand and Carn kept up, and she was impressed with their fitness. Carn dripped with sweat, and Rand's dark shirt was damp at the armpits and in a single track down his spine. Rand pulled out his phone and dialed, dropping back as the other side connected.

"He's been on that phone almost constantly. Who the hell is he calling?" Carn asked.

"His rich, powerful, and influential friends. He's desperate to get out of here," Emma said. Carn tilted his head to one side.

"Do you think he'll be successful? Because, if so, I'm happy to tag along."

Emma shook her head. "Doubtful, but the possibility is well worth keeping him around for."

Carn glanced at her. "Why doubtful?"

"Because the US is being rebuffed in its attempts at assistance and this situation requires a bigger response than any individual, no matter how wealthy, can manage."

Carn looked back at Rand. "But one thing is certain. If he gets taken hostage, he'll be able to buy his way out." Carn pointed to himself and then Emma. "Whereas, you and I will be held for a very long time."

"Well, there's that. But it's far more likely that you and I will be killed rather than taken hostage." Emma said. Carn closed his eyes for a second and then opened them again.

"That's beyond depressing. Are you always such a pessimist?"

"I'm a realist. When it comes to my life, I don't play. I figure out the best option and take it. I'll leave others to tilt at windmills. I intend to survive."

They continued walking while Rand dialed yet another rich and powerful friend.

18

The afternoon shadows elongated and, while the heat didn't abate, the insects around them shifted from those that loved the sun to those that favored the night. Emma batted at small gnats and dreaded the thought of the mosquitoes of the evening. She had insect repellent but wanted to wait as long as was safe before coating herself in a sticky, chemical sheen.

The sun sank lower and turned an iridescent orange-red color, streaking the few clouds with the same beautiful hue. Savannah grasses waved in the breeze, and the buzzing, creaking, and chirping sounds of night insects began. The air cooled, only a few degrees, but enough to be noticeable. Emma stopped to retrieve her repellent. Both men slowed and then halted. Carn took a mouthful of water from an aluminum container and offered it to Rand.

"I'll drink mine, thanks," Rand said.

Carn watched Emma spray herself. "May I borrow some? I ran out weeks ago and haven't had the time or the funds to get more."

"Of course." She gave him the can, then put her arms over her head and stretched backward, while first he, then Rand, used it. Her shoulders ached from the pack's straps. She was in the process of rolling them to work out the kinks when she froze. "Do you hear that?"

Carn looked up from inspecting the interior of his own pack, and Rand stopped spraying. Both paused, listening.

"Hear what?" Rand asked.

There came a whipping noise, coupled with the jumbled sound of pounding. As if a large herd of animals were making their way through the heavy grasses. Emma spun in a slow circle as she squinted into the distance.

"Wildebeest?" Emma asked.

Carn tilted his head to one side. "No wildebeest in Senegal that I've ever seen. Antelope, panthers, lions, giraffes, elephants, yes." The swishing, rumbling noise grew louder and then in a rhythmic overlay, came a pounding.

"Drums," Rand said.

"It's the insurgents. They're driving the animals in front of them." Emma felt the tingling as adrenaline started working through her system.

"They got here fast." Carn spun in a small circle, looking around him. The darkening sky lengthened his shadow. Soon it would be full night.

"Too fast. Perhaps it's a small advance troop," Emma said. She hoped it was because the three of them were in no way prepared to fight off a large one. She reached into her pack and removed the pistol, standing as she checked it. Rand and Carn exchanged glances, and Rand removed his gun.

"You said you can't shoot well. But you can shoot, right?" Emma asked him.

Rand nodded. "As well as anyone who's taken one course and been to a shooting range twice."

"Carn?" Emma asked.

He shook his head. "Like I said, I don't believe in guns."

"That's not what I'm asking you. I'm asking can you shoot?"

Carn paused. "Yeah, I can shoot."

"Better than Rand?"

"I did two years military training. I can shoot."

Carn is getting more interesting by the moment, Emma thought.

"Then take this." She offered him the gun.

He shook his head. "You keep it."

She reached out, picked up his hand and gently placed the pistol in it. "I'm going to run, and I'm going to continue running until they're far in the distance."

Carn opened his mouth to argue, but Rand waved him off. "She's an ultra runner. One hundred miles at a time or more," he said. Carn looked at Emma for confirmation and she nodded. "So, when she says she'll keep running, she means it. She'll make the border before the insurgents do."

"But, in this case, I'm just going to head straight across and wait at that ridge to get a sense of what size force we're facing. You two keep going. I'll catch up."

She grabbed her backpack and slipped it over one shoulder. Rand reached out and held the other strap as she shrugged into it. Carn adjusted his own pack. The setting sun threw its color on the waving grasses, turning them from brown, green, and beige to a dull red, like the color of blood after it hits the air and begins to congeal. The intermittent trees became black forms as the light left the savannah. The dull pounding noise grew louder, and now Emma could make out the individual beats of hooves. Emma swallowed to wet her suddenly parched throat.

"We need to run. Now," she said. Even as she spoke the words, she felt the stirrings of panic washing over her. The vast, flat plain gave no cover. In the far distance was a smallish ridge, not really a hill but definitely higher than the land all around. There, the trees were denser. Emma pointed to it. "To that ridge. At least it has some foliage that can act as cover as we climb over."

She sprinted away, accelerating with each step, until she was running at what she estimated was an eight-minute mile. Carn and Rand were keeping up, but already she heard Carn's harsh breathing.

"Slow it down into a steady pace that you can sustain," she told him. "I'm going flat out until I reach the ridge. I'll turn at that crooked tree," she pointed to a small, stunted-looking tree at the base of the ridge. "I'll lay down some cover fire when I see them. You go at a forty-five-degree angle ahead."

Neither Carn nor Rand spoke, but both adjusted their trajectories and she split off, putting on a burst of speed. From her left, the noise of the herd grew, and a cloud, darker than the air around it, filled the horizon as they churned up the dirt. She kept in a line that would traverse theirs and ramped her speed to 6:45s, which, given the terrain, was pushing her limit. It was a speed she knew she could only sustain for five miles, maybe six, but might get her to the base of the ridge before the herd was upon her. After that, she'd have to slow considerably in order to conserve her energy.

She was halfway to her destination when the first animals crossed her path. Fleet antelope veered all around her, careening right and left, slamming into each other as they did their best to avoid her. Their musky smell filled the air. One large buck knocked her on the shoulder, spinning her into another oncoming animal's withers, and she bounced away, stumbling. She gasped, and dirt filled her nostrils and lodged in her throat. The noise was deafening. She couldn't continue on her axis, there were simply too many animals around her. She'd fall and be trampled to death. Instead, she curved with them, running as they did, and doing her best to stay in a consistent line so they could swerve around her. They whipped by.

A large panther pulled alongside, slowing to keep pace, and it turned its head to look at her as if sizing her up for a kill. She kept running, waiting to see if it would pounce. There came the sharp crack of gunfire, and the panther reacted by stretching out, its long sinewy body uncoiling. It was gone with a speed that Emma marveled at and wished she could produce. A giraffe galloped up to take the panther's place but it, too, moved on.

The crowd of animals surged by as quickly as it had come. Soon, Emma was running with the slowest of them, and then even those were ahead of her. As their noise dissipated, the pounding of drums took precedence. Drums played by humans, not the drumming of animals' hooves. The insurgents were coming.

19

Emma slowed her pace and glanced behind her. Headlights from several trucks gleamed back at her. They were spread out and approaching side by side, in formation. Emma counted four sets, coming on fast. She turned sharply left and ran to the ridge, tripping into the divots that the many hooves had created in the dirt. The sky was full dark, and she couldn't see far in front of her. She had a headlamp that she kept in her pack, but she was loath to either take the time to find it or wear it, thereby signaling her presence. She stumbled forward, the rhythm of her breaths mingling with the drums' cadence.

The thrumming sound ignited an almost primeval fear in her. As if she'd been transported back millions of years and was the original cave dweller being chased by an enemy tribe. If she'd seen burning torches and pitchforks behind her, instead of headlights, she wouldn't have been surprised. The memory of a story she'd read about a man being hunted like prey ran through her mind, but she couldn't remember the title. "The Dangerous Game"? Maybe, but this wasn't a game. She was the prey, and she didn't have any real idea of how to escape—except to keep moving and disappear into the tree line, where the vehicles would have a harder go of it. Forcing them out of the trucks and on foot would level the playing field somewhat. They would still have the numerical advantage.

She reached the ridge and started up the soft incline. The drum noises were louder now, but only a lone small animal shot past her. All the others had fled. A glance over one shoulder let her know that the trucks were nearly upon her. They maintained a straight formation, though, and wild hope sprang up because maybe they were unaware of her existence. Maybe they would drive right past her.

The first shot at close range shocked her, and she flinched at the noise. Nothing hit her, and nothing hit around her. Wherever they were aiming, it wasn't effective. She continued to the first set of trees. They weren't trees, really, but more like a collection of small bushes. Not acacia, thank God, because they didn't have sharp needles. Emma scrambled behind them and crouched down, keeping her head low. Then the full import of what they were doing came clear.

The trucks had stopped in a straight line. In the glow created by the headlights, Emma could see the fighters, a ragtag group of men and some teenage boys, dressed in shorts and t-shirts in various stages of wear and cleanliness. Several had handheld flashlights strapped to their heads with bandannas to form makeshift headlamps. Uniform throughout were the guns. All carried AK-47s, and two carried rocket-propelled grenades, the weapon of choice for guerrilla armies everywhere. The simple, easy to use, and massive-damage-producing RPG-7s were grimy with dirt, oil, and gunpowder, but Emma had no doubt that they'd function and function well.

Two of the trucks carried drummers but, in the distance, Emma could see the bobbing flashlights and even two burning torches—an eerie and strange form of light even in poverty-stricken Africa—of a crowd that advanced on foot. She presumed there were more drummers in this group, as well.

The reason for the torches became clear when the soldiers walked to some scrub, touched them to the branches, and set them on fire. They would lay waste to the savannah to instill fear in the population and drive off the animals. Fifty percent of Senegal lived in poverty and went hungry. When the insurgents were done, that number would skyrocket.

The men riding in the backs of the trucks jumped out, aimed at a spot far to the right and front of Emma, and fired a series of rapid rounds. They hopped back onto the flatbed. One pounded his palm on the cab's hood, and the pickup took off past Emma and in the direction that Rand and Carn had gone.

Emma counted the men as the pickups streamed past. Though she couldn't see the entire troop in the intermittent light, she estimated there were sixteen men in four flatbeds and an additional eight—one driver and one passenger each—in the cabs. She looked at the foot soldiers and counted seven bobbing headlights and at least twenty others. All told, a troop of fifty-one men with Kalashnikov semiautomatics and RPG-7s, against three with two pistols and limited ammunition. Not great odds.

She was going to have to find a way to empty their gas tanks and steal whatever rounds and warheads that she could. She directed her attention to the foot soldiers. They trudged along, looking nothing like the men in the trucks. These fighters appeared worn and tired. They'd probably been marching the whole day in the hot sun, blasted by the Harmattan winds.

From somewhere in the back lines came an ululating cry and the foot troops stopped. The men carrying the torches yelled something incomprehensible, and the guerrillas separated into several groups and created a circle. Two women carrying loads of branches across their backs, which were held in place by cloth slings, walked into the center of the circle and began to build a pyramid of dried sticks, grass, and dung. One of the torchbearers lit it, and the fire kindled slowly at first but soon engulfed the pile. Emma heard a cell phone begin to ring with the patter of a famous pop song from America. The mundane mixed with the surreal.

Within half an hour, the camp was in full swing, with some soldiers cooking whatever raw meat they had over the bonfire, while others drank from filthy bottles and talked. Several set up rickety tents, which were constructed from ripped canvas and bent tree limbs. Barely enough to create cover but, presumably, they were the lucky ones. The rest rolled out thin blankets to sleep. Several were army green, and Emma made out the logo of the Peace Corps on two. Trophies of their pillaging, she supposed.

After a few minutes, the trucks returned and parked at the camp's perimeter. Those inside dropped the tailgates, and several laid out blankets and bedrolls in the backs. Others made their preparations in a separate section of the camp. Something seemed different about the truck soldiers. After a moment, Emma realized that they were the only ones carrying semiautomatics or RPGs. Few of the foot soldiers had such prized weaponry. Most carried machetes and a very few had pistols strapped in holsters around their waists.

Emma revised her statistics. Out of the possible fifty-one assailants maybe twenty-five were armed. The rest were prepared only for hand-to-hand or very close combat. This realization buoyed her hopes. She shook her head. How absurd to be heartened by only twenty-five well-armed attackers.

Yet, the knowledge that the troops were not a professional military machine—such as one would find from some of the better-funded insurgencies, like Al-Qaeda—raised her spirits.

She kept low and moved up the small hill, taking care to avoid stepping on any dried branches or loose stones as she did. After thirty minutes of the slow ascent, she reached a denser section of wood and settled in behind a large baobab tree. She removed her arms from the backpack's straps with a sigh. As she did, her phone vibrated in her pocket. Surprised that she had a connection at all, she pulled it out and glanced at the screen. The display read *Unknown Caller.* She answered and put it to her ear.

"Yes?" she said.

"So what the hell are you doing in West Africa during a coup? Woman, have you no sense?"

She recognized Wilson Vanderlock's smooth voice and slight South African lilt, and relief flooded through her. A blend of African and hip hop music began playing in the camp below and threaded its way toward Emma.

"Where are you? I hear township music," Vanderlock said.

"Hiding behind some bushes on a ridge overlooking an insurgent camp. Somebody must have a battery-powered boom box they keep nestled next to their Kalashnikov."

"How many?"

"Small. About fifty."

"Ah, probably the Red Hand. It's a small but vicious group. They're like locusts. They burn, pillage, rape, and then kill everyone they encounter. If you're safe where you are, stay there until they leave."

"I was hoping you'd come and get me out of here. Where are you?"

"Guinea-Bissau at the Senegal border. Drinking a warm beer, because the electricity has gone off *again,* and wondering how the hell you get into these situations."

"I was on a humanitarian mission. Busy saving the world while you're drinking beer and ogling the nearest woman."

"First of all, I never ogle. Second, I'm alone because all the women have fled from the immediate vicinity. The guerrillas in Casamance are on the move."

Vanderlock was a slender man with longish, dirty blond hair and light eyes that crinkled when he smiled. He habitually wore jeans or khakis that hung off his hips, with gray t-shirts, and either a battered set of cowboy boots or equally battered combat boots. A cigarette inevitably hung from his lips, and he walked with the swagger of a confident, but affable, man. Men laughed with him, women trusted him, and governmental authorities saw him as no threat, which was good because he often skirted the edge of the law.

"I highly doubt you're alone, especially if your protection is needed. Or, if you are, you won't be for long but, listen, do you still have your plane? Can you get to Kayes at the Mali border?"

"Yes and no. The plane is here, but currently waiting for a spare part to meander its way up from South Africa. I was quoted a week, before the unrest, now they're shrugging and making no promises. They've put it on the ground route, which you know will be a series of bush taxis, bicycles, and camels. Figure three weeks at best."

"I'm traveling with Jackson Rand."

"The billionaire? Lucky you."

"More like unlucky. I nearly put a bullet in his head a few hours ago. On top of the insurgency, he has some professional assassins on his tail. Didn't bother to tell me."

"What's he like?"

"Arrogant, rich, and a trust fund baby who thinks he's the master of all he surveys. He made an offer to the charter company to buy them an entire helicopter. If he makes the same offer to you, will you take it? Is it safe?"

"Again, yes and no. I'd do just about anything to own a new helicopter, and no, it's not safe. But, then again, when have I ever played it safe?"

"Okay, then I'll track him down and see what we can do. Can you stay put until I get back to you?"

"I'm not leaving until my plane is fixed, which means I'm not going anywhere soon. I'll check around. See if anyone can get their hands on an available chopper."

Emma rang off, then threaded her arms through the backpack's straps. She began to move slowly, keeping low and darting from bush to tree to shrub. The rising crescent moon threw some light, but she was thankful that it wasn't full. A sharp-eyed soldier might catch a flit of her shadow but, with any luck, they might assume it was an animal and leave her alone.

After twenty minutes, she'd traveled about a quarter mile. The camp had receded farther into the distance. She took a risk and straightened. Now she could cover some real ground that had eluded her while she crouched along earlier. Still no sign of Carn or Rand. After another twenty minutes, and three-quarters of a mile, she saw a shadow by a bush move. She paused. The last thing she needed was Rand to shoot her. She lowered to the ground and unclipped her keychain from a mesh pocket. It came with a tiny flashlight. She pointed it at the bush and switched it on and off in a rhythm.

"Caldridge?" Emma heard Rand's voice, soft and quiet.

"Yes, don't shoot."

She got up and jogged the rest of the way toward the bush. As she neared, she could make out the forms of the two men. She moved next to them and sat down with a sigh.

"Glad to see you made it," Carn said. "When that herd engulfed you, I thought you would be trampled."

"I nearly was. We need to keep moving. The troop has camped for the night. Let's put some mileage between us." From the distance came the roar of a large cat. Rand sat up and strained to peer into the darkness.

"Was that a lion?"

Emma shook her head. "Most likely a panther. The few lions left in Senegal are at the Mali border. Would be rare to meet up with them."

"It's the humans that we need to fear," Carn said. "Let's go."

Emma rose with the men, and they began a slow, often stumbling jog. The only sounds were the crunching of their feet on the ground and the occasional slap as one or the other batted at mosquitoes. Rand kept at his phone, texting.

"Nassar found someone to help us. He's nearby and driving a UN truck. Here's hoping he can get away for a bit and finds us before dawn."

Emma wondered how much Rand was offering the driver to divert and pick them up. She carried two hundred American wrapped in a plastic bag in the bottom of her pack. She'd hoard it until the situation became life or death.

"Would love that," Carn said.

Emma fought off an encroaching weariness and kept moving. As she did, she tried to keep from dwelling on the miles that lay ahead of them.

She failed to perceive the danger to the south.

20

Kortya sat in an open-air bar next to a courtyard and watched as his men flogged a villager in a small town off the main road. The man had done nothing to deserve the severe beating, but an example must be made, if the citizenry was to be brought into line. The ritual was the same at every village that Kortya passed. His soldiers rounded up the male population and drove them into the town square. Then, if it was dark, as it was now, they circled their trucks and switched on the headlights.

The men were brought forward, one by one, and flogged in the harsh glare for supposed transgressions against the insurgency. Drinking alcohol was one, gazing at a woman another. Any show of defiance merited instant death, a fate that three men had already suffered. Farther away, more of his men were feeding bits of the villager's possessions into a bonfire. Kortya watched as a wooden kitchen chair was thrown on the pile.

At the very end of the yard, women and young girls were collected. Kortya expected to turn to them next. They wouldn't be flogged, at least not initially. First they'd be raped and *then* they'd be flogged for "allowing" the men to defile them. This village contained a girls' school, which was a piece of real luck. Thirty girls ranging from twelve to twenty in one place. He'd ordered them removed from their sleeping quarters and dragged through the village into some waiting vehicles. They screamed and cried along with their mothers, and his men beat off the older women, who attacked them in an attempt to free their daughters. Now the girls sat in the back of trucks, shackled, and covered with burqas, as they should have been from the beginning. Kortya would drive them into Mauritania before selling them on the open market as wives for the insurgents in Syria.

He sipped his beer and watched as a beaten man was dragged away by the armpits, the flesh of his back in tatters. Some wouldn't last the night. His right-hand man, a small Yemeni named Mamo, stood to his left. Mamo was a true sadist. Kortya didn't like him much, but Mamo idolized Kortya and would leap to do his bidding. Kortya found such loyalty refreshing. Most in the insurgency would turn on their own mothers if they thought there was money in it.

"Who are these that we're watching?" Kortya asked him.

Mamo shrugged. "Like you, I wasn't here when this village was taken. It's a mixture of townspeople and others from a bush taxi the second troop intercepted on the road."

A guard walked over and whispered in Mamo's ear. When the guard left, Mamo tapped Kortya on the shoulder.

"There's a group camped not twelve kilometers from here. Fifty strong."

Kortya took his eyes off the proceedings to look at Mamo. "ASIS?"

Mamo shook his head. "Red Hand. Maybe a splinter group. Our sentries couldn't tell in the dark. They're likely to have scouts. And RPGs."

"And Rand?"

Mamo shook his head. "No sign. We did find an empty village, though. When the men searched it, they discovered this." Mamo waved at a piece of titanium luggage at his feet.

Kortya snorted. "Rand's for sure. So he passed through the village."

"And warned them to flee." Mamo sounded bitter at the loss of his usual fun for the evening.

Kortya didn't give a rat's ass about the lack of villagers one way or the other. It was the Arab who held his attention.

"We need to find Rand and fast. What have you arranged to accomplish this?"

Mamo shot Kortya a nervous look, which Kortya thought didn't bode well for what the man would say next.

"We have three advance scouts combing in a thirty-kilometer radius from the hit site. They're expanding outward."

Kortya slammed his beer bottle onto the wooden counter, and the hammering noise echoed through the courtyard. Mamo jumped, and the floggers paused and glanced over, an expression of concern and fear on their faces.

"Thirty kilometers when they could be hundreds away by now!" Kortya grabbed the front of Mamo's shirt, filthy with flecks of blood that had sprayed when he'd crowded around the floggers to watch. Mamo flinched but didn't attempt to break free. "I want twenty more men on the search, *now*."

Mamo looked alarmed. "That leaves only ten to take the villages! And if they leave now you will have no one to stop the Red Hand. I told you, they're out there, in the darkness, and close. They could bring a rocket down on your head before you even know it's coming. Better we send out some sentries to secure this area first."

Kortya pulled the stinking man closer. "I'll deal with the Red Hand. I expect you to make a few calls and get me one hundred more men. Pull them off the perimeter at Thiès, if necessary. I want Rand's, and the Darkview soldier's, heads on a platter and ready to ship to Edward Banner. Do you understand?"

Mamo's eyes widened. "Banner? What has Banner to do with this?"

"Rand travels with a Darkview operative. A woman."

Mamo swallowed and nodded up and down. "Yes, yes. If this is true, then we need more men. I'll have some sent down from the Dakar blockade."

Kortya shoved the man away and fixed the floggers with a glare. They resumed their whipping. The latest victim fell unconscious and was dragged away. The next was pulled forward, an announcement made that he had been caught drinking, and the flogging began. Kortya swallowed his beer and brooded. His cell phone rang and the display read *Tobenga*.

"Shit." He picked up, hit the button, and said, "What?"

"You lied to me, you stinking pile. Rand was tipped off and fought back. The Arab called."

Kortya closed his eyes, took a deep breath, and reopened them. "It was unexpected. Anyway, we're on his trail. He won't get away."

"Where is he?"

"Three kilometers north," Kortya lied. "We're at a nearby village, restocking. When we're done, we'll go kill him."

"Forget restocking. Go now."

"The men are hungry, and you haven't paid me yet, remember? I have over fifty to feed and no money. If they don't get fed, they won't follow me. Then what will happen, eh?"

"Shoot whoever doesn't follow you. Show them who leads and who is a sheep that follows."

"I will."

"Kill Rand and get the Darkview woman's head on a platter, then I'll be happy."

"Be at peace. I will do this," Kortya said.

"You'd better because, if you don't, the Arab will hunt you down, drag you into the Sahara, and bury your body in the sand with the body of a camel, like some worthless Bedouin."

"I will *not* fail," Kortya said, but he was greeted by a beeping tone as Tobenga had hung up.

21

Emma, Rand, and Carn stood on a small rise five hundred meters away and looked down at the village and the circled trucks. From their vantage point, they saw the girls being rounded up and the men being flogged in the center, as well as the series of supply trucks parked off to the side. Farther away, a bonfire burned and several soldiers strolled around it.

Carn watched the scene below them through Emma's small field binoculars. The captors dragged a new man forward and Carn gasped. Emma shot him a quick glance and then strained her eyes to try to see what he had but, without the field glasses, it was impossible.

"What is it? Do you know him?"

Carn nodded and handed her the binoculars. Her heart fell when she saw that the next victim was the man who had bartered half his mother-in-law's seat to Rand.

"The man from the bush taxi," she said.

Rand stepped next to her. "Do you see Rhonda?"

Emma scanned the group of women off to the right. None looked like Rand's assistant.

"No, but that doesn't mean that she isn't there," she said. She lowered the glasses a moment, and Carn exchanged a worried glance with her but said nothing.

"Do you see anyone else from the taxi?" Rand asked. Emma returned to watching the circle.

"Yes, but only two of the younger girls." The assembled women shifted. "Wait, there's another." The crowd shifted again, and Emma saw Sinclair hovering near the rear of the crowd.

"There she is." She grasped Rand by the arm and handed him the binoculars. "In the back, to the right. See her?"

Rand exhaled in relief. "Yes. Thank God she's alive."

"From what I can tell they haven't targeted her," Emma said.

"Not yet they haven't, but their focus is on the men for the moment. That's going to change when they're done with them," Carn said.

"We need to get her out of there," Rand said.

Carn shook his head. "Us against thirty? No. Not happening."

Rand wheeled on him. "Quit talking like that. We're not leaving her to them."

Carn fixed Rand with a glare. "We can't attack. It's a fool's mission. We'll die and so will she."

"Care to guess what's in those trucks?" Emma asked, interrupting them. Carn looked back at the village.

"Not food. They never carry their own but, instead, loot each village's stocks," Carn replied.

"I say guns," Rand said.

Emma nodded. "And lots of ammunition. If we're right, we need to pilfer some. This group is nothing like the one we just left. They look well funded."

"Too well funded to attack outright," Carn glanced back at Rand, ready to resume their argument. Emma dropped her backpack on the ground and took out her pistol.

"Too well funded and too large," Carn said again. Rand put the binoculars back to his eyes, watched the village, and said nothing.

"I'm not planning on an attack," Emma said. "Just a little search and steal. Maybe blow up whatever remains before they finish with the men and start in on the women." She shoved the pistol into her waistband. "I don't like to walk past carnage. Do you?"

Carn shook his head. "Not at all, but suicide missions aren't to my liking, either."

"No need to join. It might actually work better if just I go. Stealth reconnaissance. If the plan heads south, please try to get a message to Banner."

"What type of message? 'She died in a hail of gunfire'?" Carn sounded sarcastic, but underneath she could hear the stress. "This is stupid. Don't do it."

Emma put a hand on his arm. "I'm going to get whatever will explode. When I do, I'll bring it back. Then we're going to start a little fire…distract them."

Rand made an irritated sound and removed his own gun from his pack. "Hold on, I'm coming with you." He spoke in a grudging voice. Emma thought he secretly agreed with Carn but was too stubborn to admit it. She shrugged.

"You're under no obligation. But, if you're joining, then follow me. I'm going to make a wide circle. Come back up behind that last truck."

"What about sentries? If you think they're all watching the floggings you're wrong," Carn said.

Emma nodded. "I agree. No way would they leave their guns unattended…unless they're truly stupid. And stupidity is something I never like to assume. But if you see one sneaking behind us can you make some noise?"

Carn nodded. "I make a great screeching owl squawk. Perfected it when I was a boy. It carries far, so I have no doubt you'll hear it."

"Excellent. Let's go," Emma said.

She hauled her pack onto her back and loped off. She heard Rand behind her. As she moved through the night, she made plans. Heading to the farthest truck seemed the best first step. She'd peer under the tarp and see if they'd speculated right about the cargo.

After ten minutes, they were down and around on the far side of the village. The sound of the floggings was louder here and, to her right, she saw where the victims were being left. There was a muddle of bodies—the dead ones were prone, the live ones were sitting. A couple of bored-looking guards stood sentry. They passed what looked like cigarettes back and forth, but Emma suspected it was actually khat, the mild stimulant prevalent in Africa. The men would be pleasantly buzzed and somewhat less effective.

She crouched next to a tree trunk and waited for Rand to catch up to her. When he did, he settled next to her and took a deep breath.

"You okay?"

"A little winded. I'm not used to all this running," he said.

Emma saw one guard hand off the cigarette, reach down and grab at something near his feet. When he straightened, she saw that he held a bottle in his hand. He took a healthy swig and, when his friend addressed him, he handed it across.

"Better and better," Emma whispered. She turned toward Rand and pointed to the far vehicle. "Head to the right of that last truck. The one near the large bushes. We should be able to look inside without anyone seeing us."

"Then what?" Rand asked.

"Then we take what we can carry, but focus the most on any guns that we don't have and the matching ammunition. Two packs of ammo for every gun we steal. If luck shines down on us, and they've stashed guns with attached carry straps, then take two guns, but no more. I don't want us laden down and unable to flee. And be sure that you hang the guns on separate shoulders so that they don't clang together."

"And then?"

"And then you take off back to Carn and build your own bonfire off to the right. Get them going in that direction and, while they do, I'm going to stay and try to blow up the rest."

"How?"

"If we're right about the cargo, they have enough explosives to light up half of Senegal. I'll dump it and explode it."

"And yourself with it."

Emma waved him forward. "I hope I can avoid that. Come on, let's go."

He grabbed her arm. "Wait, I'm still unclear on the plan."

She returned to a crouch. "What's the problem?"

"We build a bonfire and they come straight for us."

"Only until I blow up the rest. Then they return to annihilate me."

22

Emma moved slower, taking care to stay down, and doing her best to avoid stepping on stray twigs. The winds still blew, rustling branches in the trees and whistling around the open spaces, and the guards kept their backs to them, shielding their cigarettes while they lit them.

Her breathing picked up as she neared the camp and she fizzed with anticipation. She tamped down the rush as best she could. While a certain amount of adrenaline was good, too much might lead her to make dangerous choices. Her phone started vibrating in her pocket, breaking her concentration. She did her best to ignore it while she swerved left and crabbed to the next bit of coverage. Rand stayed with her. Now they were only two hundred meters from the gathering, and the indistinct murmur of voices and rhythmic sound of the beating became recognizable. With each step, Emma could feel the fear emanating from those in front of her. It was as if a cloud of sweat, panic, and blood was carried on the Harmattan wind.

She targeted her next move. Another clump of bushes was fifty feet away. She counted down from three in her head and took off, sprinting. She crossed to the foliage and was relieved to see that the sentries still watched the proceedings. All she saw were their backs.

Rand sidled up next to her, his breathing ragged. The most dangerous section lay before them. An overlay of smoke, and the stench of unwashed bodies, burning hair, and rotting meat floated on the air. Emma looked to the right and saw that the sentries were throwing the bodies of the dead into a burning pyre. She almost retched at the sight of the limbs sticking up through the flames. Next to her, Rand made a small moaning sound. One woman knelt next to the fire and began wailing in an uncontrolled keening that set Emma's teeth on edge. One of the sentries hit her in the head with the butt of his gun, and she dropped to the dirt. The remaining guards laughed amid a smattering of applause from the others.

"Jesus, this is awful," Rand whispered. "What kind of animals are they?"

"The kind at war. Those who glorify it don't live it."

Three men threw another body on the bonfire and the rest cheered again. Emma was horrified. She crouched lower and waved Rand onward. He followed close behind her. The men were passing bottles around and drinking with abandon. Emma could see them loosening up as they did. She made it to the far side of the covered trucks. Now that they were closer, the stench became overwhelming. Emma could smell a disgusting mixture of blood, manure, and garbage carried on the wind. Red and yellow flashes flickered over the side of the trucks, all thrown by the light of the fire. She pressed up against the cool metal side of the truck and prayed that none of the men would think to stroll that way. She'd given up trying to keep her jumping nerves under control.

On the back of the truck, a shredded piece of rope held a tarp down in only a few places. Emma reached up and lifted it slowly. Long wooden boxes, just the right size for rifles, filled half the truck bed. Two crates—stamped in black with a red logo and the initials of a famous explosives manufacturer in South Africa—sat next to the rifle crates. A graphic of an exploding bomb below the logo left no doubt as to the contents of the crates.

"Is that dynamite? What does ANE stand for?" Rand whispered.

"Not dynamite, ammonium nitrate. A different type of explosive. ANE stands for Ammonium Nitrate Explosives. It's the largest manufacturer of explosives in Africa," Emma said. She lifted the tarp a bit higher, and a shaft of light fell on a spare gas container and another set of boxes further down the truck bed. The word RAND was stamped on the side. Emma turned her head to see his reaction. Rand stared at them and a grim look passed over his face.

"I thought you said all the boxes were accounted for," Emma said.

Rand nodded. "They were. I have no idea where these came from."

"Someone has breached your security," Emma said. Or you're lying, she thought. But, once again, she had no time to engage him in a discussion. "At what temperature will smallpox be destroyed?"

She reached in and pulled at the lid of one of the ANE cartons. She managed to open it. Another roar came from the direction of the burning pyre and she did her best not to jump. Inside were plastic bags containing small round white beads.

"I can't believe they're driving around with these in their truck and stored so close to gasoline."

"What are they?"

"Prills of ammonium nitrate. They'll absorb the fuel and, when you light them, they'll create a massive explosion. Here," she said, handing him the gas can. "Just pour this on some branches and start a fire. That will have to do for a distraction."

"What are you—"

"Go!"

Rand clamped his mouth closed, turned and, after a quick glance around, retraced his steps to the closest cover.

Emma sidled down to the long cases in the bed. She reached in and tried to pry off the lid of one. It rose a bit on the end but was held in place at the box's center by a gate latch secured with a padlock. She wouldn't be able to remove anything without first either breaking the latch or snapping the padlock. Another scream rent the air, and she moved to the end of the truck to steal a glance at the men.

Her attention was focused on the burning pyre, so she didn't immediately hear the whistling of the incoming rocket. By the time she did, it was overhead. The guards, villagers, and the small group in the clearing all froze and stared up into the night sky.

23

The rocket landed on the far end of the village and exploded in a deafening mass of heat and fumes. Emma stumbled backward, touched a hand down to catch herself, straightened back up, and then began to run. The whistling sound of another incoming rocket hijacked all of her attention, and she didn't care about being seen, shot at, or captured. None of these would matter if one of the incoming rockets hit the trucks. They'd all incinerate in a ball of chemical fire. The second rocket hit one of the vehicles in the circle. It exploded in a mass of flying metal, shrapnel, bits of wood, and tire rubber. Chaos reigned, and the villagers ran in all directions. Two soldiers pulled alongside, running for all they were worth and not sparing a glance for her. The whistling sound of another grenade directly overhead made her run even faster.

This grenade struck the ground next to the prill-laden trucks, exploding and sending dirt flying. Somebody had the good sense to fire up the remaining vehicles in the circle, and Emma threw herself sideways to avoid being hit as a truck sped by. At fifty feet away, it was hit by a grenade. Emma saw a man tumble out of the passenger side. One sleeve was on fire, and he dropped and rolled to put it out. Emma kept sprinting, running back to Carn, back into the safety of the darkness, and as far from the village as she could be. She sensed rather than heard the last rocket and glanced behind her in panic, afraid that it was headed for her. Instead, she saw that it was on a direct path to the prill-laden trucks.

It hit and, for a moment, Emma thought the world had stopped. After a second's pause, the truck incinerated in a massive ball of yellow and red fire. The explosion knocked Emma down, even though she was several hundred yards away. A wave of singeing heat rolled over her, and she felt it cover her face and line her eyebrows and lashes. Screams rent the air, but it was impossible to see where they were coming from, or who was making them, because the sky was thick with dust and dirt in an enormous, choking cloud.

A series of smaller explosions followed, and Emma scrambled to her feet. A soldier ran up to her and, from the singed sleeve, she could see that he was the one who'd tumbled out of the exploded vehicle. He was thick and squat, with a shaved head and narrow, mean eyes. Those eyes locked on her face and his expression twisted into one of rage. He held a knife in one hand and reached out with the other to grab her arm. His fingers bit into the flesh of her bicep, and she yanked it away and out of his grip. His ragged fingernails scraped, leaving a trail of blood on her skin. He slashed at her with the knife, aiming for her face, as if he sought to mutilate her, as well as kill her. She dodged the first wild slash, spun, balled her fist, and punched him in the face. Her angle to his side made it difficult to hammer his nose, which was what she wanted to do, but she still managed to land a solid hit onto the soft section of his cheek below the bone. The top of her knuckles vibrated with pain as they skimmed his cheekbones.

His head whipped to the side with the blow, and he screamed an obscenity and threw himself at her. She staggered at the extra weight and fell sideways into the dirt, with him landing on top of her. She felt his fingers around her throat and smelled beer on his breath. She lunged up, opened her mouth, and closed her jaws on a section of his cheek, ripping at it as she yanked back. He screamed and released her throat as he hauled a fist back to hit her. She rolled to the side, unbalancing him, and jamming an elbow into his midsection. He collapsed forward, and she was once again up and running. She spat out a bit of skin as she did. Another catastrophic explosion sent the ground shaking and a massive cloud of dust landed on her. She inhaled and sucked in a mouthful of grit and ash and started choking. A quick glance behind her let her know that the man was chasing her, his hand reaching out to grab the pack on her back.

She had little doubt that she could outrun him, and so she kept up a blistering pace, coughing and spitting out ash particles as she did. Within thirty seconds of the chase, he faltered and she slowed to conserve energy. More explosions rent the air and the dust grew thicker, obscuring her vision even more. Her pursuer disappeared in the cloud, and she was forced to pick up her pace to keep ahead of him. She settled into the new level and did her best to keep moving in a straight line away from the village. She heard screams and the intermittent roar of engines but didn't waste her time trying to analyze the various sources. The dust and chaos made it impossible.

She ran for thirty minutes at the faster pace, before slowing to a nine-minute mile. Fast enough that the average person couldn't sustain the speed without training, slow enough that she could maintain it for at least twenty more miles before she would have to walk. With any luck, the force would scatter into a million different directions, and she wouldn't have the killers on her trail. The chaos would work in her favor.

An hour later, she was still running. The darkness worked against her but she was through the dust cloud, and the half-wedge moon helped to illuminate the terrain. Twice, she'd fallen into a hole, bending her ankle but not so violently that she felt pain. The sudden divots made by animal hooves had proven to be her worst enemy because, if they caused her to sprain her ankle, then her only method of escape would be gone. The men had long since faded into the background as she tore up the miles, the trucks also. There was only Emma, darkness, the scratching of insects, and the sound of her feet crunching on dirt.

After another twenty minutes, she slowed to an easy pace and settled in to run all night.

24

Sumner must have dozed, lulled by the movement of the train. When he opened his eyes, the man traveling with the shepherd was holding the younger one against the wall with one hand around his throat and punching him in the head with the other. The others in the car, including the man without the tea, were watching with stony expressions. The husband and wife had lit a small oil lamp and placed it on a sandbag, hollowing out a hole to keep the lamp from falling over. The gently swaying flame illuminated the area, and the two men were at the edge of the light. Their shadows flickered as they moved.

Aaliyah had squeezed into the corner and was holding Risan with both arms, covering his face as she did. The remaining men in the car watched the attack with impassive faces.

"Stop it," Sumner said.

The man kept punching. The shepherd held his hands over his head but didn't attempt to fight back or resist, despite the fact that he appeared to have three inches and twenty pounds over his attacker.

Sumner stood up and immediately regretted doing so. His head swam, and spots appeared before his eyes as the blood emptied. He used his left hand to brace himself against the wall.

"I said stop it," Sumner repeated. The man turned his head to look at Sumner but didn't release the younger man's neck. He said something in what sounded like a local language to Sumner.

"What did he say?" Sumner asked Aaliyah.

"He says that the boy is his slave and to watch your own affairs."

"Tell him no one is a slave, and I expect him to stop now," Sumner said.

Aayilah swallowed. "You don't understand our ways. Slavery exists here. It always has."

"Don't give me that cultural crap. Slavery is a wrong against humanity. Tell him to stop it immediately, or I'll make him stop."

"Please, don't interfere. The boy knows he's a slave, that is why he doesn't fight back." Aaliyah's voice held a pleading note.

"Tell him to stop, or I'll kick the shit out of him," Sumner said.

Aaliyah said something to the man, who turned all the way toward Sumner, letting the boy go. He spoke in a rapid flow of words.

"Translate it," Sumner said.

"He says that the boy's mother, grandfather, and great-grandfather were all slaves in his home."

"Tell him he lies. Wealthy men with slaves don't travel in an open iron ore car."

Aaliyah repeated what Sumner said, and the man rattled back.

"He says that the train is the fastest way to get to Choum and he needs to be there. The passenger cars are crowded and this is best. Please believe him. He tells the truth."

"Tell the boy to come over here. Tell him he is no longer a slave."

"That's not a good—"

"Say it."

Aaliyah spoke. The young man, who appeared to be in his late teens, perhaps just turned twenty, eyed his attacker. He rose slowly, and the other man spat words at him that Sumner couldn't understand. The boy stopped and looked at Sumner, waiting.

"He told him to stay there," Aaliyah said.

Sumner took two long strides across the car and was in front of the man, who pulled his hand back to hit Sumner. At that precise moment, the train gave one of its tremendous lurches and both men stumbled. Sumner recovered first and grabbed the other man by the front of his shirt. He hauled him forward and down, taking a rapid step backward while the man hit the metal floor, face first. He grabbed the man by the hair and smashed his face into the metal, then, with his other hand, he clutched a large part of his shirt and dragged him to the car's edge, lifting the much lighter man until he was folded, face down over the ledge.

The wind whipped at them both, and the end of Sumner's head scarf flapped against his shoulder in a rapid pattern. He felt the vibrations of the train's movement through the man's body. The man yelled what Sumner assumed was an oath and his hands scrabbled against the outside of the car's walls as he tried to push himself to reverse into the car. Sumner hammered his elbow into the small of the man's back, making sure to hit the soft section on the right of his spinal cord and then pulled out his pistol and slammed the muzzle into the soft tissue. The man yelled again.

"Tell him to tell the boy he is free or I drop him in the Sahara. He can die there for all I care."

Aaliyah was up and at Sumner's right shoulder, the husband at his left. Sumner noted that the husband didn't make a move to assist the man, nor did he demand that Sumner release him. The rest of the car's passengers remained silent. Sumner couldn't see if they'd risen to get a closer look at the proceedings, but he didn't feel them at his back, and so felt fairly confident that they weren't going to intervene on the man's behalf.

Aaliyah spoke in rapid words. The man responded.

"He told the boy he was free."

"Tell him to say it again. Louder."

Aaliyah spoke and the man yelled from his upside-down position.

Sumner looked at the young man. "Did you hear that?"

Aaliyah translated.

The young man, wide-eyed, nodded.

"Then tell him to get to my side of the car and I'll protect him until Choum."

Aaliyah spoke, and the young man grabbed a small sack and scrambled to the far corner, where he slid down next to Risan.

Sumner let go of the man and walked back to Risan and Aaliyah. He turned his back to the wall and lowered until he was sitting. He kept the gun in his hand for all to see. The attacker clambered off the edge, moved to his side of the car, and stared at Sumner as if staring at a madman.

The husband returned to sit on his carpet and the wife did as well. Sumner thought he saw a flash of satisfaction in the wife's eyes, quickly masked. The other men resumed puffing on the hookah.

The man without the tea regarded Sumner through lowered lids and in silence. He hadn't moved during the entire altercation.

The train continued through the cold desert night.

25

They chugged into Choum as the sun was rising. Aaliyah, Risan, and the shepherd, whose name was Yann, had fallen asleep, as had all the others in the car, with the exception of the man without the tea. His steady regard of Sumner never wavered, and Sumner knew that it meant nothing good. Yet he hadn't made a move toward Sumner or threatened him in any way. It was the husband who warned everyone that they were at Choum. No official announcement was made, and Sumner was thankful that the man thought to warn them.

As Sumner and his ragtag band of travelers jumped down from the train, a large group of men surrounded them, all calling out.

"What do they want?" Sumner asked Aaliyah. She waved at the row of dented and ancient pickup trucks, Toyota Hiluxes, and Mitsubishi Pajeros parked thirty feet away.

"They will drive us to Atar. Three thousand ouguiya for a seat and eighteen hundred to ride on the roof."

Sumner stared at the roofs of the cars. All had luggage racks packed with duffels, backpacks, rolled carpets, and bent cardboard boxes tied with string.

"Six dollars to ride on the roof! Do you sit on top of the luggage?"

Aaliyah nodded. "It's not comfortable at all."

Yann said something and Aaliyah translated. "He wants to thank you for taking him and says you are his master now."

Sumner shook his head. "Ask him if he speaks French, and tell him that I'm nobody's master. He's free."

Aaliyah translated and listened as the boy responded. She turned a troubled face to Sumner.

"He says that you do not understand. That without the protection of a master he will be shunned and possibly killed."

Sumner contemplated the situation and the unintended consequences of bringing freedom to someone in a society with institutionalized slavery.

Sumner nodded. "I understand, but I am *not* his master. Where will he go?"

Aaliyah asked him. After some discussion, she turned a troubled face to Sumner.

"He has nowhere to go. His family is gone, and he is afraid to return to Nouadhibou."

Before Sumner could respond, a loud cry rose up from somewhere near the transport, and a man loped toward the assembled crowd. He spoke in rapid sentences and the crew all talked at once. To Sumner, it appeared as though they were firing questions at the newcomer.

"What's going on?" Sumner asked. To his surprise, a man in the group answered in English.

"The insurgency has taken Thiès and a second branch of the same group has crossed into Mauritania from the east. They're marching this way and claim that they will reach Tidjikja by nightfall, Atar after that, and Nouakchott soon after."

"From the east? That's the border with Mali. Between there and here is sand. They'll need fuel," Sumner said.

The man nodded. "They'll get that in Tidjikja."

"How are they traveling?"

The man stroked his beard as he thought. "Likely by four-wheel drive. Camel possibly, but only for shorter distances. They will want to stay well ahead of any United Nations authorities, and camels can be overtaken by pickups." The man indicated Aaliyah, Risan, and Yann. "Your wife, son, and slave must go now."

"He's not my slave," Sumner said.

The man looked surprised.

"Mauritania banned slavery over thirty years ago. He is not a slave," Sumner said. And this time he put some steel into his voice.

The man held up a placating hand. "As you say. I mean no disrespect. But if you care for these people you must get them on the trucks, now. There are only a few seats left."

Sumner saw the truth in what the man was saying. The trucks, already loaded with luggage that rose higher than the height of their cabs, were surrounded by a throng of people, all jostling to get inside. Sumner waved Aaliyah over.

"It appears as though the insurgents have breached the border and are headed this way. I've already paid for the three of you to travel inside a car to Atar. I won't be joining you. I have to be elsewhere, and I'm afraid my presence will only draw attention to you. Here." He placed his backpack on the ground, removed one of his wallets, and handed her one hundred dollars.

"There's over three hundred dollars still inside. Some in a hidden compartment." Aaliyah's eyes had widened at the sum he'd quoted, and she watched with interest as he showed her the secret zipper set into the side of the wallet and under the card slots. He covered the opening again and handed the wallet to her. She shook her head.

"It is an enormous sum. I don't need it," she said.

He pressed the wallet into her palm. "Take it. But promise me you'll keep Yann near and share some of the money with him. I don't want him to starve due to my actions."

Aaliyah blinked several times. "You are a savior to me. Thank you for saving me and Risan. I will not forget your kindness."

Sumner smiled at her. "In that first sleeve is my business card. Dial the number on it if you ever need me. Either I will come, or I will send someone to help you."

Now Aaliyah didn't bother to hide her tears. Her eyes gleamed.

"Thank you."

"Promise me you will call me if you require my help."

She inhaled a deep breath and nodded. "I promise."

"Good. Let me say goodbye to the others."

Sumner knelt in front of Risan. "Your mother has my number, and I've instructed her to call me if she needs to. If you need me, you call me as well. Do you understand?" Sumner knew that he had butchered the French, but the boy nodded. Sumner pulled the boy by his thin shoulders toward him and gave him a hug. Risan wrapped his arms around Sumner and squeezed him with what Sumner imagined was all the might in his small body. When he let go, Sumner gave him a smile. Then Sumner stood and took Yann's hand and put the hundred dollars in it. The young man stared at it in wonder.

"I've given money to Aaliyah, as well. If you can, stay with her to help," Sumner said in French. Yann answered with a long series of sentences in his native language.

"He asks what you will do," Aaliyah said.

"I need to find my friend in Senegal, possibly near the fighting. I will go there."

Yann spoke again.

"He has offered to go with you. To help find your friend. He thinks it may be dangerous to go alone," Aaliyah translated. She laid a hand on Sumner's arm. "I think it's dangerous, as well. You should not go alone. Accept Yann's offer. Please."

Sumner shook his head. "Thank him for his generous spirit but tell him that, if he stays with you, it will put my mind at ease and leave me free to do what I must without worry. This would be a great service to me."

Yann listened to the translation and nodded.

Sumner put out his hand and, after a moment where he thought Yann wouldn't know what to do, the young man solemnly reached out and clasped it. One of the drivers interrupted with a stream of instructions and Sumner watched as Risan, Aaliyah, and Yann climbed into the back of a pickup truck. Within seconds it tore off, one of many in a long line. Sumner watched as the boy Risan waved at him, nearly jumping up and down in the pickup bed, swinging his arms in long sweeping motions. Sumner waved back until the cars were mere specks and he was sure that Risan could no longer see him. Then he picked up his pack, removed his phone, turned it on, and dialed Banner. As he waited for the phone to connect, he looked around. The only truck left was a rusted Peugeot. The owner, a dark-skinned man, stood next to it with a mixture of pride and determination. The call to Banner failed to connect and Sumner walked over to the man.

"Can you drive me?"

The man nodded. "Where?"

"To the Senegal border."

"That is far and I'm low on gasoline. We will have to refill in Tidjikja." The man waved at the car. "I'm Denal and this is my car." Sumner shook his hand.

"Why no other riders?" he asked, more out of curiosity than anything.

Denal frowned. "I used to be a slave. They avoid me."

Sumner waved at the car. "Then their misfortune is my great fortune. Thank you."

Denal smiled and, within minutes, they were barreling toward Tidjikja.

26

Emma woke at dawn. She'd run most of the night, stopping only when she came to an abandoned grass hut. Not one to pass up an opportunity, she'd gone inside to see what she could salvage from it. The interior smelled like dust and had been stripped of all the essentials. She found some broken pottery, a bale of rope, empty aluminum cans, three stools, and a low table. The night had been hot, and she'd dragged the table outside, pushed it against the wall of the hut under an overhanging portion of the roof, and laid down on it to sleep.

Now she sat up and looked around her. A quick glance downward confirmed her instincts to raise herself off the ground. Not far from the table was a small anthill. The ants must have found some food because they were busily marching in formation around the corner.

Her back ached from sleeping on the table and she stretched. A shifting breeze blew, bringing with it the sickening stench of decay. She coughed and covered her nose with her hand while she slid off the table to investigate. She knew enough to follow the ant trail. If an animal had died, they would make use of the carcass.

She turned the corner and found the dead bodies of what must have once been a family, the corpses stacked on top of one another in a crazy collection of limbs and torsos. A man's head, severed from its body, was placed on top of the pile as if a trophy.

She dropped to her knees and began dry heaving. Her muscles contracted over and over as she emptied the meager contents of her stomach. When that was empty, she brought up thin, watery bile. The breeze continued to blow the stench of blood and death toward her, and she stumbled up onto her feet and staggered away, back around the corner.

She grabbed her pack and started running in blind panic, with the image of the terrible stack of humans in her mind's eye. After fifteen minutes, she slowed long enough to shove her arms through the straps to carry the pack properly. Another ten minutes and she reached a small circle of huts. She stood outside the perimeter and saw no one and heard nothing. No sounds of voices floating on the air, children playing, or music. She stopped and warred with herself. Should she investigate? Or run? She took deep breaths, using her sense of smell to see if she could identify what might lie inside the circle of huts. The last thing she wanted was to be caught by surprise again.

The wind blew from the wrong direction, and she would have to circle the area to try and detect any decay. She walked forward, slowly. With each step, she felt her heart beating faster and her stomach clench. She made it to the edge of the first hut and stepped around it. She got no further. She didn't have to. She could see the stack of human remains. This time she didn't retch. Not that it mattered. There was nothing left in her stomach anyway.

She made a large circle, angling around the huts, and doing her best not to look right or left but ahead. She began to jog and then run.

Emma came upon the refugees an hour later. At first, she ran past the stragglers and small children walking with their mothers. As she continued, she found people marching in groups of ten or more. She came upon a dirt road and slowed to stare.

There was a line a people as far as she could see. The women carried huge bundles of their belongings on their heads, while their children walked next to them, some walking goats on rope leashes, some pulling carts loaded with belongings. The lucky ones had donkey carts loaded to the brim with household items, though Emma wondered just how much effort would be needed in the coming days to continue to pull the cart forward. Perhaps a better strategy would be to carry only the essentials.

"Lady, is it you?" Emma looked behind her and saw the two women from Carn's village who had given Emma the extra pistol.

"I thought you were going to the bush," Emma said. The woman with the white hair frowned.

"We tried, but the road to Kayes was blocked. The ASIS swarmed down from Mali like the locusts that they are. They were killing all in their path and we turned back." She looked around Emma. "Is Carn here? Is he all right?" Emma could hear the strain in her voice.

"When I left him last night he was fine. We came upon a small group of insurgents marching from the east. I went to stop them and left Carn in the back."

"Did he have a weapon?"

Emma nodded. "Yes. I gave him the gun and told him to use it if he must. Whether he will or won't is up to him."

The woman sighed. "Ah, yes, that is out of our hands. Come, walk with us. You can't go back toward Thiès, because it has fallen, and the others are boxing us in from the direction of Mali."

"Where does this road lead, then?" Emma asked.

"To Bakel. It's on the border with Mauritania." The woman grimaced.

"That's where I was supposed to go to meet a friend," Emma said. "I'm pleased to march this way. You're not?"

The women both shook their heads. "They think they're better than the rest," the white-haired one said. "They view Senegalese as thieves that are beneath them." She snorted. "Their land is nothing but sand and garbage."

Emma refrained from commenting. It seemed that Senegal would soon suffer the fate of its neighbors, if the insurgency could not be put down and soon. She couldn't imagine that the world community would allow Senegal to fall. It was one of the rare democracies where peace and relative harmony prevailed, but it was surrounded by war-torn Africa.

"Have you heard if the United Nations will come? Stop this?"

The woman nodded. "France has retaken Timbuktu. They march toward Bamako and are driving the insurgents toward Senegal. I believe they will prevail, but we'll take the beating. The ASIS are little better than animals and, if they reach us, we will die."

There seemed nothing to say to that. Emma walked with the women in silence and did her best to keep the horrific image of the murdered family from her mind.

Banner watched the pickup below his helicopter as it barreled through the desert. As he flew the chopper, he kept a steady eye on a small tablet computer that was propped on the seat next to him. The screen showed a blinking dot that corresponded to the truck below. The copter received a hail, and he answered the radio, speaking into the mouthpiece attached to his headset.

"It's Caldridge. I'm on the move and alone. Any news on obtaining a helicopter?"

Banner smiled. "I'm in one and currently headed toward Atar, in Mauritania. Where are you?"

"On my way to Bakel. It's on the border with Mauritania. And I have terrible news." Banner listened as Caldridge told him of the carnage at the two villages. "I've learned that the ASIS isn't far from here. They're working a pincer movement, spreading outward from Thiès and, on the other end, marching in from Mali."

The pickup below Banner's helicopter slowed and stopped. Banner swung around to fly in a large circle above the vehicle. Banner kept his eye on it while he listened to Caldridge.

"The ASIS have kidnapped some US embassy personnel, and we're preparing a counterstrike to rescue them. If you can—" Banner swore and jerked on the cyclic to haul the helicopter to the left. Below him, the truck's driver had stepped out and was now aiming a rocket-propelled grenade at him.

"What's going on?" Caldridge said.

Banner spun the copter in a circle and jerked it back and forth in a zigzag formation. The driver fired. The blades over Banner's head drowned out the sound of the gun, but he could see the backblast from the RPG and saw the grenade release. He jerked the chopper to the right and was relieved to see the rocket whiz harmlessly by. He flew higher and away from the pickup below. When he was sure he was out of RPG range, he began another loop in order to keep the helicopter moving parallel to the truck's path.

"I was following a suspected insurgent below me, and he just stopped his truck and shot an RPG. It missed. I'm going silent. Keep moving, and I'll try to call you in a bit."

Emma rang off and continued trudging with the women. The hot winds blew sand in her eyes and grit in her nose, but she was alive, and for this she was grateful.

27

S he reached Bakel several hours later as the sun was setting. What she found was chaos. Hundreds of refugees encamped on the border, erecting tents and makeshift shelters. Groups of Mauritanian soldiers lined the road or sat in the back of open transport trucks. Campfires dotted the area, and the smell of burning wood and the stench of human waste floated on the air. Emma made her way through the crowds, looking for a Peace Corps officer, United Nations officer, or missionary. Anyone that could speak English and give her a report. As she worked her way through the crowd, she saw the unmistakable erect posture and white skin of Rand. She jogged up to him and he turned to her with a smile.

"You made it!" To Emma's surprise, he wrapped his arms around her in a bear hug. When he pulled away, she saw Carn walking towards them. He also pulled her into a hug.

"We were afraid you were hit by the explosions," he said.

"How did you get here so fast?" Emma asked. Carn jerked a thumb at Rand, who answered.

"One of my Saudi contacts came through. A friend of a friend of a friend was driving a UN relief truck here, and he convinced them to lend aid to those near the blast. They found us and transported us," Rand said. "Now I just need to find Rhonda, and I'm hoping to pay someone to drive us the rest of the way through Mauritania."

"What about the villagers? Where are they?"

Rand shook his head. "By the time the dust settled most of the villagers were gone. Carn and I stayed put and tried to hike back to check, but all we found was a blackened, burning hole. When the UN truck arrived, we drove another quick circuit but saw nothing. I can only hope that Rhonda fled with them."

"What's the story here?" Emma asked, pointing to the makeshift tent encampment.

"Like the others, we tried to cross into Mauritania, but the soldiers are refusing. No one's allowed to cross."

"Not even you?" Emma asked Rand. "With your money and a US passport, I would think you'd be allowed through."

Carn shook his head. "I told him not to risk using his real name. And, frankly, he shouldn't go flashing cash around anywhere near them. With his white skin and obvious Western looks, it's more likely that they'll happily take his money but then set him up, instead of helping him. Offer him safe transport, get halfway into the desert, and then hand him over to the insurgency to be held hostage."

Rand glanced downward a second, before looking back up. "It doesn't matter. I won't leave until we find Rhonda."

"Wouldn't that best be accomplished by using your contacts to gather a force?" Emma asked. "Assuming that a force could be mustered."

"That's a big assumption at this point. I'm not leaving, and I'm not even going to try to until we locate Rhonda. And to that end..." He held up his phone. "My cell died. Can I borrow your solar charger? Once that's done, I can try to locate some help for us."

Carn glanced between the two of them, and the look on his face gave Emma the impression that there was more to the explanation. She made a mental note to ask him when they were alone. She handed over the charger and Rand hooked up his phone. It began charging immediately, and the relief on his face gave Emma an idea of how stressed he really was by the whole situation.

"I would think they'd accept refugees," Emma said.

Carn grimaced. "They're afraid that the influx will drain their already low resources. What really gets my goat is the fact that they stand there refusing us entry, but they're also holding up the aid supplies that are intended for the displaced."

Emma looked around. "What do you mean? I don't see any supplies."

Carn waved a hand. "They're on the other side of the border. Eight trucks filled with water, food, mosquito netting, and solar cookers. They were purchased by several humanitarian foundations to ease the refugees in the Sudan. They'll never make it there with all this fighting, but the supplies would really come in handy here." He waved a hand. "There's no more firewood to build a fire for cooking, and it's not safe to drink the water without boiling it first. If we don't get these supplies, the children will contract dysentery and start dying."

"We've got to get out of here," Rand said.

"So does everyone else," Carn snapped back.

Carn was right. The few fires that burned were fed with dung, that much was clear, but there wasn't enough dung in the area to light the hundreds of campfires that were required. The land, already stressed by the stripping of its natural resources, was unable to give back.

"Where exactly are these supplies?"

"They're literally just sitting on this very road, parked, while the Mauritanians decide what to do. The drivers have fled and the supplies are ripe for stealing," Rand said.

"How far away?" Emma asked.

"No more than three miles." Carn shook his head, frustration plain on his face. "Might as well be a hundred miles, for all the good they're doing."

Emma gazed at the soldiers. They sat in trucks and stood lolling against the sides. Even though they carried guns, they didn't appear too menacing.

"How about a bribe?" she asked, looking at Rand.

"I tried. Or, rather, Carn tried, because we thought it was safer than me going up to them. Offered fifty American. No one was willing to take anything but cash, and I have to save the rest for bribes once we enter Mauritania. But none were willing to risk it."

"That's as much as some Mauritanians make in a quarter. And yet no one would take it?" Emma shook her head. "Just what the hell is going on here? How afraid are they?"

"They said that the supplies are guarded by a small group of the Red Hand and, if word got around that they were assisting, they would be hunted down and killed."

She looked at Carn. "Do you believe that? Or were they just angling for more?"

"I believe it. One guy grumbled that the rich guy like me would flee north and they would be left to pay for their actions."

Rand's wealth, and its limitations, surprised Emma. Before this mission, she would have said that while money couldn't buy everything, it could get damn close. Now she wasn't so sure.

A thought came to her. "How long have you both been here?"

"Only one night. Why?" Rand asked.

"Do these troops get relieved at night? Is there a second shift?"

Rand shook his head. "Not that I saw. Carn?"

Carn shrugged. "I didn't see it either. Why?"

"So, by nighttime, this group is going to be tired. And tired soldiers fall asleep."

A slow smile ran over Rand's face. "And then?"

"And then we cross the border and steal the supplies. You in?"

Rand nodded. "I am."

Emma looked at Carn. "You?"

He nodded. "Yep. When?"

"I'll find you at midnight. Get some sleep until then."

Emma walked with the men to the older women's tent. They greeted Carn with enthusiastic hugs. Emma sat on the ground with her back against a pile of luggage and plotted their heist.

28

Emma shook Rand awake five minutes before midnight. He opened his eyes, sat up, and reached over to Carn to wake him.

"Bring the pistols and a backpack with water. Do you still have the field binoculars?"

Carn nodded. "I'll bring them. I won't use the pistols, though. Each of you take one."

"And I have a compass and my phone," Emma replied.

Ten minutes later Emma, Rand, and Carn headed out, keeping parallel with the border. A couple of soldiers played dominoes around a campfire, but the rest either dozed, using their packs as pillows, or drank, sitting on the ground with their backs against the transport truck's wheels. Emma struck out, keeping the pace to about a ten-minute mile. Still fast for the untrained, but manageable. Rand and Carn jogged alongside. After a mile, Emma waved in the direction of the border.

"Let's turn here. We'll make a wide circle and come in from the north." They ran in silence. As Emma had thought, no one guarded the border.

"Where are the soldiers?" Rand asked in a whisper.

"Not enough manpower. I'd figured as much."

"This is going to be a breeze," Rand said.

Emma shook her head. "No, it's not. They're bound to have someone guarding the supplies."

"Carn said the drivers all ran off."

"But that doesn't mean that no one's there."

"She's right," Carn said. "This is Africa. The only thing that you can be certain of is the generosity of the people and the corruption of the government."

"That's depressing," Rand said.

"But true," Carn replied.

They ran for another half hour. Rand and Carn were both laboring. Emma could hear their rapid breathing, but neither complained. When she'd decided they were parallel to the road, Emma turned ninety degrees and slowed to a walk.

"Let's walk in." She consulted her compass. "I think the supplies must be about a mile in front of us. Or at least the road is. Once we get there, we may have to break and reconnoiter to find the exact location. We could have either run too far or not far enough."

She turned to cross the border and stopped so suddenly that Carn bumped into her.

"What?" he said. She put out a hand to stop Rand, who was passing on her left. Both men waited and the night sounds rose around them.

Something bothered her. She couldn't put her finger on it, but all her instincts were screaming not to step ahead. Nothing had changed. The night sounds remained calm, and the amazing display of stars above her head glowed. If not for the wretched circumstances forged by the world of humans, the night would have held a magical, vast quality that few get to experience in this world. She ran through her mind everything she knew about Mauritania and its soldiers.

"Let's go," Rand said. His voice held an impatient note.

"No," Emma said. "This is too easy."

Rand snorted. "You're just having second thoughts. You've said that the soldiers can't watch the entire border. They don't have the manpower. That's why this section is left wide open."

"I know what I said, but that doesn't mean that this area isn't protected. Perhaps I didn't think this through enough." She looked at Carn. "Do you know anything about Mauritania?"

"Seventy percent is desert. Nothing grows and drought is common. You do *not* want to be lost in Mauritania. You'll end up dying of thirst on a sand dune in the hot desert sun. I'm pretty sure the guards know this and so don't worry about border crossers who try to go off the main roads."

Emma held up her compass. "That's why this is the most important piece of equipment we have."

Carn nodded. "Followed by a watch. You need to time how long you're moving, or you'll think you've been out there shorter than you have, and you won't have a sense of the time it will take to return."

"What else do you know?"

Carn thought a moment. "Slavery prevails today. Most live in poverty. And the area to the north, when crossing into or near Morocco, is protected with land mines."

Land mines. Emma had some experience with those from her time in Colombia, where large swaths of the jungle were rigged with them. She waved at the darkness in front of them.

"What if this is mined? Would explain the lack of interest in protecting it."

Carn inhaled and blew out a breath. "You had to suggest that? Just when I was ready to cross?"

"Is there any way to tell?" Rand asked.

From their left came the sound of an engine.

Emma slid behind a nearby baobab tree, and Carn and Rand hid behind a second. After a moment, Emma saw a pair of headlights coming her way. As the car neared, she could make out that it was a white SUV. It barreled past her. In the moonlight, she could see multiple bullet holes on the car's exterior, and the passenger windows had been shattered. Once it was out of sight, Rand appeared at her shoulder.

"What the hell do you think happened to that car?"

"It took some fire. Were you able to see the plates?"

"Not me, but Carn might have."

At that moment Carn walked up. "US consular plates on that Suburban," he said.

"What a stroke of luck. I'd heard that some embassy personnel were kidnapped. I'll bet that whoever is driving that car either has them or knows who does," Emma said.

Rand snorted. "I don't see how that's lucky. You think they're guarding the supplies, you'd better believe that they're guarding those hostages. They're worth a hundred times more."

"Banner is looking for the officials. If we can get the word to him, then they'll join us here. That means soldiers, equipment, and backup. We'll have everything we need to recover the supplies." Emma held her phone and was texting Banner as she spoke.

"That will take too long," Carn said.

"Maybe not. He was headed to Atar last time I spoke to him. In a helicopter."

She finished texting and waved the men forward. "But our land mine problem is solved. Let's follow that SUV. Walk in the tire tracks. And something tells me the supplies are that way."

After another few minutes, Emma's hunch paid off. The sound of music, voices, and barking dogs indicated an encampment somewhere ahead of them.

"Bold assholes, aren't they?" Rand said. "They just set up shop on a main artery in Mauritania? Aren't they afraid the UN troops will find them?"

Emma had to agree. If ASIS was behind the kidnappings, then they seemed to be operating with complete impunity.

"Could they have paid off the Mauritanian officials?" she asked Carn.

"I don't know. I guess anything's possible."

"Let's move a hundred yards to the left and take it slow. Keep dodging for cover whenever you can."

Emma kept her eyes on her compass, hitting the indiglo button only sporadically to check her direction. After another fifteen minutes, she spotted the fires, propane lights, and headlights of a camp. She made her way to the same tree that Carn and Rand huddled behind. She shrugged out of her backpack and rolled her shoulders to release the tension. Just seeing the encampment had her heart racing and the rest of her ready to fight.

"Looks like we found them," Rand said. He handed her the binoculars. "They're not night vision, but you can make out a line of what looks like transport trucks to the left."

The supply trucks came into focus. They sat in a group about thirty feet from the main encampment. She turned her attention to the rest of the camp and took her time, looking at each person that she could see with any accuracy. Most appeared to be African. None looked like hostages. She kept sweeping her view and, at the far right side of the camp, she saw the men who'd been in the circle of insurgents from the day before. The one who drank beer while he watched the others being flogged and his lieutenant. She handed the field glasses back to Carn.

"We've got trouble. It's the same group we ran from yesterday."

Rand gave a short moan. "I don't want to risk getting blown up again, do you?"

Emma sighed. She hated to admit it, but Rand was right. She'd hoped to find the supplies guarded by a group of Mauritanian guards, who would be all too happy to take a bribe to release one or two of the transport vehicles. She hadn't counted on facing, yet again, the well-organized and well-funded ASIS.

"We'll have to wait for Banner," she said.

"No! Look at that far truck." Carn's voice was a furious whisper. "It's pretty far from the camp's center, and their sight lines are blocked by the other trucks. We could come around the far end and drive it off."

"With what?" Rand said. "We'll need a key. Our whole plan was predicated on paying off any Mauritanian guards, not stealing the transports."

"You can bet those trucks have the keys in the ignition."

Emma shook her head, "You don't know that for sure, Carn."

"I can't be one hundred percent certain, but the odds are I'm right. Those earlier guards didn't run off with the keys because they wouldn't want to be accused later of stealing. They would have left the keys with the trucks."

"We'd have to make it over there unseen, check the ignition and, if the keys are there, fire it up and take off. But you can bet they won't just let us go. They'll give chase, and that SUV can go a lot faster than any one of the transport trucks," Rand said.

Emma used the binoculars to view the trucks again. From what she could make out, Carn was right about the sight lines. But she had to agree with Rand about the relative speed of the two vehicles. Someone would give chase, and they'd have the advantage. She lowered the binoculars.

"We can't risk it. We'll have to wait for Banner and backup."

Before she could stop him, Carn took off at a dead run toward the farthest truck.

"Is he crazy?" Rand asked.

"Yes. What the hell is he thinking? He'll be killed." Emma wanted to catch Carn and shake him until his teeth rattled. Instead, she put her compass back in her pocket and slid her arms back into her pack to prepare to follow. Rand grabbed her arm.

"You can't run off after him. That's suicide. Why should you die for a bleeding-heart liberal with shit for brains?" Rand sounded furious. Emma grabbed her gun and checked it.

"I don't give a damn about his politics but, crazy or not, he'll need cover. Does your cell still have a charge?"

Rand shook his head. "Died again because I pulled it off the solar charger before it could finish. Don't do this."

"Here." She shoved her compass at him. "Take this and head due west for forty minutes then south for another forty and then east. That should get you back to Bakel." She stood to run and Rand rose with her.

"Wait! Don't you need this to get back?"

She shook her head. "I have two. The other is a basic magnetic, so I'll be fine."

She wrenched her arm out of his hand and ran after Carn.

29

Emma darted from tree to tree, keeping low and moving fast. She had no trouble closing the distance between her and Carn because he, too, was sprinting from cover to cover. He stopped at a tree that was a mere ten feet from the far transport vehicle. She ran up next to him and crouched down.

"Don't do this," she said.

Carn was breathing heavily, and the look he gave her was filled with determination.

"I'm tired of being a chess piece in a world of rich and corrupt assholes," he said. "Do you know how many refugees just one of those trucks could feed?"

"I'm not saying that we can't get our hands on them, I'm just suggesting that we wait for Banner."

"And if he doesn't come? Then what?"

Before Emma could reply she heard a man yelling commands.

"What's he saying?" she asked Carn.

"He's telling them to be ready to move in an hour. He says there are UN troops coming." Carn shook his head. "That's it, I'm going."

And he was gone. Emma swore under her breath and sidled around the tree, keeping her weapon up and doing her best to watch for threats. She watched as Carn made it to the far truck without appearing to raise any alarms. The camp had gone from somnolent inactivity to a mad scramble. The center of everyone's attention seemed directed at a covered military deuce and a half cargo truck. Emma moved to another tree to get a closer look. From that angle, she could see the camo paint on the vehicle and the star indicating that the truck was a former US military transport. The tattered cover flapped in the breeze.

An insurgent opened the passenger-side door, and another jogged toward the driver's side. Emma heard the engine fire to life, and she watched as it backed up to clear the truck next to it. A yell rose from somewhere to the right and the truck stopped. It idled, and a small cluster of insurgents moved out of the way as another dragged a hostage forward. The victim had a black hood over his head and his arms tied behind his back. He wore dress pants and wingtip shoes. The insurgents pulled him forward and brought him to the back of the transport vehicle. Even at a distance, Emma could see from the hostage's wrists and arms that he was white. Emma had little doubt that she was looking at a member of the embassy staff.

The attackers turned the victim around and helped him onto the truck's bed. Once he was seated, they poked him with their rifles. He got the message and scooted farther into the transport and out of Emma's sight. One of the insurgents hit their hand on the side of the truck, and the rest jogged back toward the group that they'd left. Emma watched as the truck's white backup lights came on and the vehicle began a slow reverse out of the line. After a moment, it stopped again, and the lights went off. The soldier from the passenger side exited and headed back to the main part of camp.

Emma turned her attention toward Carn's truck. She couldn't see him, a good sign, she supposed, because that probably meant that he'd successfully crawled into the vehicle. After a moment, she saw the taillights flash as the truck came to life.

He was right after all. The keys were in there, Emma thought. Keep it slow and easy. Don't alert them. Emma wanted to yell the advice to Carn. It was all she could do to stay put and watch. But Carn must have had the same idea because the transport truck turned ever so slowly in a semicircle and began to drive away.

Emma's mouth was dry and her hand slick on the pistol. No one from the clustered group of insurgents noticed that the supply truck was moving. Carn proceeded slowly, methodically, and without screaming tires or creating a scene. For a moment, Emma thought he was going to make it and just simply drive away. But she watched the first man in the group glance over and he hit his buddy next to him on the arm. The second man reacted. He gave a loud cry and pointed to the retreating supply truck. Within seconds, the others responded. Emma raised her weapon and targeted the first, waiting to see if he would shoot.

Surprisingly, he didn't. Instead, he did what Emma and Rand had feared. He jumped into the battered SUV, falling into the driver's side while three of his cronies joined him. The SUV roared to life and backed up in a rush, kicking up a cloud of dust only a bit darker than the air around it. Emma switched her focus from the car to the wheels, aiming at the nearest.

Before she could squeeze off a shot, the reverberation of another gun firing split the air. A dent formed on the SUV's side nearest the driver's wheel.

Rand, Emma thought. Despite all his complaints, he'd stayed to assist.

Two more shots in rapid succession also landed on the SUV's side wall, missing the tire. From the angle of the shots, she could tell that Rand was firing from the tree where she'd left him.

Not bad, Mr. Rand, but let me help you, she thought.

She held the pistol at eye level and fired three times—twice at the front wheel, once at the back. All three hit their target and she saw holes rip into them. None deflated, however. They were run-flats and of the highest quality because they must have taken similar hits during the initial skirmish. Emma could only hope this second assault would render them useless, and soon. The SUV plowed onward, turning toward Emma as it chased Carn. She worked her way around the tree as the car hurtled past.

Emma watched the car plow after Carn with growing frustration. She needed wheels to give chase, and the only ones were there, in the camp. She contemplated the truck that held the hostages, now idle on the edge of the encampment. While she did, Rand jogged up and crouched next to her.

"I thought you were leaving," Emma said.

"You were right, guy as stupid as that needed backup," Rand whispered. "You think he can outrace that SUV?"

"I hope so. I put three into its tires. Eventually, they have to fail."

Rand nodded. "I figured that as well."

"What about that truck?" Emma said.

"The one with the hostages? What about it?" Rand asked.

"Think we can pull a Carn and drive off with it?"

"No." Rand's voice was flat. "They're not going to fall for that twice. Look, they already have three guys guarding it."

Rand indicated three insurgents who'd returned to the truck and now leaned against it. One smoked a cigarette, and the other two worked on some khat.

"Rhonda could be in that truck," Emma said.

"Rhonda could have died in the blast back there on the savannah," Rand said.

Emma shook her head. "She was on the far side of the camp when it blew. They all scattered initially, sure, but I'll bet they went back and rounded up anyone they could find. As a Westerner, she would be a high-value hostage."

"Which one do you want to hijack?"

"That farthest one. Once it starts moving, they'll have to respond. Perhaps the ones guarding the hostage truck will break and follow."

Rand remained quiet. Emma thought he was mulling the chances.

"It's too risky."

She watched the guards and looked back at the group she'd encountered on the savannah. The leader paced back and forth, yelling into a phone. His lieutenant sat next to him, glaring at his boss. Bandages covered his burned arm. Emma made a mental note that, if she ever tangled with him again, she would make it a point to hammer that injury.

"I agree it's risky."

Her phone buzzed and the display read *Banner*. She hit the answer key and heard him say, "Got your text. That was some quick work. Are you sure?"

"Yes. How far away are you now?"

"Far. But I'm in a copter and heading your way. Three hours, no more. And I notified Stromeyer to let Secretary Plower know. I would imagine the DOD is already working on an extraction. Can you stay put? Monitor the situation?"

"Not for long. I have very little cover and, once the sun rises, I'll have none. I'm headed back to the refugee camp at the border. But first I'm sending you the coordinates from my phone."

"I have those," Banner said.

"Then, God willing, they'll still be here when the DOD begins its extraction."

30

Thirty minutes outside of Choum, Denal checked the rearview mirror and frowned.

"Wake up, sir. We're being followed."

Sumner opened his eyes and glanced in the side mirror. A truck drove behind them, coming on fast.

"Perhaps they're just another group of travelers," Sumner said.

Denal shook his head. "I saw a gun. That car has the look and smell of trouble."

"Can you outrun them?"

"No."

"How far are we from Tidjikja?"

"Twenty miles. The next town is there, just ahead."

In front of them was a collection of small huts with canvas walls and grass roofs. Hardly a town. More like a small way station. Sumner glanced again in the side mirror. Denal was right. The men riding in the truck looked like soldiers, not civilians. Azhan had found him. Sumner collected his pack from the back seat and checked his weapon.

"When we reach that village, stop. I'll get out. Then hit the gas and get out of there as fast as you can. Whatever trouble this is, it's after me, not you."

Denal flicked a worried look at Sumner. "I would stay and help."

Sumner shook his head. "No. But I thank you for the offer."

They neared the first hut and Denal slowed and then stopped.

"Goodbye, my friend," Denal said. "May peace be with you."

"And you as well," Sumner said. He got out of the truck, closed the door, and stepped back. Denal waved and hit the gas. The truck's wheels bit and he drove off in a cloud of dust.

Sumner held his gun in one hand and turned on his phone and dialed Banner with the other. While it connected, Sumner turned to see the following truck skid to a halt a few feet away from him. It remained there, idling. After a moment, the driver cut the engine, and a man stepped out and stood in front of him, aiming an AK-47.

Sumner froze. He heard Banner's voice through the phone.

"I'm in a town outside of Tidjikja. Under attack," Sumner said.

Behind him, he heard the sound of engines. He turned his head to look, slowly, so as not to startle the man with the gun. Four pickups drove towards them, their wheels kicking up a large cloud of sand and dust. They wheeled around and stopped in a semicircle with Sumner in the center. The doors flung open, and men stepped out from all sides, all carrying weapons. Last out of the trucks came the man from the train, the one who'd traveled without supplies to make tea.

"Hang up. Now," he said in English.

Sumner clicked off the phone.

"Give the gun and phone to me."

Sumner handed them over and watched as the man powered down the phone.

All of the assorted fighters wore army fatigues, most wore turbans, and several carried a second weapon at their waists. They stayed in place at the sides of their vehicles and remained silent. Several glanced toward the first car in the circle, a dark green Land Rover. From the expectant expressions, it was clear to Sumner that whoever was in that car was the head of this particular group of soldiers. The driver's side door opened and a man got out and walked toward them.

He was tall, with dark eyes, and wore the same style fatigues as Sumner's captor, along with a blue turban that wrapped around his eyes and mouth to protect him from the sand. His khaki-colored shirt had a collar and rolled-up sleeves, and he wore a silver box necklace around his neck on a leather cord. He walked with a confident stride and held a rifle in one hand, by the barrel rather than the butt. He flicked a glance at Sumner and turned to the man without the tea.

"Where did you get him?" he asked in French, which surprised Sumner, who had expected him to speak in either Arabic or Tamasheq, the Tuareg language.

"On the train. He speaks English and he traveled with her."

"Where is she now?" the leader asked.

"On a desert taxi to Atar. It shouldn't be hard to catch her."

"Why didn't you hold her as well?"

The man jutted his chin at Sumner. "He carries a weapon and the transports were there. Too many for one man to control."

The leader turned to Sumner and looked him up and down. He walked over and batted Sumner's phone out of the other man's hand. The device fell on the ground, and he stomped on it with the heel of his boot. Bits of plastic sprayed onto the sand.

"Did you touch Aaliyah?" he asked Sumner in English. The question said it all. It was Azhan. Sumner stared at what he could see of the man's face, doing his best to commit it to memory.

"I did not," he said.

Azhan stood a moment. Sumner could smell the oil from the weapon, mingled with the unique scent of Oud, a perfume that he'd only smelled in the Middle East.

"I'll shoot him," the man without the tea said. He raised his weapon. Azhan raised a hand to stop him.

"Not here. Drive him into the desert and leave him there. That way is easier. No body to dispose of, no blood to clean, and no wound that would point to murder. His body may never be found but, if it is, he'll be just another man who died after getting lost in the Sahara." Azhan spoke in French. He looked back at Sumner.

"You'll be so thirsty by the time the jackals come to eat you that you'll thank them as they tear you to pieces."

Sumner kept his face impassive. It was clear that Azhan believed that the sentence he'd just handed down was a horrible fate, but it was all Sumner could do not to show his relief. A drive into the desert with one man gave him a chance to escape in a way that an immediate bullet in the head did not.

"And shall I come back here?" the man asked. Azhan shook his head.

"Go to Atar and bring her to me."

"And her son?"

"Kill him," Azhan said.

The man without the tea motioned Sumner toward one of the pickups with the tip of his gun. Sumner walked forward, keeping his backpack with him. Azhan watched him as he passed, his eyes filled with hate. Sumner gazed ahead and didn't engage or glance at him. He moved to the back of the truck, stood at the pickup's lowered tailgate, and waited as the man without the tea stripped him of his pack, trussed his wrists behind his back, and hammered the tip of his AK into Sumner's spine. Sumner grunted with pain and crawled onto the bed as best he could without the use of his hands. The engine fired up, and the truck took a slow curve to point toward the west. Azhan ignored them completely as they drove away.

Sumner pressed himself against the side wall to avoid tumbling around, as the truck bed rocked up and down on the rutted desert track. While he did, he plotted possible escape routes. The leather ties that bound his wrists held firmly, cutting off the blood to his fingers, and he felt a numbness settling in. He ran through several possible scenarios. He could try to kick the man as he lowered the tailgate, but an extended fight with only his feet seemed impossible, as long as the other man held a gun. He could try a bribe. But he suspected that, once he retrieved the money from Sumner's backpack, the other man would simply leave him in the desert anyway.

The truck bounced and lurched, following the heavy tracks laid out across the desert. It was as if they'd been carved by a gigantic knife and then preserved in stone. Blowing sand occasionally obscured a portion of the trail, but never for long. The sun continued to climb in the sky and with it came stifling heat. Sumner still wore his sunglasses, but the wind had ripped away the scarf from his mouth and eyes, and he was battered with grit. The truck barreled forward and Sumner estimated it hadn't gone below sixty miles per hour since it started.

After half an hour of driving, the truck slowed and then stopped. Sumner sat up straighter, waiting for his captor. The car shook as the man exited and slammed the door. He came into view and sauntered to the rear of the truck and lowered the tailgate.

"Get out," he said in French.

Sumner scooted down. As he did, it was clear that the man was taking no chances. He stepped back, well out of kicking range, and kept his gun leveled at Sumner. Sumner slid off the pickup bed and stood.

"Take me with you to Atar and I'll pay you," Sumner said.

The man shook his head. "There isn't enough money to tempt me to cross Azhan. He wants you to die out here in the desert, and that's what you'll do."

"Five thousand American," Sumner said.

The man stilled. Though the scarf wrapped around the man's face kept most of his features hidden, Sumner could still see his eyes, and it was clear that he was mulling the offer.

"I can also assure you asylum across the border in Morocco."

Sumner was not at all sure that he *could* get the man across the border, but he'd worry about that eventuality later. Now he needed to sway his attacker. The man shook his head.

"No. Azhan will kill my family in retaliation. There is nothing you can give me to cross him." The man unbuckled Sumner's watch, pocketed it, and ran a hand down the outside of Sumner's legs in a quick pat down.

Sumner tried one last attempt. "Then at least untie me. Let me die holding my hands up to my maker."

The man contemplated this request. After a pause, he slid a long knife from a holder that hung on a string around his waist. He kept his gun up and trained on Sumner as he walked around and insinuated the blade between Sumner's hands. Sumner could feel the cold steel on his skin. In one quick cut, the leather ties broke. The man strode past Sumner to the pickup, climbed in, and drove away without a glance back, taking Sumner's backpack with him.

Sumner stood in the blazing sun and began to plot his survival.

31

Banner had heard the few words Sumner said before the phone line went dead. He switched on the tracking device and saw that Sumner's signal was racing along the road outside of Tidjikja. His phone lit up and he saw the message from Caldridge about the hostages. He hit a button and dialed the only person left in the area with a possible helicopter.

"What's up?" Vanderlock's voice came over Banner's headset.

"What's the ETA on your helicopter repair?"

"No word. Why?"

"Sumner's under attack in the desert in Mauritania, and Caldridge may have located the embassy personnel that were kidnapped near Dakar and driven to the border. I need someone in the area that can fly and a machine to fly in."

"Not happening here. But there is one option."

"And that would be?"

"Caldridge's buddy, Richard Carrow, is in Johannesburg. His band is playing a gig there. I understand that they travel in style. Gulfstream jet."

"A helicopter would be better. More nimble."

"But a jet is fast."

"Will he lend it?"

"If Caldridge asks he will."

Banner contemplated the idea. "Hold tight." He clicked off and dialed Stromeyer.

"What's the name of Richard Carrow's band?" he asked.

"Rex. Used to be Rex Rain and they shortened it."

"Can you reach him?"

"Would take me endless calls through layers of publicists, agents, and managers. Caldridge has his cell. She can speak to him in a second."

"I'm not sure she's in a place where she can receive a call. My last communication was a text. She thinks that she found the embassy personnel." He ran down Caldridge's text and Locke's suggestion about the Gulfstream, and heard Stromeyer whistle over the phone.

"I think Vanderlock's right. Get Carrow to lend the plane, fly it to the border on the Mauritania side, and send in a small force to free the hostages. When that's done, they can be flown out of there to Casablanca."

"Does our contract with the DOD include reimbursement if we destroy a Gulfstream?"

"Absolutely not. Even used, we're looking at twenty million. Insurance won't help because damage due to an act of war is a standard exclusion. Whoever flies it better not trash it."

"Call Plower. I should think the secretary of state can get the DOD to agree to cover the cost of the jet. We're talking people's lives here."

"Agreed. I'll argue that if they're not willing to negotiate with kidnappers, then they'd better put their money into rescue."

"I'm headed towards Tidjikja and then back to Choum. Send me a text. No calls."

Banner rang off and turned the helicopter towards the last known ping for Sumner's location. As he did, he watched his fuel level. He'd had enough to make it across Mauritania and carried a can in the back, so levels weren't an immediate concern, but he wasn't sure how long it would take to locate Sumner.

Half an hour later, Banner hovered over a pickup truck as it barreled across the desert on the track toward Atar. The GPS device that he'd given Sumner indicated that Sumner was in the truck. Banner flew lower for a closer look and saw Sumner's backpack bouncing in the bed. He sank even lower and flew alongside, looking to see if the truck had a passenger. There was none, and he flew up and over to the other side to check out the driver. One glance told him that it wasn't Sumner driving the car. The driver kept turning his head to look at the chopper and, with his right arm, he was maneuvering what looked like a semiautomatic rifle across him to the window.

Banner flew straight up, aimed his own front-mounted guns at a spot in front of the truck and laid down fire, keeping it far enough in front to ensure that the truck had time to avoid getting hit. He wanted the man scared but not dead. He needed information.

The truck swerved and skidded, kicking up a cloud of sand and dust. Banner climbed higher. He didn't need his engines to get clogged with sand. After another minute, he laid down another line of fire, and the truck swerved the other way. Banner swung up ahead and lowered down, flying backward until he faced the truck.

"Stop now, or this time I'll aim for you," he said over the chopper's loudspeaker, both in English and repeated in French. He said the word "stop" over and over in both languages.

After a moment, he saw the pickup begin to slow. He swung around to the back of the truck, and the brake lights glowed as it came to a halt. "Get out and lay face down." Banner repeated the instructions while he hovered above the truck, close enough to keep the man in his sights and far enough to avoid taking fire, should the man step out and let off a volley from the assault weapon. He watched as the driver came out of the cab, unarmed and with his hands in the air. The man dropped to his knees and lowered himself until he was face down on the sand.

Banner descended, keeping far enough away to ensure a quick exit, if necessary, but doing his best to place his skids onto the track to avoid having dust enter the moving parts. He cut the engine, grabbed his gun, and jumped out, keeping his head down to avoid the propellers. He jogged to the prone man. As he passed the truck's bed, he snagged Sumner's backpack and carried it with him. He frisked the man, removing a cell phone, a wallet, the truck keys, and a lip balm from the man's pockets. He kicked the sole of the man's shoe.

"Look at me," he said in both languages. The man looked up. Banner held the pack in front of him. "Where is the man who owns this?"

The man rattled off a sentence in French. Banner's command of the language was rudimentary, but he understood that Sumner had been dropped in the desert somewhere.

"Alive?" Banner asked.

"*Oui*. Alive," the man repeated.

Banner fished around in Sumner's backpack until he found the map that he knew Sumner carried. He laid it in front of the man.

"Show me," he said.

The man rose to a kneeling position and studied the map. He pointed to a place not far from Choum and about three miles from the road. Banner wasn't sure if the man was telling the truth, but there was one way to find out.

"Stay down," he said.

He went to the truck and popped the hood. He fished around in Sumner's backpack and found what he knew he would—inside a plastic food storage bag was a small rag. Banner had suggested that Sumner carry one to clean his gun while in the desert. Now, Banner wrapped it around his hand and reached into the engine, taking care to avoid touching any hot metal, and located the spark plugs. He removed one, closed the hood, grabbed the man's AK-47 from the front seat, and returned to show the two items to the man.

"I'll keep these. When I find him, I'll come back and give you the spark plug and the keys to the truck. The gun's mine."

The man exploded in a string of French. From what Banner could understand the man was terrified that Banner would leave him there in the desert to rot.

"If you're telling the truth I should be back in two, maybe three hours at the outside," Banner said.

"Wait!" the man said. "He's probably here." He pointed to another spot on the map in the exact opposite direction from the place he'd indicated previously.

"Is he on foot?" Banner asked.

"Yes."

"Who do you work for?"

"No one," the man said. Banner pointed the gun at the man's face.

"Then no one will care when I kill a common thief," he said.

"Wait! I work for myself, but I was forced to take your friend."

"Forced?"

The man nodded. "Azhan. You may know of him. He owns everything and everyone. He demanded that I kill your friend. But I didn't. I did him a favor, even, and untied his hands."

"And then you left him in the desert to die."

"I had no choice!"

Banner shrugged. "And neither do I. If I don't find him, then you'll pay the same price, and you'll die here." Banner headed to the helicopter. The man scrambled to his feet.

"Mister! Take me with you. I will help you find him."

Banner shook his head. "You'd better get in that cab. The sun is hot." He tossed Sumner's backpack, the AK, and his own gun into the helicopter, dumped more fuel from the can into the copter and strapped into the seat. Once the chopper's rotors reached speed, he rose up and flew in the direction the man had indicated. He only hoped he'd find Sumner before Azhan realized that his man had been taken.

32

Sumner stared at the desert landscape for a moment before lowering to a crouch. The sun directly above told him it was noon. He reached to the inside of his pant leg and removed a flat compass. It was a gift from Caldridge, who'd insisted he carry one at all times. She'd even gone so far as to have a seamstress sew hidden pockets in most of his pants legs.

"No matter where in the world you are, if you have a compass, at least you can choose a direction and keep with it," she'd said. "Even if the direction ultimately proves to be wrong, you won't have expended wasted energy walking in circles."

The thought of Caldridge calmed him. She, of course, would have just picked a direction and started running, continuing for one hundred miles until she came upon a village, but he didn't have the stamina or training that she did. While in excellent shape by most people's standards—he could run ten miles at a fast pace and without getting too winded—he didn't engage in the endurance training that she maintained.

He estimated that they'd gone west from the village and so, now, he held the compass and walked east. His sunglasses were a godsend, as was the scarf that he wrapped around his face. While the scarf compounded the stifling heat, he didn't need to add sun poisoning to his list of discomforts. Sweat streamed down his arms, the center of his back, and pooled around his waistband. His feet sweat in their lightweight combat boots.

The landscape held nothing but sand, scrub trees, and a few rocks. Every once in a while, he'd spot an insect, but that was the only beast out in the noonday sun. Every other living being in the desert knew enough to seek shade and lay low. Within thirty minutes, Sumner's parched throat began to ache, and his eyes were watering from the bright sunlight, despite the sunglasses. The intense heat and blowing wind seemed to suck every bit of liquid from him. His shoulder wound ached and his knife slash throbbed. He kept his heading east and never let the compass needle move at all. He stared at the device, enthralled with the fact that it was this, and this alone, that kept him moving forward and not in circles. He said a silent thank you to Caldridge because, without the compass, he wouldn't have been able to hold down the panic that occasionally bubbled up. With the compass, he could tamp it down with a silent, You're going the right way because the compass doesn't lie.

Three hours into his ordeal he heard the sound of an approaching aircraft. He stopped and shielded his eyes as he gazed upward. The helicopter came into view, and he strained to see any markings that would tell him who owned it.

The craft turned toward him and, when it was a hundred yards away, it began a slow descent. Sumner watched it lower and rock from side to side as it settled onto the sand.

"Sumner, come on over. I need a co-pilot." The words streamed from the copter's address system. Sumner's legs almost collapsed in relief at the sound of the familiar voice.

"Absolutely," he said out loud, though he knew Banner couldn't hear him. He jogged to the waiting helicopter and climbed inside. Banner slapped him on the shoulder and handed him a headset.

"I can't tell you how relieved I am to see you," he said. "Elated, actually."

"You're relieved and I'm ecstatic. Do you have any water?" Sumner asked.

"Behind your seat." Banner focused on getting the copter airborne while Sumner rooted around in a cooler and grabbed a bottle of water. He chugged it down, relishing the cool liquid.

"You need one?" he asked. Banner shook his head.

"No. But the guy we're heading to might. I left him without transportation somewhere on the road to Atar." He waved to the back. "I tracked your backpack. It's there. I also have your Dragunov in the back.

"I hope you beat the shit out of the asshole that left me there."

Banner shook his head. "I figured you'd want that pleasure."

"I would. After I get some answers out of him."

Banner laughed. "I thought the exact same thing. He claims that Azhan ordered him to leave you in the desert. That true?"

Sumner nodded. "I think it was Azhan." He told Banner about Aaliyah and his trip in the iron ore car.

"So this Azhan will be hearing soon that his orders weren't carried out," Banner said.

"And then he'll send the next guy to get her."

"We need someone there to intercept the next one. We could use any information that he could give us. About Azhan and about where the ASIS will head next."

"Exactly."

"I'm headed to the border. I'm sorry, but I can't leave you this chopper after all. I'm going to have to use it to retrieve the embassy personnel. But take this." He handed Sumner a spark plug. "And these." He gave him a set of keys. "You're now the proud owner of a ten-year-old pickup truck."

"I'll take it."

"What should we do with the former owner?"

"Leave that to me," Sumner said. "I'm going to discuss his options with him. One will be to join me."

"And if he doesn't?"

"Then I'll let him know that I'll be sure to get the word out that he messed up on the one thing Azhan ordered him to do. He won't have much time to live after Azhan hears about it."

"Something tells me that you're going to have his full cooperation."

Sumner stared out of the windshield, watching the endless waves of sand as they flew back to the truck.

33

The early morning sun's rays rose over the horizon, and a beam hit the metal side of the trailer, spraying light onto Emma's face. She came awake in the back of the truck that Carn had stolen. He'd opened the doors to the trailer, and they'd pushed aside crates and boxes to create a makeshift sleeping area. Carn slept against the far wall and Rand in the center. Somewhere in the distance, a child cried and was hushed by its mother. Emma sat up and did her best to work out the kinks from sleeping on the hard metal surface. While not as comfortable as the ground, it had the advantage of being away from any crawling bugs. The flying ones, though, were another story. She scratched at a random bite on her leg.

She moved to the edge of the trailer and looked out over the refugee camp. Hundreds of sleeping people lay on the ground in a mass of blankets, the occasional makeshift tent, and even a few battered old bush taxis. Most of the displaced people who'd fled from the oncoming insurgency brought only what they could carry on their backs. Emma stood in the trailer's doorway and stared out over the hundreds huddled in front of her and, for a moment, thought that she could feel their sadness as a tangible thing. As though despair was a disease one could catch instead of a state of mind.

Carn stretched and stood up. He looked first at the hordes of sleeping people, and then at her.

"You look grim," he said.

Emma waved at the scene. "This." She had no words.

Carn inhaled. "I've been here for years, and this is the worst that I've experienced. It seems as though Africa always has some country at war, but to have the attackers coming from all sides...." He shook his head. "We literally have no place to go."

"But we have to move. Staying here, for us and them, means certain death."

Carn snorted. "Just where do you want to go?" He squinted into the glory of the rising sun. "That way is Mali, where the ASIS is massing. And there," he said, pointing south, "the insurgents from Casamance march this way. And there," he said, pointing west, "is filled with the Red Hand working their way toward us." Then he pointed to the Mauritanian border guards lolling half asleep on their flatbeds. "While those jokers stop everyone in their tracks." He picked up and flung an empty box at the wall of the truck. It bounced off and tumbled at Emma's feet. "And even if we got past the Mauritanian border guards we'd hit the land mines in the north as we tried to cross into Morocco."

Emma knew he was right, but to stay and be killed by inaction felt like giving up. And giving up was something that she rarely, if ever, did.

"I just can't sit here and wait to be killed. I don't have it in me to let fate just take its course."

Carn contemplated her with a serious look. "What about 'God will provide'?"

"Well, there's that," Emma said. "But perhaps God will provide while we're on the road to Morocco?"

Carn's lips tilted in a bit of a smile. "Maybe you're right and God doesn't care where we are when the provisions come."

"I'm supposed to be helping Banner rescue those embassy officials. I can't stay here. But I'll help you unload the cookers and mosquito nets."

Three hours later, Rand, Carn, and Emma had successfully distributed over four hundred cookers and double that number of mosquito nets. Emma wiped the sweat from her forehead as she watched a child accept the last of the nets.

"Wish there was water to go with those cookers," Rand said.

Carn nodded. "And food."

Emma's phone was charging in the sun. She picked it up and sent a text to Banner telling him to call. He rang her within seconds.

"Where are you?" he asked, and the strain in his voice was clear.

"With a group of refugees at the border between Senegal and Mauritania."

"That's what I was afraid of. You've got to get the hell out of there. Now."

"What's going on?"

"The insurgents breached Thiès four hours ago. They're headed to Bakel."

Emma swallowed. Her throat remained dry and her lips were chapped. "How about Mali? Have the French taken it back?"

"They have, but by driving that group along the Mauritania and Sudan border. It's only a matter of time before they get to Bakel as well. It's a pincer movement."

"So where do I go?"

"North into Mauritania is still the best option. You're going to have to slip over the border. When you do, head in the direction of Atar. But, before you go, check Rand's bags."

Emma glanced at Rand, but he stood ten feet away and was deep in conversation with Carn.

"Why?"

"He may be carrying stolen vials of smallpox."

"He told me," Emma said. She ran down the story that Rand had supplied regarding the vials. "He claimed to have notified the authorities."

"He did. But he told them it was smallpox vaccine, not the actual disease."

"So he lied."

"Yes. Check his things before you go and send me a text. And after that I want you to get as far away from him as possible."

"Because of the virus?"

"No. Because I think he deliberately invited you on this trip in order to hand you over to the insurgents. They need a trained chemist and he's providing them one." The dry wind blew Emma's hair into her face, but she hardly noticed. She ran the events of the past few days through her mind and it all fell into place. She could see the outlines of the plan and the role they'd designated that she would play in it.

"That bastard," she said.

"With the virus out of his control, he only has you to barter with. Search his bags and get the hell out of there. I'll try to find you on the Mauritanian side."

Banner rang off, and Emma watched as Rand and Carn walked away. Rand carried his backpack. She would wait until he fell asleep or set it down.

Funny how the lack of possessions made life easier, Emma thought. There was no place to hide anything in their current circumstances.

But that was the only bright spot. Emma hated that there was nothing they could use for shelter. In the distance, she heard the chop-chop sound of a helicopter in flight. Someone was headed their way. She only hoped they were friendly because the wide-open expanse left the entire camp open to attack from above. She scanned the sky as she waited to find out.

34

The helicopter appeared like a black speck that grew larger as it approached. The rhythmic sound of the spinning blades increased and soon the people massed on the ground ceased their activity to watch. Kids stopped their running and women their cooking. Several men, who were sitting in a circle preparing tea, rose from their crouch to shield their eyes. Emma could feel the mounting tension and fear, as the collected groups assessed the incoming stranger.

Details emerged as the chopper approached. It appeared to be military, green, with large sections covered in gray, which Emma thought was actually primer. One black runner, bent at the back, gave the machine a decidedly battered appearance, and black smoke poured out of the engine, leaving a trail.

"That machine has taken a beating," Carn said as he walked up to her. He kept his eyes to the sky and watched the chopper approach.

"Probably military. Good?"

Carn rocked his hand back and forth. "That could be good or bad, depending on which military." Rand joined them, still wearing his backpack. Emma thought she saw the gleam of an upcoming negotiation in his eye. Doubtless, he intended to offer the pilot whatever he could to hitch a ride out of Senegal.

"Do you see a gun mount?" she asked.

Carn shook his head. "No."

The helicopter flew directly over them, and several children clapped hands over their ears as it hovered above, belching black smoke. Every few seconds came a grinding sound of metal on metal.

"Thing is falling to pieces." The din forced Emma to yell this last comment into Carn's ear. He nodded.

After a few moments, the helicopter began a slow descent and the children scattered in its downdraft. Emma, Carn, and Rand backed off, putting more distance between them and the lowering machine.

Dust kicked up and began to swirl as the blades beat above the dried earth. The acrid smell of burning oil, and the shrieking of mismatched metal gears, filled the air with a nails-on-a-blackboard note that set Emma's teeth on edge. She squinted, as bits of sand and dirt flew into her eyes and blew her hair around. Then she stepped back farther and watched the chopper rock itself to the ground before settling into a lopsided landing. After a moment, the engine stopped and the blades' rotation slowed. The belching smoke cloud lightened as the winds blew at it, but it was still impossible to see the pilot. After a moment, a side door opened and a man climbed out. He jogged toward them, keeping his head low. A slow smile crossed his face.

"He's smiling at you. Guy's chopper is nearly dead and he's smiling. You know him?" Carn asked.

Emma nodded. "I do. That's Wilson Vanderlock. We all call him Locke."

Vanderlock strode in her direction, and his smile grew. He wore dust-colored cargo pants, battered black combat boots covered in dust, a gray t-shirt, and his habitual nonchalant air. His long, light brown hair hung to his collarbone and looked as though someone had chopped it with a knife. He headed straight to Emma, with his arms wide open, and she laughed and walked into his embrace. He smelled like dust and sweat and oil and cigarettes and man, and all of it was welcome. She gripped him tightly. He responded by lifting her off the ground and holding her in the air for a moment before lowering her back to earth.

"Part came for the helo lots quicker than I expected," he said. "Not that it mattered. Thing's broken again, as you see."

"How'd you find me?" Emma asked.

"Stromeyer. She's been tracking your phone."

He put her down and glanced at Carn and Rand with a question in his eyes. Emma waved at them.

"This is Carnegie Wendel and—"

"Jackson Rand. I know. The helicopter service called me and said you were offering a new helicopter for anyone willing to fly you out of the hot zone." Vanderlock shook Carn's hand and then Rand's.

"Offer still stands. But can that thing fly?"

"Not as far as you need to get out of the hot zone. I took some damage over Thiès. It fell a few hours ago."

"No gun mount?" Emma asked.

"None."

"What kind of damage?" Carn asked.

"Some idiot with an RPG got lucky and grazed me with his shrapnel. He managed to hit the same damn place that I just fixed. But he didn't do the real damage." Locke shook his head in disgust. "Sometimes I don't know why I bother repairing this thing. But I come bearing gifts. Let me show you." He waved them toward the helicopter, which now listed on the ground, its blades still. Emma glanced under the carriage and watched as a drop of oil fell from the engine.

"Who did the real damage? You're leaking oil."

Locke nodded. "Not the guy on the ground, someone in the air. Another helicopter."

"Rare for insurgents to have helicopters, isn't it?" Emma asked.

Locke opened the copter's door and shot Emma a knowing look.

"Beyond rare. I got a look at the pilot, and while he covered his face, I thought I saw some Arabic lettering on the copter's fuselage."

"Saudis?" Emma asked.

"Or from Yemen. But, whoever it was, the guy could fly. He maneuvered really well. Kept me on my toes, I can tell you."

Locke's reputation as a pilot was legend, so the fact that he was praising another one was telling. Whoever shot at him was no novice. Emma pondered this new and sobering information as she watched Locke remove several boxes from the back of the helicopter's cargo area. He handed them first to Carn and then to Rand. The third, a long, thin box that resembled a flower box, he handed to Emma.

"What is this?"

"A rifle. Courtesy of the government of Guinea-Bissau."

"Stolen," Emma said flatly. Locke pretended to look outraged.

"Borrowed. The government official who had it in the back of his car had just received it as payment of a bribe. In my view, all's fair in love and war...and blackmail."

"Hmm," Emma said, as she opened the lid to peer at the gun. It was a shiny new Heckler & Koch. Next to it was a small box of Davidoff Demi-Tasse cigars, Emma's favorite brand. She held the box up. "This is the real gold. How did these get in here?"

"They're for you. I know they're your favorites."

"I only smoke one or two a year—New Year's Eve and to celebrate something wonderful."

Locke nodded. "Then we'll smoke them together when we reach Morocco."

"Your government official isn't going to forget about this HK."

Locke shrugged. "It will be just one more theft in a country rife with it. But, if it worries you, I can keep it."

Emma shook her head. "I'm not that outraged."

Locke laughed. "And you shouldn't be." He handed her two bullets.

"That's it for ammunition?"

"I'm sorry to say it is, so save them for the right moment."

She waved at the boxes that Carn and Rand were busy opening. "What's in there?"

"Food. Military rations, ready to eat," Locke said. Emma picked up a bag.

"MREs. The packaging looks grim."

"Also known as 'Meals Rejected by Everyone,'" Locke said, laughing.

"How many?"

"Not enough. A few hundred."

Emma sighed. "It's never enough, is it?"

Locke swept his gaze over the mass of humanity dotting the field. "These people need to move, and now. The insurgents are coming, and they're like the ancient Huns, pillaging everything in their path."

Emma thought about the village where she'd spent the night. She wondered if the image of the dead would ever leave her. "How bad?" she asked.

"Terrible. They're killing the men, raping the women, and collecting the young women to hold as captives for the fighters. Slaves." He pointed his cigarette at her. "You need to flee this place ahead of the rest, with your white skin and American features. You're the first one they'll attack."

"Banner told me to move. I'm going to finish up something for him and meet him over the border."

"Banner's here?"

"No. He's in Mauritania. So the world's taking notice?" Emma asked.

"I don't know if 'notice' is the right word. They're bickering over who'll have to absorb all these refugees."

"Forget absorption. Is anyone willing to fight? Bring a force?"

Locke shook his head. "None yet. The UN peacekeepers are stretched thin, the average American citizen is tired of fighting everyone else's battles, Congress is afraid to rile up their constituents, and the European nations don't have a force of the size needed."

"And, so, we sit here and fight piecemeal."

"And, so, we sit here and get destroyed." Locke ground his cigarette stub into the dirt. A shriek from the direction of his helicopter made them both turn around. Several children huddled around the open door, peering inside. One was already seated in the pilot seat with her hand on the cyclic, pretending to fly it.

"Hey!" Locke yelled something in another language and the kids scattered, with the girl who'd been sitting inside tumbling out of the cockpit and running away as fast as she could.

"What did you say?" Emma asked.

"Get out, or I'll hang you by your thumbs."

"Nice. Good thing you're not a father."

"If I was, I'd be plotting ways to get these kids over the border." Locke stepped closer. "I'm not kidding. We have to get these people out of here."

Locke's concern rattled Emma, because his usual demeanor was relaxed and unworried, whether his helicopter was hemorrhaging smoke and ready to fall out of the sky, or he was being targeted by an enemy.

"How much time do we have before they arrive?"

"Eight hours on the outside."

"Eight hours to move three thousand people across a guarded border into a vast desert where they might die anyway."

Locke sighed. "That's the way of it."

"Why is life here so hard?" Emma kicked at a rock and sent it flying.

Locke shook his head. "I don't know. But I don't want to stay around to watch the carnage. There's only so much darkness that I want residing in my brain." He gave her a sidelong glance. "You've lost weight."

She shrugged. She didn't see Locke often enough to keep him up to date on her life, but things had been stressful back in the States, and she'd been happy to have the excuse to travel. Now the problems in the States seemed benign compared to this.

"I haven't eaten in a day."

"I don't think it's a matter of one day," Locke said. She should have known better than to try and fool Locke.

"I'd been doing a lot of training before I came here. Marathon season is coming." It wasn't the complete truth, but not a complete lie either. She had been training hard before she'd agreed to the charitable mission.

Locke pulled on his cigarette while he contemplated her, and she had the distinct impression that he knew more than he was willing to say. After a moment, he looked back at his helicopter.

"That thing won't get far. In the meantime, let's make a plan." Locke tossed her an MRE. "But, first, eat."

Emma tore at the package and, for a moment, had the ghoulish thought that it might be her last meal.

35

Emma stood next to Locke and watched as the refugee camp came alive with the rising sun. It seemed impossible that a small fighting force could control such a vast amount of people, but she knew that Locke was right. Without weapons and training, the refugees would be captured...or killed.

"Is there a plan to move?" Locke asked.

Emma shook her head. "Not that I know of. The Mauritanian army..." she said, pointing to the guards by the line of trucks at the border, "are stopping people from crossing."

Locke snorted. "That's all? Good luck holding them back. The border is porous. They can't monitor it all. They'll be able to move across, despite what those guards want."

"But move into what? Mauritania is just a vast desert. If they cross, they need to stick to known routes or risk dying of starvation or thirst. And, if they do stick to known routes, the army will just round them up and ship them back. Or worse, harass them until they want to go back."

Locke rubbed his neck as he thought about what she'd said.

"How bad is it in Mauritania? Can they find food while they pass through? If they can, perhaps they could promise to keep marching to Morocco."

"But if Morocco won't take them?" Emma said.

"Impasse."

"Exactly." She watched a young girl shuffle through the dirt. "What about turning around? Facing the insurgents?"

Locke shook his head. "They would need weapons and training. These are women, children, and old men, and none of them are trained to fight. How can they possibly rally a force strong enough to overcome a semiprofessional army?"

Rand and Carn stepped up to listen to the conversation. Rand, in particular, seemed grim.

"I would think that a peacekeeping force would get involved with this one," he said.

Carn grimaced. "That's not going to happen."

"Why? You mean they're just going to let us all die? Either by dying of thirst, hunger, or by being fired upon by a hostile insurgent group? Or, in this case, groups?" Rand's voice rose along with his anger.

Locke pulled a pack of cigarettes from a shirt pocket and knocked one out. He put it to his lips, lit it, and inhaled, shaking out the match. He exhaled a stream of smoke.

"Why are you still here? I would think a man with your resources would be long gone."

Rand raised an eyebrow. "You think I haven't been trying? Everywhere I turn I hit a wall. I had help getting here, but that was in trucks, and—"

"Way too dangerous to travel surface roads through Senegal," Locke said.

"Exactly. And you know the state of air travel. Or the lack of available air transport. And then everyone keeps warning me about my white skin and kidnapping."

Locke kept a steady stare on Rand as he smoked. Emma tapped him on the arm.

"Walk with me. We need to talk."

Locke nodded, and Emma waved him away from Carn and Rand.

"I don't trust that guy," Locke said, when they were out of earshot. "Someone has to be crazy enough to fly into here to get him. Especially when the payoff is a new piece of equipment."

"The Maraad has promised to get him."

Locke snorted. "Those snakes. But money talks the world over and Africa is no different. What's going on with him?"

Emma shook her head. "I don't exactly know." She told him about Banner's contention that Rand carried the smallpox virus.

"I'm supposed to check that pack he wears."

Locke contemplated the new information for a moment, then shook his head.

"Something's off. I mean, the guy knew he was targeted from the beginning and went so far as to test his fancy netting on the vehicle. Then he claims to have discovered the tainted vaccine and now claims to be stuck in this hellhole." Vanderlock jutted his chin at the sea of people camping all around them. "You see any other billionaires in this camp?"

Emma sighed. "It's beyond odd, but to what end? You and I both know that the Maraad might just as well kidnap him as save him. He's truly in danger here. We all are. And he risked his life to help get some of those cookers you see." She pointed to the aluminum circular cookers dotting the landscape. "But I guess none of that changes what I have to do. Here." She handed Locke the HK. "Hold this and follow me. I'll talk and you can be my wingman."

"Sure," Locke said. He took the weapon and walked next to her as she returned to the open trailer, now empty of boxes.

Carn and Rand sat inside with their backs against the metal wall. Rand's backpack was next to him.

Emma hopped up to join the two men in the trailer while Locke stayed outside. The HK hung from his right hand, and he worked a cigarette with his left. Rand and Carn both watched as Emma walked to the pack.

"What's up?" Rand asked.

Before he could protest, Emma grabbed the pack by its shoulder straps and carried it with her to the edge of the trailer where she jumped down to stand next to Locke. She upended the pack onto the dried earth and crouched next to the dumped contents.

"Hey!" Rand stood up and headed to the trailer's edge.

"Nope," Locke said. He raised the gun's muzzle in Rand's direction. "Stay there a minute."

Rand looked outraged. "What the hell are you doing?"

Emma sorted through the assorted possessions in the pack, moving aside a small plastic see-through bag that carried toiletries and a sleek, black leather passport wallet that bulged with cash. Once it was clear that the main body of the pack contained nothing of interest, she began working her way through the smaller, zippered pockets. It was there that she found a small box stamped with the Rand Pharmaceuticals' logo. About the size of a cigarette box, it was made from a shiny metal that might have been titanium, and had a keypad on the front. The weight and construction of it seemed solid and indestructible.

"What's in here?"

"Vaccine," Rand said.

"Really?" Emma held the box up for Locke, Rand, and Carn to see. "What's the unlock code?"

Rand shook his head. "I'm not telling you."

"Put it on the ground. I'll shoot it open," Locke said. Rand took a step toward them, and Locke raised the gun in his direction. "Back off."

"You can't shoot it open, so don't even try. The military arm of Rand Pharma developed that container. It'll take any number of hits from a weapon and the worst that'll happen is it'll suffer a couple of dents."

Locke slid his glance sideways towards Emma. She nodded.

"I don't believe much of what he says, but that I do believe. Besides, the last thing I need is for you to hit a vial of smallpox virus with a bullet and spread it into the air."

"You know that's not the virus. It's the vaccine," Rand said.

"Now why would you go to such lengths to protect some vaccine vials?" Emma asked. "I don't believe you. I think this high-tech box holds live virus."

Rand snorted. "Is that what this is about? I told you before, I found the smallpox vials, removed them, *and* notified the government. Those are two regular doses of smallpox vaccine." He pointed a finger at Emma. "Doses enough for two people."

"Enough to save your sorry ass when your Maraad buddies release the live virus, eh?" Locke said.

Emma tossed the box at Locke, who caught it in midair. He put it in his shirt pocket before resuming smoking.

"You're going to have to fly that out of here in that rickety copter of yours," Emma said. "Banner's on his way, but I don't think that virus should be anywhere near Rand. Meet up with Banner on the Mauritanian side. Tell him about this." She waved her hand to indicate the camp. "Someone has to step in and stop their march."

Locke nodded. "Not a problem. Here." He handed her the HK and then looked at Carn. "You want to join me?"

Carn shook his head. "She should have that spot. I know you're friends."

"I'm not leaving with him," Emma said. "I have another ride on the way. And Rand here has the Maraad."

"I want my vials back," Rand said.

"No can do," Locke said.

"You don't understand. My life depends on it." For the first time, Emma thought Rand sounded desperate.

"On ordinary smallpox vaccine?" Emma raised her eyebrows.

Rand began pacing.

Locke rolled his eyes.

"It's time to come clean," Emma said. "Unless you want to die here. And, right now, that's looking like a real possibility, for all of us."

Rand glanced from Locke back to Emma and the HK.

"If I don't deliver those vials to the man who wants them, someone very close to me will be killed."

Well, that's a new story, Emma thought.

"Who's going to do the killing?" Locke asked.

"I can't say."

Locke snorted. "Come on, Carn. Let's go."

Carn took a step toward Locke and Rand did as well. Emma raised the gun and Rand stopped.

"Who?" she asked.

"Nassar," Rand said.

Locke whistled. "You travel in some very rich circles."

Emma shook her head. "I don't believe it. You told me Nassar was your friend. He's as wealthy as they come and he doesn't need the trouble that those stolen smallpox vials represent."

"Nassar's not the one doing the killing, he's one that's been threatened as well. He's agreed to be the conduit only."

"And so? Who's the one that's been able to strike terror in two of the wealthiest men on this planet?"

"Drakkar Kortya."

Now Emma *was* alarmed. Kortya controlled a vast network of insurgents throughout the Middle East and, rumor had it, through Europe as well. He was radical, unhinged, and oddly compelling for a subset of young men who needed an excuse to kill. His zealotry frightened even those who ran their own insurgencies, and he'd been kicked out of several terrorist groups. He alone would be crazed enough to start a worldwide scourge. The damage he could do by disseminating the live smallpox virus would be incalculable.

"How did they rope you into this?" she asked.

Rand resumed his pacing. "They threatened to kill me." He waved a dismissive hand. "At first, I wasn't concerned. The odds of someone like that coming near to someone like me was remote, at best, and I thought it was an Internet troll, nothing more. But the threats increased. I never responded to them, but I did ensure that if anyone really wanted to get at me that I would have something to bargain with. So, I took two of the discovered vials and secured them elsewhere and then sent the rest to the CDC for storage. In the past months, more threats were sent through our Israeli subsidiary's hacked email network. We secured the server and went on about our business. Two weeks later, the vice president of our subsidiary was gunned down on her way to work. Two weeks after that, Nassar called. He said that he'd been threatened as well, but they went a step further with him. One of his wives and three of his children were kidnapped. Then our CFO disappeared. They said I was next. That's when I decided to help."

Emma watched Rand closely as he delivered his story. It sounded plausible, but the holes in it were enormous.

"What in the world made you two think you could access smallpox virus and then spread it, without the governments that held the vials finding out?"

"No one would believe that I would carry live virus on my person. I knew that, if I did, I would avoid most questions. I fly private, so getting through customs wasn't an issue, and the box was in my luggage. It was the ideal way to transport it."

Locke whistled. "Nice con. But I'm not buying it."

Rand's face turned red with his anger. "Who the hell cares what you think? You're just a drug jockey flying a rusting bucket of nails held together with duct tape."

"So you were just going to hand over smallpox to Kortya." To Emma the entire exchange was surreal. Locke seemed unconcerned that he held a box of deadly virus, with only a thin cotton shirt between it and his skin, and Rand believed that he would outsmart a man who was battling the world's armies. "Too bad cold-blooded murder is not my style because I swear I'd give it a go in this case," she said.

Rand took a step back. "I told you, it was to save Nassar's family. We were planning on capturing Kortya and his men before they release the virus."

"How?" Locke asked.

"Nassar hired the Maraad to handle the exchange."

"Well, if anyone is capable of turning on their master, it's the Maraad," Locke said. "Clearly the exchange never happened, or you wouldn't still have the virus."

"We arranged to hand the vials over in Dakar, and the Maraad operatives were going to tail them. While they did, we were going to notify our respective governments. But as

Ms. Caldridge can attest, Kortya didn't honor the agreement. We were attacked on our way to the last vaccine event."

"They wanted the virus *and* to kidnap you. Two for the price of one," Locke said. "But the Maraad is not a whole lot better. They'd as likely help Kortya as kill him. They work for the highest bidder, you know that."

Rand nodded. "And I'm one of the richest men in the world. No one outbids me." Rand's voice held a note of pride.

He really thinks he's untouchable and money will buy anything, Emma thought. What rattled her more, though, was the fact that Locke held two vials of live virus in his shirt pocket.

"They'll run circles around you," Locke said. "Hell, they already have."

"Oh, yeah?" Rand said. "I got the vials here, didn't I?"

"So, the whole vaccine trip was a way to smuggle the virus into Africa?"

Rand snapped his mouth closed.

"Don't worry, they're in good hands." Locke patted the box in his shirt pocket.

Rand pointed to the listing helicopter. "In that piece of trash?"

Locke looked offended. "Hey! That machine has gotten me back and forth across this continent for years. It has enough juice left in it for one more flight into Mauritania."

Rand moved closer. "Listen. My offer still stands. You get me through Mauritania to Casablanca, and I'll buy you a new one."

Locke shook his head. "I can only carry one. And that person has to be prepared to be ditched in the sand in case of a malfunction." He looked Rand up and down. "You don't look the type to be able to survive a crash landing."

Rand's eyes narrowed. "You'd be surprised at what I can survive." He held his hand out. "I want my virus back."

"I'll make you a deal," Emma said. "Call Nassar and tell him that I expect the Maraad to join you here and guard this camp. I also expect him to bring as many vehicles as he can. Tell him to make them large transport trucks. I want to move as many people over the border as I can. Once we're there, I'll ask Banner to arrange security for both you and Nassar."

Rand shook his head. "What about Nassar's wife and children? Have you forgotten? They'll be killed."

Emma hadn't forgotten them.

"I'll do what you should have done from the very beginning. I'll ask Banner to request that the entire might of the United States Department of Defense be given the job of locating where they're being held. They'll find them and free them."

Rand snorted. "The United States does not negotiate with terrorists, you know that. And find them? In this vast desert? They never found the journalist who was beheaded. Or the captured soldiers who shared the same fate. You expect me to believe that? And, don't forget, they've promised to kill me, too."

"It's the best I can do. You're not getting that virus back."

"I'm out. Carn?" Locke jerked his head to the battered helicopter. Carn grabbed his backpack and jogged to the copter.

"Take me with you," Rand said. Locke shook his head.

"You call Nassar and arrange the muscle. I'll drop this," he patted the box, "and send Banner here while I fix the chopper and come back."

"I'll be dead by then." Rand's voice was tight with fear.

"Did it ever occur to you that you're safer without your precious virus? Once Kortya discovers that you lost it, he'll give up chasing you and go after Locke here," Emma said.

Locke tilted his head as he contemplated Emma. "Well, that's a real pisser. Thank you."

"You're welcome. You're the toughest guy I know, which is why I give you the riskiest assignments."

"I'm touched, really I am," Locke said. "But a bigger crock of shit I've never heard. You sure you want to wait for Banner?"

Emma eyed the listing helicopter.

"I'm good. He's not far."

"I insist you take me," Rand said. "You don't and I'll destroy you. You'll never make a penny flying in Africa again."

He's chosen the wrong man to threaten, Emma thought.

Locke snorted. "Spare me the theatrics. No one controls Africa. Least of all some billionaire blowhard. Don't be a coward." He pointed to Emma. "She's staying here, and you don't see *her* begging to be saved."

Rand swallowed but said nothing.

Locke walked over to Emma, who glanced at him from the corner of her eye. She kept the gun pointed at Rand.

"Don't let me interrupt you." He kissed her on the cheek. "Get the hell out of here. I stuffed a bunch of MREs into your pack and left some for him." Locke glanced at Rand. "'Course, if you decide to shoot him, then there'll be more for you."

"You're a fool," Rand said. "You could've had a brand-new helicopter. Now you're going to die in that death trap, and you've sealed the fate of an innocent woman and three little girls. Not to mention the two of us." Rand glared at Locke.

Locke leveled a glance back. "Kortya placed them at risk, not me. I'm putting my faith in Banner to find them. And better I die in a crash than let Kortya bully me into harming half the world." He turned to Emma. "If we crash, what will happen to the virus? Assuming I'm broken in half and unable to do anything."

"Make sure the fuel tank goes up in flames. Extreme heat will kill it. Throw that container in the fire and hope for the best."

Locke closed his eyes, opened them, and then shook his head. "You really know how to make a guy feel special."

"Next time you see me I'll be fat and happy," Emma said. Locke smiled. "I'll hold you to it."

He walked to his chopper. Emma held the weapon on Rand and didn't waver, even as she heard the blades begin to rotate. The machine belched and stuttered but soon it was clear, from the regular rhythm of the blades, that the copter would fly. Only then did she take her attention off Rand.

The helicopter hovered fifty feet above them. The black smoke remained, but the chopper gained loft. After a few more minutes, it rose even higher before turning in midair. It flew toward Mauritania and freedom.

"You just sealed my death warrant. And yours, too," Rand said. He looked stricken.

Emma didn't respond. Instead, she grabbed her now bulging backpack, slung it over one shoulder and the HK over the other. She pulled her phone out to call Banner while she walked away. She never looked back.

36

Banner sat at an outdoor bar drinking from a cold beer for which he'd paid triple the going rate in the States. Atar boasted more amenities than he'd expected from such a poverty-stricken country, but it was clear that the entire village was determined to get a piece of the Westerner's cash in some form or another. Two women had walked by and made soft suggestions that he purchase some brightly colored cloth to make a dress for his wife, but in such a quiet manner and undertone that, at first, he thought he'd imagined it. He told them that he didn't have a wife, but instead requested two water bottles and paid triple for them when they arrived. He finished the beer and started on the water while he waited for his phone to ring.

But it wasn't Caldridge who called him first. It was Stromeyer.

"You in a place where you can talk freely?" she asked without preamble.

Banner turned to lean his back against the counter and surveyed the area around him. The two women loitered against a wall about thirty feet from him, and the bartender unloaded a cart at the side of the open-air bar nearly twenty feet away. From his previous interactions with them, it was clear that none spoke English with any fluency.

"I think so," he said.

"The situation is much worse than we expected. There are four different insurgent groups marching to the location at the Mauritanian border where Caldridge's phone is emitting a ping, someone fired on Locke's helicopter and it took damage, and I can't raise Sumner at all."

"What do you mean you can't find Sumner? I just left him with a truck and instructions to head to Atar. I'm waiting for him here."

"He switched off his phone and isn't checking in. You sure he's okay?"

Banner wasn't, of course.

"No. But I assume so."

"Assume nothing. Or at least nothing good. The only interesting information I have is from Locke. He's flying around in a battered helicopter with live smallpox virus in a metal tin in his pocket." Banner's mouth fell open. For a moment, he thought he'd heard her incorrectly. The bartender unloading the cart glanced over and paused as he caught a glimpse of Banner.

"Okay?" the man asked.

Banner closed his mouth, nodded, and waved him off.

"Are you still there?" Stromeyer asked.

"Yes, sorry. I wondered if I heard you correctly."

"I know, scary, isn't it? Locke seemed to think the container was sealed properly and he acted unconcerned, but you know how Locke is. He'd never admit to being nervous. He also gave me some insight into why Rand is doing all of this." Banner listened as Stromeyer brought him up to date.

"So Nassar and Rand thought that they'd be able to contain this thing?" Banner sighed. "Sometimes civilians wear me out."

"I know, it's maddening, isn't it? But a desperate father will do anything, and the VP's assassination was a clear warning to Rand."

"I remember when that happened. Some at the DOD assumed that she'd gotten caught up in some dirty dealings. So, what's the plan?"

"You need to drop everything and be prepared to meet Locke. He's going to fly as far into Mauritania as he can before his equipment fails. He'll try to set down safely and then send us coordinates to retrieve him and the virus. He also has a passenger named Carnegie Wendel with him."

"Don't know him. Should be we worried?"

"I checked him out. He's a Brit. Started with a Peace Corps trip to Africa and signed back on with the Red Cross. He's been working throughout Senegal for a couple of years now. He's a pacifist, votes socialist, and stayed when he began a relationship with a local woman who died of malaria a year ago."

Banner gave a soft whistle. "Talk about the odd couple. I can't imagine anyone farther from Locke in temperament. But, if he's flying with him in a broken chopper and knows about the virus, then he must have guts."

"Or he's crazy. But nothing in his profile suggests mental illness."

"Unlike Locke."

Stromeyer laughed the low-voiced laugh of hers that Banner loved to hear. "Unlike Locke."

"Tell me about Caldridge."

"She's in some trouble. I'm not going to sugarcoat it. She can probably cross into Mauritania fairly easily, but only because she can navigate the desert with her compass. You'll need to be prepared to pull her out on a moment's notice because, once inside, she'll have to head to a village or die out there in the sand. And, to reach her, you'll likely be forced to fly over some advancing Red Hand troops."

Banner checked his watch. "What if I left now? Can I beat them to her?"

"No. And there are the embassy personnel to think about. Secretary Plower gave me specific instructions. You're to first secure the virus and *then* the embassy personnel."

The bartender finished unloading his cart and clucked at the emaciated donkey hitched to it to move on out. Banner watched as the cart shook and shivered away. The two women pushed off the wall and headed toward the main part of the small town. One languidly fanned herself with a magazine as she walked. Once they were out of sight, Banner sat down at a nearby wooden picnic table.

"I disagree with those priorities. We need to secure living human beings first. After all, they're in imminent danger. The virus, virulent as it is, currently resides in a safe place."

"If you want to call a tin can in Locke's shirt pocket a safe place, then I guess I agree."

"Safety is relative."

"Perhaps. But that doesn't change the fact that Darkview's contract with the DOD requires us to follow their orders or risk that they'll withdraw their support."

"And their funding."

"That, too," Stromeyer said. Banner waved at a fly that dive-bombed toward his water bottle.

"How much firepower is Secretary Plower willing to put behind these two rescue missions?"

"Not as much as I'd like. She's green-lit Sumner's hire; Locke, or someone like him; an assistant; you; and, if Caldridge gets free, she'll pay for her as well."

"I'll need a couple of standing military. Seals, Rangers, anyone she can spare."

"That's going to be a tough sell. The US still hasn't agreed to get involved in this particular conflict. If the governments of Senegal and Mauritania learn that we're throwing our military into the country, that'll be met with alarm. They'll think we're looking to take over."

Banner snorted. "Take over what? Senegal has something but all Mauritania has, that I can see, is sand. What else is here?"

"Iron ore."

"Okay. But there can't be a massive demand for that, is there?"

"Actually, prices are falling worldwide. But it's all Mauritania has. Well, they've discovered some oil offshore but, first, they have to extract it and then they have to hope prices rise or the supply flags. Because, right now, Saudi Arabia is losing its shirt on oil."

"So, tell Plower to call the Mauritanian government and give them the heads-up that we'll be operating in their country. No need to make it sound alarming. Call it a charitable mission. Just let them know it'll be for a limited time. I'll do my best to handle things quickly and discretely."

"I'll give it a shot. But, in the meantime, you'd better play it safe and head out to get Locke."

Banner's phone beeped and the screen displayed Caldridge's name.

"Caldridge is on the other line. I'll talk to her. Once I know where she is, I can get a handle on the situation there."

"Get to Locke as soon as you can. I'll pass on your request but, for now, we can't afford to ignore Plower's explicit instructions."

"I'll see what I can do," Banner said.

"You're hedging. I can hear it."

"Gotta go," Banner said. "Duty calls."

"Don't forget, if we head into a war zone without authorization we're on our own."

"That's why I'm counting on you to sway Plower to flip those priorities."

He clicked off and started running towards his helicopter.

37

Emma listened as Banner gave her the sobering news that Locke's assessment was not only correct but brighter than the actual situation.

"So, there's little chance anyone's coming here to save these people."

"Extremely little."

"Where are you?"

"In the air. I'm headed to the coordinates that you gave me to find the embassy personnel."

"What about Rand? Do I just leave him here?"

"That's entirely up to him. The moment I set eyes on him I'm going to take him into custody for pulling this stunt."

"Odds are then that he'll wait for the Maraad."

"Good luck to him."

Emma agreed.

"What about Locke? Have you heard from him?"

"Negative. And I'm getting worried."

Emma began to pace back and forth with her head down. She watched as puffs of dust rose around her boots with each step.

"I'm a bit away from the camp but going back to cut through it and slip over the border now. I can't cross on either side of it due to possible land mines."

"If you cross the border again, be prepared to slam right into the Red Hand."

"I've already seen what they do, and I'm not willing to get anywhere near them. Maybe I try to go toward Mali?"

"No better."

"And if I stay here?"

"You can't stay there. Not with your Western looks. Once the Maraad appears it's more than likely that they'll hold you hostage. And you need to get as far away from Rand as possible."

Emma's started sweating with the force of her anger. The idea that Rand had intended to hand her over to the insurgency the entire time had been tough to hear, and she'd been struggling with how to fit that fact into everything else she was trying to figure out.

"I'm out of ideas and so angry right now that I'm having a hard time thinking straight. Tell me what you'd do and I'll do the same."

"I'd risk the border crossing. Head toward Atar."

"That's one hundred miles from here."

"Yes. Didn't you run across Death Valley? Maybe just think of it as another ultra."

The Badwater 135 Ultra passed through America's Death Valley. Temperatures soared so high during it that sometimes the rubber on a runner's shoes melted to the asphalt.

"The Death Valley portion is brutal, but there are handlers available to assist. And you're running much of the time on asphalt, not sand. Tough on your bones, but it allows you to make some time. Tell me that, once I cross, I'll be traversing salt flats, at least."

"Sorry, no. Deep sand. How long do you think it'll take you?" Emma made a quick mental calculation. "It took me thirty-five hours to run through Death Valley on asphalt and packed earth. When you add the additional challenge of deep sand, then I think you have to add at least another twelve."

"It's the best option. But, when you cross, try to keep off the road during the day. The Red Hand has the same logistical problem we all have. It's impossible to off-road for long because the sand slows you down and eventually clogs up the machinery."

Emma checked her watch.

"I'm out. Wish me luck."

"See you in Atar."

Emma clicked off before she choked up. She tracked the rising sun and wished she hadn't wasted the past two hours but had struck out at first light, instead.

She heard an ululating wail carried on the Harmattan wind. Worried, she turned back to camp and picked up her pace. The haunting noise grew, as more and more took up the call. The open-throated tones raised a primeval and strange fizzing through her veins. Every muscle and fiber went on alert. An enormous dust cloud on her right billowed into the morning air.

When she reached the camp's edge, it became clear that the rising and falling keening was a warning of impending danger. Women grabbed their children and meager belongings and started running toward the border guards, who were still wiping the sleep out of their eyes. Emma fought through the panicked people, cutting a perpendicular path through the crowd. The dust cloud grew closer, and now she could hear the drums pounding and the engines roaring.

The insurgency was coming.

38

She returned to the trailer, only to find it empty. People streamed all around it as they ran for the border. She clambered into the bed, hoping for protection from the stampeding hordes, and to gain some height to see over their heads. The trailer faced east. She peered around the edge to look to the south.

Ten open trucks of various makes and models—one carrying a dozen or so men and the rest empty—barreled toward the camp. The sun glinted off their weapons, which many held high in the air. It was clear from their open mouths that they were yelling, but she couldn't hear them over the din made by the pounding feet of hundreds of people.

Emma turned north in time to see the Mauritanian guards scrambling to stop the stampede across their border. Some hammered the butts of their guns into whoever they could reach, while others yelled and pointed their weapons. One man stood deeper into Mauritania and let off a volley of bullets, spraying the ground before him in a warning. Screams erupted, but the crowd, rather than slowing, surged even more. The leaders of the crowd ran past the shooter, bashing their shoulders into him, spinning him. He spun one way and lost his footing, stumbling like a drunk as he fought to stay upright, before careening into another and bouncing the other way. The third hit did him in, and he went down amid the bodies and disappeared.

The ten trucks split and started directing the edges of the crowd. They herded them inward. The width swath of people narrowed, and a second truck sped past the first, taking a turn at the border and driving in a line perpendicular to the first, much like Emma had tried to do on foot. The trucks, though, had the advantage and the lead people stopped short, to avoid running directly into the vehicles. Those behind them piled into their backs, and soon there was a mass of people collecting on the side of the trucks.

A second group of trucks came from the other side and the stampede stopped. Emma watched as the people slowed and started milling around. One man in a truck started speaking through a megaphone in a language that sounded like Wolof. The people settled down as they listened to the address. The loudspeaker man's voice rose at the end in a question, and Emma watched as the crowds began to look around them. A disturbance in the middle of the circle of trucks caught her eye. The crowd parted to reveal Rand standing alone.

The loudspeaker man handed his megaphone to another and jumped off the flatbed. He strode toward Rand and, as he did, the gun hanging from a strap across his shoulder banged against his side. When he reached Rand, he held out a hand. Emma watched the two men shake.

The Maraad, Emma thought. They'd come to rescue Rand, and they'd brought the empty trucks that she'd requested. She jumped down from the trailer. No sense framing herself in the open for the Maraad to see. She hunched down next to the truck wheel. The massed bodies around Rand, and the Maraad, once again hid them from view, something Emma welcomed, because they would not see her make her way north along the edge of the crowd. Only the dozen or so men riding in the back of the first truck would be high enough to spot her, but she was counting on the distractions all around them. She hoped that no one would look her way.

She began skirting the far edge of the crowd, doing her best to move slowly and carefully through the people. Most stood and craned their necks, in an attempt to see Rand and the Maraad commander, and so few looked her way. She was halfway toward the open expanse that led to the border when the crowd began to move. Once again, she found herself walking opposite the crowd. This time they seemed to be moving toward the empty trucks. She reached a tree and stayed near the trunk, allowing the rest to pass.

"Lady, are you okay?"

Emma turned and saw the white-haired woman from Carn's village. She held the AK-47 in her hand and next to her stood a most remarkable-looking person. Clearly a man, but dressed in women's clothing, including an intricate white head wrap and a long, flowing, bright green dress. He was wearing lipstick, rouge, and heavy foundation makeup with mascara, and had unhooked the veil from his face, revealing a five o'clock shadow.

"Who are you?" Emma asked.

"Victoria." Victoria spoke in perfect American English and a heavy, man's voice.

"How the hell did you end up here, Victoria?"

"Call me Vic. I was kidnapped from a traveling theater group by the ASIS. Bastards." Vic looked at the white-haired woman from the village. "Sorry, Biba," Vic said in French. The white-haired woman waved Vic off. "I got away just in time to get caught in a civil war. I always did have awful timing, except on stage...there I'm wonderful. Best drag performer next to RuPaul.

But you can't stay here, honey. Why, you look like the girls from Connecticut, where I grew up, who used to go to the private Catholic schools in their plaid uniform skirts." A man bumped Biba's shoulder and the older woman gave him a sour look. He glanced at the weapon in her hand and muttered an apology.

Biba turned to Emma. "You must leave. These men are not trustworthy and you'll be taken," she said.

Biba's quick read on the Maraad impressed Emma. "I agree, but how can you tell?"

She gestured in the direction of the trucks with the muzzle of her gun.

"See how they're loading the trucks?"

Emma watched a moment. The men yelled orders and chose those that would ride. The first three trucks held a mixture of men and women and children. The men waved up families but denied access to single men and women. Families filled the second truck, as well. The third truck, though, held only young women.

"You mean the young women in the third truck?"

Biba nodded. "They aren't here to help us, but instead to steal our girls. The rest is theater only."

Emma watched as the men weeded out the young women and then offered them a ride. Many of the women hesitated and, when they did, the men broke into smiles that never reached their eyes.

"They take advantage," Emma said.

"They will take them away and their parents will never see them again," Biba said.

Emma's heart twisted at the thought. "We must stop them." She took a step toward the trucks, but Vic held her back.

"No. It's their only chance to live. Those that remain behind will either die of starvation or be killed by the insurgents. And the rest of us, who march through Mauritania, might die of thirst in the desert. Those girls will live and perhaps some will later find a way to escape."

"How is that living? To be a slave?"

"Oh no, we have a do-gooder here," Vic said, but his voice was kind. "To be *alive*. But they're actually better off than you are, though I know that you don't think so. You can't go there. They won't offer you a forced marriage but, instead, hold you as a hostage under terrible conditions. I know, because I was held for a month."

"It's the same thing, just a different type of prison," Emma said.

Vic sighed. "Perhaps. But I'm here to warn you. If you choose to join them, at least be aware of what's really going on, not what those men will tell you is happening."

"Thank you for the advice," Emma said. She turned to Biba. "This is the second time you've saved me." She shrugged one strap of the backpack off her shoulder so that she could reach inside. She removed four twenty-euro bills and held them out to Vic and Biba.

"Please take this. You may need it to pay bribes. I want you to have it."

Both shook their heads. "That is not necessary," Biba said.

"Please," Emma said. "I'm in your debt."

Biba paused, then took the bills and handed two to Vic.

"You should really get a face veil to cover your light skin, or even a burqa, with a grill to view through, so that no one sees your light eyes. It's the best way to travel incognito." Vic reached inside his sack and removed a brightly colored head scarf. "Use this to cover your face. Don't let them see that you're a Westerner. I have another and I know how to navigate my way. I'll be okay. But you? With that straight brown hair and white skin? You haven't a chance." Vic shook his head.

Emma took the scarf and wrapped it around her head.

"I'll never forget your kindness," she told Vic.

"Hell, honey, don't be so serious. We're all getting out of here now. Biba and I are just going to run across that border and head north. Anyone tries to stop us, Biba will shoot 'em down with her AK."

"You're running into miles of nothing but sand. Pure desert. One hundred miles to the first town." Emma looked at the sack slung across Vic's shoulder. "You have any food and water in that?"

Vic shook his head and this time all the false bravado was gone.

"Here." Emma gave him two MREs. Not gourmet, by any stretch, but it's food."

Biba reached out and hugged Emma.

Vic took the food, blinking back tears.

"I'm Emma, by the way."

"May you go in peace," Biba said.

"See you in Casablanca. We'll drink a toast to Bogie," Vic said in his whiskey-laden voice.

Both stepped into the crowd and allowed themselves to be rushed along with the rest. Emma watched them disappear and wanted to call them back to come with her. Instead, she turned toward the northeast and to the border. For a moment, she wished she'd never met Rand, never been talked into the charitable trip that was sold to her as a mission of mercy.

But one thing she'd learned—after all these years of taking dangerous missions the world over—was that you only had the present. The past was done and the future uncertain.

She started to run.

39

Sumner stood on the second floor of a seedy hotel on the border between Senegal and Mauritania and watched as the hotel proprietor in the courtyard below chased the one live chicken left to eat. He had declined the offer of fresh poultry for dinner, and so he wondered why the proprietor was still attempting to kill it. There were no other guests in the hotel. Indeed, there were no other people in the town at all. All had fled in the path of the oncoming insurgency. He got the answer when he saw three men, two with ammunition belts slung across their chests and one balancing a rocket launcher on his shoulder, step into the courtyard to watch the action.

He moved to hide by the window's edge and flicked aside the filthy mosquito netting that hung from a curtain rod above his head. He reached behind his back and pulled a pistol from his waistband. Something told him that the three weren't going to let either the chicken or the man live.

The chicken eluded capture and ran across the courtyard with a loud squawk. One of the soldiers tried to kick it as it ran by but missed. Another took out his own pistol and squeezed off a shot. The noise cracked through the night and the hotel owner flinched. But the bullet went wide, and the bird continued to race around the enclosed area. The man with the gun pointed it at the proprietor and gave him a guttural command. The owner nodded several times in rapid succession and chased after the bird with a desperation that was difficult to watch. He caught it by one wing and pulled it toward him, turning his head away as it flapped and screeched. He wrung its neck and the protests died. The man scurried away, and the soldiers sauntered back into the hotel and out of Sumner's sight.

The small border village was a ghost town, and the desolation in the air was hard to ignore. For Sumner, the emptiness created a tension that he couldn't shake. He waited for the bombs to fall and the violence to erupt. As far as he knew, the three soldiers, the hotel proprietor, and he were the only people left. A dim yellow bulb hung from a wire strung across the courtyard, between a light pole and a nail pounded into the hotel's side.

He gazed into the darkness and his eyes lit on a bit of movement in the distance. The moonlight allowed for some night vision, but the distant shadow was too indistinct to allow Sumner to pinpoint what was heading toward town. Whatever it was, it moved toward the hotel in a regular, albeit awkward, gait. As it neared, the edges came into focus, and it became the shape of a human, either male or female, he couldn't tell, but it kept a direct line to the town. The awkward gait appeared to be the result of a limp or injury.

Sumner waited. If it was another soldier, then the last thing he needed to do was reveal his position in the second-floor window. If it were a townsperson returning home, he would have to intercept. Sumner wouldn't allow an innocent to march into certain death at the hands of the insurgents.

He shoved the pistol back into the waistband of his jeans and reached to the nearby corner where the Dragunov sniper rifle rested. It was his favorite weapon, a variant of the standard Dragunov that allowed for auto- or semiautomatic mode. He set it to semi—no need to waste bullets unless required—and slung the carry strap over his right shoulder. He returned to the window to check on the incoming party. The person had covered an impressive amount of distance in the few short seconds it had taken Sumner to grab the rifle, and the lurching gait was gone. Sumner felt a frisson of familiarity run along his spine as he stared at the newcomer. The straightened strides were regular and unhesitating, and now the person ran, giving the definite impression of determination. Sumner had seen that loose, fluid, rhythmic pace on one of the few elite runners that he knew. He raised the weapon and peered into the telescopic sight to get a better look. He exhaled as his gut reacted to the view.

Emma Caldridge ran straight toward him.

My God, she's alive, he thought, followed by a burst of joy. His second reaction was concern because he knew that she likely had no idea that the town had been taken. As he watched, she darted sideways to a bush and crouched behind it. Relief flooded through him. He should have known that she'd proceed with caution. She was far too savvy to run straight into any new situation. He wished there was a way to call her. Let her know that her careful approach was the right one. He looked around the small room, and his eyes fell on the flashlight that he carried in his pack and that now rested on the top of the nightstand. He snatched it up and returned to the open window.

There were no screens, a problem if one were trying to avoid malaria or dengue fever but, in this case, a boon because there was no metal to reflect back the light. He pointed at the bush where Emma was hiding. In the dark, and without the telescopic sight, it was impossible for him to separate her shape from that of the branches, but it was an inconsequential problem. He didn't need to see her, she just needed to see him. Or, more accurately, his flashlight.

He switched on the beam and began turning it off and on in a repeating sequence. He kept the rhythm to the short and long bursts of an SOS code. Anything more elaborate would have been too difficult to arrange, given the flashlight's limitations. He stared at the bush, but nothing revealed whether she'd seen the light or not. He kept on. The switch made a clicking noise as he flicked it back and forth. Below him, the hotel proprietor came into view. He carried a tray with glasses and what appeared to be three bottles of clear liquid. He stopped and glanced up, catching the sequence before Sumner could flick the flashlight off. For a moment, they locked eyes. In the weak glow of the courtyard's single yellow bulb, Sumner saw the word *Vodka* stamped on the side of one of the bottles.

A shout came from the main room downstairs. The proprietor lowered his head and hurried forward, out of Sumner's sight. Shortly after that came the sound of clapping. Clearly, the soldiers were happy to see the bottles of alcohol.

A light flashed from the bush. Sumner leaned out of the window, once again narrowing his eyes to try to catch a glimpse of the woman hiding among the branches. As he did, a second burst of light came from the bush. This one was in the same SOS pattern that Sumner had been using. Sumner responded with his own SOS. Then he moved the light up and down in a nodding motion. *Yes.*

She imitated the nod.

The hotel proprietor burst into the courtyard with the soldiers hard on his heels. The lead man held the vodka bottle in one hand and a gun in the other. He fired a shot, and the hotel owner dropped to the ground, moaning, and holding his leg where the bullet had entered the calf. The soldiers laughed, and the lead one sauntered over and kicked the owner directly over the injury. The man howled from the ground. A second soldier leaned over and slashed at the man's leg with a knife. He laughed as the proprietor shrieked in pain. The soldier handed the knife to the next, who took his turn slashing. The owner screamed again, his cries echoing in the courtyard and piercing the quiet night.

Three more soldiers walked into the courtyard, whether attracted by the screams of the dying man or not, Sumner couldn't tell. They nodded at the three attackers and strolled past the man on the ground, ignoring him. They disappeared into the hotel. The first group continued slicing at the owner. Blood covered his arms and legs and was dripping onto the beaten earth, leaving a wet, black stain that spread outward.

"Shit," Sumner said out loud. His options had whittled down to bad and worse. Either watch the soldiers flay the hotel proprietor alive, do nothing, and lose his own soul in the process, or shoot them down and reveal his position, leaving the probability that he'd die along with the owner. While he had no doubt that he'd have time to kill at least two of the three, the third stood at least thirty feet away and watched. He faced Sumner's window and an AK-47 hung loosely from his hand. Sumner decided to kill him first, then one of the attackers second, and hope to squeeze in the third, before he responded or ran. Still, Sumner estimated that he'd get all three.

Which left the three in the hotel. Once his position was revealed, they'd retaliate. All had been armed, that was to be expected, but he wondered just how skilled they were at firing those weapons. Likely they'd had a lot of opportunity to practice in the last few weeks.

The hotel owner screamed as one of the soldiers ran the knife in a long cut from his upper thigh, past the knee, and down to the ankle, opening a long slit in the man's leg.

Sumner put his eye to the sight and shot. He took out the watcher thirty feet away, with his back to the courtyard wall, by shooting him dead center in the chest. The man slammed against the wall and began a slow slide downward. Sumner didn't bother to watch him fall. He swung the muzzle to the left and took out the guerrilla who had just made the long cut. He was still leaning over and he fell directly onto the hotel owner.

The third attacker spun to face Sumner, but he made the fatal mistake of looking at eye level, not up to where Sumner stood. Sumner dispatched him with another chest shot and heard, rather than saw, the reaction of the three in the hotel. From below came the pounding of shoes on dirt. They must have run to the door, but none were stupid enough to enter the courtyard.

Silence fell. A moth flew in swooping circles around the bulb on the wire, and a few gnats danced in a semicircle. A night bird hooted, but Sumner couldn't tell if it was an owl or some other creature. The hotel proprietor moaned but didn't try to rise. Sumner took that as a sign that the three were in the doorway, looking at him, and the hotel owner must have decided to lie still, so as not to provoke them.

The floor outside Sumner's door creaked.

They're better than I expected, Sumner thought. They'd managed to get up the wooden stairs and outside his room without making a sound. He took one large step to the side, placing himself outside of the direct line from the door and two feet from the open window. He figured that only one had climbed the stairs. He didn't think two could have managed it that quietly. That left two in the lower level and probably both covered the courtyard.

He reassessed his options. Jumping out the window was one. Fifteen feet down, give or take. If he rolled as he landed, he had a decent chance of keeping his leg bones intact. Firing at the one on the landing was another option, but that would only work if the guerrilla were moronic enough to stand in front of the wooden door, where Sumner's caliber bullet might pierce it. Sumner wasn't willing to try to shoot through the walls. They appeared thick enough to absorb the impact and he'd only manage to waste his time.

He lowered down to a crouch to wait.

40

Emma stared into the town, watching the building where the SOS had originated. As quick as it came, it vanished. Whoever had sent it needed help, that much was clear from the gunfire. She'd seen the muzzle flash from the same location. The only question in her mind was whether it was a guerrilla holed up and fighting off angry villagers, or a villager fighting off the insurgents. She needed to get closer.

The building itself stood on what must have been the very edge of town. The road in front of it stretched away, out of her sight. One or two more buildings lined the road further down. The moon's glow was the only source of light, other than a lightbulb hanging over the first building's yard.

A second small clump of bushes, about one hundred yards closer to the town, was the only thing between her and the building. She checked the HK and its last bullet. She'd used one bullet to ward off two attacking animals the night before and now wished she hadn't. She counted to three and sprinted toward the bushes. Her right leg throbbed from the sudden motion, but she ignored it. She made it to them, scrambled down behind, and waited to see if there would be any reaction from the town.

Silence. In fact, since the gunfire from the second floor, there had been only silence. While it was possible that the sender of the SOS had been hit, she didn't think so. She moved to the side of the bush to peer towards the building.

Now she was close enough to see that it was a squat, square, two-story building made of cinder blocks laid over rebar. Pieces of the rebar poked out from the roof. The builder hadn't bothered to trim it. The rusted round metal rods looked like spikes and stuck out from each of the building's corners. Also from the new distance, she could see the faded sign nailed into the wall that declared the building to be a hotel or pensione. The shabby construction and tattered fabric that hung in window frames, which were devoid of glass, added to the depressing sight. Actually, given the location, the surprising thing was that there was a hotel at all.

She watched the building for a full five minutes, saw no movement, heard no talking or sounds, and the SOS flashes had not returned. Either the second-story gunman was dead, or he was waiting out someone still in the area around the hotel. If the latter, she would have to approach very cautiously. A moan floated to her on the breeze, filled with agony and definitely human. She was unable to tell if it came from the open hotel windows or from some other source.

She weighed whether she should stay where she was and watch to see what happened next, or if it would be better just to retrace her steps and take off, leaving the SOS person to their fate. If she took off, she'd have to sleep outside and the idea of sleeping in a bed, albeit even one as miserable as the slovenly hotel exterior suggested would greet her inside, was so tempting that Emma thought it was skewing her perceptions. She decided to get closer and figure out what was going on. The rest of the town looked deserted. The only action had come from the hotel.

She inhaled, did a mental three count, and burst from behind the bush, running straight toward the low wall that surrounded the hotel. Her shoes made alarmingly loud crunching noises, but she reached the wall without incident. This close she could hear the rattling of the gas generator that provided the meager light for the hotel. She crouched against the crumbling stone and caught her breath before rising in a slow ascent to peer over.

In the meager light, she could see two men lying in a pool of blood in the courtyard's center, one atop the other. The moaning appeared to be coming from one of them. Two others were clearly dead, one sprawled in the dirt, the other slumped against a wall. To the right, Emma saw another two men crouched on a small outdoor terrace furnished with cheap plastic chairs, a battered wooden picnic table, and two benches. Insects flitted around the remnants of a half-eaten meal, deftly avoiding the guttering flame of a candle stuck in an empty wine bottle. An overhang roof sheltered the terrace and the men hiding below. They kept their backs to the courtyard and flanked a wooden staircase as if waiting for someone to come running down. Both held AK-47s and, from the tension in their bodies, Emma could tell that they were itching to make a move.

A crashing sound came from above, followed by gunfire. Emma watched in astonishment as a man leapt from the second-story window. Her initial surprise turned to shock when she saw that it was Cameron Sumner. A soldier with a gun was framed in the window above, and the two men below moved closer to the stairs. Emma recovered, raised her gun, and aimed at the man in the window. He must have sensed something because he moved to the side as she did, and her bullet only seemed to nick him. He disappeared back inside the room. The two below jerked at the crack of her weapon.

Sumner landed on the earth and rolled while the men shot at him in semiautomatic mode. Bullets peppered the earth around him, and Emma heard the high-pitched scream of a woman. She stopped to take a breath and, when she did, she realized that she was the one screaming. Sumner kept rolling as she launched herself upward. She dropped her gun, put a foot on the wall and flew over it, like a runner navigating the hurdles. She landed in the courtyard and took two short leaps to the dead man slumped against the wall, throwing herself onto his body. Her entire concentration was on the gun that he held in his lifeless hands. His limbs felt cold and the flesh rubbery. She ignored all of that as she scrambled to get the gun. She didn't try to remove the strap from around the dead man's shoulders, but instead lay on top of the corpse and simply raised the gun, shoved his finger away from the trigger and added hers. She fired from that position, lying on her side on top of the dead man and doing her best to sweep the weapon in a side-to-side motion.

She managed to hit the two waiting by the doorway and watched them scramble around a corner. One limped and the other moved freely, so her hits weren't lethal. She looked up to the window, to see if any more attackers would appear, but there were none.

Sumner had rolled until he was against the wall and rolling was no longer an option. He stayed there, pressed against the stone and motionless, but Emma couldn't see any blood or exit wounds. She prayed that he was playing dead while deciding what to do.

Silence fell again over the small courtyard. She needed to move before they regrouped and came at her. She removed the strap from the weapon and released it from the body before she crabbed over to Sumner. He remained pressed against the wall and his eyes were closed. For a crazy minute, she thought he was dead. As she reached out to him with a shaking hand, he opened his eyes and looked at her.

"So, it *was* you out there," he said in a low voice.

She became a touch lightheaded, her relief was so profound, and she exhaled in a rush. She wanted to kiss him, yell at him, hug him close, and dance for joy all at once. Instead, she went straight to the important question.

"Are you hurt?" she asked.

He moved his arms a couple of inches so that she could see his torso.

"No hits."

"We need to move. The one on the second floor is still alive. I only hit him in the shoulder, and he'll have a clear shot at us when he recovers his courage to try. Jump over the wall."

Emma rose, took a few steps back and ran to the wall, leaping over it. Sumner followed by scissoring his legs over the edge. A shadow flitted in the second-story window, and Emma grabbed Sumner by the shirt and pulled him down behind the wall. She turned to say something but a volley of automatic gunfire hammered into the other side. Bits of stone flew, and she pressed her eyes closed against the tiny shards. They huddled there, taking what shelter they could.

"He's got his courage back, if not his aim," Sumner said.

"It's amazing he missed the first time," Emma replied.

"All of them suffer from a combination of bad wine and possibly chewing khat. This is Africa, after all."

"How much ammunition do you have?"

"Last clip. Did you kill the ones on the terrace?"

Emma shook her head. "Nicked them, but they're mobile. With any luck, they'll take off." From nearby came the grinding noise of an old engine starting. It kicked into gear with a roar that was followed by a squeal of tires.

"Damn," Sumner said. "They hot-wired the truck."

"What truck?"

Sumner pulled a set of keys out of his pocket and dangled them in front of Emma.

"The truck that these belong to. But they won't get far, thing only had a drop of gas left."

"Don't count on it. They might be able to find some more. They must be advance scouts for the insurgency. Why are you here? I thought you were out of the game."

Sumner put his palm on her cheek. "I came here to find you."

Emma placed her hand over his and leaned in to kiss him on the lips. He kissed her back with an intensity that was the mark of this man. Emma always knew that Sumner's feelings ran deep and often dark, but this kiss contained a hint of wildness that he'd never revealed before. She pulled him close, overwhelmed with the idea that he was there and had almost died in front of her. When she pulled away, she saw the relief in his eyes.

"I'm torn between joy at seeing you and concern that you're here and risking your life for me. Who sent you here? Banner?"

"I sent myself. I came to help you."

She sighed. "It appears as though God played a joke on us because now we have to help each other. Ideas?"

"The two from the terrace are pretty lit but, if they drive around that wall, we're done. Even a drunken idiot would hit us at this range. Especially a drunken idiot driving a truck."

"Move left? What will we see when the wall ends?"

"The main street runs perpendicular. It heads into the center of town. If that's what you can call this hellhole."

"Are there any more insurgents?"

"I don't know. These showed up and I was trapped in my room. But, if the rest aren't here now, they will be soon. How did you come to this village of all places? And alone? I was told you were traveling with Rand."

"I've been following some high-value prisoners. Embassy officials out of Dakar. They drove in this direction."

"You think the hostages are in the vicinity?"

She nodded. "If they haven't been assassinated."

"Unlikely. Too much money riding on their ransom."

"Good point."

She looked around. Beyond the wall, the sandy savannah stretched, with only a few trees and small mounds to offer cover.

"I just came from back there, and I can verify that there's no place to hide in that direction. And the Red Hand is on the march and headed this way."

"And I came in from the east," Sumner said. "Nothing there, either, except the insurgents from Casamance." He waved left. "Let's get to the corner and check it out. We might be able to move from cover to cover. It's our only play, in any event."

She nodded, and they crouched low and moved to the corner, kicking up dust that rose around them. She did her best not to cough and was thankful for the darkness. The dust cloud would have been easy to follow in the light. She waited, while Sumner peered around the wall's edge.

"Street is dark as hell, but I don't see anything moving. There's another that bisects this one, half a block down. After that, only sporadic houses."

In fact, the town, if one could call it that, was tiny. Ten houses spread out among the sand. It appeared as though only the shabby pensione had electricity. Before Emma could reply, she heard the sound of an explosion far in the distance and the faint sound of engines. The Red Hand was coming.

41

S umner heard the trucks as well.

"We're going to be outnumbered very soon," he said.

"We already are."

"We need wheels. A truck, motorcycle, anything."

From the distance, the sound of engines grew louder.

"Ideas?"

Sumner nodded. "I suggest we split up, go around the hotel, and meet at the front. From there, we can watch when the joker on the second floor decides to run. He won't stay in that room long. When we get our hands on him, we shake some information loose."

He turned and began working his way back to the far corner. Emma waited until he disappeared before crabbing her way along the wall on her end, stopping to pick up the HK that she'd dropped in the dirt before leaping into the fray.

Stepping out on the new angle felt far riskier. She wished she had a sense of the direction in which the other two had run. She moved down the side wall and stopped at a point three-quarters from the end because the wall had collapsed. She took a deep breath, rose, and sprinted the rest of the way, coming to a stop at the front of the boxy two-story pensione.

Sumner huddled across the street, against the corner of a small shed, no bigger than a garage, and peered down the main street. Emma stayed with her back against the wall opposite the pensione's door. She heard no sound nor saw any movement. Sumner jogged across the street and joined her against the wall.

"We need to flush him out."

From around the corner, Emma heard shuffling, and a man emerged on the street. Both she and Sumner aimed at him. He threw his hands up. Only then did Emma see that it was the injured man from the courtyard center. Sumner waved him over.

"It's the hotel owner," Sumner said to her in a low voice.

The man limped to them, pain on his face. Somehow, he'd managed to get out from under the other body and then bind his wounds, but blood was still dripping down his leg.

"Take me away with you in your truck," he said to Sumner in a voice equally as low and in perfect English.

"It's been stolen," Sumner said. "Is the shooter still on the second floor?"

The man nodded. "He'll stay up there. Without his friends, he has no courage. They are all cowardly people. But here." He handed Sumner several boxes of ammunition. "It's theirs. I stole it some hours ago while they drank, in order to minimize the shooting that I knew would begin soon. And I believe we can find your truck."

Sumner raised an eyebrow. "Yes? How?"

The man pointed down the dusty main road. "They encircle an *adwaba* about an hour's walk from here. Use it as their base of operations."

Sumner frowned. "Adwaba?"

The man nodded.

"What's that?" Sumner asked Emma.

"They're villages. Most of the people who live in them are slaves, or former—"

The man interrupted. "No one worries about Mauritania. In Mali, the French care, in Senegal, everyone cares, but here?" He shrugged. "Nothing. We have no industry beyond the iron ore shipments. No tourism, now that the Dakar Rally is gone, and no more agriculture. As the Arabs say, 'No one chooses to live in the Sahara.'"

"They'll care if the insurgency leaks into the neighboring countries," Emma said.

"Yes, now it is beginning to matter. But only because their precious Senegal is at risk."

The old animosities between Senegal and Mauritania still simmer, Emma thought.

The man winced. "I must treat my wounds. Please, sir, take me with you."

Sumner glanced at Emma. She gave a small nod.

"Only as far as the next town. You'll find that it's not healthy to be near us," Sumner said.

The man gave him a small smile. "I have seen you shoot, sir, and watched your friend leap the wall to join the battle. In my humble opinion, it is not healthy for *them*."

"Can you walk?" Emma asked.

"As far as the adwaba, yes. I have these." He held out a hand and showed them a prescription bottle with its label torn off.

"What are they?"

"Carfentanil."

"That's used by vets as an elephant tranquilizer. How on earth did you get those?"

The man shrugged. "It's all I have."

"Never mind. Let's get going," Emma said.

"Show us this place," Sumner added.

They followed the limping man down the main street. Sumner and Emma kept to the edges, flitting between buildings, and stopping in doorways. The man, though, marched down the middle, walking as if on an evening stroll, with no attempt to hide. Emma worried that his newfound confidence might be misplaced. After all, they were only three against many insurgents, but he seemed emboldened by them as companions. Sumner carried his Dragunov rifle and moved quietly, keeping to the shadows. Emma did the same. The sound of engines remained in the distance. She wondered how far away they actually were, as sounds were magnified in the desert, and something that sounded close could, in reality, be very far away.

The mud- and straw-walled houses dwindled, and soon they saw only square tent-like structures, with tattered fabric and canvas walls held up by narrow sticks at each corner. The tent city appeared abandoned. Not even a mangy dog or emaciated donkey could be seen. Now Emma and Sumner walked with the man, as there was no longer anything to hide behind.

Emma glanced up and gasped. Stars lit the sky, their pinpoints of light glowing white against the black. The larger ones scattered among many tiny ones, but all glowed with an intensity that she'd never before seen in a night sky. In all her years of traveling to remote locations, she'd never been in one as vast and empty as the Sahara.

"What a beautiful display," Emma said.

The limping man looked up.

"There is no artificial light here and so the stars shine brightly."

"It's breathtaking," Emma said.

The man nodded. "I used to think so."

She looked at him. "Used to?"

"Yes. When I was young and still believed I could grasp the world in my hands."

"How old are you now?"

"Thirty."

Sumner raised an eyebrow. "Not old, then."

The man sighed. "But old enough to know that the world is beyond my reach." He looked at Emma. "I would trade that view for opportunity in an instant."

Emma watched the man limp along. "Where did you learn English?"

"From my master."

Sumner frowned. "What do you mean, 'master'?"

The man shrugged. "I am a slave."

"I thought you owned the hotel."

The man shook his head. "I run it for the true owner. He lives in Nouakchott."

"Does he pay you?" Sumner asked.

"No. I work for free. As I said, I am a slave."

Emma's anger surged at the word. "You understand that slavery is banned in Mauritania?"

The man gave her a knowing glance. "What I understand is that, if I leave the house, I will have no place to sleep, no way to get work, and no way to eat. As I said, I would trade this view," he said, sweeping his hand in the direction of the star-studded sky, "for opportunity."

"And those at the adwaba that we're headed to see. Would they say the same?" Emma asked.

The man shot her a sidelong look. "They don't think they have any choice in how they live."

"We will free this place." Sumner's voice held a resolve that was familiar to Emma. Sumner's intensity most often remained well masked and simmering under the surface. Only rarely did he allow it to show and usually only to Emma or Banner or Stromeyer, those he trusted. Yet his reaction seemed to be coming from a new place. There was a grim set to his features.

The man sighed. "I don't believe so."

Sumner stopped walking. "You doubt me?" He ground out the sentence. The man stopped as well, put up a placating hand, and shook his head.

"Not you. Them. Their slavery is here." He pointed to his head. "And here." He pointed to his heart. "As is mine."

Emma wasn't buying this particular form of blaming the victim. While she believed that people could be cowed from years of oppression, the oppressor needed to take ownership of what they'd done to the people. Sumner started moving again. The tension between them stretched. A cold breeze passed over, and the hairs rose on Emma's arms at the sudden change in temperature.

"The desert cools," the man said. "What are your names?"

"Cameron Sumner and Emma Caldridge. You can call me Sumner. What's yours?"

"Mansur." He gave a short bow to them. "I am pleased to meet you both."

They continued walking. Sumner brooded as he did and Emma struggled to keep her own thoughts in check. Soon, they would be confronting the enemy, and she needed to focus.

Twenty minutes later, the adwaba came into view.

42

The only sign of the adwaba was a series of tree branches, their ends stuck in the sand and used to form a loose wall of upright sticks. The bleached and sandblasted wood glowed white in the moonlight. Lengths of tattered canvas hung from the branches, creating a barrier. Mansur waved them to a stop at three hundred meters away.

"Look to the right. There is your truck."

In the weak moonglow, Emma could see a dented pickup truck parked in the sand.

"No sign of the thieves," Emma said. Mansur waved at the adwaba.

"Likely they are there. Eating or drinking. Can you smell the smoke of the fires and hear the sounds of the village?"

Emma nodded. Bits of light glowed through the gaps in the upright sticks and the canvas cover.

"How many in there?" she asked.

Mansur tilted his head as he thought. "Twenty or thirty. They rely on each other and wait for their masters to come for them."

Sumner pulled Emma aside. "Every time he says 'master' I get a twinge. We need to free these people."

Emma contemplated the bedraggled encampment. "I don't see any guards or chains. If Mansur is right, and they enslave themselves, it's going to be a tough sell getting them to go with us. We'd better have a plan." She waved an arm to indicate the vast emptiness around them. "If we 'free' them, then we're responsible for getting them food and shelter. Otherwise, they'll die in the desert, which is not the desired result, by any means."

Sumner's jaw was set and his cheek twitched. Emma wondered at his obvious emotion about the adwaba encampment. She played a hunch.

"Did you have an encounter with someone claiming to be a master before I got here?"

He nodded. "I had the misfortune of bumping into a lieutenant of Azhan's. We fought, and I ended up freeing a woman that Azhan had forced to be his wife. Later, I bumped into a young man who was being treated as a slave. I freed him."

"Where is he now?"

"I don't know. I gave him, the woman, and the woman's son some money and told them to get to Atar."

"How much money?"

"Over a hundred American."

Emma smiled and touched his arm. "That's three years' salary in Mauritania. Well done."

But Sumner didn't seem mollified. "It's not enough. Especially if Azhan finds her."

"With any luck, he won't. Things are heating up here. Banner's flying in some personnel to find the missing embassy officials and the various governments are gearing up to repulse the latest insurgency. The world won't sit by while Senegal falls. It's one of the few real functioning democracies in Africa."

Mansur walked up to them. "There are insurgents here, but also some new villagers."

From the encampment came raised voices and the sound of scrambling feet. A young boy, no more than seven years old, squeezed between two poles, took a few steps into the desert, knelt down and scooped some sand into his mouth.

Emma gasped. "What is he doing?"

"He's hungry. The sand fills his stomach," Mansur said. "It will stop the pains for a while."

Emma covered her eyes for a moment before removing her hands.

"Sumner, you're right. We're getting these people out of here. Now."

Sumner looked down at her. "Thank you. I needed your help."

She turned to Mansur. "I see Sumner's truck. Are there others?"

Mansur nodded. "Several on the far side of the adwaba. But these soldiers will guard them with their lives because to lose them means they will be killed."

Emma removed the strap of the HK from her shoulder. "I think we can convince them."

Mansur looked between her and Sumner.

"Yes," he said. "I believe you can."

She waved towards the wall of branches and canvas. "Let's get a sense of what we're facing. Mansur, can you ask that boy to come over here? Translate for us?"

Mansur whistled between his teeth and the boy looked up from the sand. Mansur waved him forward. The boy came freely enough, curiosity on his face, and stopped before them. He showed all the symptoms of malnutrition—a bloated stomach, skinny arms, and drawn features. Intelligence shone in his eyes. Mansur held a whispered conversation with him.

"He says there are five men. They brought a large group of foreign women with them, all dressed in black." Mansur tilted his head to the side while he thought about that. "He must mean that they wear the abaya or the burqa. He said the men are seated in the center, drinking alcohol, and eating all the food that was left in the village. His mother sent him away because she said there will be things happening soon that he should not witness."

"Ask him if they are armed."

Mansur asked the question and listened intently as the boy answered.

"He says yes. They keep their guns next to them, always."

"How drunk are they?"

Mansur asked the question, but the boy looked confused and answered in a halting sentence.

"He says most in the adwaba are Muslim and drinking is forbidden. He has never seen someone drunk. These men are drinking, and he says that they laugh too loud and act strangely, but they seem fine."

Emma thought it likely that they were well on their way to being stone drunk, but she kept that opinion to herself. "Ask him if he can take us to a place where we can see through the sticks without them noticing."

Mansur translated and the boy nodded. He spun and started running toward the opening in the sticks from which he'd come. Sumner, Emma, and Mansur, who was limping badly, followed. The boy crouched at a gap, two feet wide, a bit larger than the others and not covered by canvas. He gestured to it and stepped aside to let them see. Emma moved close to Sumner and peered through the opening. She heard Sumner's breathing hitch in surprise and wanted to ask him to explain, but they were too close to the group and they would be able to be heard through the flimsy canvas.

About thirty people sat in a circle at the edges of the adwaba walls. At least twenty of them Emma recognized as the stolen girls from the camp. The rest consisted of a mixture of women and young children, but there were two white-haired men, as well. Just as the boy described, the soldiers sat in the center around a burning campfire with their guns beside them, drinking and laughing. One ate with abandon from an earthenware bowl, using a flat piece of bread to wipe up every bit. Emma noted the hungry eyes of the women and children pressed against the wall.

Through gaps in the far side of the wall, Emma could just see a series of heavy, open-backed trucks. Boxes filled the bed of the closest one, which had the Red Cross symbol on its side. She gestured towards them. Sumner nodded his understanding, and they backed away slowly, with the boy and Mansur keeping pace.

"Did you see those young girls? They were rounded up by the Maraad when they came to rescue Rand. They went from a refugee camp to a slave camp. And those women in black are some of the young women that were kidnapped from a nearby village." Emma described the attack, the night of the deadly bonfire, and the explosive prills.

"More stolen aid supplies in those trucks," Emma said.

"Remember me mentioning the woman, her son, and the man I freed?"

Emma nodded.

"They're in there. Against the far wall. You mentioned the explosives. You don't happen to be carrying any of these ammonium nitrate prills, do you?" Sumner asked in a hopeful voice. "We could throw one outside the wall, let it explode and then, when they come out to investigate, sneak around and take the trucks."

"Create a distraction, you mean?" Emma said.

"Exactly."

"No prills, sorry. They're incredibly dangerous to carry around."

"What about the boy?" Mansur asked. "He could go to them. Say that he saw some soldiers out here. They might come to investigate."

"We have nowhere to hide." Sumner swept his hand to indicate the endless, flat sand all around them. Only one spindly tree rose from a pile of small rocks about fifty feet away. "They'll pick us off."

"Not if he leads them out the front. We can work ourselves around the sides while he does," Emma said. "Use the wall as cover." She watched as Sumner pondered her suggestion.

"They'll leave someone to watch those trucks. One of us will have to pick off the scouts while the other hits the guards."

Emma glanced around again, looking for something—a plant, a tree, a rock—anything that they could hide behind or use as cover.

"Okay. Let's assume a distraction just leads to one of us getting killed in the firefight. How about slipping them a Mickey? Putting something in their drinks, so they nod off? Mansur, you willing to sell me some of those Carfentanil pills you have?" Emma pulled out a twenty-dollar bill and Mansur's eyes grew wide.

"How many do you need?" he asked.

"Five. One for each of their drinks."

Mansur shook out five pills and handed them to her. She walked to a nearby rock and placed them on it before pulling out her knife.

"I'm going to cut these in half and then crush them." She began working on the pills, taking care not to allow the powder to migrate off the rock.

"Who's going to slip them in the drinks?"

"I will do this," Mansur said. "They will not notice me. I am just another slave."

Emma glanced at Sumner in time to see him grimace at Mansur's statement. She finished crushing the pills.

"Can you empty your container so I can add the powder?"

Mansur transferred his remaining pills to his pocket and handed over the container. Emma carefully filled it with the powder.

"How much for each?" Mansur asked.

"Two pinches, no more. And best if you add it to a glass. If you only have a bottle to spike, then you should add the entire amount and hope that they all drink from it."

"They were passing one back and forth,' Sumner said.

"I saw that, too," Emma said. "But you know how it is. Each man will have a different uptake rate, depending on their weight, the amount they ingest, and how deep into the alcohol they are."

Mansur took the bottle and rose. "Don't worry. I'll try to get the powder into all of them. Stay here."

He limped toward the wall with the boy at his heels. When he turned the corner to the entrance, the boy peeled off and returned to peer through the opening. Emma waved Sumner forward, and they watched as Mansur stepped into the enclosure.

43

The men continued drinking and laughing as Mansur stepped into view. Two glanced up at him. He ducked his head once in deference and slid down next to one of the women against the wall, saying nothing. The soldier watched him for a moment before reaching out to the bottle that was passed to him. They continued eating, and Mansur stayed against the wall, biding his time. After fifteen long minutes, during which Emma began to wonder if their plan would work, one of the men barked an order to a nearby woman.

Mansur rose and took two rapid steps toward them. He bowed and murmured something. The man flicked a hand at him and repeated his order. Mansur left the enclosure, making his way to the first truck. He opened the passenger side and leaned into it, keeping his back to the wall. Emma saw him reach into his pocket.

"He's doing something," Sumner said. "Did you see him remove the bottle?"

Emma nodded.

The soldier yelled towards Mansur. His obvious annoyance at the delay worried Emma. These men would think nothing of shooting Mansur if they decided he was too slow in serving them. But Mansur kept his back to the wall.

"Come on," Sumner muttered. The tension stretched as Mansur continued his delay at the truck.

The soldier who'd barked the order rose, annoyance and irritation plain on his face. He yelled again, speaking in a staccato, rapid-fire fashion. He reached down for his weapon.

The other soldiers stopped their talking and glanced at their comrade. All held the expectant look of someone waiting for something to happen.

"I don't like this," Emma said.

Sumner nodded and pulled his gun off his shoulder. "Be ready to fire," he said.

"We don't have a clear shot." As if to emphasize her point, a young girl walked past the seated soldiers, right across Emma and Sumner's line of fire.

The standing soldier pulled a pistol out of his waistband and raised it.

"Get ready to run," Sumner said, as he slid into position, aiming through the narrow opening.

Mansur turned out of the vehicle, holding a bottle of whiskey high before him. He called out to the standing soldier before shuffling his way forward and back into the enclosure. The soldier waited but kept his pistol aimed in Mansur's direction. The rest of the adwaba fell silent. Emma, too, put her weapon to her shoulder and waited.

"He's going to take that bottle first and then shoot him," Sumner whispered. Emma swallowed as she waited. She hoped Sumner was wrong.

Mansur took several lurching steps closer to the soldier, all the while holding the bottle high. As he neared the soldier, he extended it toward him. The soldier took the bottle with his left hand, raised his pistol, and Emma watched as he flicked off the safety with his thumb.

Sumner fired.

The women screamed, and the soldier dropped to the ground. The other soldiers sprang to their feet, surprise on their faces. The one closest to them turned and fired in their direction, but the shot went wide. Sumner shot him in the shoulder and he flew back.

Pandemonium erupted. Women screamed and grabbed at their children. They darted this way and that, flitting through Sumner's line of fire.

"Get out of the way," Sumner muttered through gritted teeth. Emma waited, targeting a soldier on the far side of the fire.

"I've got the skinny one," she said.

The soldiers turned in unison and aimed.

Emma dove left and Sumner right, as a line of bullets punched through the canvas and hit the upright sticks. Slivers of wood exploded around her and Emma closed her eyes as they flew around her face. One embedded itself into her cheek and she swiped it away.

The gunshots kept coming, forcing Emma and Sumner to continue moving. Emma rolled onto her front and pushed off the ground with her gun, gaining her feet. The stick-and-canvas walls shook with the blows of bullets, and bits of wood, dirt, and fabric rained down on her. She sprinted around the corner, but the soldiers must have been able to see her through the gaps in the tattered canvas because they began tracking her, firing the whole time.

People swarmed out of the adwaba, running into the desert and around the standing trucks, using them for cover. Emma caught a glimpse of one of the soldiers through the wall. He stood facing her while he squinted into the darkness. He squeezed off two more shots, and one whizzed by her ear.

She stopped and fired back, hitting him in the shoulder and spinning him around.

Two soldiers bolted out of the adwaba, firing the entire time, one in her direction and one in Sumner's. Their shots went wild, but they effectively held both Sumner and Emma in place while the soldiers headed to the trucks. A third took off toward the lead truck in line. The soldiers kept firing and struck one of the white-haired men, who dropped to the ground and lay there, motionless. Sumner hit the soldier who'd been firing at him, and Emma shot the last one standing in the upper back. He toppled over onto the dirt.

The lead truck engine roared to life, and the vehicle's tires spun, as the driver lay on the gas pedal. The vehicle took off, skidding sideways in the heavy sand, before the wheels bit and it straightened. The truck roared away in a spray of sand and a cloud of dirt.

Silence fell. Emma rose from her crouch and watched as Sumner stood up as well. After a moment, Mansur limped out of the adwaba. He held the tainted bottle in his hand. Emma inhaled slowly in an attempt to slow her racing heart. The entire attack, so fierce and fast, was not what she'd expected. The white-haired man sat up, blood running down his sleeve, but the wound appeared superficial. Several people came into view from behind the trucks. More and more joined them. Soon the entire group stood in a semicircle around Emma, Sumner, and Mansur. The young boy who had helped them remained close to his mother, who kept a hand on his shoulder. Another young boy ran up to Sumner, his eyes shining with happiness. Behind him came a young woman, this one in white, and a young man who looked relieved. The woman spoke first.

"This is the second time you have saved us," she said in French.

"This is Aaliyah, her son Risan, and our friend Yann."

From the body of one of the soldiers came the static of a handheld radio. A man's voice spoke in quick staccato bursts. Several people jerked to attention, and Mansur stepped closer and bent his head to listen.

"What are they saying?" Sumner asked.

"The man in the truck is calling for reinforcements. He says that they were overcome by twenty American Army Rangers." More words flowed from the dead man's radio. "He says that they fought through the evening, and he escaped after killing ten of the Rangers, but he thinks they are headed to the border village and asks that they join him there to fight off the rest."

Emma raised an eyebrow at Sumner. "Twenty Army Rangers? Trying to put a heroic spin on things, are we?"

The radio spat out some more sentences. Now the women and men surrounding Emma and Sumner began murmuring. Mansur put up a hand and barked out a word, and they fell silent again.

"They reply that they have fifty men, who have just entered the village. They told him to wait at the pensione for them, to give a further report in person, and then they will come back to the adwaba and kill everyone here."

One woman began keening, and another clutched at her young daughter, who appeared to be about nine years old and stood in front of her in a shapeless shift dress and bare feet. The girl's arms and legs were thin sticks.

"Tell them to stop. I need to think," Emma said. Mansur gave the order and the crowd fell silent again. Sumner stepped next to her.

"We need to take the trucks and head toward Atar. Banner was supposed to meet me there," Sumner said.

"I have bad news. Banner's chasing down Locke and some kidnapped embassy officials at the border first." Emma looked at her phone. The display showed no service.

"I can't reach him." She held the phone up for Sumner to see. "No service."

"It's doubtful that you'll have any service until twenty minutes outside of Atar," Mansur said.

"Then we can't wait. Can you drive a truck?"

Mansur nodded. "Yes."

"Good. Sumner and I will each drive one, you the third, and we then need one more. Please ask if anyone in the crowd can drive."

Mansur called out his question and a young woman, one of the girls stolen from the village, walked forward. She looked about nineteen and stood tall.

"I can drive," she said to Emma in British-accented English.

"You're from the village. One of the schoolgirls?" Emma said.

She nodded. "I was home from my studies in Dakar. I'm taking a degree in hospitality. To work in the hotels there. One must speak English and French."

"What's your name?"

"Zahara."

Emma walked to the dead soldier, fanned some mosquitoes away from his cooling body, and pulled the radio off his belt. His blood stained the holder that clipped it on, and Emma wiped it clean on the man's shirt. Then she held the radio out to the woman, who raised her eyebrows in alarm and reared back a bit. Emma waited. If the woman didn't have the guts to take the radio of a dead man, then it was unlikely that she'd be of long-term assistance. Finally, Zahara reached out and took it, and Emma decided that she'd do well.

"We're all set. You mind taking up the rear?" she asked Sumner. "It's likely to be the most dangerous position."

"If it means I'll be the one firing on those soldiers, then yes, I'll be happy to be at the end," Sumner said.

Mansur had been walking around the dead man, giving him a critical look.

"I think we should take his uniform. He looks about Yann's height, and it might come in handy to be dressed like one of them."

Emma waved at the soldier. "Have at it."

Mansur spoke to Yann, and they went about stripping the body. Then they redressed it in his white robe and disappeared behind a remaining bit of canvas. Yann stepped out, dressed in desert fatigues, standing straight. With his cropped hair, and in combat boots, the difference in his appearance was remarkable.

"What a difference clothes can make," Emma said in French. "It's amazing."

Yann smiled. "Thank you. Where do you want me?" He spoke in broken French.

Emma pointed to Zahara's truck. "Meet Zahara. I'm going to take the lead and she's going to drive second, Mansur will be third, and Sumner will take up the rear."

Within ten minutes, all of the occupants of the adwaba, their meager possessions, and several sets of utensils for making tea were distributed evenly among the trucks. All of this was done by the light of a campfire.

"Douse that, could you?" Emma said to Yann. He dumped a few handfuls of sand on it. Zahara switched on the headlights and Emma squinted in the sudden glare.

"How will we travel in the dark? It's dangerous," Sumner asked.

"Less dangerous than in the light. They'll be on us soon. We need to move, and we have to follow the tracks. Without them, we could end up spinning our wheels in the sand." Emma pulled out her compass and showed it to Yann. From her left, she heard Sumner give a soft laugh.

"Was going to offer you the one you sewed into my pants leg. Remind me to tell you how it already saved me once on this trip."

Yann moved closer and stood next to her shoulder while she consulted the compass.

"Good idea, that," he said.

Emma checked it, went to her truck, started the engine, and led the unlikely convoy north.

44

Kortya's driver pulled up next to a dead body near the adwaba and cut the engine. The early morning sun threw its light across the grisly scene.

"Here is where the worthless live," Kortya said.

He slammed out of the truck and walked to the prone figure—a man dressed in a white robe. As he neared, Kortya could see that it was one of his sergeants. A younger man who Kortya remembered as a good fighter, though not particularly bright. That he was one of those killed by a bunch of weak civilians was not surprising.

Two more pickups, all filled with soldiers, pulled up nearby and stopped. Kortya ignored them, as he paced around the shredded walls and pummeled wooden sticks of what remained of the adwaba. Thirty schoolgirls stolen, at least thirty more hostages, and three soldiers dead. The damage done seemed right for a group of Army Rangers, but something about the story didn't ring true to Kortya. If there had been twenty Army Rangers within a hundred miles of the adwaba his spies should have called it in. Yet, he'd received no warning. He waved over Mamo, who was kicking at the remains of a fire, sending the charred wood remains into the air.

"Bring the soldiers to me who say that they survived this."

Mamo swallowed. "I can't. They fled. When we got to the village, they were gone."

Kortya's eyes narrowed. "Cowards. Let everyone know that I'll reward the man that brings them to me."

"I'll kill them myself," Mamo said.

"No, you won't," Kortya snapped back. "I said *alive*. Or don't you listen to me?"

Mamo blanched. "Yes, yes, many apologies. Alive. Of course."

"And well enough to speak. Don't bring me men without tongues."

"Of course."

Kortya continued his walk around the adwaba, searching for clues. One of his soldiers ran up to him, holding something in his hand.

"They left these behind. American soldier rations," the man said. "Perhaps the Americans are here." The man seemed rattled by the thought.

"Are you so frightened by them?" Kortya's voice was soft.

The soldier quickly shook his head. "Not at all. They cannot win against us."

Kortya held the man's gaze a moment before flicking his hand in dismissal. In truth, if the Americans had managed to infiltrate this far without being picked up by his spies, then he had a much larger problem on his hands than a few Rangers. And always at the back of his mind was the Arab, waiting to kill him, slowly and painfully, if he failed.

He continued his reconnaissance, walking close to one of his own men's trucks as they watched him. From beneath their wheels ran a line of indentations in the hard-packed sand. One set made by the recent trucks, but they overlapped what looked like a second and third set. He began tracking along the crisscrossing imprints, following them out. At about thirty paces they diverged, with one set heading north, in the opposite direction to where he and his soldiers had come from, and the second at a forty-five-degree angle from those. He walked back to the parked trucks. The assembled soldiers fell silent as he did. He pointed north.

"They headed that way. Call back to the village and tell them to get here. We're heading north. I want these people found. Then kill the slaves and recapture the girls. I'll lead the convoy. This must be done before news travels to Azhan. For, if he finds out, then we are already in the land of the dead. Do you understand me?" Kortya spoke loud enough for the assembled group. At that moment, his radio buzzed—a call from the small group he'd left to watch the border village. "What?" Kortya barked into the speaker.

"The Maraad called. They say they have a high-value hostage, which means they need to speak to Azhan."

"No one speaks to Azhan but me. You know that," Kortya said. Azhan maintained strict anonymity. It was the only way he'd been able to stay alive, for the past four years, as the head of the insurgency.

"The Maraad say it is an American billionaire named Jackson Rand."

Kortya froze. His target was alive and safely in the hands of the Maraad. If Kortya could get to him first, then he could kill him and complete his mission. The Arab would be pleased and Kortya would live.

"Ask them where they are. I will come personally to speak with them and relay their message to Azhan."

The radio remained silent. Kortya waited, holding his breath, and hoping that the Maraad would be foolish enough to reveal their location over the radio. It came alive with static once more.

"They say that is not possible. They will send an envoy to meet you near Atar and will send the coordinates to you by text once he is in position."

"Tell them I'm in the middle of stinking Mauritania, and my phone does not receive. The fact that I'm able to speak over the radio is miracle enough. Tell them to give me the coordinates now and I'll meet them there."

Silence. Kortya waited. Sweat beaded down the side of his face and a large fly buzzed near his ear. He flicked it away. The sun hurt his eyes and he squinted.

"They refuse. They also say that someone is aware that they have Rand. A woman in the border camp. Rand spoke of her. She is a Darkview operative and chemist."

Kortya wanted to spit. Once more, this woman was thrown in his face. He wanted *her* dead more than Rand, and that was remarkable, given how badly he wanted Rand dead.

"I've heard of this woman before. She will die. The Maraad can be sure."

"They say that they will give you coordinates once she is dead. They want no witnesses to know that they are the ones who last saw Rand alive."

So they're clearing their way, Kortya thought. Scorching the earth behind them to be sure that no one learned of their perfidy. Kortya doubted that their precautions would work. All knew of the Maraad's reputation for treachery. Well, at least all in the African world. Whether the Europeans and Americans held the same view, was another question.

"Tell them this will be done, and soon. They aren't the only ones who want her dead."

And not the most dangerous ones, either, Kortya thought. The soldier on the other side of the radio transmission rang off. Kortya waved at the soldiers to get back into their trucks and climbed into his own vehicle. The driver fired it up.

"Follow those tracks," Kortya said.

The air filled with the noise and rumble of engines. Kortya watched a buzzard make its first sweeping pass over the site. Soon the bodies would return to the sand and dust from which they'd come and their souls to hell or paradise, depending on how they'd lived their lives.

Kortya didn't want to go to either place just yet. He sat in the truck and plotted how to find the chemist and kill her.

45

Banner spotted the burning helicopter an hour and a half into his flight to the border. Black smoke belched from the chopper and billowed behind it as it flew lower, spinning, and declining erratically. He opened a channel.

"Locke, is that you burning up in front of me?"

"Yeah. I'm...Carn, get ready to bail," Locke said. "Listen, Banner, my headset's shot and I've got you on an open mic."

"How bad is it?"

"We're going to have to jump."

"Then do it now. You'll need time to open your chutes."

"No parachutes."

Banner heard someone in the background yell, "Shit!"

"That's Carnegie Wendel?"

"Apparently he expected a parachute," Locke said.

"So, what's the evacuation plan? Because, from where I'm sitting, you've got about ten minutes to impact," Banner said. He watched as the chopper descended in another series of loops, spins, and back-and-forth bobs. From this distance, Banner could see the flames leaping out of the chopper, and the black smoke increasing. Locke was doing a good job of keeping it level, but it was a battle that was bound to end with the copter slamming into the sand.

"Get as low as we can and roll out the side door. Hey, Carn, when you jump out the side, you need to fall, bend your knees on impact, and immediately start rolling away from the chopper. You got that?"

"All I got is that you're crazy. Where are the God blessed parachutes?" Carn shouted at Locke and sounded panicked as hell.

As he should, Banner thought, because even though Locke was doing an excellent job with the tools at hand, it was still a distinct possibility that the machine would explode into a fireball on impact.

The damaged helicopter flew lower and then began to level off at about twenty feet above the ground. Locke held it there, and it flew in a straight line for a moment, holding the elevation. Then the tail started to shimmy forward, once again throwing the chopper into an unstable rocking motion.

"Jump now. I can't keep it here for long," Locke said.

Banner hovered in place, watching. After a second he saw a man leap from the helicopter, feet first. His black dreadlocks flew upward as he catapulted downward. He hit the sand, his legs collapsed, and he began rolling.

Nice job, Banner thought.

"He's out. Locke, jump."

Banner watched as Locke stood framed in the doorway a second before leaping out of the helicopter. He hit and rolled away as the machine plunged nose first into the ground. It plowed through the sand for a few yards, creating waves that flowed off on either side, until it came to a halt. Seconds later, it exploded, spewing a massive fireball that shot into the air in a column of red and yellow flames.

Banner reversed and flew around behind the two men, both now on their feet and running away from the downed chopper. He flew another three hundred yards before beginning his own descent. Once his helicopter settled onto the ground, he switched it off and began unbuckling. He grabbed two bottles of water from a cooler behind his seat before getting out and heading toward the men. Carn reached him first. He accepted the bottle of water without a word and chugged it down. Locke strolled up behind him and took the other bottle.

"You sure know how to make an entrance," Banner said.

Locke nodded. "Second time I've been told that." He looked at Carn. "You okay?"

Carn finished swallowing but Locke's helicopter exploded in another fireball before he could respond.

"You're certifiable, you know that?" Carn said to Locke, who just grinned.

"You have the virus?" Banner asked. Locke finished gulping his water before pulling out a metal canister from the leg pocket of his cargo pants. He held it out to Banner, who paused a moment before reaching out to touch it.

The weight and construction of the box surprised Banner with its heft and quality. Rand must have been well aware of the virulent nature of what he was carrying and arranged to construct a container that would withstand severe impact.

"This is well made," he said to Locke.

"He claimed it could take a high caliber shot and not be compromised," Locke said. He looked around. "Are we anywhere close to anything? The instruments on the helicopter went out at least an hour ago."

"We're two hundred miles from anything in all directions. The border is that way," Banner pointed to the south, "and Atar is that way," he pointed to the north. "And in between are the embassy officials that I'm supposed to be tracking."

"We saw some cars," Carn said. "They were heading north at a pretty fast clip."

"Did you spot anyone that looked like the embassy personnel?"

Carn shook his head. "Sorry, no. They're in SUVs, not open trailer beds."

"How far?" Banner asked.

"Thirty miles, no more," Locke replied. He pulled a cigarette pack out of his shirt pocket, shook one out and put it to his lips. After a second, he pulled it back out and spit to the side. "I ate a ton of sand just now." He patted around his chest a moment. "You got a lighter? Mine must have fallen out."

Banner shook his head.

"I don't smoke."

Locke shrugged and headed to the still burning helicopter. He dodged some of the higher flames, instead working his way around to a section of low-lying wreckage. He held the cigarette out and leaned in, placing the tip into the fire. The section next to him whooshed upward when it hit some fuel and he leapt back.

Carn shook his head. "That man is nuts. You know this, right?"

Banner nodded. "Yep. But he's one hell of a pilot."

Carn sighed. "I hate to admit it, but he is. Helps that he's so cool under pressure."

Banner wondered just what actually went on in Locke's well-hidden interior, but now was not the time to delve into that. Locke walked back up, smoking the now lit cigarette.

"Time to move. Both of you strap in. And don't worry. There are enough parachutes for all," Banner said.

Carn sighed in relief. "Now that's what I'm talking about."

46

Emma led the procession across the desert. She followed a dirt track that wound north to Choum. Both Sumner and Mansur warned her that to deviate from known trails meant possibly grounding the trucks in deep sand. The upshot of this requirement, though, meant that they would have to pass within a few yards of any soldiers who were riding south to intercept them.

The dawn sun rose. Bright beams of light shot over the sand dunes, turning the world a golden yellow. Despite her extreme exhaustion, thirst, and worry, Emma stared at this display with awe. Nature held its own force, despite humankind's attempts to bend it to their will. And that force would burn them all unless they made their way to an oasis.

The lack of vegetation was astonishing. For some stretches, nothing grew except the occasional spindly tree and scrub bushes. She wondered at the toughness of the men and animals who could navigate such a stark and forbidding landscape. No water, no food, few plants. Only scorpions…and miles of sand that blew into everything, clogging engines, and sending grit into her eyes. To her right, a pack of jackals loped by, their narrow faces and skinny legs giving them a dog-like appearance. She picked up the radio.

"Hey, Sumner, you see that pack of jackals? Ask Mansur if they attack humans."

After a moment, Sumner replied. "He says it's rare and usually when they're starving or disoriented with rabies. They stay near villages now because they can't survive in the desert. The fact that we're seeing them means that we must be getting close to a town. Perhaps even Choum."

Emma hoped that was true because every step closer to civilization would make it more difficult for the insurgency to attack. While the insurgents were pushing into Mauritania from Mali, their roots had not yet grown so deep that they could attack at will. Or at least that's what she hoped.

"Mansur tells me that a group of soldiers are behind us, riding north from the adwaba," Sumner said. He'd collected all of the functioning walkie-talkies and tuned two of them to a different channel, leaving one open to spy on the soldiers. Mansur drove behind Sumner, translating any conversations that transmitted.

"Anything else I should know?" Emma asked.

"They've gone silent," Sumner said.

"I don't like that."

"Me, either. Maybe we stop here and talk about the next steps."

Emma slowed and stopped. She watched in the rearview mirror as Sumner swung out of his truck and jogged up to her. He stepped up on the running board to get even with her and took off his aviator sunglasses.

"Isn't it a little dark to be wearing sunglasses? Can you see anything with them on?"

"It's a hassle, but the sand is worse. I feel like I have a layer of it coating my eyes. The sunglasses keep it from grinding in."

Emma winced. "Now that paints a graphic picture."

"Mansur thinks we have a decent chance of driving safely through the next town if we swing to the left. He says the sand is deep, but he doesn't have any better ideas."

"And if we get stuck?"

Sumner rubbed his face and Emma could see that exhaustion was taking a toll on him. "Then we'll have to get unstuck as quickly as possible. We have five guns—your HK, my Dragunov, and three AKs taken from the dead men."

"Did you give one to Mansur?"

Sumner shook his head. "No. I need him to stay with the radios and transmit to us. I gave one to Zahara, and the other two to an older woman named Rena and to Yann."

The other trucks idled behind them. The noise of their rumbling engines seemed to fill the desert, though she knew that such a thing was impossible. She hoped the sound would travel slower in the hot air than it would in a cool environment. Still, she waved to Zahara and Mansur and made a cutting signal across her throat. The trucks silenced. Both drivers climbed out and walked to her. Yann, too, stepped out and joined them. The women, men, and children riding in the back of the trucks stayed put.

"I have some very bad news," Mansur said when he reached them. "There are two teams of soldiers headed this way."

"I thought they'd gone silent?" Emma said.

"They did. But just now they communicated their positions. They're thirty miles that way." Mansur pointed north. "And twenty miles that way." He pointed south.

"You mean they're coming at us from all possible directions?" Emma said in a tight voice.

Mansur nodded. "We have no choice but to turn into the sand."

Zahara shook her head. "We can't. There are great dunes in both directions. The trucks will stall."

"Can we make a stand?" Mansur waved at the trucks. "We have over forty people here. We must outnumber them."

"Not enough guns," Sumner said. "We need better weapons."

"And there's a *haboob* coming," Mansur said.

"What's that?" Emma asked.

"A sandstorm."

Sumner flinched.

More sand in his eyes, Emma thought.

"Which direction?" Sumner asked.

"From the south. They describe it as over one thousand feet high."

"How long does a haboob last?" Emma asked.

"Hours."

"What's it like in a sandstorm?"

Mansur shook his head. "Terrible. So dense that the day turns to night and one can see nothing. The Bedouins tell the story of a storm that engulfed an army of fifty thousand near the Siwa Oasis. It killed them all. Buried their bones."

Sumner frowned. "Are you talking about the legend of Cambyses the Second? It's said that he lost an army that marched from Thebes to the Siwa."

Emma raised an eyebrow. "Herodotus. You know your mythology."

Mansur shook his head. "It's not a myth but a true story."

"It's been proven?" Sumner asked.

"Not by the West, but the Bedouins know of the valley of white bones where the army is said to lie. And I believe it occurred because I've been in a sandstorm and it's a fearsome thing. The grit flays you. This is one reason we dress to cover all skin, and you must as well." He pointed to his cheek. "We must find a scarf for you to cover here."

"Will the vehicles be operational after the storm?" Emma asked.

Mansur shrugged. "Perhaps. I'm not sure. This storm makes me think that we must get off the track and hide."

Emma stepped off the road and began walking to the left. The surface changed from packed to soft in the span of only ten feet. And this section, she could see, was a dense spot. After another ten feet, her heels sunk into the sand. She could only imagine what would happen to the heavy truck wheels. She returned to the group and did her best to maintain a calm exterior. No need to add to the problem. Zahara looked panicked, Mansur grim, and Yann's jaw was twitching. Only Sumner remained impassive, but Emma knew that inside he was casting about for an answer to their problem.

"Did we check every nook and cranny in those trucks for weapons?" she asked.

Sumner nodded. "I did. But let's do it again, in case I missed something in the dark."

They split up, and Emma headed back to her vehicle. She looked under the seats, behind them, and found nothing. Then she headed to the covered back portion.

A soft canvas top—draped over arched metal spines and added as an afterthought to the vehicle—covered the bed of the truck, where ten people hovered. Three men, three women, and four children gazed at Emma, and all of their faces held an anxious, worried expression. She switched to French and asked them to search inside for weapons. One of the women nodded and translated to the others in a language that Emma assumed was their native tongue. Emma watched as they checked under, and around, a couple of boxes marked with the Red Cross logo.

One small boy, with a proud smile, brought her a shoe box that held two screwdrivers and a set of pliers, their handles wrapped in duct tape. Emma smiled back at him.

"That's wonderful, thank you!" she said in French. The boy ducked his head and sidled back to stand next to his mother.

"The boxes?" Emma asked. One woman opened the lid and held up a mosquito net in a plastic holder.

"*C'est tout*," she said. That's all.

"*Merci*," Emma replied. The woman frowned and tapped her heart with her fingers. Emma just nodded. It *was* sad.

She returned to the passenger side and opened the glove box. Inside, she found a yellowed registration paper from Sierra Leone dated over five years earlier, and a worn and creased operator's manual. On top of it all was a folded letter from the truck manufacturer marked Final Notice. The letter warned that the truck had still not been brought in for replacement of its defective airbags. The bags could explode unexpectedly, sometimes with deadly force, and most often in hot climates.

Sumner appeared at her right shoulder. "Find anything?"

Emma held the letter up. "Just a friendly note from the manufacturer that the airbags are deadly in hot weather."

Sumner snorted. "Nice. Especially since it'll probably be close to one hundred by late afternoon."

"If we live that long. If the soldiers don't get us, exploding airbags will. You find anything?"

He shook his head. "We'll need to chance it in the dunes."

Emma leaned back against the truck and looked across the vast space in front of them.

"That's so risky. What if we get stuck? And, if we do, the insurgents will just pick us off. And, if we manage to evade them, then we'd have to navigate the rest of the way on foot.

I don't know if the children or the older people will be able to walk as far as will be required to get to the next town. Not to mention that we're low on water and food."

Sumner removed his glasses and rubbed his eyes. "I hear you. I just wish I had a better idea."

The panic that Emma had held in check through it all was now starting to bubble up again. To have gotten this far, only to once again be hemmed in by insurgents from every side was devastating. She balled up the recall notice and threw it into the truck. Several people in the back of Zahara's truck stared at her, silent. In the eyes of some, panic, and others, resignation, and all seemed to be looking to Sumner and Emma to find a solution.

"There is literally no place to hide. If we go into the dunes, we could get stuck and die of thirst before we get to the nearest town. And, if we stay here, these soldiers bearing down on us are going to wipe us out." She wanted to swear and scream and cry, but her throat was so parched and her lips so dry that she didn't think she could muster up enough liquid for tears, and the enervating heat made anger difficult to sustain. "Can I take a drink of your water?" She pointed to the bottle attached to Sumner's belt.

"They're only fifteen miles away," Mansur said.

Sumner just glanced sideways at him before handing his water bottle to Emma.

The liquid cooled her throat and, after a couple of gulps, she forced herself to stop. "I'm parched as hell, and it's not even that hot yet." She handed Sumner the bottle back. "You're right. We have to risk the sand, don't we?"

Sumner blew out a breath. "I don't have any other ideas and, depending on their speed, they could be only half an hour away."

She glanced at the balled paper. Something about it jogged her memory. She reached into the footwell and retrieved it, spreading it out on the seat, taking the time to read it again. Sumner stepped closer.

"You look like you have an idea. What is it?"

"The airbags. Weren't these part of a massive recall in the States, as well?"

"I think so, why?"

"I know a bit about the recall stateside. You asked about the prills. Those were ammonium nitrate. And this," she said, holding the paper up, "happened because the manufacturer replaced a stable gas, designed to explode on impact, with an unstable one that exploded with much more force and in the heat. Guess what the chemical was that they replaced it with?"

A slow smile spread across Sumner's face. "Ammonium nitrate?"

She nodded. "The cause of a couple of the deadliest explosions in history."

Sumner shook his head. "That's crazy. You said the prills were far too volatile to carry around, but the manufacturer added the same chemical compound to airbags?"

She nodded. "Ammonium nitrate is far cheaper than the usual substances. The airbag manufacturer claimed that a cooling chemical, when mixed with it inside the inflator, would stabilize it enough to render it safe." She waved the notice in the air. "Clearly that didn't work."

"Is there a way to safely remove the inflator and use it as an explosive?"

Emma nodded. "It's worth a try."

Sumner put his gun down and took off his glasses. "Let's go, then."

Emma looked at Mansur. "Have you heard anything more over the radio? How much time do we have?"

"I'm not sure. They're silent again."

"Send someone with sharp eyes up that dune." Sumner pointed to a high dune about fifty feet away. "Tell him or her to call out when they see anyone approaching."

Mansur limped away toward his truck and Yann stepped up. "You have a plan?"

"We're taking out the airbag inflators. They're the explosive ones under recall," Sumner said.

Yann frowned. "You know how to do this safely?"

"I've never done it before, but we have to try. We need access to the chemical in them."

Yann nodded slowly. "Okay."

Sumner stuck his head inside the driver's side of Emma's truck. "Looks like the driver's side airbag is in the center of the steering wheel." He ran his hands along the edges of the airbag console. "We need tools to pop this off. Probably an Allen wrench of some sort."

Emma walked to the truck seat and picked up the shoe box. "We only have these. A flat-head screwdriver and some pliers."

"How about the tools for putting on the spare tire? Don't most cars come with tools built in?" Zahara asked.

"Good idea," Sumner said.

"I'll check." Emma returned to the bed of the truck and waved the passengers away. She found the compartment that held the spare tire and jack and pulled the cover up by the release tab. Her heart fell when she saw that it was empty. There was no tire, not even a temporary donut tire, and no jack at all.

She hopped down from the trailer and went to Sumner.

"Bad news. The compartment is empty. No jack, no tools,

and no tire. Looks like someone either stole them or they used them on another truck."

"Well, here's some good news. It looks like this particular airbag module is held on by tabs in the back. Here, check out these access holes."

Emma ran her fingers along the back of the steering wheel console and felt the deep access holes.

"Does the screwdriver fit?"

Sumner nodded. "It does. That's one module we can access. Let me check on the others." He handed the tool to her and turned to Yann and Zahara. "Let's go. Each person works on their own truck. I assume that we should be removing some sort of fuse or electrical current that operates the thing."

Emma popped the hood of her truck and leaned into the engine compartment to gain access to the battery. "We should take the poles off of the batteries, at least."

"That should help, but be aware that it'll take some time for the remaining electricity to discharge," Sumner said.

"I don't think we have time for that."

Sumner nodded. "I know, but give it a couple of minutes."

Pulling the leads off proved to be easy. Emma returned to the driver's seat to remove the module. The square, injection-molded plastic centerpiece connected to the steering wheel and was stamped with the vehicle brand logo. A seam running around the piece showed that it was snapped onto the center of the steering console and not an integral part of it. Emma telescoped the steering wheel out as far as it would go and angled in so that she could see the back. There were four tabs where the box containing the airbag clicked in.

Here we go. Take it nice and easy, she thought.

The sun beat through the windshield onto the back of her head, and a bead of sweat ran down her face as if to remind her of the airbag inflator's volatility in the heat. She put the square tip of the screwdriver against the tab and lowered it until it cleared the edge. The seam between the box and the steering wheel console widened a tiny bit. She worked on the next three and all unclipped easily.

"Now for the hard part," she said aloud.

Rivulets of sweat were pouring down her sides, soaking her shirt, and not all of it was from the heat. She stayed to the side of the wheel in case the bag exploded while she pulled on the plastic box containing the airbag, lifting it off the center. Two cables clipped to the back of the inflator ran from it and disappeared down the interior of the steering wheel column and into the bowels of the engine, where Emma assumed they ended at the truck's battery. As she reached to unclip the leads, she heard someone yell from a distance.

The insurgents were coming.

47

Sumner jogged up to Emma, cradling his own airbag module in his palms. Behind him came Zahara and Yann with theirs.

"The passenger side of the other trucks requires an Allen wrench, so we're out of luck there," Sumner said. "Yann, you go reconnect all the batteries. We need to get these vehicles back up and running."

Four square modules, each a bit bigger than a hockey puck. Emma pulled her module out of the injection plastic cover and weighed the piece in her hand. The ammonium nitrate portion was encased in a square metal holder, which was fastened on all four ends with screws and bolts. She assumed it was these metal pieces that turned into projectiles when the bag detonated with too much force.

"We're guessing they're three miles away," Mansur called from the second truck.

"Will they explode when a truck drives over them? We can bury them in the dirt on the road," Sumner said. "Mine it in both directions."

Emma nodded. "They should, if the truck drives right over, but what if they miss?"

"Not good."

Emma once again weighed the piece in her hand. It could be thrown, but there was no guarantee that it would explode once it landed. She thought perhaps it would require more heat and more force. She glanced at Sumner.

"Are you as good at skeet shooting as you are at everything else?"

Sumner raised an eyebrow. "You're looking at the Champion of the Minnesota Gun Club three years running. You thinking of throwing it?"

"Yes. Directly at them. But you may have to shoot it out of the sky to make sure it detonates. I'm not sure that merely hitting the ground or the side of a vehicle will be enough."

"I can do that. How do you want to transport them?"

Emma picked her backpack up from the passenger seat. "In this." She placed the pack on the ground, flipped over the top flap, and expanded the opening. She left her folded clothes inside. "The clothes should protect them from bouncing around too much. We need to place them out of direct sunlight." She lowered the first module in, then placed the other three on top. "Ready."

Sumner put his sunglasses back on. "Now the only question is which direction will they come from first?"

The boy on the hill yelled something.

"He sees a dust cloud. Coming from the north," Yann called from the far truck, where Mansur stood next to him and relayed the information.

"North it is," Emma said.

"Everyone, let's go." Sumner called to Mansur, who translated for the others. Soon those who'd been sitting on the ground, in the shade of the vehicles, were up and crawling back into the trucks. Zahara pulled herself into the cab of hers, while Emma waved at Mansur.

"You need to drive mine and find someone to drive Sumner's."

She jogged up to Zahara and stepped up on the running board to speak to her.

"You're going to be first. It's the most dangerous place to be. Sumner and I will be in the back, preparing to throw the modules. If you don't want this position, tell me now, and I'll ask Mansur, or see if Yann can drive."

Zahara shook her head. "I am not afraid. My heart is strong and my soul is clear. Tell me what you wish me to do." Emma swallowed the sudden emotion she felt at the woman's bravery.

"We're going to ride right behind the cab. I'll throw the module and Sumner's going to shoot it. I expect it to explode and spew bits of metal and the bolts that hold it together. But that's not the worst I expect."

"You expect them to be shooting at me the entire time," Zahara said.

Emma nodded. "I'll try to divert their attention to me, but you'll be up front and a clear target." Zahara closed her eyes a second but, when she opened them, Emma could see her resolve.

"I would rather die than be taken prisoner again." Zahara started the engine, and the truck began to vibrate.

Zahara's was the only truck with an open back and the high, wooden slatted sides designed to hold cargo in place. Now it was jammed with people, but Emma waved them aside and headed to the portion directly behind the cab, making sure to place the backpack gently on the truck bed next to her. Sumner joined her. He had a dark scarf wrapped around his face, leaving only his eyes free, his Dragunov in hand and his sunglasses on. He climbed the slats, and Yann and a young woman, one of the kidnapped girls, stood behind him, holding Emma's HK.

"I've asked Yann and his friend to be prepared to hold us in place once the truck gets going. I was going to tie myself to the slats but, as the fight heats up, I need to be able to move freely. She's also going to hand you the modules and hold the HK, depending on what weapon you're going to use."

"What's your name?" Emma asked the girl in French.

"Silwa," she said. She stepped up behind Emma and handed her the HK. Emma took it and glanced at Sumner.

"No sand in your eyes, I hope?" Emma asked.

Sumner shook his head. "I'm ready."

She climbed up the slats and, when they reached her waist, she stayed there, hanging a bit over the edge.

"How's your throwing arm?"

"Good enough, I guess." Emma blew out a breath, put on her own sunglasses and pounded on the cab roof. Zahara hit the gas and Emma swayed back a second as the wheels bit and the truck started to move. She grabbed at the slats to hold herself in place.

The truck convoy rolled out.

48

It took only five minutes more before Emma could see the dirt cloud created by the oncoming soldiers. While it was impossible to tell how many they were facing, they did kick up an impressive amount of dust. The dry wind hit her face, and she felt bits of sand and grit in the air. The truck bounced over the occasional pothole, and Emma clenched her teeth and watched the backpack vibrate on the truck bed below her. Yann stayed next to it, keeping it upright, as they barreled into trouble. She leaned into Sumner.

"Can you make out the numbers?" she yelled over the sound of the wind and engine.

"Not yet," he said.

Emma glanced behind her at the other trucks. First came Mansur's, then two other trucks driven by men from the adwaba. They'd decided to place the mothers and children in the two middle vehicles, leaving the last pickup to cover the rear. They stayed in single-file formation by necessity, because to deviate even by a few feet risked being bogged down in the sand.

The road passed between two massive dunes, and then it angled downward and straight. For the moment, she saw nothing behind her, but the dunes blocked the view. Their now low angle worried her because, once the chasing crew passed between them, the insurgents would have a nice shot at her convoy from above.

She returned her attention forward and squinted into the telescopic sight on the HK. Now she could make out the oncoming soldiers, and what she saw made her mouth drier than it already was, if that was possible.

There were only two trucks, but the first sported a gun mount manned by a fighter. More men rode behind him on the flatbeds.

"You see them?" Emma asked Sumner, who was squinting through his own gun's sight.

"Now I do," he replied. "I'm targeting the guy behind the gun mount first."

"I'm going to take out the driver."

"Good idea," he said. "Fire on my signal."

Zahara kept the truck on line, barreling forward on the pounded sand track. The cab's metal top heated in the sun, and Emma was glad for her long sleeves because each time she brushed against the cab's roof she could feel the heat through it. Every so often, the vehicle hammered into a pothole, and Sumner and Emma's guns clattered against the metal. Each time, Yann and Silwa reached up in unison to hold the two of them in place.

The truck in the distance filled the trail and drove straight at them in a terrifying game of chicken. Emma watched as one soldier held a set of binoculars and stared in their direction. His mouth moved, and Emma wished she could read lips. But she supposed it didn't matter in the end. What really mattered was their superior firepower. She didn't see any RPGs, but she knew that the insurgents rarely traveled without them. Her forearms burned, as the heat penetrated the fabric of her sleeves. She lifted up a bit to cool down. The motion set her to swaying as she lost the stabilizing effect of the roof and Silwa pressed her back against the slats.

"Get ready," Sumner said. He lowered the muzzle of his own weapon onto the top of the cab and sunk down until it sheltered most of his body. Emma did the same. And waited.

"Now," Sumner said.

She squeezed the trigger, feeling the gun respond and the recoil punch into her shoulder.

49

Emma winced at the sound of Sumner's gun firing so close to her ear. She saw, rather than heard, the soldiers return fire because they moved with the recoil as she had. Both she and Sumner ducked behind the cab. Bullets flew overhead, and one ricocheted off the metal cab hood with a metallic bang and split up in the air, moving too fast for her to see where it went.

"Up," Sumner said.

She rose with him, swinging her rifle over the cab hood and aiming once again at the oncoming soldiers. Now she could make out the people in the trucks without benefit of the scope and, when she put her eye to it to aim, they jumped into view and swayed as their trucks barreled forward. Several wore black scarves wrapped around their faces, the others, white. The man in the foreground, manning the machine gun, was the only one not completely covered by a scarf. A navy bandanna covered his face.

Sumner fired, and one of the black scarves dropped and disappeared from view. The others fired, and now Emma could see them move, and the crack of gunfire was simultaneous. Both missed, but Emma heard the bullets hit the cab and her heart beat in her chest with fear and adrenaline. The truck slammed downward, and the floor pitched under her feet as Zahara hit a pothole. The scope jolted upward, scraping across her eyebrow, and Emma's ribs slammed against the edge of the hood. She grunted in pain. Silwa pushed her hard against the cab, compressing her ribs against the hot metal.

Emma regained her balance and aimed again. She fired back at the soldiers, hitting a white scarf in the shoulder in a shot that would have been dead-on had she not been jolted yet again by the movement of the truck. Still, she watched him buckle and grab at the wound. Not dead, but injured.

Sumner fired and punched a hole through the windshield of the first truck. The front tires twisted to the right and the entire vehicle swung sideways, tossing the soldiers in the back against the bed walls. The injured white scarf catapulted over the side and landed on his back in the sand. The driver of the second truck slammed on the brakes to avoid hitting the one in front. His truck shimmied and swayed, then stopped a few feet from the other and began reversing, the now spinning wheels kicking up a plume of sand. The truck that had angled sideways stayed put, its entire length now facing them.

"Get the modules. That gunner's almost in range," Sumner said.

"Tell Zahara to slow down, or we'll drive right into that blocking truck."

"She can't. Look behind you."

Emma glanced back.

In the distance, she saw the glint of metal as the rising sun hit a second convoy of trucks.

"Air bags," Emma said, holding her hand down to Silwa, without taking her eyes off the trucks in front. The second one kept reversing backward, and its fighters occupied themselves by holding onto whatever they could, to avoid being flung off, like the soldier in the sand.

The short-lived triumph of the retreating second truck was shattered as the machine-gun operator in the sideways vehicle swung his weapon on its tripod to aim at them and began firing.

Emma ducked behind the cab just as Zahara slammed on the brakes. Now it was their turn to shimmy as the wheels bit into the dry sand. Bullets pounded through the cab and some hammered through the back window over Emma's head. Bits of glass flew everywhere, and she closed her eyes to protect them.

Please let Zahara be alive, she prayed.

The first truck began reversing, picking up speed, and swaying back and forth. The insurgent's machine gun continued to fire and bullets flew, but Zahara started the truck up again and Emma heaved a sigh of relief. Sumner rose up just high enough to clear the cab and fired again.

The machine-gun fire stopped.

"Got him," Sumner said.

The sideways truck roared to life, and it swung around and started driving away. A dark scarf soldier grabbed at the machine gun and pointed it in their direction, but didn't fire.

"Out of ammo?" Sumner said.

"Must be," Emma said. "They're running away."

The two retreating trucks fell into a side-by-side formation, keeping only a few inches between them as they picked up speed. They began to pull ahead and, within thirty seconds, the new tactic became clear. Clouds of dust rose off their back wheels and hung in the air. At their current pace, Emma's convoy would drive right into it. Silwa slapped a module into Emma's hand, but she waited to throw it, watching as the trucks in front drove away. She bent down to peer into the back window. Zahara's dark eyes gazed back at her through the rearview mirror.

"Are you hit?" Emma asked.

Zahara nodded. "In the arm. A flesh wound only. I can still drive."

"You see what they're up to?" Emma asked.

"They want to blind us."

Emma nodded. "And then the soldiers behind us can pick us off. Can you go any faster? Create our own dust cloud?"

Zahara shook her head. "Only a bit. The friction will burn the rubber off the tires."

Emma rose back up to stand next to Sumner.

"Zahara's worried that, if she goes faster, the sand will delaminate the tires."

Sumner kept his aim on the soldiers in front, who were fast disappearing from view as the cloud of dust grew.

"She's probably right. What's going on behind us?"

Emma swung around to look. The following soldiers and trucks kept chase, but none were looking their way and, to her relief, none were firing. But Emma's relief evaporated when she saw what approached.

A churning wall of sand and dust poured from between the two massive dunes, boiling through the narrow passage and ripping sand from either side, covering the entire horizon and enveloping everything in its path.

50

Emma pounded on the cab roof and bent into the back window.

"You see the storm?" she asked Zahara. "We need to risk those tires."

Zahara simply nodded, and the truck began a slow acceleration. Yann and Silwa stared at the storm with frightened eyes.

"How bad is it?" Sumner asked, never moving from his station, or taking his eye from the Dragunov sight. Emma returned to her position next to him, grabbing at the hood as the truck bounced.

"Bad. Terrible. We're going to be engulfed, and Zahara will have to stop. The risk of falling off the road will be too great. She's a smart driver. She's going faster, but no spinning wheels, just an easing upward in speed."

Sumner nodded but kept his view forward. "These guys in front are hightailing it out of here. They're trying to stay ahead of it."

"And so should we," Emma said.

The wall of sand behind them would soon engulf the chasing soldiers. The ones in front barreled away, firing only occasionally and in a desultory fashion. Emma stared through the HK's scope and saw them gesturing at the enormous wall of sand. They pounded on the cab's hood.

"They're just as desperate to stay ahead of that storm," Sumner said.

"Silwa, tell me, what happens when the sand hits?" Emma asked.

Silwa shook her head. Emma realized she'd spoken in English. She tried again, this time in French, but again the woman shook her head. Sumner ripped the radio off his belt and handed it to her.

"Ask Mansur."

Emma returned the module to its soft place in the backpack and slid down to sit on the bed floor, her back against the cab. She radioed Mansur.

"Best ways to protect ourselves in that cloud?"

"You must take cover. Stay in the bed. Remember the valley of bones. Wet your scarves and cover your noses. This will help filter the sand and keep it from filling your lungs and suffocating you. Keep your eyes closed, if possible, and find something to cover those bullet holes in the back window, or the sand will fill the cabin."

Emma slapped the radio back onto Sumner's belt.

"I need something to stuff in these bullet holes in the window."

"Take my shirt," Sumner said.

"What about your skin? You'll be flayed."

"I'll curl up in a corner of the bed when the time comes."

Emma handed Silwa the gun, much to the young woman's surprise, and turned to pull up Sumner's shirt. She worked it up his back. His skin felt smooth and warm as she did. He moved away from the cab to allow her to raise the front. She took his gun out of his hand and held it while he yanked the shirt over his head. As he did, she saw the wound on his stomach, the angry red line running across and ending at the hip bone, before disappearing into the loose waist of his pants.

"What's that?"

Sumner took his gun back and, before he could answer, the truck hit another pothole and he fell against the hot metal hood.

"I forgot about that. Knife fight."

Emma handed him back his shirt.

"Forget it. I'll use mine. You need to keep that wound covered, or the sand will infect it."

He waved her off.

"Use it."

She gave it back to him. "Later. First mine."

She jerked the shirt back over his head and held the Dragunov while he put his arms through. When he was done, he returned to aiming, and she pulled off her own shirt.

As she did, she noted Yann's eyes grow wide, but she ignored him. She wore a black sports bra, which in the West would be considered a running top, but in the conservative Muslim country would be scandalous, indeed. She took the shirt and began shoving the fabric into the bullet holes, trying to stretch it across to cover them all. After a moment, Yann waved her off and finished the job.

"Good," he said, with an approving nod.

Emma waved at Silwa to help.

She felt the truck slow and glanced through the glass at Zahara. Before she could ask why the slower pace, she heard the radio on Sumner's waistband beeping. Mansur was calling.

"I'm listening." Emma leaned against the back of the cab and stared at the incoming storm, which had engulfed the soldiers approaching from the back. She could see nothing of them. The enormous cloud boiled toward Mansur's vehicle and the two others. The air buzzed with the sound, a roaring train noise with a high-pitched whistle on the top, as the wind swirled. It poured ever closer, and it was clear that they were not going to outrun it forever. Soon they would be swallowed up as well.

"Get everyone into the cab that you can fit," Mansur said. "It's safer there. I'm sending two of the children from the third pickup to join your group. The rest of the trucks are closed, but you'll be in grave danger in the open flatbed. Tell Zahara to stop a little to the left of the road, but not too far, because the sand will accumulate quickly and she'll be bogged down."

"Can you see the men behind you?" Emma asked.

"No. The storm has them."

Emma relayed the information and Zahara began a slow deceleration.

Sumner pulled his gun off the cab roof and slid lower to sit next to her on the bed of the truck. "You, Silwa, and Yann can fit into the cab. I'm too tall. I'll ride it out back here," he said.

Emma shook her head. "Not a chance. I'm staying right next to you. Anyhow, Mansur's sending two of the children. They'll have to squeeze in. Just give me a minute to check on Zahara's wound." The truck ground to a halt, and she jumped over the side, with Yann and Silwa right behind her. She stepped up on the running board and Zahara lowered the window.

"Show me your wound." Zahara turned so that Emma could see her right arm. An angry slash oozed blood, but it had already begun to coagulate. "Use the water bottle to rinse it and try to cover it with something." Zahara just nodded. "And tell Yann and Silwa to get in the cab." A girl and a boy, both about ten, ran up next to Emma and she waved them into the car. "Roll up the windows and stay there until the storm passes."

"What about you?" Zahara asked.

"I'm staying in the truck bed with Sumner."

"We can all fit. Please, let's try."

Emma shook her head. "No. But, remember, keep that wound clean. You're an excellent driver in sand and we need you. Turn the truck around to face the storm. Sumner and I will need the cab to block some of the sand. Be sure to face backward in the seats. That way if the windshield fails you won't get a face full of sand and glass."

Zahara nodded, but she looked grim and panicky. Emma didn't blame her one bit. She went to the passenger side and, once the children were inside, did what she had seen Carn do a lifetime ago. She pressed the door shut.

By the time she'd climbed into the flatbed, the storm's edge was only two hundred yards away. Debris flew all around and the wind howled. Sumner waved to her, and she clambered next to him in the corner of the bed, lying with her back against the side wall.

"The corner walls should help," Sumner said. He poured water onto the front of his shirt, lay down next to her, wrapped his arm around her and pulled her against his chest.

"I wet my shirt. Feel free to use it as a mask to filter the sand." He smelled incongruously of beach and sweat. She only wished they were at the ocean, instead of in a vast desert and soon to be engulfed in sand.

She hugged him close, pressing her body against the entire length of his.

"Don't you dare get hurt," she said.

51

The storm hit with an intensity that made Emma gasp. Stinging bits of sand flayed the naked skin on her arms, and the truck rocked and creaked as the wind buffeted it, pushing it up and then down on its suspension. Sumner held her against the wall but had to reach up and hold onto the edge, to keep in place as the gusts battered them.

The storm howled, and sand began to fill every open space. While the cab deflected some, the wind swirled, rather than blew in a straight line, and sand soon covered the metal floor and accumulated around her, rising as fast as flooding water. Except, in a flood, she would have had a chance to keep her lungs clear. In this storm, she seemed to be drowning in sand and dust with each breath. She kept her nose pressed into Sumner's chest in an attempt to filter the grit, but it still managed to find its way into her lungs. Sumner sneezed and she knew that he, too, was suffering. As the truck rocked and the wind howled, an image of the tornado scene in the Wizard of Oz rose in her mind's eye. She half expected a witch on a bicycle to fly by, screaming at her.

The sand built ever higher and, when it covered her torso, she began to panic. She shook her head to keep it from accumulating on her face.

"It's getting too deep. We need to sit up," she said to Sumner. "I'll curl up on my knees but keep my head down."

He let go, and she curled up and over onto her legs. The moment she moved from the side wall, the wind gusted and she fell back against it. Sumner inched closer, pinning her against the wall with his body. He wrapped his arm over her and once again braced her against the wind.

"How long will this thing last?" he yelled into her ear.

"A haboob usually lasts only a few hours."

"I don't know if I can take this for a few hours."

Emma agreed but kept her thoughts to herself. Speaking was too difficult anyway and just let more sand into her mouth. Grit lined her teeth, and her throat felt raw and dry. The wind picked up, and the truck began rocking again, creaking and cracking on its suspension.

Their activity narrowed to three things—shaking off the sand that accumulated around them, take turns alternating their grip on the side wall, and digging into the drifts that built against the cab and threatened to engulf them both.

An hour and a half later, it appeared as though they would lose the battle. Ironically, it was the periodic slowing of the wind that threatened them the most. While it blew hard, the cab deflected enough to keep drifts from accumulating on the other side. But during the lulls—as the wind slowed—the storm hung in place longer. The sand seemed to fall straight down, rather than be driven sideways. They'd push the sand down toward the truck's end, shoving it over the edge. Then, when they returned to the top, a new drift would have formed, and they would have to push at it. With only their hands as tools, it was an arduous task.

Two hours into the storm, sand overfilled the bed and piled against the cab back, while more drifts grew along each end.

Drifts on the side reached as high as the windows and Emma worried that soon the entire truck would be buried, and Zahara, Silwa, Yann, and the two children with it. She stood now against the cab, and the sand reached her thighs. She and Sumner kept digging away, clearing it enough to move their legs, only to have it collapse around them again. She'd clear the back window and through it watch as the crammed inhabitants of the truck coughed and hacked. The darkness made it impossible to see with any clarity, but she could hear a high-pitched whistling sound as the wind blew through the bullet holes in the windshield.

The back window collapsed a half an hour later, after a massive gust of wind shook the cab and the steel frame twisted with the movement. Shards of glass fell onto those inside, and Emma heard one of the children shriek. The relentless storm continued, and the sand rose some more, piling into the cab from the back. Both she and Sumner blocked the window as best they could with their bodies but, as the drift rose ever higher, it was clear that they'd have to move soon to save themselves. While the cab interior was filling, the rate remained slow compared to that of the truck bed.

Now the truck ceased to shake because the sand pressed in from all sides and held it in place. The line covered the doors. Unless it stopped soon, Zahara and the rest were going to have to climb out the windows to free themselves.

"This sand gets any higher and we won't be able to move. Climb onto the roof," Sumner yelled into Emma's ear. She put her foot on the broken window ledge and hauled herself upward, but the drift pulled at her legs and sucked her downward. After the second try, she cleared the worst of it and fought her way up onto the cab roof, only to be battered by the wind. She lost her grip on the cab edges, and the wind forced her backward. Sumner grabbed her shirt as she slid, and it was only this that kept her from flipping head first into the sand. She settled onto the roof on her stomach, keeping her eyes closed tight against the storm and Sumner wrapped an arm around her and pressed her tight against his body. A jumble of images crossed her mind—Sumner fighting side by side with her against paramilitary fighters in Colombia, then battling Somali pirates in the Indian Ocean and a gunrunning cartel in the Caribbean. In all of these cases, their enemy had been human, relentless but ultimately conquerable. Nature, though, held a power that no human could match. You didn't play against nature, because nature held all the aces. Emma lay on the roof with Sumner bracing her as the storm flayed them, and she held this man tight, adding her strength to his.

"Don't you dare get hurt," Emma said again, but the wind ripped the words from her lips.

The storm stopped as abruptly as it had begun. First the wind died, then the sand ceased to fill the air. Then, at last, the sun shone again. Emma and Sumner remained in place, face down on the cab roof.

Emma loosened her grip on his waist. His breathing remained slow and his eyes closed. Sand covered her back, and she turned to her side and faced him, to allow it to roll of the cab roof rather than onto him. He moved, too, taking his arm away and brushing at his face as he lay there.

She sat up, slowly, squinting into the sun, expecting a transformed landscape. But they remained surrounded by sand dunes and empty skies. And the road was gone, swallowed up by sand in both directions. There was one thing that did remain though.

Before her stood the man who'd been thrown off the back of the truck in front of them and left to die. He knelt in a drift and held a rifle aimed at her head.

52

Banner spotted the convoy carrying the embassy officials twenty minutes after takeoff. He waved at Locke and pointed to the cars below.

"That them?" he said.

Locke nodded. "Yep. Moving fast."

"I can only follow for a short while. I'm running out of gas and will need to head back to Nouakchott soon. Flick through the radio signals. Maybe we can intercept something."

Locke did, stopping at an active channel. A man rattled off words in a language that Banner assumed was Wolof.

"Carn, can you understand that?" Locke handed Carn his earphones and attached another set for himself. Carn listened a moment and then nodded.

"Sounds like you have two groups talking here. One is outside Atar waiting for a man named Kortya to appear."

Locke frowned, and Banner gave a small shake of his head. He didn't want to alarm Carn. But Carn noticed the motion.

"What? Who is this Kortya guy?"

"A mean son of a bitch," Locke said.

"Head of an insurgency. What's the story? Is Kortya headed to Atar?"

Carn rocked his hand back and forth. "They thought he was but, the last time they heard from him, he was reportedly chasing some escaped hostages and headed into a massive sandstorm."

"Escaped hostages? Where?" Banner asked.

"They aren't saying."

"Hold on. I'll get hold of Stromeyer."

He switched to another signal and called her. She answered immediately.

"I need the coordinates of a sandstorm somewhere between the Mauritanian border and Atar."

"You got it. And Banner?"

"Yep."

"We've managed to obtain one Mi-24 Hind helicopter equipped with a jerry-rigged laser missile firing system and one missile. It's in Nouakchott."

"Been a long time since I've flown one of those," Banner said.

"Your sandstorm is massive, and it's about fifty miles outside of Atar and moving north."

"Close. Good. I've intercepted a transmission that Kortya is somewhere along that storm's route, if not right in the center of it and chasing some escaped hostages."

"Escapees? That's good news. Will you have time to get the Hind going and head back?"

"Hard to say. If he's in the thick of it, he may be stationary and trying to ride it out. But, as I recall, aren't laser sights subject to a lot of backscatter in this environment? Especially if we're talking flying into a sandstorm."

"Yes. And the vertical climb on this beast is slower in anything over seventy degrees. I'll leave it up to you if it's worth heading back to get it."

"Out."

Banner clicked off and Carn leaned forward.

"What's backscatter?"

"It's when a laser targeting system's beam gets reflected off of particles in the air. It scatters the energy, and the missile misses its target."

"Particles? Like sand?"

Banner nodded. "Like sand. I wouldn't even attempt to fire it in a sandstorm. Waste of a good missile."

"What do you bet Caldridge has something to do with those escapees? That sandstorm is right along the route she'd be running," Locke said.

"And possibly Sumner. I left him in a truck outside of Atar, as well."

"Looks like we're all heading to the same place. Time to have a party," Locke said.

"I am *not* interested in any party with escapees and the enraged head of an insurgency," Carn said.

Locke slapped him on the shoulder. "What, you don't like fireworks?"

Carn groaned. Banner hoped fireworks weren't in the future as he followed the SUV convoy. After a few minutes more, he saw a man lean out of the side window of the lead vehicle to look up at them.

"It's about time they noticed us," Banner said. He watched as the man below tilted back into the SUV. Seconds later, the barrel of a rifle emerged from the same window.

"Better move out," Locke said.

Banner spun the helicopter and darted sideways as the man below began firing. All the shots missed and Banner flew in a large circle. As he did, Locke unbuckled and moved to pick up a rifle shoved into some netting on a side wall in the back.

"Not sure that's the best idea," Banner said. "You might hit the wrong guy."

"Well, that one we know isn't the right one. And, if I get him, we'll be sending the correct message, don't you think?" Locke headed to the open side and hugged the wall. "Can you swing back around and get me in position for a shot at him?"

Banner finished the turn and once again began following the convoy. The man with the gun still hung out of the side window of the first vehicle.

"Not too bright, is he?" Locke said.

"He sees that we don't have any gun mounts and thinks that means that we don't have any weapons," Banner said.

"Yeah, well, let's prove him wrong, shall we?" Locke aimed and fired three shots in a row. None hit the man, but one hit a panel next to his head. He ducked back inside.

"Won't see him for a while," Locke said in a satisfied voice. "So, where we heading?"

To Nouakchott. Can you fly an old Hind?"

"Alone?"

"I'll be flying this one."

Locke looked at Carn. "You want to help me?"

"Forget it," Carn said, shaking his head.

"Didn't you say you had two years' military service?"

"That was compulsory, and all I learned was the basics. How to shoot. Drive a tank. They didn't teach us anything about helicopters. Besides, I'm not getting into any helicopter alone with you ever again." He glanced out the windshield. "That guy below is regaining his courage."

Banner waved at Carn. "I've got a second rifle in the case strapped against the wall. You're free to use it."

Carn shook his head. "I'm a pacifist. I'm against guns."

Locke fired another shot, and the man jerked back into

the SUV. Locke shoved the rifle back into the netting and returned to his seat. "Why against guns?"

"They kill people," Carn said.

Locke nodded. "That they do."

"And I'm against killing people."

"Me, too. In general."

"And specifically? Who needs killing, specifically?"

Locke put his headphones back on and strapped into the seat.

"Specifically, those that are trying to kill me."

Carn sat back and said nothing. Banner thought that he wasn't convinced. Either way, they'd have an opportunity soon enough to test everyone's resolve.

53

Banner landed at a small airfield outside Nouakchott, which consisted of one small Quonset hut and refueling pumps next to a dirt runway. He kicked up an impressive amount of dust as he did, and the air around him turned a deep yellow from the sand. He landed near a stationary Hind helicopter that had seen better days. When he cut the engine, both Carn and Locke jumped out. Banner followed at a slower pace. Locke headed straight to the new helicopter and crawled into the pilot's seat.

"Come have a look," he said to Carn, who climbed in the other side. A few seconds later, Carn jumped back out.

"Seen enough?" Banner asked.

"Can't read a thing in the cockpit. It's all in a foreign language."

"That's a Mi-24 Hind. Russian made."

"Ah, that explains it," Carn said. He stayed next to Banner, gazing at the helicopter. After a few more seconds, Locke climbed back out.

"Think you can fly it?" Banner asked.

Locke nodded. "Sure. These are the preferred ride in Africa. Built like tanks and easy to service."

"So, climb back in and let's go. Why'd you come back out?"

Locke waved at something behind Banner and Carn. "That's why."

Banner turned to see a well-dressed African woman walking briskly toward him. She carried a briefcase and wore a navy suit and flat black oxford shoes. She carried herself like a soldier, but her hair could only be described as civilian. She wore it in a natural style, with each strand twisted, which resulted in a curled halo around her head. The effect was stunning. She stopped a few feet from Banner.

"Mr. Edward Banner?" she asked.

Banner nodded. "I am. How did you know? I don't believe we've met."

She raised an eyebrow. "I've seen photos, of course."

Locke snorted and, when Carn looked confused, he leaned over and whispered, *sotto voce*, "It's his pretty face. The women all swoon when Banner gives a press conference. He hates giving them, but Stromeyer hates them more, so he loses."

"I can hear you, Locke." Banner threw Locke what he hoped was a quelling glance, which failed to move Locke at all. He merely smiled and pulled his pack of cigarettes out of his pocket.

"Indeed, it's just those press conferences that I've seen." She put out a hand. "I'm Janel Taylor, vice president in charge of risk management for Worldwide Insurance. We handle the kidnap and ransom insurance for Rand Pharmaceuticals." She handed each of them one of her business cards. Locke glanced at his and then placed it in his shirt pocket while he shook out a cigarette.

"Smoke?" he said, offering the pack to Taylor.

"Only cigars," she said. Locke looked intrigued and Carn gave a small smile.

"Ah, I wish I could accommodate, but I gave my last pack to another woman I know who has the same excellent taste."

"Thank you for the compliment." Her lips quirked in a small smile.

She turned her attention back to Banner and once again appraised him. He thought he detected a hint of amusement in her eyes. He shook her hand and introduced both Locke and Carn.

"I was unaware that Mr. Rand had been kidnapped," he said.

Taylor shook her head. "Not Mr. Rand, his Chief Financial Officer, Sophia Bertrand. She disappeared over two months ago, and we've been having intense negotiations since then."

"Fruitful, I hope?" Banner asked.

"They will be, as soon as I receive the container that I understand your people have confiscated."

Banner noticed that both Locke and Carn kept their faces impassive.

"I'm not sure I understand what you mean."

Taylor raised an eyebrow. "I understand that Darkview employs a chemist named Emma Caldridge for the occasional mission and that she stole a container that belonged to Mr. Rand. I further understand that she passed that container to you."

Now it was Banner's turn to raise an eyebrow. "Stole is a strong word. She's currently somewhere in the Sahara, but I believe that she would take issue with the characterization. What did Mr. Rand tell you was in that container?"

"The one thing that will save Ms. Bertrand's life."

"And that is?" Banner asked.

"Smallpox vaccine."

Banner shook his head. "I'm afraid that your client has

lied to you. It's our understanding that there is a very good chance that Mr. Rand was actually transporting the smallpox *virus*, not the vaccine. And he claimed to be doing it to ransom some small children who'd been taken hostage."

Taylor tilted her head to the side. "I'd heard a rumor to that effect, but all of the virus should be under lock and key in the United States."

"Exactly. I'm glad we agree, Ms. Taylor."

Taylor shot him a cynical look. "We agree on nothing. Do you have the container? I understood that you did."

"Who told you that?"

"Secretary of State Plower. She's authorized me to take possession of the container and verify its contents. I intend to do just that."

Locke lifted his head and blew out a couple of smoke rings, keeping his gaze steady and unperturbed. Carn stayed quiet.

"I'll need to verify this, you understand."

Taylor nodded. "Of course. I believe that if you contact Secretary Plower's office, they'll confirm."

"Excuse me," Banner said and walked down the runway, opening his phone as he did. Thankfully, he was able to receive a signal, and Stromeyer answered on the first ring. He ran down the conversation with her.

"I was just going to call you about that. She's correct. Plower approved her taking possession of the container. Apparently, she's trained to handle all sorts of high-risk transfers and has some sort of quick and safe way to test the vials. There's a whole security team standing by in town. They chose not to create a scene by flanking her. Thought it was safer to let it appear as though she was simply handling a business transaction."

"Given that Azhan has spies everywhere, that's probably wise. But do you think this is a good idea? Seems to me she would be more than happy to hand over the vial, no matter what it contains. Presumably, it would save her company from paying out on the K&R policy."

"We have no reason to doubt her and no authority to say no, for that matter," Stromeyer said.

Which is an excellent point, Banner thought.

"Any news on Caldridge?"

"No, but lots of chatter coming from near Atar. Be careful."

Banner hung up and walked back to his helicopter, retrieved the container, and brought it to Taylor, who weighed it in her hand.

"Heavy," she said.

"And locked. I don't have the code to open it."

"We'll manage," Taylor said. She smiled at Banner. A dazzling smile, and Banner thought she'd make an excellent choice to handle a press conference. "Thank you."

"You're welcome."

She glanced at Locke and Carn. "Gentlemen."

Locke reached out to shake her hand.

"Next time we meet I'll be sure to bring some cigars," he said. She smiled again.

"I'd like that, thank you." She shook hands with Carn and walked back to the Quonset hut. The flimsy screen door slammed behind her. A few minutes later, Banner heard the sound of an engine starting and a green Jeep Wrangler, complete with grill winch, came into view. Taylor drove away without a glance back.

Locke pulled the card out of his pocket.

"She lives in Johannesburg. Lucky me," he said.

"Here's hoping that luck carries you through Atar because you're going to need it. Let's go," Banner said. He turned to Carn.

"What's your next move?"

Carn looked startled. "I'm going with you. I want to help any way I can. Half my village is caught up in this, and I want to see them safely to Morocco."

"Climb in," Locke said.

Carn shook his head. "Not you, him. I'm never getting in another helicopter with *you*."

"Are you sure? There's no guarantee that your group is in Atar."

Carn nodded. "I'm sure."

"Then let's go."

Banner refueled, strapped back into the cockpit, and began the process of starting the helicopter. While he did, he handed Carn a 9mm pistol in a holster.

"I told you, I won't use a gun," Carn said.

"I know what you told me, but I want you to carry it, anyway. Sometimes the threat of a gun is enough to stop an attacker."

Carn paused but, after a moment, reached out and took the holster.

Banner took the helicopter airborne and turned toward Atar.

54

Emma stared at the man with the rifle for a minute before sliding off the roof and dropping into a three-foot drift of sand piled up against the driver's side door. Zahara and the others also stared with wide eyes through the windshield at the man.

"*Arrêtez!*" the man yelled in American-accented French, as he rose to a standing position, still aiming at her.

Emma shook her head. "I'm not stopping. This sand has to be removed, so the door will open."

"Uh, Caldridge, he's got the gun, and ours are in the cabin," Sumner said in a low voice.

"I'm aware," Emma said. "But I'm just about done with it all. And you!" she called to the man pointing a gun at her, "I hear your accent. You're American, and you look about sixteen years old. I don't know what you're doing with those killers, but they dropped you in the desert and left you to die so, if I were you, I'd rethink my priorities and get over here and help me clear this sand so we can get moving."

"I'm going to shoot you if you don't stop," the man said in perfect American English.

"Huh," Sumner said. "You *are* American. Where the hell are you from?" he asked.

"None of your business. Tell her to stop."

Sumner shook his head. "She won't listen to me, either."

"I'll kill her!" He became agitated and took a step toward Emma.

Emma ignored him and continued using her hands to claw at the sand blocking the driver's door. Out of the corner of her eye, she saw Yann reach into the footwell in slow motion and begin maneuvering her HK upward. She caught his eye and shook her head. He paused with a puzzled look on his face.

Sumner remained on his stomach on the cab roof and directed his attention back to the teenager.

"I wouldn't do anything rash. She's pissed and holds all the cards."

The man turned his rifle on Sumner. "Holds the cards? I'm the one with the gun. How about I kill you, too?"

Sumner gave an exaggerated sigh and rose to a sitting position, shaking sand off his back as he did. Bits fell onto Emma and she sneezed.

"Sorry," Sumner said. He jumped down into the drift next to Emma and began helping her.

The man stood there, holding the rifle.

"You two are crazy. I should kill you both."

"Oh, please. Knock it off. That weapon's filled with sand and you know it. No one's dying from *that* gun," Emma said.

The man swallowed and lowered the gun.

"You look like a Somali. Let me guess, from the diaspora in Minnesota," Sumner said. "I know because I'm from Minnesota. Minneapolis. Great city and I sure wish I was there right now, rather than in this desert fighting for my life."

The man swallowed. His eyes took on a bit of a sheen.

"He's going to cry," Emma said in a low tone to Sumner. "But he better save his tears for someone else because they're not moving me. He sure was happy enough to try and kill us from that truck."

Sumner bent back to the job of moving the sand blocking the door. After a moment, the man stuck his gunstock into a nearby sand pile and then walked over to them.

"Let me help," he said.

"Only if you let me pat you down," Sumner said. The man held his arms out.

"Go ahead."

Sumner patted him down and then went over to the gun, pulling it out of the sand pile.

"This is empty." Sumner glanced back. "You threatened us with an empty gun?"

The man shrugged. "I thought you were trying to kill me."

Emma snorted. "No, you didn't."

"You did before."

"Just dig," Emma said.

The man bent down and added his hands to the project of shoveling out the truck.

"What's your name?" Sumner asked.

"Daoud."

"Okay, Daoud, how did you end up here?"

Daoud kept digging, but Emma could see him set his jaw.

"I came because my imam said that there was important work to do here. Stop the infidels."

"You mean kill people."

"Only other insurgents. Never civilians."

"Quit lying," Emma said. "You tried to kill us and we're civilians."

Daoud shook his head. "No, you're not. They said you were with the Red Hand."

Emma glanced at Sumner.

"You believe everything you're told?"

Daoud shook his head. "Not anymore. Not since coming here. I think that I was lied to by that imam. But he was like a father to me, because my own father died in Somalia right after I was born."

"Why did you stay?" Sumner asked.

"I had no choice. When you get here, they take your passport and all your money. Once you're here you stay. If you try to leave, they kill you. Two of my friends slipped away. One made it. The other was caught and told to dig his own grave before they shot him in the head. He was twenty."

"How old are you?"

"Nineteen."

Emma kept digging and steeled herself to keep from caring. Talk was cheap in the desert. For now, they needed his help, but she'd watch him closely. They finished and Emma pulled on the door. It opened far enough for Zahara to slip out.

"Daoud, go and help that truck back there," Emma pointed to the second truck in line. Daoud nodded and headed that way.

"Who is he?" Zahara asked.

"A teenager from the States who got roped into a war."

Yann climbed out next and handed Emma her HK.

"Teenage boys are stupid," Yann said. Zahara frowned at him.

"You're a teenage boy."

Yann nodded. "That's how I know they're stupid."

Sumner snorted and waved the children out of the cab.

"Mind those. Don't jostle them." He pointed to the modules, which they'd stacked in the corner of the footwell before the sand came. The children nodded and clambered out of the cab.

"Go ahead. Find your families," Sumner said.

As they ran back, Sumner worked his way around the truck, analyzing it from all angles.

"This thing is in deep."

Emma nodded. Sand drifts nearly three feet high surrounded the truck. While this was bad enough, even if they could free the vehicle, they faced the task of trying to drive through more sand because the road had disappeared.

"I'm wondering why we should even bother digging out. All we'll do is get it free and then drive into trouble."

"Ideas?"

Emma had none. After a moment, the group from the trucks behind gathered around, Mansur in the lead.

"Any injuries?"

"No. We're all intact."

"And the trucks?"

"All buried as badly as this one is."

The radio on Mansur's belt crackled and a flurry of words poured out.

"And?" Sumner asked.

"The group behind us are radioing to their friends ahead. They've instructed them to dig out and head to Atar immediately. They say they will dig out as well and drive on to finish us off and then meet them in Atar."

A woman moaned and two of the children started crying.

"Then that settles it. We start digging. We need to get these trucks mobile again before they get here. Go. Now," Emma said. She waved at Yann, Zahara, Sumner, and Daoud. "Let's work on this one. Everyone take a wheel."

They bent to the task. Daoud knelt next to Emma and started digging with his hands, pushing the sand away from the wheel well.

"Lady, you know that this man behind us is Kortya?"

Emma nodded. "I do."

"Then you know what he will do when he catches us."

"He's not going to catch us," Emma said. She kept at the driver's side wheel, digging away at the drift. "And I don't know why you're worried. You're safe."

Daoud shook his head. "I failed in my mission. When he sees me here, he will kill me."

Emma reached under the front of the wheel and worked to pull the sand away from the truck.

"I'll tell him that we captured you."

Daoud shook his head again. "It won't work."

"Then I suggest you keep digging."

Daoud kept at it, helping her to free more sand built up under the chassis.

"Lady—"

"My name is Emma Caldridge. Call me Caldridge."

"Do you believe there's life after death?"

Emma stopped, grabbed him by the front of the shirt, and pulled him toward her. He looked surprised at her sudden movement.

"I certainly hope so, but none of us knows what's after death. This much I *can* tell you, I'm not giving up and you're not either. Now dig."

She released him and they returned to battle the endless sand.

55

They'd dug for almost half an hour, and the bulk of the sand on all of the trucks was shifted. Emma and Daoud finished their section, and she stepped back to view the results. They'd managed to remove a two-foot section away from the truck's front, and she thought there was a good chance that the vehicle could pull itself over the initial drift. Then it would be a matter of laying down tracks for the trucks behind to use.

"Ask Mansur if he's heard anything more on the radio," she told Daoud. He nodded and loped off. Sumner walked up to her.

"We should talk," he said in a low voice. He waved her away from the truck, where Yann and Zahara sat in a small patch of shade thrown by the flatbed. Emma slapped her hands together and they walked a short distance away.

"We have two guns and the modules. If we ride in the trucks with the others, we're going to forever be disadvantaged because they have superior firepower."

Emma nodded. "Agreed. Do you have an idea? You seem to."

He grimaced. "I do, but I don't know how you're going to feel about it."

She tilted her head to the side. "Try me."

"We need to attain some sort of advantage over them. Surprise them. I suggest that you and I take all the available weapons and crawl up that dune." He pointed to a tall hill about one hundred yards away. "If we hide over the top and wait, we can ambush them as they drive by. Pick off as many as we can."

Emma stared at the dune and then back at Sumner.

"That's suicide. We'll empty our guns, and they'll stop, come find us, and kill us. There's nowhere to hide."

Sumner nodded. "I know. But we'll have scored a hit, inflicted some damage, and slowed them in the process, buying time for this group to widen the gap between them."

She looked back at the other trucks. Daoud walked toward them, speaking to Mansur as he did, and behind them the women, children, and men hovered around the vehicles. She knew that Sumner was right. They were at a severe disadvantage in this fight, and only the two of them had the weapons and expertise to mount an effective ambush.

Mansur walked up, a grim look on his face. "They're on the move. We must be, as well."

"Then get everyone into the trucks. Let Zahara take the lead again. Her truck has four-wheel drive. She'll lay down some tracks, and everyone else should do their best to follow them. Single file. Each truck deepens the groove. Hopefully, in this way, you can cut through the sand."

"And if her truck stalls?"

"Then be prepared to dig her out each time."

"You should let the air out of the tires. It increases their footprint and they travel easier through the sand," Daoud said. "We sometimes take them all the way down to 10 psi, though at that low rate there's a danger of the tire separating from the rim. Fifteen or twenty is safer."

Mansur gave Daoud an assessing glance. "That's a smart idea."

"Shall I get started?" Daoud turned to the first truck. Emma put a hand out, and he paused.

"No." She turned to Mansur. "You supervise it, please."

Daoud flushed. "You don't trust me."

"I trust you as much as I trust anyone who was trying to kill me just a few hours before. Do you think I'm wrong?"

Daoud sighed. "No."

"Come with me," Mansur said. "Let's get this done." Daoud turned toward the first truck, and Mansur threw Emma a reassuring look. "I'll watch him." He followed Daoud and soon was issuing orders in his native language to the others.

"And?" Sumner asked.

"And I agree. Let's stay behind and ambush them. I'm done being chased around by a bunch of madmen. Besides, if I'm going to die, it won't be because I was too afraid to attempt a plan that had a shred of hope. Better die fighting strategically then by being picked off."

"Then let me try to revive that sand-filled gun of Daoud's. If I can clean it enough so that it'll function I think we should give it to Yann."

"I'll get the modules and help with the tires."

Fifteen minutes later, they reconvened at the lead truck. Mansur had briefed everyone on the plan. When he was done, Sumner handed Yann the gun.

"I got as much sand out of it as possible and put some ammunition on the seat of the last truck. I'd like you to ride there and be prepared to use it, if they get close."

"I will be happy, sir, to fight alongside you and the lady."

Sumner shot Emma a look.

"We're not coming with you," Emma said. "Sumner and

I will climb that hill," she said, pointing to the dune, "and take up positions behind it. We'll have our weapons and the modules. When the group passes, we'll fire on them from above."

Zahara started in alarm and Yann looked stricken.

"You must come with us. That idea will lead to nothing but both your deaths," Zahara said.

"Zahara's right, that's madness," Mansur said.

Emma put up a hand.

"We've decided. Thank you, my friends. Now go, before we lose whatever advantage we have."

Zahara stepped forward, bowed, and said, "May God go with you." Yann and the others followed suit. Emma thanked them and nodded as each stepped up. Her throat felt tight.

It's as if I'm at my own funeral, she thought. But she pushed that idea away. She'd upbraided Daoud for giving up and she wouldn't either. Even in her thoughts. One of the last ones in line was the young boy who they'd seen at the adwaba eating sand. He bowed in a jerky motion and then ran back to the truck where his mother waited.

Finally, Aaliyah and Risan came forward, and Aaliyah gave Sumner a stricken stare. "Please come with us."

Sumner shook his head. "Don't worry. I have no intention of dying anytime soon."

She struggled to stay composed, but Risan stepped up and wrapped his arms around Sumner's waist, hugging him with all the strength in him. Emma watched as Sumner hugged the boy back, his own struggle to remain calm apparent on his face. Mother and son returned to the truck, and Mansur helped them into the bed.

A few seconds later, the engines started, and Zahara began to move. Her truck bumped and teetered over the first obstruction, but the flattened tires bit and the vehicle kept going, plowing tracks through the sand. The others followed, riding in the same grooves. By the time the third truck came through, the tracks were beaten and compacted.

They moved out, with those in the back waving goodbye. Emma noticed that Daoud was in the last truck. He waved long after the others had turned to face forward.

Emma stood next to Sumner in the hot sun and wiped her mind clean of sorrow and fear. Neither emotion would help them survive.

56

Banner spotted the gathered trucks two miles outside of Atar. There were three large covered personnel carriers, the SUVs, and three pickup trucks loaded with what looked like a collection of men, women, and children. Various soldiers lounged around, carrying weapons. To the right, in a circle, sat a group of people, all with their hands tied behind their backs, and further to the right of that was a large group of young women. Banner flipped his headset to a clear channel and called Locke.

"You see what I see?"

"Yep, jackpot. Looks like they expect zero resistance."

"A valid assumption, since no country has been able to muster an army against them yet."

"Do you have permission to fire on them?"

"Official permission? As in a green light from the DOD to engage in a battle with the insurgency? No," Banner replied. "But I do have permission to find and save the embassy officials."

"That's enough for me. And, remember, I'm not an American citizen, I'm not hired solely by the DOD, *and* I'm flying a Russian Hind from God knows where, so I'm going to have no trouble firing this missile if I need to," Locke said.

"Carn, you'll find a set of binoculars in that pack behind my seat. Can you take a look around and tell me what you see? I'll curve around to get you a better view."

Carn retrieved the binoculars and peered out the windshield.

"The group to the left are Westerners. Your embassy officials, I bet. To the right is…" Carn paused.

"The group to the right?" Banner asked.

"Sorry, I got a bit emotional there. The group to the right are people from a village in Senegal that I helped evacuate."

"So they made it this far. And the rest?"

"The last group are women from the refugee camp. And there's Rand and Rhonda, his secretary!"

"Are you sure?"

"I'm sure. They're sitting with the embassy group."

"Free?"

"Nope. Shackled."

"So the Maraad turned on him."

"So it appears."

"And the crowd in the pickup trucks?"

"I have no idea who they are."

"Do you see anyone who looks like Caldridge?"

Carn scanned the area for a moment.

"Sorry, no."

Banner tamped down his disappointment.

"Relay this information to Locke. Tell him that we're going to lay down some fire and then open a channel and hail them."

"Who's going to lay down fire?"

"You are," Banner said.

"No, I'm not. I refuse to kill people."

"I didn't ask you to kill anyone, I told you to lay down fire. Feel free to shoot at their feet, but I'm going to ask you to drive that group of soldiers away from the collected people. Once we've isolated them, I'm going to give them one warning and then have Locke fire his missile. You think you're a good enough shot to do that?"

Carn nodded. "I am. I'll get them moving."

"And I'll give them a chance to surrender."

He tilted the helicopter in a circle while Carn readied the rifle. He headed to the side and leaned against it, preparing to fire out a window provided just for that purpose.

"Go around and come in from the west and hover just above that second pickup truck. I'll start with the soldiers lagging from the first group and drive them toward the second."

Banner did as Carn asked, flying in a circle, and beginning a descent to hover over the truck.

"Better start firing fast because those soldiers are watching us with interest. This chopper isn't marked, so they don't know if we're friend or foe, but I don't need to wait for them to figure it out. One lucky shot and this chopper is going down."

Carn began firing, laying a precise line of fire around the feet of the lagging group. Their reaction was immediate. They began running toward the second set of soldiers, and Carn continued to fire, laying down a semicircle of shots that kept them moving in a group.

"Locke, open a channel and tell them to throw down their weapons and surrender. If they don't, fire that missile."

"Got it." Locke's voice came through Banner's headset.

Seconds later, Banner heard the loudspeaker on the Hind scratch to life and Locke's voice repeating a command in several languages.

"Keep the pressure on," Banner said to Carn. Carn fired again at the soldiers' feet, and they jumped and scrambled while Locke's demand for surrender continued to blare out of the loudspeaker. For a brief moment, Banner thought they would comply. But their disarray didn't last long. Rather than lay down their arms to surrender, as Locke demanded, several to the right turned and aimed their weapons at the shackled prisoners in preparation to kill them. Two lifted shoulder-held missiles, which they pointed at Banner's helicopter.

"It's a suicide mission. They're going to mow down the hostages and fire those rockets at us," Carn said.

"See that?" Banner asked Locke.

The loudspeaker fell silent. Banner saw the missile launch from the Hind and seconds later it hit slightly off center. It exploded in a burst of fire, smoke, and flying debris.

"My God, one shot and they're all gone," Carn said.

"Not all," Banner said. The clearing dust revealed that Locke had targeted the armed group at the right. Locke's demand to surrender blared again through the loudspeaker. The remaining insurgents threw down their arms and lowered to the dirt, face down.

"Nice shot," Banner said into his headset. "But I'm a little surprised that you didn't just aim dead center."

"I took a calculated risk. I thought most of them just needed some encouragement to surrender and the ones targeting you were clustered together. I guess Carn's rubbing off on me. Tell him I admired his precise shooting," Locke said.

Banner waited until the dust from the missile settled enough so that he could safely land, without sucking in the dust and debris, and began his descent. Thirty minutes later he walked up to Rand, who Carn had freed from his shackles.

"Mr. Jackson Rand?" Banner asked.

Rand nodded. Banner noted the man's gaunt appearance and the deep circles under his eyes.

"I want to thank you for freeing me," Rand said.

"Don't thank me yet as I may have to take you into custody."

"The smallpox," Rand said.

"Yes."

"It's safe."

"Carrying it around in a lock box, no matter how high tech, does not constitute safe."

Rand shook his head. "That box didn't contain the actual virus. It contained a synthetic version designed to mimic it under test conditions. My scientists developed it."

Banner raised an eyebrow. "Why didn't you mention this before?"

"Because I needed everyone to believe it was the virus or they wouldn't release Sophia."

"And the story about Nassar and his children?"

"That was a lie. I thought Caldridge would agree to let it go if she thought children were at risk."

"Why Caldridge? Why drag her into this?"

Rand tilted his head. "I needed assistance on the mission. And her reputation precedes her. I figured if the whole thing went south she'd be the one to fight her way out."

"You took a risk with her life."

Rand colored, the first sign Banner saw in the man of any kind of apology.

"I know. I'm going to try to make it up to her when I get back to the States."

Banner walked away before he felt compelled to say anything further. A part of him understood Rand's desperation, but another part was angry at the entire situation—the insurgents, the kidnappers, the victims all around them.

An hour later, Banner had arranged for the transportation of the entire group. Stromeyer confirmed that the insurgents in Senegal had been scattered by a UN peacekeeping force that drove them back over the border. It wasn't a complete win, though, because they scattered into small cells and Banner had little doubt that they'd return again in force one day. Such was the nature of insurgents.

A woman walked up to Banner. Her head remained uncovered, and she stood tall and straight. Banner estimated her age to be about twenty.

"The man named Carnegie Wendel suggested that I tell you this. Your friend, Emma Caldridge, and Cameron Sumner remained behind…about two miles, not more…to block a second set of insurgents that attacked us. I don't know if she lived." The young woman's eyes shone with tears.

Banner nodded. "Thank you. I'll take the chopper and find them."

57

Emma turned to look behind her and gasped. In the distance, a vast expanse of water gleamed in the sun. She watched the rays shimmer off the sparkling water and her spirits lifted.

"Sumner, you see that?" she pointed. "Am I going crazy or does that appear to be an ocean shimmering in the distance?"

Sumner groaned. "It's a mirage. A trick of the light. I don't think we're anywhere near an ocean."

Emma's spirits plunged as quickly as they had risen. Of course he was right. It was a trick of the light—the heat rising off the sand and the horizon meeting in a beautiful, watery illusion.

"Like an asphalt road on a hot day. It looks so real. It's cruel," she said. "But I know you're right. If it's only an image from where the refracting light and the horizon meet, it'll fade as we climb the dune, right? We'll have changed the angle of view?"

"I think so," Sumner said. "Let's see."

She and Sumner crawled up the hill, their rifle straps slung over their shoulders. Sumner carried the modules in a pack. The sun beat on his back and Emma prayed that they would get to the top before it heated up the pack's interior.

They reached the top, turned around, and scanned the horizon. The miraculous sight of water was gone. Just miles and miles of golden sand as far as the eye could see. Emma's spirits plunged again.

"It's gone."

"Yes."

The glaring sun made Emma's eyes tear. Or maybe it was her despair that the water wasn't real.

"We're pretty exposed here. Move back," Sumner said.

They crabbed back over the dune's top, and Sumner lowered to a position on his stomach.

"Keep the weapons low, so the sun won't glint off of them."

Emma did as he suggested, packing the sand near her down by hitting it with her hand before carefully placing the gun down.

"Let me help you out of that pack. I'll open it so that the modules will be in the shade but we can still reach them easily."

She pulled the pack off his arms, lowered it, slowly and gently, to the sand. She opened the mouth wide, revealing the modules stacked inside. "What's the plan?"

Sumner peered through the scope of his gun. "Watch until they appear and then fire first. When they're close enough for you to throw the modules, then use them."

Emma hoped they wouldn't get that close, but she didn't voice her concern.

They lay there, watching the road below. She strained her ears to listen for any noise, but the desert was quiet. When she was home in Miami Beach, she was used to a constant hum of noise, from the cars outside her window to the hum of the ever-present air conditioners. Even the airplanes overhead added to the ambient sounds of her day. She'd traveled to many places, from the jungle to islands in the Caribbean, and all came complete with their own sounds and unique smells. In the jungle, the calls of birds, buzz of insects, and hooting of the howler monkeys added to a mixed concert that continued at all hours. At the beach, the shore birds wheeled and called, and the waves crashed into the rocks in a constant rhythm. Until the Sahara, she'd never really focused on the blanket of noise that the tools of civilization and the animals created.

But there was none of that here. Here there was only the sound of the wind as it scoured the sand and the occasional clicking of a lone desert lizard. Everything else hid from the unrelenting heat. The sun beat on her back and the sand warmed the front of her. She'd retained Vic's brightly colored scarf and she pulled it lower over her forehead. It held a masculine scent of expensive cologne. She wondered if Vic and Biba had reached Morocco.

Please, let it be so, she thought.

Sumner crossed his arms on the sand and rested his cheek on them, turning to her. His face was only a few inches from hers and he gave her a searching look.

"How have you been since Mary's death?" he asked.

Emma blinked. Her best friend since childhood had died four months earlier of a rapidly spreading cancer, and Emma was still dealing with the fallout. Mary had been vibrant and fun and lighthearted. She laughed from morning to night and was a perfect contrast to Emma's serious nature. When Emma's fiancé died, it was Mary who remained by her side, urging her to leave the house and stay active, when all Emma wanted to do was to sleep and cry. Emma's job took her away for months on end but, when she returned, she and Mary would always pick up just as before. Mary had been a big fan of Sumner as well, teasing them both that they needed to lighten up.

"It's been tough. I miss her so much. And it's the small things that I miss the most, you know? The phone calls and coffee and clubbing." Emma shook her head. "I can't believe she's gone."

Sumner batted away a gnat that was bouncing in the air between them.

"I've been worried about you. You've lost so much weight, and I was concerned that you were sliding into depression. Which isn't like you."

"It's not, but the grief comes in waves and at unexpected times. I lost my appetite completely. Without the nutrition, though, it was hard to train. I'd get lightheaded. It's been a mess, really. That's why I took this mission with Rand. I thought helping others would ultimately help me to see beyond the grief and my own problems. And look how that turned out." Emma realized that she sounded bitter.

"We'll get through this," Sumner said.

Emma leaned into him and kissed him. He kissed her back, and she was once again surprised by what she thought she sensed in him. There was a shift, somehow, but she couldn't say in what way.

She'd always been circumspect with Sumner, keeping him at somewhat of an arms' length. His intensity often resulted in him pulling into himself. He wasn't the kind of man that one could throw oneself at and expect a warm response. Serious to a fault, he required the same level of seriousness in his companions. Women loved his quiet calm and did their best to draw him out but, more often than not, they failed. Once Sumner set his sights on you, he would never waver, this much Emma knew. It was all or nothing with him. As a result, she'd moved very slowly, because she wouldn't toy with him and, between building her business and traveling for it, she never knew when she'd be home or in what shape.

When she pulled away, he gave her a small smile.

"We will make it through this," she said.

"Hold that thought," he replied. He lifted his head to glance at the horizon. "There they are, coming on fast."

A hazy cloud of sand and dust rose to meet the blue sky. At first, it seemed benign, like a small dust devil swirling in the breeze. But, after a moment, Emma could make out the metallic parts of the trucks and their black tires as they churned through the sand.

"How many do you see?" Emma asked. "After that mirage, I no longer trust my vision."

"Two, no more."

"That's enough."

Sumner nodded. "Yes, it is."

The dust cloud grew and the trucks came into sharp focus. They were pickups, with open beds each containing several fighters. All were armed and all scanned the area. Most had their faces covered. The trucks rocked as they crawled over sand piles. Twice the tires on the lead truck spun, kicking up a plume of sand, before catching and moving forward again. Whoever drove the vehicle had experience, because it slowed each time it seemed to ground out, rather than dig a hole with a spinning tire. She supposed she should have expected as much. Anyone living in a desert country would have vast experience driving under these conditions. The trucks kept coming. Now they were within a few hundred yards of the tracks made by Zahara.

"Once they meet those tracks they'll move a lot faster," Emma whispered.

Sumner grunted. "I'm going to fire at the driver long before they get there. Take him out, then aim at the second truck, while you fire on the guys in the back of the first. Keep them on the defensive."

They drove ever closer. Emma peered through her own scope and waited.

"Soon," Sumner said.

Thirty seconds later he fired. Emma targeted the man standing directly behind the cab and fired within seconds of Sumner. The man moved just as she did, but she hit him in the shoulder and he dropped.

The advancing force turned in unison, and their yelling voices mixed as they dove for cover in the open beds. The lead truck shimmied to the side and slowed. Sumner's shot must have hit home.

The following truck stopped and the men poured out of the flatbed. Emma aimed at them as they jumped, hitting one and missing the next two. So far, none of the men had fired on them, but she knew that was only due to the element of surprise. Already they were regrouping behind the vehicles.

"Here it comes. Close your eyes against the shrapnel and move back," Sumner said.

The sand around her exploded as the bullets peppered it. Emma crawled backward, dragging the HK and pack with her, shielding the last with her body because one stray bullet would explode the modules. Sharp bits of sand and rock hit her face and head. Some flew so hard that they managed to cut through her hair into her scalp. A scorpion, dislodged from its hiding place under a rock by the flying bullets, catapulted into the air with the sand and landed in her hair. She shook her head, and it fell down next to her shoulder, bristling and feinting at her.

"Move left and then back up. We'll shoot again," Emma said.

She rose to a crouch and shifted sideways, stopping after twenty feet to begin the climb back up, with the pack now slung over one shoulder and the gun in her hand. She could hear the men below yelling to each other, and wished she understood their language to better prepare for the next round. Sumner crawled upward in unison with her. When she got to the edge, she inched up and slowly rose so that she could see to aim.

The crowd below hid behind their trucks. None moved, but Emma knew that the lull wouldn't last long. Once they agreed on a plan, the group would come at them.

The back of the second truck contained what looked like a gasoline can strapped to the side wall with a bungee cord. Emma targeted it and fired off two rounds. Gasoline poured out of the bullet holes. She hadn't expected it to blow up, as only an incendiary bullet could provide the necessary spark, but anything she could do to disable the vehicles was worthwhile. The gas appeared slick and black with flecks of electric blue where the sun caught it. It coated the truck bed. Heartened by the small win, she targeted and hit the gasoline can strapped to the sidewall of the next truck. Silence fell as they all stopped firing. The brief lull didn't last. After a few seconds, she saw the tip of a grenade launcher pop into sight.

"Get up and run," Emma said.

The grenade hit seconds later.

58

The sand exploded in a wave of heat and grit. Emma heard Sumner yell, but she couldn't see him because it had turned suddenly dark. The surface under her feet shifted, and she stumbled and then fell to her knees, as the sand moved sideways to fill the hole made by the grenade. She inhaled and immediately started coughing, sucking in sand along with the oxygen. Somewhere behind her, she heard Sumner coughing, as well, and seconds after that came the sharp crack of his weapon. Perhaps he could see to fire, but Emma couldn't. She kept her hand on the HK and the pack on her shoulder.

Below them, the trucks roared to life.

She scrambled to her feet and attempted to run along what she hoped was the upper edge of the dune but could have been anywhere in the clouded mess and shifting surface. With each step, her shoes dug deep into the soft sand. Pulling her feet out and up each time took enormous effort, and she stumbled when the tip of her right shoe didn't clear a hole. The engine sounds grew closer. Sumner appeared next to her.

"Keep running. I'll cover you." He knelt, facing the direction of the oncoming trucks.

"No, Sumner, run. With any luck, the trucks will slip and stall as they climb."

"I can't run. I've been hit."

Emma turned and knelt next to him, aiming toward the sound of the trucks.

"I said go," Sumner said. "Run while you can."

"I'm going nowhere."

She dumped the pack on the ground and pulled out the first module. Now she could make out the trucks, and it was as she feared—one crawled up the dune while the second stayed stationary. The men in the second group kept up a steady stream of gunfire, but the dust cloud must have kept them from seeing as well because the bullets whizzed past, four feet to her right. The truck riding up the dune managed to keep traction and the three men that rode in the bed held onto the side walls and hid behind the cab. Emma had no doubt that they would pick her and Sumner off, once they reached the dune's peak. She grasped the module.

"I'm going to throw this when they're at fifty yards. Get ready to shoot it."

She glanced at Sumner to see if he heard her and gasped.

Soot covered his face, and a jagged tear in his pants leg revealed a long bleeding slice along his right thigh. At the top of the slice there appeared to be a stick of some sort embedded in the tissue. He knelt on his left knee but kept his right leg straight out to avoid stretching the slash. No matter what happened, from that moment Emma knew that running was out of the question. They would have to make their stand here.

"Ready?" she asked and was relieved to see Sumner nod. He held his gun high and waited.

She glanced to the two trucks below, raised her own gun and fired three rounds in succession. Two hit the men in the back of the first truck, and she watched them drop, one falling over the side and the other backward. He knocked into a third man, who stumbled with the hit. She turned her attention back to the climbing truck.

"Now." She rose to her feet and threw the module as hard as she could. She aimed for the truck cab but hoped to hit anywhere close.

To Emma, it seemed as though the module flew in slow motion. She watched it arc through the air, spinning around as it did. Her aim was true, but the truck chose that moment to slide. It shimmied sideways and down the slope as it lost traction in the sand. The driver overcorrected, and the truck cab shifted downward while the bed shifted up towards them, leaving the men hiding in the back now fully exposed. Each carried a weapon, and they shouldered them in preparation to fire, but the sliding truck and slanted bed made for some difficult footing, and they struggled to aim. Above their heads, the module, rather than heading for the cab, was now going to land somewhere toward the back. Not an ideal location.

"I'm throwing the second." Emma heaved it into the air.

Sumner shot the first out of the sky when it was ten feet over the truck bed. It exploded in midair in a blast of noise and black smoke. The force contained in the small module was impressive in its fury, as the ammonium nitrate combusted, creating a fireball. The module splintered and bits of plastic and metal spewed outward. The shrapnel from the module rained down on the men in the truck bed. One screamed and held his eye, where a piece had embedded itself, while the others ducked. They wore scarves over their faces, which protected their skin from the projectiles.

Sumner waited a bit longer to shoot the second module, letting it drop further before he fired. This module, too, exploded in a flash of fire and smoke. It flew downward, like a falling comet of heat and flame, and landed in the truck bed.

Ten seconds later the truck bed exploded, as the fire lit the spilled gasoline. The combination of fuel and ammonium nitrate detonated with a force that knocked Emma down. Flames engulfed the truck, shooting twenty feet into the sky. Black smoke roiled from the vehicle, licking near the fuel tank, and setting the tires alight. Another explosion rocked the truck, and the front joined the rest, disappearing in a black fireball of smoke and flame.

Emma rolled to a kneeling position and grabbed at the final module.

59

A man jumped out of the passenger side of the disabled truck, holding a gun and bellowing at the remaining soldiers, who remained hidden behind it. He screamed again, and one of the soldiers rose up, fired one shot that went wild, and then returned to crouch behind the vehicle. The crazed man screamed again, pointed in Sumner's direction, and then ran around to the hidden side of the vehicle and fired at the men. He took another step toward them, and they streamed out from the other side of the truck.

"He's firing on his own," Sumner said. "Driving them out into the open."

Emma shoved her weapon at him.

"Take this, it's empty. I'm going to use the burning truck as cover and throw this last module."

"Don't. That crazy man is going to pick you off."

"I have to get closer to throw the module."

"No. I can't give you effective cover. I'm down to five bullets."

"Which is why this module has to hit its target," she said.

She took off, running down the dune's slope, slipping and sliding in the sand, all the while doing her best to keep the module steady. Having seen its lethal force, the last thing she wanted was to have it explode in her hand. Twenty-foot tall flames licked upward from the truck, and black smoke poured into the sky. The acrid smell of burning rubber, fuel oil, and soot made her want to gag.

The soldiers below streamed out from behind the truck, firing upwards in a random fashion, all in the direction of Sumner. That they were equally afraid of the screaming man as they were of Sumner was clear.

That's Kortya, Emma thought. Only this man had the reputation of fearlessness and insanity that would mark a man so consumed with anger that he'd fire on his own soldiers. She saw Sumner shoulder his rifle and shoot, hitting one of the soldiers. Unlike them, Sumner remained cool under pressure. Kortya turned his attention from the soldiers to Sumner. He stood straight and aimed his weapon and fired.

Emma saw Sumner dive into the sand as Kortya fired. He lay on his side and pulled the gun to his shoulder and fired back. Bullet number two was gone. Three left. She slipped as her heel lost its grip and skidded out from under her. She slid down, landing on the lower part of her back. The deep sand cushioned the fall. A lucky thing, as she was able to keep the module steady.

Kortya aimed at her and she rolled to the right. The bullet hit next to her hip in a burst of sand and dust. It appeared that Kortya, like Sumner, was still able to function under pressure. She scrambled back to her feet and lurched downward once again, doing her best to zigzag as she did to throw off his aim.

Now the combined heat from the burning truck and the sun became scorching. She sidled to a stop ten feet from the conflagration and lowered to a crouch. She transferred the module from her right hand to her left and held her arm straight in an attempt to keep it from the heat.

More gunfire rang out from below, followed by a single shot reply from Sumner. That he was still alive was good, but now he was down to two bullets.

She crawled to the front of the truck engulfed in flames and peered around the corner. Two of the soldiers were dead, presumably from Sumner's gun, and she could just make out the shoes of the third, who lay behind the truck. Kortya must have shot him.

Kortya stood behind the truck's front, working on something that he held low, out of Emma's line of sight. After a moment, he stepped back, and she saw that he held the RPG launcher. There was no way Sumner would be able to move quickly enough to dodge the grenade. She rose up, transferred the module to her right hand, and threw it.

Again, she watched it fly through the air, end over end, the metal flickering in the sun as it did. Kortya finished loading the RPG and lifted it to his shoulder as the module began its downward trajectory. She heard a gunshot from behind her and Kortya staggered as Sumner's bullet hit him in the arm. He stumbled and the RPG fired.

"No!" Emma screamed as the grenade shot out of the launcher. Sumner fired again and the module burst apart. Bits of metal and sparks flew. She heard a whooshing sound as the truck bed ignited and exploded in a burst of flame and shrieking metal. Kortya's jacket set on fire and within seconds his entire body was engulfed. The gas tank on the truck detonated and Kortya's body disappeared in the blast.

Emma turned and clawed her way back up the dune, slipping and sliding and falling and pushing herself back upright with her hands before slipping again. Smoke and bits of ash and soot floated in the air around her, and she coughed in the rancid taste of melting vinyl and the toxic scent of scorched rubber. Tears ran down her face as the smoke burned them. She ignored it all. Her only thought was for Sumner.

She found him lying face down next to a ten-foot wide, blasted hole in the sand, with his fingers still wrapped around the rifle. His leg wound dripped. She reached him and knelt next to him, placing her hand on his back. He felt warm and she saw his body rise as he breathed.

"Sumner, it's me." She brushed the sand off his face and cleared it from around his nose. His eyes fluttered open and he began coughing. The relief at seeing him move made her lightheaded and her vision blackened and bits of light began dancing. She put a hand down to the ground and lowered herself next to him, wanting to get low before she passed out. She stretched out the length of him, wrapped her arm over his back, and placed her cheek against his hair. He coughed again and she saw his eyes flutter open.

"I told you we'd make it," he said in a soft voice.

She closed her eyes and put a hand to his face, letting her tears fall on him.

After a few minutes, Sumner shifted, and she moved so that he could sit up.

"Can you walk if you lean on me?" Emma asked. He nodded.

"Let's go."

She gathered the pack and the HK, leaving Sumner to carry his rifle. He wrapped an arm around her shoulder and together they began the long walk to Atar.

Twenty minutes later, Emma heard the sound of a helicopter coming toward them.

60

Emma walked into the open courtyard bar in Casablanca where Banner, Carn, Sumner, Locke, Aaliyah, Risan, Yann, Mansur, Daoud, and Zahara sat, along with another woman, who Emma didn't recognize. The group waved her over to a waiting chair between Locke and Sumner. Banner sat two seats away at the head of the table and waiters scurried around bringing small plates of food and carrying carafes of wine.

"We're celebrating," Banner said.

Emma smiled and accepted a glass of wine. She'd showered and wore clean clothes for the first time in over a week, and that was enough of a reason to celebrate, as far as she was concerned. But there was more, of course. Stromeyer had arranged refugee status for Aaliyah, Risan, Yann, and Mansur; Daoud would be allowed to return to Minneapolis; and Carn had arranged for Zahara to join him back in London. The two had made an instant connection, and Carn smiled more since meeting her than Emma had seen him smiling the entire time that she'd known him.

Locke stood up and waved a pack of cigars at Emma.

"Set out for a quick smoke?" he said. "It's a celebration, after all."

Emma laughed. "Just one."

Locke rolled his eyes. "Two a year won't kill you."

Emma wagged a finger at him. "Don't forget, I'm a chemist. I know exactly what's in those, and yes, too many and they *will* kill you."

Emma took one of the small cigars from him and followed him to the far corner of the open area. A group of Moroccan men sat in a circle placidly puffing on hookah pipes. The sweet scent of herbal smoke and the bubbling sound from the water pipes filled the air.

To Emma's surprise, the dark-haired woman from the table walked up, and Locke handed her a cigar, as well.

"Caldridge, meet Janel Taylor. She shares your excellent taste."

Taylor smiled a smile that dazzled with its brilliance.

"You're the K&R executive that Banner mentioned."

Taylor nodded.

"Any news on Ms. Bertrand?"

"Safe."

"Did you have to pay out?"

Taylor shrugged. "Can't say." She smiled again.

Before Emma could ask another question, a man stepped up next to her. Emma glanced up and gasped.

"Vic!" Vic stood before her, no longer in his bright green gown and elaborate makeup, but now dressed as a man.

"I told you we'd share a drink in Casablanca, didn't I?"

"How'd you find me?"

Vic waved a hand in the air. "Honey, the hotel is filled with chatter about the group of Westerners newly arrived from the fighting in Africa." He leaned in between Emma and Taylor. "Who's Mister Gorgeous?" Taylor laughed and Locke snorted.

"Edward Banner, head of Darkview. But, be careful, he's taken."

Vic waved a hand. "So am I. But doesn't hurt to meet him."

"Did Biba make it?"

Vic nodded. "She headed right back home. Said she wanted to clean up and get back to her life. As for me, I'm headed back to the States tomorrow."

"Join us for dinner," Locke said. "Come on, I'll introduce you around." Vic gave a quick bow to them both and followed Locke to the table.

"Who's taken Banner? I understand he's single," Taylor said.

Emma shrugged, not willing to say. Taylor raised an eyebrow but didn't push it.

"I met your friend Cameron Sumner. Still waters run deep with that one."

Emma nodded. "Yes. They do."

"I wanted to thank you for your assistance in keeping Rand safe."

Emma wasn't sure how to respond to that. After a moment, she decided to be frank.

"I didn't do anything, really. He saved himself."

Taylor raised an eyebrow. "I'm not sure I agree, but I understand your reticence. But you have my company's, and my, thanks."

She reached into her pocket and handed Emma a card.

"Next time you're in South Africa give a call."

Emma smiled. "I will."

Locke waved at them both from the table and Taylor started back. Emma remained in place, enjoying the sight of her friends, safe and laughing. The thought of Mary sprang to her mind and, for one of the first times, the memory didn't engulf her with grief. Sumner caught her eye from the table and rose, picking up a champagne flute in each hand. She watched him limp over. He handed her the flute.

"For a toast."

"Okay. To what shall we toast?"

"Well, the table's preparing to toast to freedom and peace. But I have a private toast for you. It's an Arabic quote that I just learned and conveys my feelings exactly."

Emma was intrigued. He held the flute up before him and she did the same. He held her gaze.

"Every one of my heartbeats is a poem for you," he said.

Author Note

Those who have read my other Emma Caldridge novels know that I often sprinkle real facts in among the fictional. The story of smallpox vials that survived for years in an old closet of the NIH building is true. A quick Internet search will lead you to articles about the alarming discovery.

Although the insurgent organizations named in the book are fictional, there exist several real insurgent groups scattered around West Africa.

Slavery in Mauritania was only banned in 1981, and some articles written about the country in recent years noted that there still exists a culture of servitude, despite the official ban.

Ammonium nitrate is the volatile chemical added to the airbag inflators that are the subject of a worldwide recall and this is a deadly explosive. They're more likely to rupture in heat.

My Emma Caldridge novels allow me the pleasure of taking the time to research areas of the world that fascinate me with their complexity. West Africa is one of those areas. The breadth of history, the depth of knowledge, and the intricate relationships of bordering nations make for a rich and interesting narrative.

Searching for Arabic quotes was a wonderful part of my research. The beauty of Arabic poetry and literature makes me wish that I could read it in its original language. I used some in the novel, but there was one that I think all readers and lovers of books will appreciate but which didn't make it into the final draft. It's below.

A book is a garden in your pocket.

Best Regards,
Jamie Freveletti

Acknowledgments

As with any novel, this new book in the Emma Caldridge series is only possible as a result of the hard work of an entire team of people. Thank you to my editor, Emily Victorson, for her efforts in shaping the story; my publicist, Dana Kaye of Kaye Publicity; everyone at Calexia Press, including the marketing and sales team; Kristen Lepionka, for her graphic design; James T. Egan, for his great cover; and Grace Coberly, intern extraordinaire. I also want to thank the "Best-Evers" book club for taking the time to review titles and give their impressions—they truly are the best ever!

And to my family—to Alex and Claudia for their patience when my eyes glaze over during dinner when an idea for a scene hits me, and to Klaus, who continues to support me in this writing journey and who cheerfully accepts that I'll be tapping away at a keyboard at all hours of the day and night.

Thank you!
Jamie Freveletti